A Girl Called Fearless

A Girl Called Fearless

CATHERINE LINKA

ST. MARTIN'S GRIFFIN ❧ NEW YORK

This is a work of fiction. All of the characters, organizations, and events portrayed in this novel are either products of the author's imagination or are used fictitiously.

www.stmartins.com

Designed by Anna Gorovoy

Library of Congress Cataloging-in-Publication Data

Linka, Catherine.
   A girl called Fearless / Catherine Linka. — 1st ed.
     p. cm
  ISBN 978-1-250-03929-3 (hardcover)
  ISBN 978-1-250-03930-9 (e-book)
   1. Science fiction.   2. Arranged marriage—Fiction.   3. Runaways—
Fiction. 4. Love—Fiction. I. Title.
  PZ7.L662816Gi 2014
  [Fic]—dc23

                                2014000128

St. Martin's Griffin books may be purchased for educational, business, or promotional use. For information on bulk purchases, please contact Macmillan Corporate and Premium Sales Department at 1-800-221-7945, extension 5442, or write specialmarkets@macmillan.com.

First Edition: May 2014

10 9 8 7 6 5 4 3 2 1

TO R.M.L.

ACKNOWLEDGMENTS

Books come into being because of the people who believe in you and what you've created. Without these champions, A Girl Called Fearless would not exist, much less be something I am proud of.

I owe enormous thanks to:

Sarah Davies, my agent, whose tenacity, intelligence, and finesse never cease to amaze me.

Mollie Traver, who took a chance on the manuscript and pushed me to write a better book than I'd imagined was possible. You taught me so much and made me love the journey.

Sara Goodman, my new editor, for her insights and judgment, which make the prospect of writing the sequel together exciting.

The delightful and talented team at St. Martin's, including Mike Slack, Anne Marie Tallberg, Sarah Goldberg, Jessica Preeg, Stephanie Davis, Anna Gorovoy, and Danielle Fiorella, who brilliantly captured the story in her cover design.

To my mentors and friends, the Vermont College faculty, who raised the bar and then raised it again. Tim Wynne-Jones, Ellen

Howard, Jane Resh Thomas, Marion Dane Bauer, Uma Krishnaswami, Cynthia Leitich Smith, Kathi Appelt, and Tobin Anderson.

To my VCFA buddies and the Throughthetollbooth.com crew, especially Tami Lewis Brown who is generosity personified.

To my critique group partners, Leda Siskind and Nina Kidd, whose thoughtful criticism pushed me to work harder and whose reassurance kept me from giving up.

To Sandy Willardson and my bosses at the Flintridge Bookstore and Coffeehouse, Lenora and Peter Wannier, who supported my dream in so many ways.

To my bookseller and SCIBA colleagues, including Andrea Vuleta, Kris Vreeland, Maureen Palacios, Kiona Gross, and Lauren Peugh—the best cheerleaders an author could ask for.

To librarians and literacy leaders, including Alyson Beecher, Mary McCoy, Lindsey Bozzani, Courtney Saldana, Sue Hodge, and Meryl Eldridge, for their unbridled enthusiasm.

To the kidlit writers who've welcomed me into the fold, with particular thanks to C.C. Hunter, Megan Miranda, and Gennifer Albin for reading the manuscript, and to Ann Stampler, Greg Pincus, and Kristen Kittscher for their amazing marketing advice.

To my SCBWI colleagues, including Lee Wind, Sarah Laurenson, Sally Jones Rogan, and Lynn Becker, for their kindness and support. And special recognition goes to Alexis O'Neill and Ronna Mandel, who gave me opportunities I never expected.

To my fellow lafourteeners for sharing the insanity of debut year, with a special shout-out to Tracy Holczer.

To my friends Jemela Macer, Deanna Bushman, Sue Wright, Dana Cioffi, Cindy Steckbeck, and Jerry Khachikian, whose emotional, business, and grammatical guidance has been a wonderful and unexpected gift.

To my sister, Lauren, for always being there, and my brothers, Ed and Pete, for their detailed instructions about how to properly handle guns.

But the biggest thanks go to Bob, Haven, and Max, without whose love, encouragement, and patience none of this would have happened. I love you more than words can say, even with extensive rewrites.

Los Angeles,
Present Day

1

Something was up with Dayla.

She stared out the window twisting a strand of hair around her finger as my bodyguard, Roik, drove us to my house. Usually, she'd be pawing through my purse for gum or lip gloss before we'd even cleared the school gates.

I tugged on her skirt, and she slapped my hand away before she caught herself. "Sorry, Avie," she whispered.

"You okay?"

She glanced at Roik. "I'm fine," she said, but I knew: Day was saving the truth for later.

Roik turned off Arroyo, and I sat up in my seat. The Lean Dog was eight blocks away. I smoothed my hair and asked the universe to grant me a favor: red light at Fair Oaks. *Come on.* I could really use one today.

Green lights shot us past apartments, the hospital, the post office and sub shop. I glanced at my phone. Damn. *We're too early.*

One block away, Roik sped through a yellow, and I set my finger on the window button, but I didn't have much hope.

Up ahead, the light was green. Bright, annoying, missed-chance green. It flipped to yellow and then at the last second, red. Roik braked.

I leaned forward to block Day, because I couldn't trust her to behave. The rules were clear: I could lower the window, smile, and give Yates a wave, but no calling out. No arms outside the car. Bodyguards had their rules, and these were Roik's.

The smell of hamburgers hit me as I scanned the café windows. I breathed through my mouth, trying to evade the memories it triggered.

I spied Yates handing a customer a bottle of ketchup, and the guy shook a fry at him. They laughed like they were sharing a joke.

Roik tapped the accelerator. The light was going to change. Look over here, Yates.

Yates brushed his hair off his face and his blue eyes caught mine. He smiled and swiped his thumb down his nose.

Hi, Fearless.

I waved back, keeping my hand inside the car. I wasn't Fearless, but I loved how he called me that. My tongue ran over my now perfect tooth as I relived the skateboard and the cement steps. Yates giving me a hand up. The crazy awe in his voice when he said, "You're fearless!"

I wanted a shot of him just like this with his dark hair falling over one eye and his sideways smile—different from the one he slapped on for customers.

But if I took one, Roik would make me hand over my cell. A drive-by was one thing. A photo? Not happening.

The light turned green.

"You two would be perfect together," Day said.

My heart skipped, and I checked the rearview mirror. Roik was watching the traffic, so he must not have heard Day. But still.

"Don't be weird," I said. "He's like my big brother."

"Oh, right." She smiled slightly and gave me a look I didn't understand.

I ignored her. She was still holding on to that embarrassing crush

I had on him when I was twelve. Yates and I had known each other forever. Even longer than I'd known Dayla, because our parents were old friends and our dads ran Biocure together.

These thirty seconds after school when I got to see Yates were the proof that someday soon, I'd have a normal life again. I'd go to college and hang out with guy friends like Yates and maybe—I'd even fall in love.

The world had changed in horrible ways, so Yates and I weren't allowed to talk or be alone together. Maybe I was lying to myself, but the connection we made through the glass made me feel that the future wasn't impossibly bleak.

Dayla huddled against the door. I didn't have any idea what was going on in her head, but it had to be bad.

2

"I'm pregnant," Dayla whispered.

My heart pounded as I tried not to look shocked.

The red eye on the security camera bore down on us. Dayla sat with her back turned to it, her legs stretched out on the lounge chair like we were just two girls innocently sunning on my balcony.

"Seth?" I spoke into my drink so the camera wouldn't get a clear shot.

Dayla blinked twice for yes, but we both knew I didn't need to ask. Her bodyguard was the only guy who'd gotten within fifty yards of her since her dad signed the Contract at her Sweet Sixteen. "Dad's going to murder me."

We looked at each other. Dayla had broken at least four clauses in her marriage contract. Sure, her dad was going to be pissed. Six million dollars, that's what Seth and Dayla had just cost him.

"What are you going to do?"

Dayla dropped her hand into the gap between our chairs and scooped the air like she was digging a hole.

"No!" She was going Underground. "You and . . . ?"

She blinked twice.

I got up and wrapped my arms around her. *No, you can't go. You can't leave me.*

Dayla buried her face in my hair, and I tilted mine toward the camera and beamed like she'd just asked me to be her maid of honor.

It was killing me, smiling like that and holding in how I really felt, but what else could she do? I made myself whisper, "Don't cry. They'll see you."

The border was at least a thousand miles from L.A., but she and Seth were going to make a run for it. Seth was looking at prison. The only choice left for them was to defect to Canada, the one country in the Americas that wouldn't send you back to the U.S. if you were running from a Contract.

3

Dayla didn't show up at school on Friday. At first, I thought she was late. Sometimes peaceful neighborhoods would turn wacko, and you'd have to take a detour.

As the morning dragged on, I couldn't stop looking at her chair. The emptiest place in the world: where your best friend is supposed to be, but isn't.

I messaged her about twenty times before lunch. "Day! It's Avie. Are you sick? Text me!"

But when she didn't get back to me by the end of school, I knew she and Seth had taken off. Maybe she was trying to protect me by not saying good-bye or telling me where she was going, but I felt like Scarpanol had just killed one more person I loved.

After school, I locked myself upstairs in my room. Dad wouldn't be home for hours, so it was just Roik, Gerard, our domestic manager, and me. And even though they knew enough to leave me alone, I didn't feel like dealing with even one of their XY chromosomes.

I tore off my uniform tie and grey plaid skirt and kicked them into the closet. Then I pulled on a pair of jeans and put in my earphones.

I hadn't played Scarp Hole's *Rage* album in a long, long time, not since freshman year when I finally got that it was better to feel numb than replay endless pain. I knew exactly how the music would make me feel, but I went ahead anyway.

The first song begins with the lead singer, his voice bitterly quiet. I whispered the words along with him.

I rage at the darkness in my life
The stolen love, the stolen light.
Death was silent, but I'm
Not silent anymore.

The drums start pounding, and the guitars scream and he cries, "I rage," drawing out his pain over a hundred metallic bars until we both jump into the next lines.

Mistakes were made
That dug a thousand graves.
The lies, the bribes, the averted eyes,
Millions had to die before we cried
This was no accident,
No, no! No accident

And I scream out the chorus.

Someone has to pay
For the pain they caused.
Someone has to pay
For the lives they lost.
Death was silent, but I'm
Not silent anymore.
Rage! Rage! Rage!
No silence anymore!

I pounded my feet into the carpet, letting every note take me back. Back to the helpless, awful days of elementary school when Dayla and I and all our friends watched our moms and aunts and big sisters get cancer and die—way before doctors exposed the killer: Scarpanol, a hormone pumped into American beef. Scarpanol didn't kill little girls like me, but we were still casualties—left behind with dads and brothers and uncles who were shell-shocked and afraid.

I danced and danced and beat my arms in the air, lost in a house where no one understood.

Maybe Dayla was already in Canada. Maybe she and Seth were safe, but once she crossed that border, it was worse than her being a thousand miles away. It was forever.

I lowered the volume, until all I could hear was the whispery sound of hushed anger. My fingers poised over the keypad.

Yates was the only one who'd understand.

I knew his cell number, but if I tried dialing it, the monitoring software would send the call right to Roik.

I closed my eyes and remembered how Yates had held my hand through the funeral when Dayla's mom died. I was ten and he was twelve, and I know his friends teased him about it later, but he didn't let go when I couldn't stop crying.

And when Mom died nine months later, he and Day huddled

over me, keeping the smothering well-wishers away so I didn't have to hear one more person tell me how kind my mother was or how much she'd be missed.

And two months later after his mom's funeral, Day and I barricaded Yates and his sister Becca in his dad's lanai and played endless games of pool, not saying a word, because even one word was too much.

I dropped to the floor. Now Day was gone, Becca was dead, and I wasn't allowed to talk to my oldest friend. How was I supposed to survive without them?

4

A silver van from H&S Monitoring was blocking the driveway when I came down for breakfast. The backseat of our SUV had been ripped out, and Dad stood over two guys whose arms were shoved elbow deep into the upholstery.

I scuffed to the kitchen, thinking how weird it was Roik wasn't out there, because that car was his *domain*. Nobody touched Big Black without his permission. Not even Dad, and he owned it.

My synapses didn't fire until I had a mouthful of juice. *Dad's monitoring Roik and me. He's freaked by what happened with Dayla and Seth.*

I choked on the nasty. Me and *Roik*? Roik was even older than Dad. And he wasn't at all hot. Not like Seth.

A hummingbird whirred past the window. Dayla and Seth had been gone for twenty-four hours. They could be in Oregon, maybe even Washington if they'd pushed it. By tonight, they'd be across the border, starting a new life.

Dayla was lucky. Seth really cared about her, not like Braden, the guy who Signed her. Braden's technoczar dad bought Day for him as a college graduation present.

I remembered the green sparks of envy I'd felt when she'd told me about all the times she and Seth parked the car after school. About the day in the abandoned picnic ground that she wanted him so bad she ripped half the buttons off her shirt. Or the time they fell asleep in the backseat, and Seth pounded a nail into the tire to prove they'd had a flat.

My finger traced a heart on my juice glass. I wanted what Dayla had, a real love, not a Signed one.

Once I turned eighteen and went to college, I'd have a lot more freedom and there was a chance I'd meet The One.

I'd imagined moving into the girls' dorm at Occidental. Running into Yates around campus. Having coffee with him between classes, with Roik sitting a couple tables away and actually giving us some privacy for once. Yates would look out for me. He'd tell me which guys I could trust and which not to.

The front door banged open. A man charged into the foyer and yelled, "Avie! I need to talk to you!" Dad was right behind him, saying, "Relax. Relax. I'll get her."

I peeked into the hall. Dayla's dad was sprinting up the stairs toward my bedroom. "Avie!"

Oh, God. I shrank back into the kitchen.

"She's not up here! Where is she?" Mr. Singer sounded angry, like he'd just lost six million dollars and I was to blame.

"Hold on, Singer. I'll get her. Avie?"

The doors upstairs were banging open and shut. I scooted behind the island. "In the kitchen," I called back.

Mr. Singer blew into the room, and I held on to the granite counter like it could somehow protect me. "Where is she, Avie! Where's my daughter?"

The Rolex Submariner glinted on his wrist. Dayla's future father-in-law gave it to him at her Signing. Job well done.

"I have no idea," I said. "Dayla didn't tell me where she was going."

"But she told you she was going somewhere!"

He circled around to make a grab for me, but Dad got between us. "Slow down. You're scaring her."

"Don't tell me to slow down. My daughter's disappeared. I've got to find her and that bodyguard before the authorities do."

I peeked around Dad. As bad as it would be if her dad caught up to her, it would be ten times worse if Day got stopped by the border patrol. "I'm telling the truth, Mr. Singer," I said. "I don't know where she is."

I wasn't lying. Sure, I'd heard about Underground safe houses where they'd hide you if you were running for the border, but I had no idea how to find one.

Mr. Singer banged his fist on the counter. For a second I felt sorry for him. "You'll tell me if she contacts you?" he said.

Dayla wasn't going to contact me until she made it across. "I promise."

Mr. Singer's phone rang, and he turned away to answer it. "Yes? Yes!"

"You'd better be telling the truth," Dad whispered in my ear.

"I am. I swear."

Mr. Singer shook his head as he pocketed his phone. "My people tracked the car to Visalia. No sign of Dayla or Seth." He locked his eyes on me. "This isn't a game, Avie. We've got to get her back."

I nodded, but inside I cheered. Day and Seth were still out there, free.

Dad didn't let me out all weekend and Roik made me hand over my Princess phone like running away was contagious. So when I walked into class on Monday, it was like being let out of jail.

But then I felt the skin on my arms prick up. It took me a minute, but I realized the posters for MIT and UCLA were gone, and a recipe conversion chart was stuck up in their place.

Ms. Alexandra stood like a model, her hair swept up in a chignon, her lipstick perfect. She had one hand on her hip and the other on the back of Dayla's chair, but only her lips were smiling.

Ms. A had handpicked our class when we were twelve, back when the Headmaster still listened to her, because she was the only female teacher left. Ms. A told him we had the most "potential." Put us all together, and we were a color wheel of smart rich girls who'd racked up enough detentions to catch her eye.

But we were more than a mission. Ms. A called us the daughters she could never have.

There wasn't an upperclassman at Masterson Academy who hadn't heard that Dayla Singer had run off with her bodyguard, but Ms. A addressed our class in the ridiculously chipper voice she used for the security camera. "Dayla's father called. Her cold is improving, and she should be back soon."

We all clapped, and Ms. A smiled at Sparrow. Two seconds later, the security camera buzzed like it was in pain. Ms. A nodded a thank-you, and Sparrow slid the scrambler she'd engineered back in her pocket.

"I know you're worried about Dayla," Ms. A said quietly, "but my sources haven't heard a thing. Keep in mind that's good news." She frowned. "I'm sure you're wondering why the posters were taken down. Last night, the American Association of College Presidents announced they were suspending enrollments for women."

Sparrow was the first one to figure out what Ms. A just said. "You mean we can't go to college?"

"But they just let girls back in last year," Sophie Park cried. "What's going on?"

"The reason they cited was their inability to provide adequate security for women on campus. They stated that until they can ensure the safety of female students, they cannot house or provide instruction for them."

We all sat stunned as if someone had lined up our dreams and shot them. No NYU theater for Portia. No biology lab for Sophie. No MIT engineering for Sparrow.

No psych classes at Oxy for me. No escaping home for the freedom of a dorm. The *nos* hammered me and I pressed my fingers to my forehead to stop the pounding.

"But they're going to figure this out, right?" Zara asked. "I mean, they'll find a way to let us back in, right?"

"Yeah," Sophie said. "Like, couldn't we take classes online for now?"

"Get real," Sparrow snapped. "How's Portia going to learn acting if she can't go onstage? Or Sophie—how's cyber lab going to work for you?"

Ms. A held out her hand for us to quiet down. "Sources within the association have told us that colleges are being pressured to keep women out. They're being threatened with funding cuts if they don't cooperate."

"I bet it's Senator Fletcher and the Gang of Twelve," Sparrow said.

I looked back at Ms. A. For the last year, she'd been telling us about Senator Fletcher and the twelve other powerful members of Congress who headed up the Paternalist Movement and seemed to control everything the government did.

"But why are they doing this?" Sophie asked.

Sparrow rolled her eyes. "Fifty million women died and the country fell apart. The Paternalists want us home safe and sound in the kitchen. Not taking jobs away from men who *need* them."

"This isn't fair!" Zara cried. "We're going to be eighteen. We're supposed to be free to choose what *we* want."

"They'll pay for this," Sparrow muttered like it was something she intended to carry out herself.

I stared at her. It wasn't the first time Sparrow said something like that, but it always shocked me, because she looked like a Renaissance Venus with soft curly hair and a perfect oval face. Not a kick-ass chick you'd expect to wreak vengeance.

Ms. A touched Zara's shoulder. "I promise you," she said, "the Paternalist Movement doesn't control everything or everyone. Don't forget there are people fighting for your rights in this country, including our president."

Sophie burst out, "But we can still go to college in Canada, can't we?"

"Yes, that's still an option."

I sank into my seat. I'd never get Dad's blessing to go to Canada. The only reason he'd sign off on Occidental was that it was twenty minutes away.

"This is why you cannot be silent, my dears," Ms. A said. "When you leave Masterson next year, you must speak out for Gen S."

Generation Survivor.

Ms. A nodded at Sparrow, and the security camera quit buzzing and went live. "Let's start with embroidery, class."

We got out our needles and thread. Last spring the Masterson Board of Trustees had revamped our curriculum. They cut back our courses in science and math and slipped in classes in child rearing and the domestic arts. With our mothers and older sisters no longer around to teach us, they wanted to make sure we were prepared to assume our roles.

But Ms. A turned embroidery defiant: a game we played against the administration and the trustees. Each stitch was part of a secret code Ms. A used to teach subjects we were denied: velocity, DNA, vectors.

We'd stitch or knit or crochet the principles into our heads and tear the stitches out after class. Chinese women used *nu shu* code to write letters to each other. We used ours to learn.

Ms. A marked out a pattern to follow on the board. Sparrow glared at the blank spot where the poster for MIT used to be. Zara was sniffling, and Portia stared at Ms. A with hollow eyes.

I tried to thread my needle with the white silk, but the thread wouldn't go through. Sophie took it from me and did it in one try.

"So you think you'll go to Canada for school," I asked her. "Your dad won't try and stop you?"

"He believes in my dream. He would never try to stop me."

I knew about Sophie's dream, because she'd shared it with us—of inventing a blood test that would reveal if Scarpanol had turned a girl's ovaries into cancer factories before it was too late to treat.

I didn't have a dream like Sophie, but I had questions I needed answered. I needed to understand why people did what they did, why they fed Scarpanol to cattle without years of testing it. Why the government let people import it from China, why the scientists cleared it so quickly when they already knew hormones could twist estrogen into cancer? I needed to understand why nobody stood up and said, "Wait. Are you sure this is safe?" I knew I couldn't change the world, but I needed to understand why greed and profits were so much more important than my mother's life.

Ms. A finished marking out the pattern and said, "Pay attention, class. Mastering this lesson is required for graduation."

Zara stopped sniffling.

"Damn straight," Sparrow said under her breath.

Anyone reviewing the security tape would think we were quietly stitching a line of ducklings following its mother, but in reality we were learning to stitch code: "We shall overcome."

Roik waited with the other bodyguards in the car lane after school. Two lines of armored SUVs curved past the fountain and rose beds. Usually, the bodyguards loitered in their suits on the steps outside the main doors, but today I smiled, seeing them stand at attention for Ms. Alexandra.

"A historic landmark!" She pointed at the white stucco mansion with its iron railings and red tile roof. "Designed by Julia Morgan, the architect for Hearst Castle! So show some respect, gentlemen, and stop tossing your disgusting cigarette butts in the flower urns."

Roik spied me, and my heart skipped a beat, because I could tell from the way his hand hugged his jacket pocket, he had a message for me from Yates.

Roik didn't like smuggling messages, but he needed the money for retirement. Dad had cut his salary when the company started hurting. Roik wouldn't do it often, and he made it clear he'd listen to any message first.

"I found this on the seat." Roik dropped an earring into my hand.

"Thanks." We got in the car, and he steered it out the iron gates.

I slipped the wire through my earlobe. I held my breath listening to Yates' whisper. "Hi, Fearless. I heard about Dayla and Seth. Don't freak. Seth's smart and I know he'll take care of her. I bet they're in Vancouver right now."

I hoped to God he was right. Dayla's dad had hired Retrievers to get her back. They'd probably staked out every airport and border crossing on the West Coast.

"Sorry I can't be there with you," Yates said.

"Me, too," I murmured, but Yates couldn't hear me. To send him a message back, I'd have to pop the earring in the little mint-box recording device Sparrow had assembled.

Roik cruised down Arroyo, and I sat up, ready to wave at Yates, but as we approached the cafe, Roik glanced at me in the mirror. "Is your seat belt on?"

"Yeah, of course."

He floored the car and tore through the intersection. "Guy behind us has been tailing us for blocks," he said, and hit Big Black's panic button for Armed Escort Service. We flew past the Lean Dog just as Yates went into the kitchen. *Dammit.* Today, when I needed a friendly face the most, I'd missed Yates completely.

I rolled my eyes as two armed escorts on motorcycles pulled up behind us, but, I told myself, this was better than the time Roik leaped out and pulled his gun on the taco truck tailgating us. Embarrassing.

Roik sped past the turn for Dayla's neighborhood and I slipped the earring from my ear. *Oh, Dayla. I hope you and Seth are gazing up at the blue Canadian sky right now, celebrating the rest of your lives together.*

The guards at the Flintridge community gatehouse waved Roik through and the armed escort peeled away. Up here on the hillsides, trees still hung over the streets and gardeners still manicured green lawns. We drove past a house where pink balloons arched over the door and a big wooden stork was plunked down in the grass. "It's a girl!"

Poor thing. But she'd probably have it easier than Dayla and me. She'd grow up in this world never knowing what she'd missed.

7

A black Land Rover I didn't recognize came out our gate as we went in. It was followed by the slick Mercedes convertible Dad's lawyer still drove, despite the sick economy.

Dad usually did business at the office unless he wanted to keep a deal hush-hush.

Roik parked in front of the house and I slipped the earring into my pocket. I tiptoed into the foyer, hoping to make it to my bedroom before Dad knew I was home.

Gerard intercepted me halfway up the stairs. "Your father's waiting for you on the terrace."

"Okay." I held up my backpack. "I'm just going to stick this in my room."

Gerard lifted it off my hand. "I'll take care of that for you." He'd put on a dress shirt and tie, which meant Dad was out to impress whoever'd just left.

"So I guess Dad can't wait to see me."

"Champing at the bit, so to speak."

"Fine." I started back down the stairs. "Looking sharp." I smiled at him over my shoulder, because even when Gerard annoyed me by enforcing one of Dad's rules, he usually took my side.

I found Dad sitting on the patio, holding a glass of amber liquid up to the light and gazing over the fish pond.

A sleek, inky green helicopter skimmed our neighbor's roof, buzzing like a dragonfly streaking over our pool. Leaves were settling on our lawn where the chopper had taken off.

Dad's face was amped with color. The last few months, his skin had turned patchy and yellow like a lab rat and I'd been worried he was sick, and too scared to ask. But today, even his eyes looked greener.

"Something good happen?" I asked.

"Avie, come sit down." Dad patted the cover of a thick folder on the table. Three more glasses stood next to it, slivers of ice swimming in the bottoms.

"You seem happy." Like a deal he was hoping for had gone through. Maybe money problems had been stressing Dad out.

"Yes," he said, smiling. "Regimen Industries has agreed to acquire us."

"Us? You mean Biocure?" I said.

Dad looked slightly embarrassed as he ran a hand through his thinning hair. "Yes, they've acquired a thirty percent stake, and they've promised to invest whatever's needed for expansion."

"So now you'll have money to grow the business?"

"Yes, but the best part is what this means for you, honey."

An electric current ran through me. *He didn't.* "What? What did you just do?"

Dad tried to smile, but when somebody knows they're telling you a big, fat, self-serving lie, the smile never comes out right. "I've secured you a place in one of the most powerful families on the West Coast. I've made sure my baby will be treated like a queen for the rest of her life."

I leaped out of my seat. "You sold me!"

The smile dropped off Dad's face.

"I can't believe it! You promised me you'd wait. You said I could go to college."

"I never promised."

"You did! You promised Mom before she died!"

Dad jerked his head. I'd nailed him, but he shot back, "I'm sure your favorite teacher told you the news. You can't go to school in the U.S. now even if I let you."

"I could go to Canada. UBC. McGill!"

"Avie, you need to calm down."

"You've ruined my life!" College. Freedom! In one breath, Dad had torn my dreams to shreds. I started to walk inside.

"Come back here and sit down," he snapped at me.

I spun around and grabbed the back of my chair, shaking it so hard Dad winced, because he knew that was meant for him. "What am I worth, Dad?"

"You're worth everything to me."

"No. How much did you get for me? You sold me along with a thirty percent stake. What was my asking price? I want to tell my friends so I can make them jealous."

Dad stood up and headed for the French doors. I cut him off and ripped the folder out of his hand. "What am I worth? Ten million? Fifteen? Tell me so I can lord it over Dayla the next time I see her. Your daddy doesn't love you like mine does. He only got six million for you."

"Fifty million." He paused and I gasped into the silence. Then: "You won't be seeing Dayla again."

And the way Dad said it, so quiet and controlled, I knew something terrible had happened. "What about Dayla?"

He reached out his hand for the folder and I handed it back.

"She was caught at the border. Homeland Security has her bodyguard in custody and she's been taken to a Fetal Protection Facility, where they'll hold her until the Contract family takes possession."

"What do you mean? The Contract family won't take her."

"I'm sure Dayla's father will find another Contract for her."

I'd heard differently. Families didn't want to take a chance on a girl who ran. "What happens if he doesn't?"

Dad wouldn't look at me.

My life was a car crash with bodies all over the road. Dayla detained. Seth in jail. Me promised to some guy I'd never met.

"So what's his name?"

"Whose name?"

"The name of my beloved. The man who bought me fair and square."

"Don't you take that tone with me. I'm looking out for you."

My eyes teared up without warning—my heart wishing that what he said was true.

"No, you're looking out for the company. I'm just an asset."

Dad frowned at me, but then he said, "Jessop Hawkins. Your Contract's with Jes Hawkins."

"So when do I get to meet Jes?"

"At the Signing." Dad tried again to get past me, but I threw my arm across the doorway.

"What do you mean 'At the Signing'? Dayla met her Contract months before her Signing."

"He's a busy man, Avie. He doesn't have a lot of time for social pleasantries."

My arm dropped and Dad escaped into the house. *He called Jessop a man? A busy man who thinks meeting his future wife is a social pleasantry.* "No, wait. Stop. Stop! How old is he?"

I caught up to Dad in the hall, but he stood with his back to me, his hands on his hips. Then he barked, "He's thirty-seven, Avie. And I did consider your feelings, because the other offer I had, he was fifty-three."

Dad stalked off, leaving me in the hall, my voice as dead as my mother.

8

The hardwood floor swayed under my feet, rolling like a 5 on the Richter scale as I ran into the kitchen and whipped out my phone. "Dad sold me!" I texted to Day and then slammed my phone on the counter. Day had left her cell in the car she and Seth abandoned in Visalia.

Dusty, my dog, came running and I scooped her up in my arms. Her little white paws bicycled the air as she licked my face.

My eyes burned with tears I was too angry to spill. If Day were here, we'd go upstairs and scream and thrash around my room, and she'd call Dad names like "fascist pig."

And after that she'd pick out a playlist and soundtrack Dad's betrayal. Then she'd curl her arms around me and let me cry until finally she'd say, "Who the hell is this Hawkins guy, anyway? Let's steal Roik's phone and check him out."

I could barely breathe.

The countdown: six months, probably, before the Signing ceremony, maybe another three before the wedding. I could finish junior year, and then . . .

Gerard came out of his office. He didn't say a word, but he didn't have to.

"I guess you heard."

He nodded. "You need anything?"

A life. Love. My best friend. Not a future in one of the most powerful families on the West Coast. Whatever that meant.

"No," I said, because at that instant I couldn't think of anything Gerard could do or say or give me that would fix a thing.

He headed for the back door. "I'm around if you change your mind."

I buried my face in Dusty's baby-soft fur. *I can't believe this is happening.*

Gerard's cell buzzed on the counter, making Dusty squirm. I went over and pressed Ignore.

His phone didn't have paternal controls, but Gerard would know if I called Yates. I set his cell down, and picked it right back up again. It didn't have purity screening, either. The paternal controls on mine would block all information on Hawkins. Living males were off-limits for searches. Historical figures didn't pose a threat to a girl's virginal status.

I silenced Gerard's ringer, and slipped the phone in my pocket. "Come on, Dusty. Let's go for a walk."

Dusty did somersaults as we slipped out to the street. I should have told Roik I was going, but right now I didn't feel like making his job easy. Besides, the streets in our gated neighborhood were monitored.

I walked Dusty up the hill, past houses hidden behind hedges and gates, so only the roof or top floor of the Spanish hacienda or

Italian-style villa or cutting-edge architect-designed house was visible. Oak leaves littered the pavement, crunching under my feet as I put distance between me and Dad.

I waited until we'd turned the corner before I took out the phone. A few taps and I had a full bio and pic of Jessop Hawkins. He wasn't ugly and he wasn't decrepit. The right schools. Collector of modern art. Major donor to the Paternalist Movement. Majority stockholder in Regimen Industries. Estimated worth: five hundred million.

Five hundred million. It didn't make sense.

Why me? If you could afford any girl in the United States—no, in the world—why spend fifty million on me? I wasn't that good-looking. I mean, I wasn't a troll, but I didn't have a body like Dayla's or a face like Sparrow's or long ballerina legs like Sophie.

The only explanation that made sense was Dad threw me in as part of his business deal, pure and simple, and Hawkins was such an incredible romantic he went for it.

I heard a car behind me and dropped Gerard's phone in my pocket, just as Big Black pulled up ahead and blocked me. Roik rolled down the window. "What do you mean, running off like that?"

"I didn't *run* off."

"Get in."

"Can't I go for a walk? Or does Jessop Hawkins have a problem with that?"

Roik shut his eyes. He was silently counting to ten.

"I won't get in the car. There are fifty cameras on this street. I'm perfectly safe and I'm going to finish my walk."

"Fine," Roik said. He threw the car into gear. "I'll be waiting for you."

He drove off and I didn't even care he was pissed. He couldn't tell me how to live my life.

Roik couldn't tell me how to live my life, but Dad could. Apparently, I was now "valuable" and when you're "valuable," there's a whole new set of rules for you.

I refused to come down for dinner and no one made me. I climbed into bed with Dusty and cried until my eyes puffed up.

"Day at least had a say in things," I said, stroking Dusty's fur. "Her dad did a Search, and she chose the guy she Signed. Braden was only seven years older than her."

But not me. Dad went behind my back and chose a guy twice my age, and never even asked once what I wanted.

I sat straight up. *Like the old, rich guy who Signed Becca.*

My heart squeezed, remembering. She was Yates' sister, but sometimes she'd felt like mine, too. I got up and went to my closet.

The box I'd stuffed in the back was right where I left it after she died. "For Avie" was scrawled on the packing tape in black marker. I set the box on my desk, fighting the urge to put it right back where I found it.

Why did you do it, Becca? Was being Signed to that man that awful?

I don't know what I expected to find when I cut through the packing tape, but there was nothing very dramatic inside: a stuffed whale, a couple paperbacks with frayed corners.

But under the whale was a plain white envelope with my name on it. *Please don't let this be a letter.* I didn't want to know what awful things she'd been through. Not really.

My fingers trembled as I picked up the envelope, but then I heard the slinky sound of a chain and I ripped it open. Becca's silver dolphin pendant.

She'd always worn it. Always. I fastened the necklace around my neck. My finger ran down the sleek silver back and caught on the fin. I forgot. Becca had taken it off right before her Signing.

The books she'd left me weren't any I recognized. I checked to see if she'd written anything inside. Nothing. But I found a photo between the pages of *The Awakening*.

It was from our last vacation in Maui, and it was me and Becca and Yates posing on the beach with our arms around each other. Our dads were in the background, lounging at the resort bar.

I stared at the picture. It was August just before Mr. Sandell surprised Becca by Signing her away to pay off his gambling debts. Our moms had both died two years before. Becca had handed me down her two-piece, because I'd just gotten breasts and my one-piece didn't fit anymore. The shiny fabric was printed with turquoise fish scales, and I felt like a mermaid, tying the skinny straps behind my neck.

I remembered Yates taking me to the surf shop and getting me measured for a board. Becca was off snorkeling when we carried the boards to the wet sand and pulled on our rash guards. Then Yates squirted zinc oxide onto his finger and swiped a skunk stripe down my nose.

We paddled out to where the waves were breaking, and sat on our boards, watching the ocean swell. The waves broke small and lazy, and we did more talking than surfing.

The resort had posted armed guards in speedboats, but Roik wouldn't take his eyes off us. He stood in the surf beside Becca's bodyguard as she snorkeled.

A big wave came along, and we paddled hard to catch it. I felt the wave grab my board and I leaped onto my feet and stretched out my hands. Yates soared alongside me, our fingers nearly touching, the wave surging under our boards, rocketing us to the shore, when I fell.

I hit the water, tumbling under the wave, and spinning, spinning as the blue pinned me down. I held my breath, fighting the fear that I couldn't get free, that the wave would hold me there forever, churning me until all the air in my lungs was gone.

Then it passed and spit me up, and when I finally broke the surface, I saw Yates swimming right for me. He'd torn off his leash and abandoned his board. "You okay?!"

I wiped the hair out of my face, and kicked to stay up. "Yeah," I said, realizing that I was okay. I had survived the spinning, collapsing surf.

Yates beamed. "You rocked out there," he said. "Ready to go again?"

I smiled back, wanting to be a girl that rocked it. "Sure."

Later when we came in, my legs had turned to Jell-O and Yates walked me to the dry sand, his arm around my waist. Roik met us and threw Yates a towel. Then Roik stood between us like a wall as he wrapped mine around my shoulders.

Becca ran up, her eyes flashing as she told us about the sandbar shark that passed ten feet below her. "When I'm a biologist, I'm going to live right here in Maui and study sharks!"

Now she was gone.

I sank to the floor, and Dusty ran over and jumped in my lap. She looked at me with her big round doggy eyes. "What are we gonna do, girl?"

Dusty squirmed and knocked the photo out of my hand and onto the carpet. That's when I saw the scribbled inscription on the back.

A, Stay free!!! B.

Chills went through me. Becca always ended her messages with a heart or a smile, not exclamation points that looked like slashes. She wasn't telling me to *be myself.*

I heard Roik downstairs and scrambled to my feet. He'd gone through the photos on my laptop last year and, in a complete violation of my privacy, edited out Yates and every other guy over twelve. I wasn't about to let him get his hands on this. I flipped through the DVDs in my bookshelf.

Titanic was piled with Mom's old favorites that Gerard had saved for me. I opened the case and took out the card with the cast list and director's comments. Before I stuck the photo inside, I took a second to look at the other one I'd hidden.

Day had Seth take it for me for my birthday. Yates was speaking onstage at a rally for justice. His fist was in the air and his motorcycle jacket was open, and I could read the Thoreau quote on his shirt: LET YOUR LIFE BE A COUNTERFRICTION TO STOP THE MACHINE.

Students crowded the lawn, looking hypnotized by what he was saying. Especially the blond girl next to him. I felt a sudden, sharp twinge right in my chest and dropped the photo on the floor.

Keep it together. I made myself breathe, trying to make the twinge go away as I tucked both photos out of sight and snapped the case shut.

When I turned around, Becca's dolphin glinted at me in the mirror.

Stay free!!! *Oh, Becca, I wish I knew how to do that.*

I wrapped my fingers around the little silver dolphin and held on tight. Becca had gone through with her Signing. Dayla had run from hers. I didn't want to end up like either of them, but I didn't see any way out.

Pending Contract

10

When I came down for breakfast, Gerard had made me cinnamon toast with chopped walnuts sprinkled on top, his version of a hug. I gave him a thank-you smile, and he gave me a latte. Then we had our usual It's Too Early To Say Anything Breakfast together, but we both knew it wasn't usual at all.

He passed me cucumber slices to put on my puffy eyes. Then he turned down the volume on the Domestic Arts Channel, because he knew I saw way too much of Martha Stewart in training videos at school.

I held the cucumbers on my eyes and thought about how I had to announce to my class that I was Pending Contract. And worse than that, I had to tell Yates. Knowing how he hated Contracts, I wanted him to hear it from me, not someone else. I'd tried to record a message back to him, but fifteen seconds wasn't nearly enough time to explain how this was Dad's deal, not mine.

Gerard was making up the grocery list on his cell when a news flash came in. Usually, he'd just glance at them and go back to what he was doing, but this time he slid the phone over to me. "I think you might want to see this."

I put the cukes down.

"Sources close to multimillionaire and gubernatorial hopeful Jes Hawkins confirmed his bid to acquire a thirty percent stake in ailing biotech firm Biocure Technologies. The acquisition is rumored to include a Contract for the sixteen-year-old daughter of CEO August Reveare."

Tell me this is not happening. There was a pic of me in my uniform standing on the Masterson front steps.

"You're kidding me! Who took this?" I shoved it so hard it smacked Gerard's cup.

"Based on the timing and where it was taken, my guess is a body-guard in need of cash. I'll tell Roik to let the other guards know you're off-limits."

What I really wanted was to be off-limits to Jes Hawkins.

Gerard pretended not to notice while I scanned the Net for any more humiliating pics. So far everyone was using the same one, but the bloggers were each applying their own uniquely cruel comments about whether Hawkins got a good deal.

In just twelve hours, my private life had turned into media food. Becoming Jes Hawkins' Intended made me a target. I would be followed, watched even worse than before.

When Dad got home, I'd push him to kill the publicity—he was always pretty protective. The problem was that, right now, he was more concerned about saving Biocure than he was about me.

11

Before we got in the car, I handed Roik the earring. "I won't be passing messages for you anymore," he said, "You're Under Contract, now."

I watched him slip Sparrow's invention into his pocket. "First, Yates is my *friend*. And second, technically, I'm *Pending* Contract," I said back.

Roik yanked open the door. "I could go to prison if anything happened. Accessory to grand larceny. They're holding Seth Brown without bail."

Coward. "Don't worry. Nothing's going to happen. Why would it?" I said brightly. "I'm Contracted to Jes Hawkins. Lots of girls would kill to marry a man like him."

Roik's voice softened. "All right. Just so's we're in agreement."

"Of course we are." I climbed into the car.

Roik drove, one hand on the wheel and the other on the automatic weapon on the seat. After Amber Saunders was taken during an ambush, he and all the other bodyguards had powered up.

If Roik wouldn't help me, I thought, maybe Janitor Jake would. He ran the "magic oven" in cooking lab. Put in an expensive pair of boots, tags still on, and a couple days later the contraband you desire appears. What would he charge me to pass a message to Yates? Prescription drugs? High-tech toys?

News vans met us at the community gates and followed us all the way to Masterson, even after Roik flashed his automatic weapon.

I cringed in the backseat behind the tinted glass and shades Roik had tossed me. The paparazzi on motorcycles couldn't see me, but they ran alongside the car, snapping at the windows like a pack of wolves.

A security team stopped the photographers at the Masterson gates, but the paparazzi yelled my name and shutters clicked at my back as I walked up the front steps. The Headmaster met me at the door and informed me that instead of going to class, I was to go directly to Mr. Hope's office.

I'd forgotten they'd make me see the Signing Counselor. I flung my backpack over my shoulder and stamped down the hall, averting my eyes from the Signing portraits: girls in crystal- and pearl-encrusted dresses who'd left Masterson their junior or senior year to get married. Only four seniors had actually graduated last spring.

I knocked on Mr. Hope's door, remembering how Dayla used to call him No Hope, because once you got Signed—

Hope pointed and I dropped into the hard chair across from his desk. He shut the door and all the air in the room was sucked out.

I glanced at his shelf, and saw that the rumor was true. Even though Hope dressed the hip academic, all tweed jacket and tortoiseshell glasses, there was a photo of him spray-tanned and oiled up for a bodybuilding contest.

"Congratulations on your impending nuptials," he said, pure business. "This is merely a preliminary meeting. We will discuss the details of the Signing and Wedding ceremonies after you've had a chance to think about what you want."

I nodded. *I want this to go away.*

"I suggest you take the next two days to think, and we'll meet again on Thursday. Normally, I would not recommend undertaking a Signing on such a short deadline, but Mr. Hawkins has assured us that with his resources and connections—"

"Wait. What do you mean, short deadline? I thought we were setting the Signing for March or April?"

"Oh, no, Mr. Hawkins was quite clear that given his campaign schedule, the Signing must be completed by November twenty-third and the Wedding no later than December first."

"December first? But there has to be some mistake. That's three weeks from now!"

"No, I can read you his instructions if you like."

I jerked my backpack up off the floor. "I need to talk to my father. This has got to be a mistake," I said, tearing the door open.

"I'll see you on Thursday, Ms. Reveare."

12

I called Dad. It wasn't a mistake. Hawkins had written the deadlines right into the Contract.

I walked down the hall as if I was lost deep underwater. I couldn't hear, couldn't feel, couldn't even cry.

Back in class, Ms. A stood below the new school crest: "Chastity Fidelity Maternity." I remembered laughing when the workmen installed it, but now I understood why Ms. A had gotten so angry.

Maternity. *In a few months, I could be pregnant with a little Hawkins baby. The first of as many as he wants.*

Ms. A signaled for me to come up to the front. "Avie has an announcement!"

Radiance, that's what you want to give off, Ms. A told Dayla when she had to make her announcement. I stood beside Ms. A, trying to glow. "I'm Pending Contract!"

"PC!" everyone screamed, and they rushed up, squealing like our team had scored. They embraced me in a huddle.

"I'm so sorry. I'm so sorry," Zara whispered.

I clenched my teeth and smiled for the camera.

Shavelle started everyone singing "Going to the Chapel," and we swayed as a group while my classmates whispered how sorry they were.

They were trying so hard, but all their sympathy made my being PC painfully real. Real and inescapable and devastatingly final.

"What's his name?" Portia asked.

"It's Jessop Hawkins," Sparrow answered.

The others looked at her. "It's all over the news," she said. Only Sparrow, with her incredible tech skills, always had access to restricted information like current events.

"When's the Signing?" Portia said.

"November twenty-third. Two weeks! And the Wedding's a week later!" The song died out. "I know," I said. "It's hideously fast."

"Will he let you finish the semester?" Sophie whispered.

Dad hadn't said anything, but once I Signed the Contract, I belonged to Jes. "I don't know."

"I doubt it," Sparrow said. "Hawkins is running for governor so he probably wants his pretty little wife out on the campaign trail with him."

Cold, hard reality snapped me awake. *Hawkins is a Paternalist and he's going to run for governor with me by his side.*

I would have to stand there and smile as he made speeches about how girls didn't need an education or to know how to drive, how they didn't need to have a say in who they married or if they had babies, because their dads or husbands would think for them.

"Two weeks until Avie's Signing!!" Ms. A clapped her hands. "This is exactly why we must double our efforts to master the domestic arts. Textbooks, everyone. Down to the lab."

We picked up our cookbooks and headed to the kitchen in the basement. The administration approved of the hours we spent kneading and cutting butter into flour, clueless that we switched to chemistry or current events when we turned on our mixers.

Today, Ms. A gathered us around her. We moved in close as she squeezed rose petals out of a frosting bag. "The American Civil Liberty Union's offices in Birmingham, Cleveland, and Philadelphia were bombed," she whispered. "Six lawyers have received death threats."

We looked at her. The Paternalists had been demanding a return to the original Constitution. All men are created equal. Men. We'd counted on the ACLU to fight for us.

"Great. Maybe the Paternalists can bring back slavery, too," Sparrow snapped.

"Indoor voice," Ms. A warned. "No one is quite sure who's behind the bombings. The President has pledged that the FBI will investigate."

"If the President's on our side," Sparrow muttered, "why do the Paternalists keep getting what they want?"

Ms. A raised her voice. "Class, get your mixing bowls out, and let's whip up some icing."

Beaters whirred as loud as engines as Ms. A went around the table. This was one of those times when she talked to each of us privately, like when she ran alongside us around the track in the morning.

When she got to me, she put a hand on my shoulder. "How are you holding up?"

"Just barely," I said.

"You know you have options."

"No I don't. I'm Pending Contract to Jes Hawkins and in three weeks my life is officially over."

"Yes." She looked right into my eyes. "You do."

A question crossed my face. Ms. A glanced at the monitor, then picked up the vanilla and pointed at the label. She leaned in close. "You can talk your father out of Signing you. You can refuse to sign the document or get a lawyer and fight it like Samantha Rowley. Or you can choose an even more *extreme* solution."

Going on the run like Dayla.

"You can marry Jessop Hawkins or not. That's a choice, Avie."

Marry Jes or not! Like that's a choice!

"You have no idea what this is like," I snapped. "Your dad didn't sign you away. You got to marry for love."

Ms. A went stiff, eyes wide, and I knew I'd hurt her.

"I'm sorry," I mumbled, instantly regretting what I'd said, but she couldn't possibly know how it felt to be Signed away. She'd been married for twenty-five years to "Rupert, the love of my life and keeper of my soul."

"You're right," she said gently. "I don't know what you are going through or what I would do in your place, but you must not think marrying Jessop Hawkins is your only choice."

We iced and decorated cupcakes and she made us take them out to our bodyguards. A man's heart is through his stomach, she always said. And we all knew, we needed our bodyguards on our sides.

13

After school, Roik took us out the back gate so the news vans didn't see us go. He barreled through the streets and barely slowed through the yellow light by the Lean Dog.

Yates was cleaning the sidewalk tables when we drove past. I sat up, hoping he'd see in my face that I had nothing to do with Hawkins or my Signing.

I went to roll down the window, but it was locked in the up position. Only Roik could release it.

Yates didn't wave or even nod, he just watched us go by.

He knew.

Shame heated my cheeks. And then anger, because none of this was my fault. I didn't ask for Dad to Sign me. And it was his stupid rules that made it so I couldn't break the news to my oldest friend in a way that kept Yates on my side.

I kept my eyes on Yates until I couldn't see him anymore, because if this was the last time I'd ever see him, I wanted every detail. The way his eyes followed me. The curl hanging over his eyebrow. Becca's name tattooed around his bicep like an armband.

"We should change routes," Roik said. "Securitywise it's a bad idea to use the same one over and over."

He let that sink in.

This wasn't about any ambush. Roik just wanted to make sure I didn't see Yates. Not even driving by.

Roik pulled on to the freeway and I smoldered in the backseat. This was so wrong, so completely unfair. My heart twinged, seeing the chrome yellow billboard with Ajax the self-defense trainer in his tight, khaki camo tee. Dayla loved to cross her eyes and yell out the headline, "Don't let your daughter be a casualty."

Now we were both casualties.

The Million Mother Wall rose up alongside, one million rosy tan bricks. Back when all the funeral plots ran out and families had run through their savings buying black market chemo, the state took over cremations so women wouldn't rot in makeshift morgues. The ashes of a million moms and sisters and aunties were baked into memorial bricks, a little heart stamped into each one.

Roik turned off the radio. His own wife was at Mile Marker Twenty-nine. He looked at the marker as it flew by, and whispered something I'd never ever caught, even though he'd said it hundreds of times.

Our family had had plots at Forest Lawn forever, so Mom was in a grave with roses and trees and a real tombstone. When we drove in, the cemetery was empty as it always was on Tuesdays.

Roik parked the car, but first he turned it around so it faced the exit. "I don't think the cameramen followed us," he said, patting the hood. "But if they did, I'll be waiting for them."

I waited by the car as Roik did a quick reconnaissance. We'd never had any trouble at the cemetery, but Roik didn't like how he couldn't see past Mom's grave. The hill sloped down and there was a dirt road from a back entrance that the gardeners used.

I walked up the grassy slope and unrolled a blanket. The branches of the sycamore in the next row shaded her in summer, but now its leaves were frayed from the November heat.

I curled up on her grave and laid my hand over where I thought Mom's heart must be. In the quiet, the sadness I'd tried so hard not to feel overwhelmed me.

Mom, I miss you so much. You won't believe this. Dad sold me! He broke his promise and sold me.

I know! It's horrible!

You'd never let Dad do this if you were here. You'd tell him money isn't as important as love.

You'd tell him he made a mistake, that Hawkins isn't right for me. You'd rip up the Contract and tell him to find the money some other way.

Tears blurred my eyes. I could almost feel her arms around me. Mom would have wanted me to be with someone I loved.

She left a letter for me to read on my sixteenth birthday and I'd read it so many times I had it memorized.

"You may fall in love many times, but try to marry only once. Choose the man who thinks you are beautiful just the way you are, who wants to hear what you have to say, who urges you to follow your heart."

Jes Hawkins was barely interested in meeting me, so, clearly, when it came to what I had to say or what I wanted, he didn't care.

A leaf dropped into my hair, but when I went to brush it away, I realized it wasn't a leaf at all. It was a note. I glanced at the car, but Roik was on his phone

I unfolded the note. Yates' scratchy handwriting zigzagged up the paper. "Go back to church."

I sat up and glanced around. Every muscle in my body tensed, and I forced myself to stay still. One move out of the ordinary, and Roik would charge up here to investigate.

"Yates? Yates!" I said as loud as I dared.

He peered out from behind the sycamore. "Over here, Avie."

Yates was ten feet away, but we hadn't stood this close since after Becca's funeral. He leaned against the tree, his hands crammed in his jeans. His cheeks were still hollow, but not as bad as before, and they looked a little tan like he'd started surfing again. But even if he had, the way he stood there told me that he wasn't the same guy I grew up with.

"Are you insane?" I glanced at the car. "Roik'll freak if he sees you."

"I heard about your Signing."

Yates didn't sound mad, but I wasn't sure. "I tried to get a message to you. It wasn't my idea. Dad didn't even tell me."

"Yeah, I guessed as much." His cobalt-blue eyes were alive and defiant, like Michelangelo's *David* sizing up Goliath. "Did you meet him—Jessop Hawkins?"

I could feel myself starting to blush. "No, not yet." I couldn't just stand there; Roik would guess something was up. So I took out Mom's pruning scissors and snipped at the rosebush.

Yates ducked down and crept behind Mom's headstone. The falling sun sculpted his arms into light and shadow, and I caught myself staring.

"You know Hawkins is on our Enemies of Freedom list. We're going to fight his election." Yates said.

"Good. Someone needs to stop the Paternalists."

He rested his back against the stone and I worked my way around the rose until he was so close we were almost touching. From here, I had a clear view of Roik tapping away on his phone, playing a game.

"I'm so happy you came," I said, "but why did you chance it?"

"I thought you could use someone on your side. And with Dayla gone—"

A smile bloomed on my lips. "Yeah, thanks."

He reached up and squeezed the ends of my fingers, and suddenly the air felt charged, and I couldn't look straight at him. I wasn't used to this closeness after years of looking at him through a window.

Yates cleared his throat softly. "This thing with Hawkins must seem unreal," he said.

"It's like watching my life being taken away."

"When's the Signing?"

"Two weeks."

"Two." Yates swore under his breath. "Just like what happened to Becca. You need to go back to church."

"It's too painful. All the memories."

"I'm serious. You need to go."

I glanced at Yates' T-shirt, relieved that even though it was black, it wasn't the one he wore nonstop after Becca's death, the one with the quote from Poe: "I became insane with long periods of horrible sanity."

Memories strobed in my head. Yates collapsed on our doorstep holding Becca's cardboard box. "Becca wanted you to have these." Roik letting him in even though I wasn't allowed visits from boys. Yates disappearing into a hospital, and Roik refusing to take me to see him.

Suddenly, I guessed why Yates wanted me to go to church. "You want me to meet Father Gabriel, the priest who kept you from—" *Killing yourself.*

Yates winced. "Father Gabe's a good guy. I think he could help you."

"But I don't think I'd ever—" *Be that desperate?*

"Father G helps people in lots of ways." Yates rested his hand on my foot. "I thought maybe you could give him a chance."

Yates was risking a Tasing from Roik, so the least I could do was meet Father Gabe. "Okay. Sure."

Yates tugged my shoelace until the bow fell apart, and then smiled like he used to when I was ten, daring me to retie it.

Roik was still absorbed with his phone. I bent down to tie my shoe. Yates leaned over and stretched out his hand, and I was intensely aware of his strong fingers and the vein tracing across the back of his hand.

He touched the silver dolphin hanging from my neck and bounced it lightly on his fingertips. "Becca would be happy to see you wearing this."

Yates' eyes met mine, and I rested for a moment in their deep blue. The charge was still there, but it felt safe somehow. Yates was my oldest friend and he understood what I was going through, and he'd do everything he could to help me.

"Miss Avie!"

I bolted upright. Roik was waving me back to the car.

"Coming!"

I slapped grass off my skirt and Yates handed me the pruners. "Women's mass is at nine. Can I tell Father Gabe you'll be there?"

"Yes. Okay. Fine." Yates worshiped Father Gabe, but I didn't see how meeting him was going to do a thing. Still, I hadn't been back to church in forever. Maybe it was time.

Roik was hoofing it up the path. "Now get out of here, will you?" I told Yates. I grabbed the blanket and shook off the grass, then hurried down to meet Roik halfway.

He tossed the blanket in the trunk, and I crawled into the backseat and stuck my earphones in so Roik would leave me alone. L.A. sailed past the window, and I felt my heartbeat start to slow.

Yates was lucky Roik hadn't seen him. Roik would have Tased him for sure.

I felt the note in my pocket and played the scene over in my head. The intense look on Yates' face when he talked about Hawkins and Father G, the silly smile when he fooled with my shoelace, the moment when we held each other's eyes. His fingers brushing my neck.

I caught myself smiling.

Stop it, I thought, wiping the smile off my face. That—whatever *that* was—wasn't anything.

Yates thinks of you like a second sister. He's just trying to keep you safe.

I stared out the glass. My Signing was two weeks away, and nothing Yates could do or say could save me from Jessop Hawkins. And even though it was probably a waste to go see Father Gabe, I owed it to Yates. I'd promised him, and it might be the last promise to him I could ever keep.

14

Hawkins' bid for governor was all over the news, which meant I was, too. By morning, the media was eating up everything about me like I was a fresh shipment of imported Kobe beef.

Reporters and photographers couldn't get past the Flintridge community gates, because Jes had kindly paid for additional guards. Once we were outside, though, they were on us. Roik kept the radio low in the front seat, but every time I heard my name mentioned, I flinched.

I didn't want to be Breaking News. Didn't want to think about my future. Didn't want to deal with the tsunami coming down on me.

I was stressing so bad I let fly when I stepped out on the track for the Daily Five. Today I pushed until the voices in my head dropped out, and for five sweet miles, all I heard was the thump of my heartbeat and the pull of my breath.

When my classmates quit, I took off up the bleachers, doing the first round two steps at a time and then down. Then the second round one step at a time and then down. Then three steps at a time and then down.

Ms. A waited at the bottom while everyone else went to the showers. "Talk to me," she said, when I'd finally run out of breath.

"I can't stand this. I feel so trapped and I wish there was some way to put an end to this torture."

Ms. A scanned the bleachers as if she was trying out what she should say. "You're not—thinking of hurting yourself?"

"No. No, I would never."

"Good. Walk with me. You need to stall your Signing. You're in a state of shock, and you need time to explore your options." She looked at me for a long moment, holding my gaze with something significant in her own.

She was right. If I didn't slow down my Signing, in a few days, my life would be over.

We did a mile cooldown as she helped me plot how to persuade my father to stall the Signing. We broke it out—what to say, how to act, what not to mention at any cost.

Plot in hand, I waited until dinner, until after Dad had finished his pork roast and glass of wine. *Wait until he's eaten and appears relaxed,* Ms. A had told me.

"I want to have a big Signing," I said.

Dad looked up. "I'm surprised to hear you say that."

Even though I'd rehearsed, I fumbled to get into character. "I know I gave you a hard time the other day."

"Well," Dad said, "looking back on it, I shouldn't have sprung the Signing on you that way. It must have come as a shock, and I apologize for that."

He didn't regret *what* he did, just *how* he did it. "Yeah, it was a shock."

"So now you want a big party? You told me when you turned sixteen you don't like big parties."

"Yeah, I know I said that, but this is different." I tried to look *expectant.* "All my friends are talking about their Signings. I guess it hit me this is the most important day in my life besides my wedding day."

Dad searched my face and his eyes relaxed, and then I knew it was just like Ms. A predicted. He really *wanted* to think I was happy.

"All right," he said. "How big are we talking?"

"Well, Ms. A says . . ." Dad's mouth got tight, which I'd expected. She'd lectured the dads every year at Open House about not Signing us until we'd finished college. "Ms. Alexandra says a Signing is the modern-day equivalent of a debutante's coming-out. She told me we need to invite not just friends and family, but people you want to impress. Like business contacts, people in government who can help you get contracts."

"Ms. Alexandra said this?"

"Yes, and Letitia Hawkins, Jessop's mother, was connected everywhere. She was a huge philanthropist. She gave money to the Museum of Modern Art, the zoo. She practically owned the Santa Barbara symphony."

Dad looked puzzled. "How do you know all that about the late Mrs. Hawkins? I don't recall telling you any of it."

I swallowed, trying to remember exactly how Ms. A said to explain it. "Ms. A did a search. She said Jes would be pleased if I knew about his mother's accomplishments."

Dad shook his head. "I'm having a hard time believing Ms. Alexandra supports Contracts."

"She's changed her thinking." I bowed my head so I'd look *penitent*. "She's realized that our fathers love us deeply and only want the best for us, and she told me I should respect your decision."

Dad couldn't look at me, and I watched him run his thumb over the cuts on his crystal wine glass. When he finally said, "All right, then," his voice was quiet and strained.

I reached for the silver folder in my lap. "So the school counselor gave me this Signing Planner. It's got sample invitations, menus, band recordings. He said if we want to use the City Club, they've got openings in January and March."

"Your Signing's scheduled for November twenty-third."

"Daddy, we can't get anything in two weeks. Everything's booked. We can't even get tents before January."

"November twenty-third, Avie."

"Please."

"No."

"You don't understand," I said. "When I told everyone I was getting Signed in two weeks, they looked at my stomach."

Dad didn't say anything.

"They think I'm pregnant, Dad, and you're rushing to Sign me off."

He stared at his plate, clenching and unclenching his hand. "I wish to God your mother was here."

"Me, too."

He looked lost, like Mom was his map and now he didn't know where anything was anymore. "I need the money, Avie. Without an infusion of cash I won't be able to make payroll. People could lose their jobs. We could lose the business."

"Oh." I hadn't realized things were that bad, but I still couldn't let the Signing go ahead.

Ms. A had told me not to get angry, but to recall a hurt I'd never get over. So I went back to the afternoon I found Mom whimpering on the lounge chair in the yard, because the painkillers had worn off and she was too weak to call for help. Silent tears rolled down my cheeks, remembering.

Dad tore off his tie. "Damn it. Don't do this to me."

"It's okay. I understand." I closed my eyes and just like Ms. A told me started counting silently to two hundred. One. Two. Three. Four. Five.

I got to seventeen, before Dad let out a sigh. "Maybe I can ask Hawkins for a loan against the Signing."

"You can do that?"

"Not sure."

"Really, Daddy, you'd do that for me?"

"I don't want anyone to question—to think you'd—"

I flung my arms around his neck. "Thank you. Thank you. I can't wait to tell everyone. Can I call Sparrow?"

"Is that a girl in your class?"

"Yeah, she and I've gotten close now that—"

Dad reached for his wineglass. "Sure, go on."

I tapped my phone as I ran up the stairs. "Sparrow?" I flung my bedroom door shut and threw my cell across the room. I'd bought myself three months, maybe four before Hawkins got his hands on me.

15

Dad didn't have the guts to tell me what Hawkins said, so he had Gerard do it.

The next morning, Gerard called me into his little office off the kitchen. On his desk was a picture of his husband, Alfonse, and their son, Lavonne, in his soccer uniform.

"How's soccer going?" I said, taking a seat.

"Better than last year. This year they know where the goal is." Gerard silenced his phone. "Hawkins' office called and they've scheduled an official portrait of the two of you."

"The candidate and his bride. Looking forward to it."

Gerard set his elbows on the desk, his fingertips pressed together. "Hawkins has agreed to delay the signing until January, but you are to meet him on the twenty-second."

"Great." I'd bought myself a little time at least. I went to leave, but Gerard pointed for me to sit.

He didn't look happy. I wondered if Alfonse would lose his job at Biocure, because of me. "Is the company going to be okay?" I said.

"Looks like it. Hawkins gave your father the money." Gerard let my fifty-million-dollar debt sink in, and then said, "In return, Hawkins asked for two things."

"What?" Suddenly, my mouth tasted like sour milk.

"He insists that you be at his side when he launches his campaign for governor."

That didn't sound so bad. I stand next to him onstage. He announces. I'm done. Not a bad deal for six more weeks of freedom. "Okay?"

Gerard frowned. He didn't want to tell me thing number two.

"You're afraid to tell me. You know I'll be pissed," I said.

He drew a tiny invisible circle on the desk. "Hawkins wants medical verification of your status."

I glared at Gerard. *Isn't it obvious I'm a virgin?*

"Your father asked me to schedule an appointment as soon as possible."

"Dad's afraid I'm not pure? That I'm going to screw up his precious business deal?"

Gerard didn't answer, and I slapped my hands on his desk. "Tell him not to worry. He won't have to return a penny of Hawkins' money."

I charged for the door, but Gerard said, "Wait. You left this in my car."

I turned. He held up a yellow tee, and I knew without asking that it had appeared on the seat of his Mini Cooper while he was out buying groceries.

I took the shirt from him. Gerard could have given it to Roik, but he didn't. "Thanks."

"You're welcome. That's a beautiful quote."

A turquoise bird sailed up from the swirly script. "Hope is the thing with feathers that perches in the soul." Emily Dickinson.

I felt hope brush my heart like a swallow flying past. *Of course Yates would pick the perfect quote.* My lip started to quiver, as I folded the shirt into a pale yellow square.

"What am I supposed to hope for, Gerard?"

Gerard got up. I sensed that he wanted to give me a hug, but touching me was expressly forbidden under the terms of his employment contract.

"I think you hope for the answer, Princess."

16

From "Scarpanol: Ten Years After"
New York Times, September 10, 2011

On September 10, 2001, Dr. Tamika Watson of Biloxi, Mississippi, put in a call to the National Institutes of Health, requesting an investigation. Dr. Watson had diagnosed four patients with advanced ovarian cancer in recent weeks, and feared that a toxin had contaminated local groundwater.

The NIH took two years to locate the source of the outbreak: beef cattle that had received doses of a synthetic hormone, Scarpanol. By then over 80 percent of African-American and Hispanic women had been diagnosed with the Silent Killer.

The Food and Drug Administration implemented a ban on Scarpanol and required warning labels on all beef and beef by-products indicating "Not for Female Consumption." Cattle treated with Scarpanol were destroyed, and major beef retailers like McDonald's and Walmart recalled seventy million tons of meat.

But despite these actions, the disease was then discovered in Caucasian and Asian populations. By 2005, the mortality rate among

females between puberty and menopause was 97 percent as chemo-
therapy drugs, already in limited supply, ran out.

Two segments of the adult female population survived unscathed:
long-term vegetarians, and women whose ovaries had been surgically
removed years before Scarpanol was introduced to the U.S.

The outbreak, while catastrophic, was limited to countries which
imported American beef. Europe and Canada had banned American
beef prior to 2001, fearing that use of hormones would cause breast
cancer . . .

Friday, November 14.

I hated Remembrance Day. There wasn't anything I wanted to
remember, but the media and Masterson wouldn't let me forget. And
today, only three days after learning about my Signing, I was so raw
and battered, I wondered how I'd survive it.

It used to be a national holiday to honor veterans, but then Scarpanol killed more women in the U.S. than all the wars we'd fought
in modern history.

For four years, Mom hid the newspapers and turned the TV off so
I wouldn't hear the daily death count or see the men in coveralls
load women's bodies into refrigerator trucks in high school parking
lots.

But Mom couldn't keep ashes from the open-air cremations from
fluttering down on our lawn like dirty grey snow.

And she couldn't keep Scarpanol from turning her ovaries into
time bombs that blew our lives apart.

Masterson Academy made Remembrance Day mandatory for all
students and their families, otherwise Dad and I would never have
come. Dad gave Roik the day off so he could attend services at the
Million Mother Wall. The state shut down the 210 Freeway all along
the wall so families could light candles and lay flowers.

Masterson arranged its ceremony on the rose garden lawn. I sat with my class in our white dresses while Dad sat with the remains of our families: fathers, brothers, grandparents, a few sisters barely older than we were, and a handful of babies and toddlers.

Ms. A stood at the end of our row, her purse fat with tissues and water bottles. I looked over my shoulder and, just as I thought, half the crowd was eyeing her.

She was the only woman her age, and she wouldn't be here except for a freak cancer in her thirties and an operation that ended up saving her life twice when it protected her from Scarpanol a decade later.

At ten on the dot, the Headmaster walked up to the podium. Behind him, the faculty were lined up in their black suits, and bells began to toll a hundred times.

The Headmaster greeted our assembled families. "We are gathered here today on this solemn occasion—"

I tried to shut out his voice as he launched into the history of the holiday I wanted to forget.

"Twelve years ago, our country took up arms against the greatest foe we have ever fought—a silent killer hiding within our beloved wives and daughters, mothers and sisters."

I could feel myself spiral down.

"Doctors struggled to find the cause, unaware that it was lurking in our refrigerators, our restaurants, and our grocery stores."

I put my head down and stuck my fingers in my ears, but that couldn't keep out the memories. No one realized the connection between beef cattle, Scarpanol, and estrogen until it swept away little girls who'd matured early and left vegetarians alone. By the time oncologists grasped how many women were dying, it was way too late. White, black, yellow, tan, it didn't matter what your skin color was, the country needed an ocean of chemo drugs, but it only had a lake.

Sophie sat on one side of me, but the chair on the other stayed empty. Partway through the Headmaster's speech, Ms. A tried to take it away, but I threw my hand down on it. "No, it's Dayla's," I snapped.

Ms. A looked at me like she wished she could do more than leave me Day's chair. I sank into the emptiness beside me.

Day, I hope someone's taking care of you today.

Dayla was always a mess on Remembrance Day, and I'd spend half my time trying to keep her from drowning in memories of the September when her mom was so desperate, she drove Day's three older sisters to a clinic in Tijuana. Weeks later, Day's mom drove back, hunched over with pain, because Mia, the only one still alive, wanted to die at home.

I remembered Day standing outside our house in her pink shortie pajamas the day after her mom died. Mom plucked Day off the front steps. "My daddy won't come out of his room," Dayla blubbered as Mom dug glass out of her foot. Mom was so calm. She made tomato sandwiches and sent us out to play under the fig tree, and she went to check on Day's dad. Dayla slept in my bed for weeks while his meds kicked in.

Oh, Day. I miss you. So much.

Mr. Hope played his cello while men walked in with nine tall brass vases and lined them up along the edge of the stage.

It will be easier if you try and hold it together until the end, Ms. A had warned us. I grabbed a tissue as the box passed from hand to hand and wiped my face.

Ms. A came down the row, passing out the yellow roses for our class. She handed me one for Mom and I saw how they'd given her too many.

"Are those Dayla's?"

Ms. A winced. "Yes."

"Can I carry them?"

Tears glazed her eyes. "Of course."

I fingered their petals as they lay on my lap. The florist had cut off their thorns, but it stung to hold them.

"Now it is time to commemorate those we have lost. Each class will come up to the stage in turn and place their roses in their class vase."

The fourth graders went first in their lacy socks and fancy dresses. They marched, their roses bouncing in their hands like they were at a party and dropping flowers into the vase was some kind of game.

Sophie sniffed. "Happy little bitches," she muttered. I wrapped my arm around her and let her rest her head on my shoulder.

Remembrance Day is all ceremony and layer cake for little girls who were lucky enough to be babies when their moms died.

The Headmaster read off names of the deceased. "Mrs. Emily Florenz. Miss Amelia Florenz. Mrs. Hannah Ferguson. Mrs. Sonia Pike . . ."

The fifth graders came up. They stood on tiptoes to drop their roses into the vase and one waved to her dad, then skipped across the stage.

"What does she think this is?" Portia said. "A pageant?"

I tried to look away as the middle schoolers went up. Tried to block out their crying and the relentless recitation of names, but I couldn't escape the vases filling with blossoms, the yellow wall of shattered hearts.

I held it together through the sophomore class, then the Headmaster called up the juniors.

We filed into the aisle. This was the part I hated the most. Now that we were upperclassmen, we recited the names of those we lost ourselves.

Felicity Reveare.

I recited it in my head as I walked up the aisle, feeling the weight of losing Mom sink into me. *Felicity.* It was ironic and cruel that *felicity* means happiness when Mom, with her big open heart, was dead.

My lips trembled as I climbed the stairs. I couldn't say *Felicity,* couldn't force it from my lips when the only name I'd ever called her was Mom.

Luckily, I didn't have to, because Sophie Park took care of that. She was about to drop in her mom's rose when two girls in the front row started to giggle. Sophie went stiff and then, before any of us could reach her, threw out her hands and shoved the vase right at them.

Water shot from the falling vase, dousing the front row. Girls screamed and the vase clanged at their feet. Ms. A swept Sophie off the stage, the choral director cued up a hymn, and the Headmaster declared we'd take a short break before the seniors.

Dad was already on his feet, and when I ran up and said, "Let's get out of here," he didn't hesitate for a second. We bolted for the car and later Dad squeezed my shoulder as I sobbed in the passenger seat. "Where do you want to go, honey?"

"Someplace where I don't have to feel anything."

"I wish I knew where that was," he said, starting the car.

For a moment, it was just Dad and me again, close like we used to be. But then his cell phone rang, a new special ring. *Hawkins*.

Today? Really?

"He's probably calling for you," Dad said. "You feel like talking?"

I shook my head, and listened to Dad apologize, that I was feeling under the weather, but he'd pass on Jessop's condolences. When Dad hung up, he looked at me. "You're going to have to talk to him sometime."

Not if I could help it.

17

Roik gunned the car though the half-dead streets to St. Mark's Church and I fidgeted with my music player in the backseat. I hadn't been back to St. Mark's since Mom's funeral and I wasn't looking forward to it.

Roik stopped at a red light. On the sidewalk, a man shook a sign with a little girl's photo on it. HELP US FIND ALMA GONZALEZ. A boy smacked a flyer to our windshield. "Hey. A man took my sister. Maybe you saw him?"

She was only eight. I looked at her chubby, dimpled face and went to roll down the window, but Roik hit the gas. "Roik! Stop! We should help them."

"How? We don't live around here."

I shrank against the seat. Maybe that was true, but Mom wouldn't have driven away. She'd have done something.

The closer we got to St. Mark's, the more I wanted to turn around. If I hadn't promised Yates, I would have told Roik to bag it.

Roik pulled up out front and I saw how St. Mark's had changed. The stained-glass windows were now covered with metal screens like they'd locked Christ up in a county jail.

A dozen bodyguards hung out in the courtyard where we used to serve Thanksgiving dinner to the homeless. I took a deep breath, remembering how Mom and Dad dished out turkey and stuffing, and I put a roll on every plate.

I looked away, but a memory of our last Thanksgiving together rolled over me: Mom squeezing my hand extra hard and saying, "We're so *fortunate*. We have a roof and food and each other."

Not anymore.

Roik opened the car door. "Meet you here after mass?" He eyed the men lounging on the benches.

I nodded. My feet felt too heavy to climb the stairs, but I forced myself.

The smell of incense met me just inside the big wood doors. Half the lights were turned off so the long room was shadowy, except for the spotlight over the altar.

I glanced at Mom's favorite pew, but sitting there now would be too awful. I scanned the room, looking for someplace I belonged.

Seats up front were filled with old ladies and girls leaning their heads on their shoulders. These pews used to be packed with families.

Two bodyguards yakked in front of me, and I saw the game up on their phones. It was Women's Mass, so they weren't even supposed to be in the church. *Jerks.*

I slipped into a pew and closed my eyes so I couldn't see the emptiness next to me where Mom should be. But I could feel it.

Dammit, why'd I listen to Yates?

I had to get out of there. I stepped into the aisle, but then I saw a priest limping toward me with his hand outstretched. He was just a few inches taller than me, not the towering, heroic type I'd imagined from the few things I'd heard about him.

"Hello," he said, his English rolling out like Spanish. "I'm Father Gabriel. Welcome." His hand swallowed mine. He was as strong as Roik.

"I'm Avie Reveare. I used to come here with my mom."

"Ah, the prodigal daughter has returned. I wish we had a fatted calf, but perhaps you will stay for doughnuts after the service."

"Sure. Thank you." It had been so long since I'd been to confession, I wasn't sure that counted as a lie.

Father Gabriel moved up the aisle. "Go on. Out!" he barked at the bodyguards. "This is Women's Mass." They hesitated for a second, then pocketed their phones and slunk out.

I sat back down, thinking I could escape once the service started. Father Gabriel returned to the front, and that's when I saw Yates. He was standing in the half-dark between the pillars, wearing robes.

It was weird. Yates had never mentioned being an altar boy again. He'd quit when his mom died, because he was so angry at God.

I watched Yates reach into his robes, and take something out. Then I realized there was a girl standing next to him in the shadows. Her back was to me, but I saw Yates lean in and press whatever it was into her hands.

I sat up straight, trying to see. Their heads were close together like they were whispering, and he held on to her hand before they stepped to the left and disappeared behind the pillar.

The little drama pinned me to my seat. Something that felt uncomfortably like jealousy flip-flopped my stomach, and I remembered when I was twelve and crushing on Yates, and he asked me to go ask another girl on the beach for her name.

Larissa.

The name set off fireworks of humiliation inside me. *I am not going there again.*

A murmur swept the room and Father Gabriel began the mass. Yates emerged from behind the pillar, and the girl slipped into the front row.

Sparrow? Sparrow who last year called the Catholic Church "the biggest oppressor of women in history"?

Talk about bizarre. Now I couldn't leave. Not yet.

I watched Yates do his duties, turn the pages of the prayer book, swing the incense burner, while a voice in my head asked what the hell was going on here.

Father Gabriel launched into his sermon, and everyone shifted in the pews as he came down into the aisle. He crossed his arms like he was cradling a baby. "A man sees his baby daughter for the first time. He is consumed by the love he feels for her and he vows that he will protect her from all harm.

"He is afraid she will be cold, so he swaddles her to keep her warm.

"He is afraid of the evil in the world, so he wraps the blanket over her eyes so she will not see it and be frightened.

"He wraps the blanket over her ears so she will not hear.

"The father wants to keep her safe, but now she is blind. She is ignorant."

Goose pimples ran up my arms. He was preaching against the Paternalists. I glanced back at the door just to make sure there weren't any bodyguards listening in.

"Still the man believes he is doing the right thing." Father Gabriel jabbed his finger in the air. "We must not be silent when we see a man so confused. We must teach our daughters to question what they see or hear.

"Truth and knowledge are the sword and shield that protect us. I ask you to carry them."

Yates stood, facing the room. He hung on Father Gabriel's words like he'd already joined the crusade. But a symbolic sword and shield weren't going to free me from Jessop Hawkins.

And me lecturing Dad on what was morally right and wrong wouldn't make my fifty-million-dollar Contract go away. Yates—of all people—should know that.

After mass, I slid out of the pew. I didn't see the point in staying for doughnuts. Father Gabe couldn't fix my life, no matter how much Yates worshiped him.

I was halfway to the door when an old lady caught my arm. "You dropped this." She held out a silver phone with a cracked screen.

"Oh, that's not mine," I said, but she pressed it into my hand.

"It probably broke when it fell out of your bag. These tile floors are so hard." Her voice was soft, but the insistent look she gave me made me stuff the phone in my bag. "Thank you," I said.

"You should join us gals for refreshments," she said. "I made the pumpkin bread."

I took a step forward and she did, too. "My bodyguard's waiting," I said.

"I doubt he's in a hurry to leave." She set her hand on my purse. I'd have to tear it off if I wanted to escape. So I took a deep breath and let her lead me to the rectory.

18

The room was full of women I didn't know. A group of them circled Father Gabe like he was a rock star. I was dying to ask Yates why he brought me here, but I wasn't surprised when I didn't see him. It was borderline acceptable for a teenage guy to help serve mass, but definitely not okay for him to hang out with the girls after.

Sparrow was in the corner, teaching girls to embroider. Her soft blond curls fell around her face like she was an angel out of a Raphael painting. Then she spied me. "Avie!"

I walked over, and she held up her embroidery: balloons rising over little red roofs. I fingered the linen. "Does that say what I think it says? 'I have a dream'?"

"Yeah, Martin Luther King. This is our little revolution factory. Like it?"

My eyes swept the room for monitors, but I didn't see any. Still, I kept my voice down. "Father Gabe's okay with this?"

"Are you kidding? He suggested it. We're spreading hope one stitch at a time."

Sparrow was clueless, thinking truth and knowledge were going to get her out of a Contract when it was her turn.

"It would be great if we could change things, but we can't."

"Yes we can," she said.

"How? We don't have any real power."

"Relax, Avie. Have a little faith."

I spied Yates through the window, handing out cake and coffee to the bodyguards, and I wondered if he was deliberately distracting them.

Father Gabriel appeared by my side. He nodded at Sparrow, then he took my elbow and guided me to a quiet corner. "I am pleased you have come back to the church," he said. "What brought you here today?"

If Father Gabe was going to be cagey, I was, too. "A friend told me I should come."

"Perhaps your friend thought I could help you." Father Gabe must have seen the big fat question marks in my eyes, because he leaned in. "I understand that your father has written a Contract."

"Yes." My mouth went completely dry.

"Perhaps I can help."

"How?" The word broke as I said it.

"You know what is meant by the Exodus?"

"From the Old Testament?"

"From throughout history. Jews, Macedonians, Tibetans, Italians. Many, many times oppressed peoples have fled their homelands. Now there is a new Exodus."

My chest squeezed. Father Gabriel's meaning was clear: he helped girls get to Canada. That was why Yates wanted us to meet. He thought I should run.

Run for the border? The thought sent shivers through me. *Dayla didn't make it and she had Seth to protect her. Yates thinks I should run—alone?*

"I don't think you can help me," I said.

Father Gabe's gentle expression didn't change. "The confessional will open in a few minutes. You should visit it before you leave today."

He blessed me before he walked away. Out in the courtyard, I saw Yates was gone.

I headed back through the church and was almost out the door when I saw the red light on over the confessional. Father Gabriel was waiting, but I didn't have anything to confess. Sure, okay, so I lied on a regular basis, but I wouldn't have to if I wasn't gated, guarded, and spied on.

Still . . . I stepped inside and sat down. The shade over the grate pulled back and I heard someone whisper, "Avie."

My head whipped up. Yates peered at me through the brass grate. "Hi." His blue eyes were ultramarine in this light.

"Hi." I leaned in until our faces were only a few inches apart. Yates smelled faintly of coffee and maple syrup.

"So did you meet Father G?"

I sighed. "Yeah. Why didn't you tell me you thought I should go to Canada?"

"I thought you should meet Gabe first. See if you could trust him."

This was all coming at me so fast. "I'm not sure. I don't know."

"He helped Dayla."

"Yeah, and look how that turned out."

"It wasn't his fault," Yates said.

"Why not?"

"Dayla's father posted a reward. Seth owed money to another body-guard and the guy gave him up."

"So they were outed?"

"They'd have made it if it wasn't for that. I'm sure of it."

I shook my head. Yates acted like this was so simple. "If I run, Jes Hawkins can hire a whole army to track me."

"Yeah, he's got a lot of money to throw around, but we know how to get girls out."

Yates didn't get it. "I haven't even turned seventeen yet and you want me to go to Canada all by myself and start a whole new life just like that?"

He dropped his eyes and a moment passed before he said in a too quiet voice, "Don't you remember what happened with Becca?"

Tears blurred my eyes. "Yes." I'd tried so hard to block it from my mind, how Becca had handed her newborn son to her husband, telling him, "Now you have your heart's desire," before she went upstairs and threw the rope over the beam in their bedroom.

"I'm not going to kill myself," I said.

"I'm not saying you would, but the things that happened to her, they could happen to you."

A shiver traveled up my legs. "Like what?"

"Well, like your fiancé starts scheduling your life. Dress fittings. Sessions with the Signing Planner. Verification appointment with the doctor. Have they sprung that on you yet?"

My cheeks flamed, and I was glad the confessional was semidark. "Yes." My appointment was tomorrow, and I prayed Yates wouldn't ask about it.

"And when you get tired of all this crap and you tell your Intended you don't like it, he takes you out of school. Now you're cut off from your friends. The next thing he does is move you into his compound, and take away your phone so you can't call your family without permission. He listens in on your calls. He restricts access on your computer. Don't you remember how we could never see Becca? How we could barely get to talk to her?"

Yates' eyes pleaded with me. I didn't remember everything that happened to Becca, but I remembered a lot.

"Becca didn't have any money," Yates said. "Not one credit card. Her husband wouldn't even let her out to go to the grocery store without her bodyguard along."

"Are you trying to scare me, because you've succeeded!"

Yates blew out a hard breath and the dark curls on his forehead stirred. "I'm sorry," he said. His hand hung on the brass grate and he stretched his fingers toward me. "I don't want anything to happen to you, and I can't—you can't pretend or wish it will all go away, because it won't."

I felt like we were standing together in a cold rain. Okay, so I had to deal with the future hurtling toward me. My first meeting with Hawkins was Saturday.

"I have to think about this."

Yates nodded. "I know. It's a big decision, so I want you to call me. I'll answer any questions about Exodus you have. You got the phone, right?"

I waved it at him through the grate.

"It works even though the screen is busted," he said. "And there aren't any patriarchal controls. I'm on the contact list under AP."

"AP?"

"Antsy Pantsy."

I smiled. "Mom's nickname for you."

"I figured if Roik ever found the phone he wouldn't know that name."

The front door of the church creaked open, and I heard men talking. Roik and another guard.

Yates turned toward their voices. "You're stronger than you realize, Fearless."

My heart pinched. I wanted to stay, but the voices were getting closer. "Roik's looking for me."

Yates dropped his voice. "I'm done at work around ten and back at my apartment by ten-thirty," he said. "So if you want to talk—"

Footsteps passed a few feet away. I nodded, and Yates sat back and disappeared into the dark.

I slipped into a pew and pretended to say penance, but my head was spinning, trying to take it all in: Yates. Father G. Exodus.

If I had the guts to run, Yates would help get me out.

19

The house was silent and dark before I brought the phone out. The screen burst bright and I closed myself in my closet. I scrolled down. There were definitely no patriarchal controls. News, politics, condoms, gambling. Anything a man could want was right here at my fingertips.

And for the first time in my life, I had unlimited phone access. I shot down the contacts list and found AP. I had to be careful. If we got caught, they'd come down on Yates harder than me. Dad would sign me off to Hawkins before even I knew it.

I heard the connection take. *Please let this be Yates, not some crazy.*

"Avie?" He sounded like he'd been waiting with his hand on the screen. The cracked screen distorted his face, but I could still see his smile.

"Thank God it's you."

"So the phone's working okay?"

"Yeah. Looks like it."

"Excellent."

I was about to ask where he got it, when he grinned and said, "You know what I was thinking about?"

"No, what?"

"Riding Buddies."

"Oh, I haven't thought about that in forever." When Mom volunteered for equine therapy, Yates and I used to go to the stable and help with the kids who had cerebral palsy and Down Syndrome.

"Remember how Bruiser followed you around like a big dog?"

I smiled, seeing this huge Appaloosa horse plodding after me. "It was the carrots. I'd stuff my pockets."

"And I thought he liked you."

"The truth comes out."

Dusty scratched at the door, and I let her in. She settled into my lap and I rubbed her tummy.

"I was remembering your mom, too," Yates said.

I tensed. It was still hard for me to talk about Mom.

"Your mom was the first person to tell me that people would listen to me, that I could make a difference in someone's life."

"Yeah, she believed in you. She saw how you helped Matt." For a year, Yates had held Matt up in the saddle until he could sit up straight and take over the reins.

"You know he's applying to Oxy for next year?"

"No!"

"Yeah. He's got an electric chair, takes him everywhere."

"You did it."

"No, it was all Matt." We sat, the quiet tying us together. "Aves, if your mom was here, what would she tell you to do?"

"If she was here, none of this would be happening."

"Sorry."

I breathed in and out, got myself centered. "No, I'm sorry."

"But if she could speak to you, what would she say?"

I wished Yates would drop it, but I knew he wouldn't. "Follow your dreams." My voice broke. "She'd say follow your dreams, because even if you don't reach them, you'll still be going in the right direction."

"So what are your dreams?"

I propped my back against the wall. "I'm not sure."

"Come on. I thought you wanted to go to college."

"Yeah, I do . . . I did."

"You could still go in Canada. They've got great schools up there."

Stop it, I wanted to say.

"I know it's scary, but you should think about it."

"Okay. I will."

Yates ignored the no in my voice. "So what do you want to study?" he said.

I'd never told anyone, never said it out loud. "Psychology."

"I can see that. You always like to know what people are thinking. But I'm kind of surprised. I'd have guessed you'd go for art history."

I felt the smile on my lips. "Really, why?"

"Oh, the way you lugged that big book down to the beach every day." Mom's book about Michelangelo. "That thing weighed—what?—forty pounds?"

"More like eight," I said.

"I remember you saying you were going to Florence someday to see the *David* statue up close."

I couldn't believe he remembered that—some random thing I'd said four years ago. "You haven't told me what your dreams are," I said.

"Keep doing what I'm doing. Fighting for justice. I'm leading the Liberty Project at Oxy, taking on the Paternalists."

Yates's face was filled with passion, his twilight-blue eyes brimming with it, and I suddenly longed to feel the way he did, committed to something that filled me with purpose.

His long lashes brushed his cheeks as he spoke, and I caught myself staring at them. *I'm turning into Dayla*, I thought, and looked away.

"Oh," I said. "I forgot to say, thanks for the shirt. It's beautiful, especially the quote."

"I thought you'd like it."

"Before I could say I did, Yates said, "Sorry, I've got to take this other call."

"Oh, okay." I didn't want to let him go—not yet.

His voice dropped and his words brushed my ear. "Please think seriously about Exodus, Avie, for me. I—care about you."

My head spun. I knew Yates cared about me, but he'd never said it that way before—like it meant *more*.

"You're all I have left now that Becca's gone."

A rock formed in my throat as I tried to swallow. "I will. I promise I'll think about it."

Yates hung up and I just sat there. *I care about you.*

Of course he cared. He was my friend. We'd been through hell together.

The weird thing was, I'd felt a little flutter—like my heart wanted to go to a new place. Dusty rolled onto her back, begging to be scratched. I ran my fingers in circles over her tummy, and thought about the last time Yates and I were allowed alone together.

It was after Becca got Signed, and Yates and I spent the afternoon riding our bikes around my neighborhood. We chucked the bikes at some point and followed the horse paths behind peoples' properties. We peered over fences and stole some figs hanging over a wall, but mostly we just talked.

We weren't doing anything, but when I got home, Dad started giving me the third degree. And then he dropped the bombshell. "Roik thinks you and Yates are too close."

I didn't get it. "What's wrong with us being friends?"

"Things are different now. You're growing up."

I remembered the squelchy feeling in my stomach and how I prayed Dad wouldn't say my body was *changing*. "So what?"

"He's a teenage boy, and they—" Dad shoved his hands in his pockets. He couldn't even look at me. "You can't be alone with him anymore."

"This is so unfair!"

"Yes, but this is the way it has to be," he said.

I hugged Dusty to my chest. *Get real.* Me thinking that things might change between me and Yates was a complete fantasy. I could dissect everything he said and put any spin on it I wanted, but we'd never be together. There was no happily ever after here.

20

Dr. Prandip's office made pre-Signing exams a priority, so Gerard got me an appointment first thing Monday morning.

Dad and Hawkins could force me to go through this humiliation, but they could not make me believe it was for my own good. I kept hearing Yates warn me about how Hawkins would take over my life step by step and my head started to pound.

Only five days until I met Hawkins. In the flesh.

The building was secure, but Roik walked me to the office like he was sure I'd bolt.

I felt manipulated from the moment I walked in the empty waiting room. The decorator had designed it to be soothing: lilac-colored walls, lavender aromatherapy diffusers, and framed pastels of Mary Cassatt mothers and children. He'd even stenciled a touching quote from Cassatt on the wall.

"There is only one thing in life for a woman; it's to be a mother."

Hypocrite bitch. I'd read Mom's art books. I knew the truth. Cassatt refused to get married, because it would "compromise her art." I reached for my nail file and tapped my thumb against the sharp metal point. The only thing stopping me from scratching out the quote was the security camera in the corner.

Then I heard Ms. A whisper in my ear. Don't do anything foolish. If you appear to resist your Signing, they'll only watch you closer.

The nurse called my name, and I put away the file and followed her like a little lamb. An ignorant, submissive, soon-to-be-slaughtered lamb.

The nurse had me strip. I waited on the exam table in a paper gown that covered me about as well as a cheap paper towel.

Prandip came in with her laptop. "Ah, so you are going to be married soon," she said with a smile. "Are you excited?"

I shook my head before I realized it. "I— It's kind of last-minute. It's a lot to take in."

The smile left her eyes, but her voice trilled, "Yes, so many details. It can make your head spin." She patted my knee. "Please lie back."

I trembled under the paper gown. "You won't find anything broken," I told her.

She nodded. "I trust you, Avie, but I am obligated to confirm your status." She looked sad like this wasn't what she'd signed up for when she went to medical school forty years ago.

Dayla had told me all about her pre-Signing exam, but that didn't prep me to lie back on an exam table with my knees spread apart, and have Dr. Prandip point a blinding lamp right between them. Sweat trickled down my legs, but I was freezing cold.

"When you're ready," she said.

I closed my eyes and let her do what she had to do.

Examined. Inspected. Graded.

Invaded.

"Your status is confirmed," she said. "Would you like to take this opportunity for premarital counseling?" Prandip pointed up at the light and shook her head.

Ms. A had warned me that women's doctors have audio monitors to prevent criminal acts like dispensing birth control or arranging abortions. "I know where babies come from," I said.

"Excellent. Do you understand your duties as a wife?"

"Yes." I looked away, because I couldn't bear thinking about doing it with Hawkins even for one second.

"As often as he wants, you understand."

"Okay."

Prandip stuck a finger to her lips and reached for my foot.

I jerked. *What the hell?* Prandip stripped off my knee sock, then she waved her pen in my face and wrote something on my sole.

"He wants it three times a day, you do it. It is essential to a good marriage." She turned my foot toward a mirror in the corner, and I saw a phone number. "Sometimes young girls have trouble satisfying their husband's needs. You understand what I am saying?" she snapped.

She paused and a big question shaped her face. She pointed at me, then moved two fingers like they were running away.

Do I want to run away?

Yes. "Yes, I understand."

"It is your duty to be the best wife you can be. Promise me if you have problems you will call me," she said, and tapped the sole of my foot.

"I promise."

"Very good. Now. We'll take some blood, and you can be on your way."

Her eyes held mine. You call me, she mouthed.

"Thank you, Dr. Prandip."

Prandip left and I stood up. The paper sheet had melted to my back, and I had to peel it off. I threw my clothes back on and huddled in the exam room trying to clear my head.

Invaded. That was how I felt. And it was only going to get worse once I met Hawkins.

21

Roik dropped me off at school, but I almost asked him to take me home. I felt as if I still had on the flimsy paper gown I wore for the exam, and everybody could see right through it.

I walked onto campus as morning break was starting. Sparrow was sitting at an outdoor table, tinkering with one of the little chargers she made out of wires and batteries and old mints tins.

She was flawlessly beautiful even in a lumpy Masterson blazer.

I sat down with her, because people usually left Sparrow alone. Right now I wanted to be invisible.

Sparrow looked up. "I guess I need to say thanks."

I blew on my latte. "For what?"

"My dad upped my minimum bid. He figures if your dad got fifty mill for you with a company thrown in, he can get fifteen for me."

"Oh." I didn't know what to say. It was kind of an insult.

"Dad's taking me to New York tomorrow to get appraised by the auction houses. I have interviews at Sotheby's and Christie's."

She wasn't boasting. Sparrow loathed debutantes. "I'm sorry."

"Yeah, well, who cares what you or I want anyway. So, where were you today?"

"Status verification."

"God, you'd have to tie me down and give me electroshock before I'd do that."

I picked up my coffee. I'd had enough Sparrow for now.

She put down her tiny screwdriver. "Sorry, I didn't mean to make you feel worse."

"I doubt that's possible."

"So did you hear what happened today with Samantha Rowley?"

"The girl who's fighting her Signing? No, what?"

Sparrow pulled out her phone and tapped away at the screen. I spied a sliver of chrome under the sequined case, not pink like the Princess cell everyone else had.

"Whose phone is that?" I said.

"My brother's. He lets me borrow it so I can sell my kits. I give him a cut."

I'd heard rumors Sparrow had a stash of cash, but now I believed it.

She muted her cell and handed it to me. "Watch this."

Reporters mobbed a man in a suit as he exited a white marble building. The camera pulled back, revealing Corinthian columns and EQUAL JUSTICE UNDER THE LAW carved along the roof. The man jogged down the long flight of steps past a line of policemen holding back protesters.

"Who is that?" I said, squinting at the signs the crowd was waving.

"That's Rowley's lawyer at the Supreme Court."

The man paused to look at the protesters, then he got in the car. It edged into the traffic and boom! The car exploded into a fireball, and flames roared out the windows.

I clamped my hands over my mouth.

"That's right," Sparrow said. "They killed him."

"This is crazy. Who did this?"

"I don't know. The Paternalists, maybe. Sending us a message that fighting Signings is too dangerous to even try. It's like the Taliban's trying to take over America."

"What's the Taliban?"

Sparrow sized me up. "You've really been protected," she said, like that wasn't anything to be happy about. "Don't you ever wonder why all these things are happening? The ACLU bombings? The intimidation? This isn't just about keeping girls safe. I think something bigger is going on."

The bell rang and I got up and tossed my latte in the trash. I'd had just about all I could stomach.

22

Run.

I traced my finger over the phone number on my foot. Dr. Prandip. Father G. Yates. They were all telling me to run. I just didn't know if I had the guts to do it.

Bad things happened out there in the real world. Girls got kidnapped from ballet class, brides got snatched off beaches. But when I thought about Becca—

Hawkins was already taking over my life. Dad would never have had me verified—ugh—if Hawkins hadn't demanded it. And if Yates was right, this was only the beginning.

I took another look at Prandip's number and repeated it under my breath until I knew those ten digits by heart. She told me to call if I needed help, but could I trust her? Or Father Gabriel for that matter?

It was almost ten, and I knew I should wait to call Yates. Roik never went to bed before eleven.

A text came in and an image flashed up on the screen. The spider-web cracks distorted the picture, but I could still make out the white marble sculpture. Michelangelo's *David*.

I felt my whole body lighten. I hesitated a second, and called. "Hi."

"Hi."

"What are you doing?"

"Nothing." I brushed my hair back from my face, before it hit me what a flirt move it was. "Just sitting here thinking."

"About Canada?"

"Yes, among other things."

"And?"

"I'm scared."

"It's scary."

We let the silence fill with the bad, unspoken things we both knew could happen.

"Why do you trust Father Gabe?" I said.

"Because he's honest. Unlike a lot of the lying sacks of sh— I've had to deal with."

"You thinking about your dad?"

"How'd you guess?"

Yates would never lie to me. Ever. "You really believe I can trust Father G with my life?"

"Yeah, I do," he said. "Exodus is full of good people. Good people who'll hide you, drive you to the border."

"How do you know they're good people? How do you know that's what happens?"

"Because I'm one of them," he said.

I was surprised, but not surprised—like I'd smacked into a door I should have known was there. "You are?"

"I'm one of the links in the chain. I get girls out of L.A. to their next stop."

I wrapped my sweatshirt tighter around me. Yates was insane putting himself at risk like this. If Father Gabe went to jail, Yates would, too. I tried to keep my voice from shaking. "How long have you—"

"Almost a year. Once I turned eighteen."

"So you'd be the person who—"

"Roik knows me, so I can't extract you, but I'd drive you to Indio or Goleta or whatever town they picked for the meet."

"But why? Why are you doing this? You could get killed."

"I made a vow," Yates said.

I was suddenly very angry, because this was Father Gabriel's fault. He knew Yates worshiped him and took advantage of that. "A vow? To who? Father Gabriel?"

He took a deep breath. "I promised Becca," he said quietly.

Becca? "But Becca loved you. I can't believe she asked you—"

"She didn't."

"Then I don't understand." Yates didn't answer, but he didn't owe me an answer. "Wait, you don't have explain."

"No, I want to," he said, then looked away. "It was my fault Becca died."

A vision of Becca hanging from a beam swayed in front of me. "But she—" I searched for a gentle way to say it. "She chose to end her life."

"It wasn't a suicide."

I gripped the phone, my head reeling. "But they found her—"

"Yeah, I know, but I couldn't believe Becca would just give up, so I tracked down the coroner's assistant."

"What did he say?"

"Her hyoid bone was broken. He can't prove it, but he thinks Becca might have been strangled."

"I can't believe it."

"I was supposed to help her escape from the hospital after she had the baby and drive her to Vancouver. But I didn't show, so it's my fault she's gone."

Not show? That didn't make sense. "No, I don't believe you deliberately left her there."

"Yeah, I could give you a list of excuses. The baby was early. I didn't know. I left my phone in a friend's truck. But none of that matters, because Becca's dead. So I made her a vow that I'd be there for other girls who needed to get out."

Now I finally got why Yates lost it, why he ended up in the locked ward after Becca died.

We let the quiet settle around us.

"Thanks for sharing that with me," I said.

Yates blew out a breath. "I've never told anyone about it before."

"Miss Avie!"

Roik's voice wrenched me off the floor. I dropped the phone in my dirty clothes and flicked on the closet light. "What?" I said, throwing open the doors. "I'm right here."

Roik was rifling through the stuff on my desk. "I thought I heard something." He did that little thing with his mouth where he squashes it shut after saying something that isn't exactly true.

"So you just barge into my room?"

"When I knocked, you didn't answer."

"I had my earphones in."

Roik frowned like that was hard to believe since I didn't have any earphones hanging around my neck. He scanned my closet and I knew he wanted to go in there, but didn't want a scene.

"Then are you done?" I said.

Roik muttered good night and left. The closet hung open, and I wanted desperately to call Yates back, but I couldn't risk Roik catching me.

I pulled my comforter onto the floor and lay below the window so I could see the moon. I thought I knew Yates, but now I saw how much I'd missed since we'd been kept apart. He'd been carrying around this horrible secret, and blaming himself. How could Yates think for even one minute that it was his fault Becca died? Tears trickled into my hair, but for the first time in a long time, they weren't for me.

The next day, Roik showed up unannounced and had the dean pull me from class. I waited in the entrance hall while Roik signed me out, wondering why the hell he was here. Roik came out of the office, and steered me to the door.

"What's the problem?" I said.

"There's a stylist waiting for you at the house."

"But I thought Elancio was coming on Friday."

"Your lunch with Jessop Hawkins was moved up."

I snatched my arm away. "To when?"

"Thursday."

Hawkins was doing exactly what Yates warned me he'd do, taking over my life one appointment at a time. "Nobody even asked me!"

Roik pushed out a breath. "Hawkins runs the show, and if he has to go to Singapore at the last minute, then you've got to change your precious plans."

I burned, looking up at the Signing portraits filling the walls. A hundred blindingly happy girls in rhinestone tiaras smiled at me. I refused to be one of them.

"Okay," I said.

A silver Airstream was parked on our driveway, a grey and rose-striped canopy popped open above the door like a party bus.

Gerard intercepted me as I got out of Big Black. "Hawkins' assistant decided to drop in," he said. "His name's Adam Ho, and I suggest you choose your words carefully."

"You think I can't behave myself?"

"I think," Gerard said slowly, "he isn't your friend."

"Gerard, block her!" Roik barreled around the car, pointing at something behind me. I turned to look. A cameraman hung from an upstairs window next door, clicking away.

Gerard hustled me into the Airstream, slammed the door, and rolled down the shades. "Even the neighbors are cashing in on you."

Thank you, newly found celebrity. Now I can't even walk outside my house.

The Airstream was a mobile salon done up in blond wood and leather. Pink roses peeked from glass bud vases. Grey-striped garment bags lined one wall.

Elancio introduced himself while Ho perched on a lounge chair, scrolling through his tablet. He eyed me like a lizard as he talked on the phone.

Outside, Gerard was raising hell with Roik about the camera.

Elancio patted the salon chair and I sat, acting ever so cooperative like the girl Ms. A had warned me to appear.

Photos of a woman I didn't recognize were taped to the mirror, and they stared back at me. Young and hopeful on the left. Older and confident on the right. My face appeared right in between them, reflecting back the same brown hair, oval face, and deep-set eyes. Even the slight upturn of our noses.

Elancio combed his fingers through my hair, and my mouth went dry. He was here to make me into *her*.

"Who is that?" I said, choking out the words.

"Letitia Hawkins, Mr. Hawkins' mother."

His mother? I started to heave. Elancio pulled me out of the chair and threw me into the tiny bathroom. I bent over the toilet, and let it all out.

Hawkins, that perv, wants to—OhmyGod, no! I couldn't even say it, it was so disgusting.

I set down the lid and crawled onto the seat.

Now I finally got why Hawkins did the deal. I wasn't a beauty queen, but that wasn't what he was looking for. And Dad was clueless. He thought Biocure was the reason.

Elancio knocked on the door. "Shall we continue, Miss Reveare?"

"I'll be out in a minute," I called back. Elancio could try to make me over into Letitia Hawkins, but I refused to be Hawkins' sick fantasy. I was not going to make this easy.

I rinsed my mouth and dabbed my face with Elancio's rose-scented towel. He handed me sparkling water as I sat back down in the chair.

I sipped and pointed to the garment bags. "Are those clothes for me?"

"Yes." He ran a finger over my brow.

"So I get to choose the ones I like?"

He held a color chart up to my skin. "No, I choose. Each outfit is in a separate bag, matched with the correct accessories."

"What if I don't like them?"

Ho snickered behind me, and Elancio turned to him. "She is your problem, not mine," he said.

A floodlight went on in my brain: I'd made a huge mistake, revealing how I felt. "I won't be a problem," I said. "I'll wear what you tell me to."

But I won't like it. You can dress me up, but I'll never be Letitia.

Elancio picked up my hand, then dropped it in my lap. "You bite your nails."

I shrugged. "Can't you do acrylic?"

"Mr. Hawkins prefers them natural." Elancio was tapping his foot like I'd just ruined everything. I stifled a smile. "When is her first public appearance?" he asked Ho.

Ho frowned and consulted his tablet. You could tell the question irked him. He had better things to do than babysit a stylist. "November twenty-eighth. Morning rally at Pasadena City Hall. Then golf in San Clemente. Major donor dinner in Del Mar."

"Your office did not mention golf. I have styled day, cocktail, and formal wear."

Now I was paying attention. This wasn't just an hour in the morning. This was all day and a couple hundred miles. "Wait, you only need me at the rally, right?"

Ho's eyes turned to slits as he smiled. I expected a forked tongue to dart out of his mouth. "Miss Reveare, as Mr. Hawkins' fiancée you are expected to attend every campaign event."

Roik knocked on the door. "Ho, we could use your input." Ho gave a little huff and went outside as Elancio handed me a smock. "I must prepare the wax," he said, and disappeared into the back.

I tied on the smock and crept over to Ho's tablet. Hawkins' campaign schedule was up on-screen, every event until the election next year. There had to be two, maybe three hundred of them from San Diego to Eureka.

And in the margin was a list of who'd be there. My name was next to every one.

Hawkins' perfect little wifey and helpmate, silently and adoringly standing at his side.

I stepped away from Ho's tablet as Elancio came back. He sat me down and started in on my brows.

Time was running out. I only had two weeks, because if I didn't get away before Hawkins' announcement, it would be too late. It didn't matter that I wasn't Signed yet, I'd be constantly surrounded by Hawkins and his men.

I wasn't ready. This was all happening too fast.

Gerard returned while Elancio conditioned and cut my hair. I half listened as he and Elancio reviewed the outfits in each garment bag.

Each outfit had been photographed on a model so I'd know exactly how to wear it. Every detail was dictated, even how I buttoned my cardi. There were three acceptable alternatives, and I was to choose one.

My anger was on simmer, but it boiled over when Elancio told Gerard, "Mr. Hawkins selected her intimate wear. It's on hold at Sweet Fantasies on Melrose and we've booked her an appointment next week."

Hawkins thinks I'm his plaything. That he bought me and he can do whatever he wants with me. But he's wrong. I haven't Signed the Contract.

Ho banged through the door, barking into his phone, "The neighbor's name is Geller. Make sure he understands that if I see even one image of the fiancée anywhere, he can kiss his house good-bye. His house, his car, his labradoodle. I will *own* him!"

Because that's what you and Hawkins do.

Elancio put down his blow-dryer, and I leaped out of the chair. "Thanks for the color and the fashion advice," I said, whipping off the smock.

"You are not done here."

"No?"

"No." He handed me the outfit for Thursday. "I must check the fit."

When I came out of the dressing room, Elancio smiled for the first time.

I saw in the mirror how he'd packaged me: Jes Hawkins Ideal Mate. He'd chosen Letitia's favorite colors, but updated them. Sky-blue dress with a yellow belt. A cream-colored cardi draped asymmetrically over my shoulder. And the pièce de résistance: a black and cream patterned headband with an unexpected dash of red. I was Letitia, but reborn fresh and new.

"This is genius," Ho murmured. "Female voters will love her no matter what political party they belong to. This girl's going to get us the fifty-plus demographic we need to take the race."

Ho and Elancio traded congratulations while I peeled off the dress. It wasn't enough that I fed some sick fantasy of Jes Hawkins, I would make his political dreams come true.

I had a hand on the door, when Elancio stopped me. He held out a crystal bottle of pale green perfume, the color of poison. "Mrs. Hawkins wore Chanel No. 19, and you will also."

"You're telling me what perfume to wear?"

Gerard flashed me a look. Don't go there.

"I assume you wish to please your husband," Elancio said.

I swallowed back the anger boiling inside me. "Yes. Thank you for being so—thorough."

The sky was dark when I stepped outside, and I realized I'd lost my chance to go to the cemetery. Along with my identity and my freedom to choose what I wore and how I smelled, Ho had stolen my time with Mom.

This was playing out exactly the way Yates said it would.

24

"How are you?" Yates said later when he got me on the phone.

I was sitting in my closet with the door cracked open so I'd hear Roik if he knocked. "Angry," I said. "I spent all afternoon being made over for Jes Hawkins and the voters of California."

"It's good you're angry," Yates said. "You should be. You ready to change your life?"

I could feel my heart going tick-tick-tick. Time was running out.

"What do I have to do?" I said.

"Tell Father Gabe you're ready."

"I can't just tell you?"

"No, he needs to hear you say it. You tell him you're ready and we pick a date and a place to extract you."

Extract. Like I was a miner trapped two miles down. "It has to be soon. The campaign starts November twenty-eighth and after that, they're making me travel with Hawkins all over the state."

"Sixteen days. Doesn't give us much time." He raked his hand through his hair, combing it off his face. "We need to choose a place where you're out in the open, and it's hard for Roik to watch you."

Out in the open? I lived behind gates. Gates at home, at school, even when I went shopping, I was checked in and out at the Beverly Center like a dog at a kennel.

"There isn't any."

"Sure there is. We got one girl out of a dentist's office. Took another out of a fancy spa. Hawkins has got you doing a lot of pre-Signing stuff, right? Any appointments coming up?"

"One next week—on Thursday at Sweet Fantasies on Melrose."

"Doesn't sound like Roik's kind of place. Maybe he'd wait in the car?"

I felt a rush. "Absolutely." Roik would rather die than shadow me in a lingerie store.

"Okay, I'll have someone check it out."

This was real. This was happening. All I had to do was tell Father Gabe on Sunday and a few days later I'd be history. Hawkins would never touch me.

"I'm glad we're doing this, Avie."

We. I had a momentary flash of us riding off into the sunset on his bike, before I set myself straight. We were planning my escape. That's all. "Yeah, me, too."

Yates studied my face. "Everybody gets a little freaked at this point. What can I do to make you feel better?"

Tell me you're coming with me.

I froze, my hand across my lips, hoping I hadn't said it out loud.

"You worried about what happens when you get to Canada?" he said.

I nodded, relieved.

"You ask for asylum at the border. Refugee Assistance will meet you and find you a family to stay with. They'll get you set up in school, and even give you money for clothes, and bus fare."

"You make it sound so easy." It wouldn't be. With fifty million dollars on the line, Hawkins wasn't going to let me disappear. "But what if—"

"They'll give you a new identity. You'll be free, Avie."

My heart pounded. *Free.* It was what I wanted, but—

"You'll be a thousand, two thousand miles away, completely out of Hawkins' reach."

"It's terrifying. Wonderful, but terrifying."

Yates gave me his sideways smile. "I'm sending you a song. This band, Survival Instincts, pops up and plays fast sets in abandoned buildings and then disappears. It'll give you strength."

"I need all the strength I can get."

I didn't know a silent pause could hold so much, until Yates said, "Listen—" I knew something was coming.

"So, you might not be able to reach me for a couple days."

My heart plummeted, and I realized I'd been counting on calling Yates when I got back from meeting Hawkins. "Why not?"

"I'm going up to Sacramento with the Liberty Project. Students from all over the state are going to protest the new amendment. You heard about it, right?"

"No. Ms. A hasn't said anything."

"Congress has proposed amending the U.S. Constitution to raise the voting age to twenty-five, but if that happens, the Paternalists will have total control and we won't be able to stop them."

"That's hideous."

"The states vote on it, so if we can keep California from voting yes, we could kill it. Otherwise we're screwed. We can't let a bunch of old men decide our lives!"

I heard the fire in his voice. "You sound excited."

"I have to do this. I can't sit on the sidelines while other people fight for our rights."

"I know. You've got to be the counterfriction."

"Yeah." He grinned.

I wished there was a way I could protect him. "Stay safe, okay?"

"I'll be fine. A nonviolent protest by unarmed students? Tons of media will be there so the police won't dare use force."

"I guess you're right," I said.

His voice dropped to a whisper. "Don't let Hawkins intimidate you. Stay angry, Fearless. Don't let him own you."

His eyes reached for mine and my insides swirled like thick golden honey ribboning off a spoon. "I promise," I vowed.

But when we hung up, I felt scared, not angry. Lately, I'd started to see the ugly truth of what people would do and who they'd hurt to get what they wanted. I hoped Yates was right about the police— that they wouldn't dare attack the protestors with the media around. I didn't know what I'd do if I didn't have him to turn to.

25

It was Wednesday night and tomorrow I was meeting Hawkins. I yanked on ripped black jeans and my RAGE tee and layered on mascara until I looked like an addict. Dad had scheduled dinner with me for the first time in days. I practiced my death stare in the mirror.

See what you've done to me.

But I couldn't silence Ms. A's voice in my head. "Try and look as young as you can. Remind your father you're still a child, one he's supposed to protect."

I drenched a cotton ball in makeup remover. When I finally came downstairs, I was Daddy's little girl in a yellow cardi, and a touch of Pink Innocence gloss.

The table was set in the dining room—spinach salad with out-of-season strawberries and grilled salmon. For some reason, Dad had told Gerard to cook my favorite foods.

I sat down, and when Dad looked up, I gave him a trying-to-be-brave smile.

"I'm glad we could have dinner together," he said. "I haven't seen much of you lately."

I shrugged. "It's okay. I get it. A lot's been going on."

Dad hated spinach salad, but he speared it onto his fork like it was his absolute favorite. "Big day tomorrow."

I picked at my salad. "Yeah, big day."

Dad ignored my pitiful voice. "We had a breakthrough this week. Our research results suggest we've finally found a cure for opiate addiction."

I put down my fork. Beating cocaine and heroin was Dad's quest. The reason he'd started Biocure. "Dad, that's incredible."

"You don't remember your uncle Mike—" Dad shook his head. "Your mom was so close to getting him off Skid Row before he disappeared."

"Uncle Mike made it to the minor leagues, didn't he?" I said, quietly.

"Yes, before the drugs messed him up." Dad squeezed my hand. "I don't know how to say this. You're a big part of this success, honey. Without Jes Hawkins' investment, we'd have had to shut the re-search down."

My mouth fell open, and I drew my hand away. *I'm the sacrificial lamb. My life taken so others may live.*

Dad launched into a soliloquy about dopamine and serotonin

and the blood-brain barrier. As if I cared one *milligram* about the biochemistry I paid for!

"Thousands of patients and their families won't suffer the agony of addiction, and they have you to thank. Not to mention the hundreds of Biocure employees whose jobs you saved. You're a hero."

Thousands of lives saved. Mine ruined. "I'm not a hero. I didn't choose to save all those people."

"Doesn't matter, you're still a hero to me."

"I'm not a hero!" I tore off my yellow cardi and ran for the stairs.

"Avie!" Dad called after me.

I slammed my door and wiped the gloss off my lips. To hell with him. I was stupid to think he cared.

I put in my earphones and played the song Yates sent me. The words drummed in my head and took my feet with them. I stomped to the beat, because "Better Learn My Name" gave my anger a soundtrack. Those six black girls were my voice in a world that didn't care what I said.

"Better Learn My Name"
By Survival Instincts

Wifey. Mistress. Angel. Babymaker
Honey. Vixen. Helper. Housekeeper

I've got a hundred names,
But it all comes out the same
I'm someone's prize possession
Not a person. An obsession

I'm not. Yours to own
Think again 'bout what you call me
I'm not yours to chain and ball me

Not your mommy. Not your whore
Not your freaking doormat
Not your sweetcakes
Cherry pie
Twinkle in a daddy's eye

I'm me!
So call me

Ninja. Warrior. Templar. Gladiator
G.I. Ranger. Samurai. Terminator

I resist your classification
Gonna build a brand-new nation
And I won't be second-class
Gonna kick you in the ass

Cause I'm a
Ninja. Warrior. Templar. Gladiator
G.I. Ranger. Samurai
And get this:
I'm your terminator

Hawkins

26

Roik waited with me by the French doors in the library for Hawkins' helicopter. The plan was Dad and I would fly out, and Roik would follow later in Big Black after showing the photographers at the community gates that I wasn't inside.

"You smell nice," Roik told me.

"Fifty million dollars nice?"

The way his eyes narrowed, I thought he'd smack me. "Don't mess this up," he said slowly. "Let me tell you, you want the deal with Hawkins to go through."

A chill shimmied down my back. "Why?"

"That guy in his fifties who bid on you. He's still interested. Keeps calling the broker and offering more money."

Blow this deal and the next one was right there, waiting. "Good to know," I said.

Hawkins' helicopter came up the canyon toward our house, then it dived for the paparazzo neighbor's roof, and hovered until the satellite dish rattled so hard it almost tore off. Ho's instructions, obviously.

The copter landed on our lawn just as Dad appeared. "Let's go."

The helicopter took off and L.A. shrank beneath us. We flew over downtown and the westside and out Pacific Coast Highway. Any other day, I would have enjoyed the perfect blue sky, and the white ribbons of waves unfurling on the water.

Beach houses lined the highway. We passed the Colony where the stars used to live and Pepperdine University. The town of Malibu disappeared, and the houses got bigger and farther apart until they perched like castles on the cliffs.

Dad pointed. "Look, you can see Hawkins' compound."

Of course Hawkins had a compound. Domestics. Security personnel. Everything and everyone right where he wanted them 24/7. From here, I could see the high gate and quarter mile of iron fencing that sealed his compound off from the road.

There wasn't a single tree or flower or blade of grass, just grey scrubby brush that clung to the rocky slope.

The main house was long and low, built into the cliff, made of glass and stone, and spread out so every window faced the water. A terrace cut into the hill like a knife blade and a sleek pool overhung the edge. The drop to the rocky beach was a hundred feet at least.

If I wanted to get out of there, I'd need a SWAT team to extract me.

The pilot touched down on a helicopter pad in the parking circle behind the house. Ho met us and led us down some stone steps past a subterranean garage big enough for twenty cars, and over to a set of double doors.

Ho threw open the doors and the ocean filled our view, a blue wall of wind-chopped waves.

"Wonder what this set him back," Dad muttered. We stood on a landing above a big room walled in floor-to-ceiling glass.

Hawkins appeared at the bottom of the stairs. "Ah, you've arrived."

Dad looked from me to him. Go on. Get down there.

My ankles wobbled in the stilettos.

I'd seen pictures of Hawkins, but they didn't prep me for the hair slicked back like an Italian race-car driver, or the European golf shirt the color of carbon steel. The Intimidator. I'd overheard Roik call him that. Now I got why.

His eyes were dark. Cold. Rust-stained concrete. And they were fixed on me like he owned me.

My thoughts flashed to the warm blue depths of Yates' eyes.

Dad gave me a little push. Go on!

"Fine." I watched Jes *observe* me all the way down the stairs.

"Magnificent view, isn't it?" he said when I got to the bottom.

"It's beautiful." I tried to ignore the thought beating its wings in my head: *I'll die before I let his lips touch mine.*

"Not nearly as beautiful as what is standing before me. Welcome to my home, Avie." He held out his hand. My muscles went tight like even my cells wanted to get away from him. I forced out a smile and shook his hand. Hard. "Thank you, Mr. Hawkins."

"Call me Jes." He wasn't inviting me, he was telling me.

"Jes."

Jes. How many times will you make me say your name? Say it like I love you, desire you? What will you do if I don't?

"Shall I show you around?" he asked.

"Yes, please."

He leaned in close and took a deep breath and I heard him moan faintly like he'd tasted me.

Nausea flooded me and visions of Becca flashed before my eyes. I could barely hear what Hawkins was saying as he led me through the room, angling around the big steel coffee table and skinny leather benches as he pointed out the huge modern paintings on the back wall, and rattled off the artists' names.

I circled the room, because the last thing I wanted was to sit down and have him wrap his arm around me. I couldn't stop imagining his lips pressed against mine or how he probably tasted like imported mouthwash.

Make him think you like him. Make him feel the admiration you have for him and his mother, Ms. A had instructed me. Our goal is to keep you away from him as long as possible.

I recognized the huge, translucent blue fish speared on a tall, metal pole, its body curled like it was fighting to get away. "Isn't that by Giacomo Perretti?"

Hawkins beamed. "My mother commissioned it."

"She had amazing taste."

"Yes, she did." He leaned in. "Which artists are your favorites?"

I'd memorized Letitia's, and I should have said, "Boyle, Simcha, and Veragatzi," but the me that refused to be her answered, "I love the Renaissance more than anything. Botticelli, Michelangelo, Raphael."

Hawkins' lips flattened, and in my heard Ms. A snap, "Don't bait him."

"Sorry," I said. "I'm not very sophisticated about art. Maybe you could teach me?"

"Gladly." He studied my face, appraising me like a new painting. "Care to go outside?"

"Yes, I'd like that." Anything to keep moving.

Stone steps led from the dining room down to the terrace. I stopped at the top, surprised there wasn't a railing. Waves crashed on the rocks a hundred feet below.

"It can be a little unnerving—the first time," Hawkins said.

I got the feeling he *wanted* me to be afraid. "It's really dramatic."

"I'll walk on the outside so you can get used to it."

What do you want from me, I thought. What kind of game are we playing?

We started down. The wind came up, fresh and clean and I ripped off my headband, and let it blow through my hair. At the bottom of the steps, Hawkins took the headband from me. "Put it back on," he said, his voice very quiet and controlled.

I looked him in the eyes, smiling ever so slightly while the rebel in me made him wait. Couldn't he see that I wasn't what he wanted, I thought as I swept my hair back and set the headband in place.

The terrace was a couple hundred feet long, completely bare except for the pool. "Where's the furniture?" I asked.

"It mars the view. Right now the view is perfect. Pristine. I like things in their places."

Pristine? I thought about my unmade bed, the clothes on my floor, and the papers and pictures on my desk. I could never fit in his pristine world.

I wiped my damp hands on my skirt. *He would make me fit.*

Hawkins steered me to the edge of the terrace. Waves dashed the rocks below us, sending my stomach into spasms.

"No railing," I said. "I guess that would mar the view, too."

"Exactly." His hand pressed the small of my back. "You understand me."

I held my breath, caught between him and the rocks. "I'm getting a little dizzy. Can we back up?"

"Yes, of course," Hawkins said, and he took my hand and kissed it.

I slid my hand away too quickly. *Blush. Look away. Pretend you're overcome. You're a virgin. Make him respect that,* Ms. A had said.

"Sorry," I said, "I'm—"

"It's all right. I understand." He touched my cheek and I'm sure he felt me flinch, so I smiled at him like I couldn't believe I was the one he'd picked.

Lots of girls would want him. Good-looking, powerful, rich.

And twisted. Only someone truly twisted would search until he found a girl who he could mold into a replica of his mother.

"Mr. Hawkins." Ho strode toward us. "The photographer and his stylist have arrived and are setting up in the great room."

Hawkins gestured to an open door. "Shall we?"

27

Upstairs, the stylist combed my hair and fussed with the headband, consulting a photo of Letitia on his phone until he got it right.

Ho slunk over to me while I waited for Hawkins to change. "Your job is to look pretty," Ho said. "You are not to speak to the reporter, not even if he asks you a direct question unless Mr. Hawkins indicates you should. Do you understand?"

"Perfectly." I'm a prop. "So where's the golden retriever?"

Ho glared at me.

"Joking," I said.

"This isn't funny."

"Okay. I get it."

Hawkins returned in a sport coat and a light blue shirt, his collar open like he wanted people to believe that even though he's rich, he's an okay guy. He smiled, and his teeth were too white.

The photographer seated Hawkins on the leather bench beneath the struggling turquoise fish. Then they arranged me, curled up at his feet, my hand on his knee like I worshiped him.

Feeling his body heat through his pants made my skin crawl.

Jes squeezed my hand and I looked at him over my shoulder. He smiled, and I caught the flicker in his eyes. Behave. Play your part.

I smiled back. Of course.

The photographer got off a hundred shots before the reporter from *People* arrived, and Dad and everyone else leaped up in adoration.

Tyce Pham was probably in his twenties, but we all knew his face, because he appeared on *Entertainment News* every week. He sat down with Hawkins and me and went on about how grateful he was to interview Jessop, multimillionaire businessman and likely candidate for governor of one of the key states in the country.

"We're giving you the cover, Mr. Hawkins," Tyce said.

It took a second for the gunshot of reality to hit me: my face was going national.

Until now, it was just local news or a few bloggers following me. How the hell could I go Underground if I was famous in fifty states?

Jes and the reporter were ping-ponging compliments about me back and forth, but I barely listened. When was the issue coming out? I had to get to Canada before that happened.

Hawkins rubbed my arm, bringing me back to attention. "Look at my future wife, she's beautiful isn't she?" he said.

"She resembles your mother."

"Do you really think so? I didn't notice. But she has my mother's taste in art."

"Who are your favorite artists?"

The question was for me. I glanced at Ho.

"Aveline." Jes squeezed my hand in warning.

"Boyle, Simcha, and Veragatzi," I said, playing my part. I felt Jes relax.

"Mr. Hawkins. You're going to marry after a long bachelorhood. Has this affected your political positions in any way?"

Hawkins beamed. "It's made me even more concerned about keeping women safe. Right now most women in this country are under twenty or over sixty, and vulnerable to being manipulated by banks and credit card companies, targeted by Internet predators, and victimized at schools and in the workplace by rapists and kidnappers." He shook his head. "I don't know what I'd do if Aveline was taken from me."

I knew he wanted me to look adoringly back at him, but I stared at my skirt.

"And how do you feel the government should deal with this?"

"In these dangerous times, women need protection. Patriarchal controls to screen the phone and Internet provide some protection. Requiring women drivers to be escorted by a male guardian helps. Assigning financial guardians to oversee a woman's banking and credit could make a difference."

"So women should not handle their own money?"

"It's not fair to force that responsibility on them."

"You've spoken out before about sexual harassment in school and at work."

"Yes, women are safest at home away from the claws of sexual predators."

My throat squeezed like Hawkins had looped a belt around my neck. He'd keep me a prisoner, force me to beg him for money.

"You have a history of helping the most vulnerable," Tyce said. "You headed the task force that created L.A.'s orphan ranches."

I sat up. Sparrow always railed about how orphan ranches exploited teen labor.

"Yes, Tyce, when the mayor called, I jumped in. Scarpanol had devastated the African-American and Hispanic communities, leaving hundreds of thousands of children and babies without a safety net. I'm proud that these children now live in clean, safe conditions and receive training in technical skills and domestic arts."

From what I'd heard, the boys were bused to pick fruit or lettuce for ten hours a day while the girls canned jam in industrial kitchens. I was sitting next to the man who'd probably invented the idea of turning a profit on abandoned kids.

"Any thoughts on the proposed Twenty-eighth Amendment to the Constitution in light of the violent student protests in the capital today?"

"Violent?" I blurted. "But they were supposed to be peaceful." Hawkins crushed my hand. I blinked at the pain while Tyce flashed me a smile, thrilled I was off script. "There was a confrontation with the capital police and several hundred protesters were arrested," he said.

"Was anyone hurt?"

Ho glared at me, over Tyce's shoulder. "I think we're getting off message."

Tyce ignored him. "The police were armed with batons and pepper spray. Several shots were fired."

My heart pounded. I had to find out if Yates was hurt, if he'd been arrested.

Hawkins leaned forward and blocked me from the reporter. "To answer your question, Tyce, I admire these young men for their idealism and conviction. For taking a stand on what they believe in. But science tells us the human brain does not fully mature until age twenty-five. Twenty-five! We don't let ten-year-olds drive cars. That would be irresponsible. So we shouldn't let eighteen-year-olds drive the nation."

Tyce radiated approval. He asked a few more questions and then suggested some shots of the two of us around the house.

"Actually," Hawkins said. "How would you like an exclusive?" He pulled a red Cartier box out of his pocket.

I shoved my hands behind my back. It wasn't a ring box. It was worse.

"Go ahead. Open it," Hawkins said.

My hands trembled as I lifted the lid. A Love Bracelet to match the one Jes had on: a gold band studded with screw heads, the most popular Signing gift a girl could get, except mine had a second diamond-pavé band.

No one else I knew had one like this. Not even six-million-dollar Dayla.

Hawkins fished a tiny gold screwdriver out of his pocket. "Hold out your arm."

"This is great," Tyce crowed. "This could be the cover shot."

I wanted to run. Out the door. Up the hill. Let them drag me out of the scrubby brush. But instead, I did as Hawkins said.

He slid the bracelet onto my wrist and the camera shutter snapped relentlessly as he locked it. "Now everyone will know you're mine."

It was gold and glittery, but it was still a handcuff. *I have to get this off me!*

"I can't wait to show my friends." My voice was so bright and chirpy, so totally not me, that I couldn't believe Dad and Roik were nodding like they thought I loved it.

"Now you can do mine," Hawkins said, retrieving a white gold band from his pocket.

The photographer snapped as I slipped the bracelet over Hawkins' hand and tightened the screws. "Now that's done," Ho said, taking the screwdriver from me, "how about a shot of Jessop at the controls of his helicopter?"

"Fantastic!" Tyce said. "Lead the way."

The guys left me behind as they went out to the helicopter pad. I spit on the bracelet and tried twisting it off, but it wouldn't go over my hand.

The ride home was endless, because all I could think about was the protest and whether Yates was okay. Back at the house, I told Roik and Dad I was going to bed early. I sat on my floor, turned on the phone and lowered the volume.

The reporter hadn't lied. Dozens of videos of the protest were already posted. "Mayhem in Sacramento." "Marchers Defy Cops."

No, Yates. You said it would be peaceful. I clicked on "Police Brutalize Protestors."

I struggled to watch the video on the tiny screen. The camera caught a sea of young men marching up the Capitol mall and wearing college sweatshirts from all over the state.

"Don't take our voice! Don't take our vote!" they chanted.

I tried searching the crowd for Yates, but the shaky video was too blurry.

The camera turned to the wall of police on the Capitol steps, zooming in on the batons and shields as big as car doors. My breath caught. The men in the last row carried rifles.

Yates, where are you? Please be in back.

The protestors sat down as a group and linked arms. "Keep it peaceful. Keep it nonviolent." My heart sank, hearing Yates' voice.

"I told you to stay safe," I whispered. "Why didn't you listen to me?"

The police spread out, walling the protesters in. "This gathering is illegal. If you do not disperse immediately, you will be arrested."

The camera focused on officers waving red bottles that looked like fire extinguishers, then panned to ones who'd trained their guns on the crowd.

"Stop, don't do this. They're unarmed," I pleaded under my breath.

The boys threw their hoods over their heads and hunched over. "You use weapons," someone yelled. "We use our voices."

A beam of thick orange mist shot out over the crowd and the protesters screamed as if they were being burned.

Then I heard Yates yell, "The world will see this!" and my eyes filled with tears. as the camera caught him staggering to his feet. "Students aren't criminals," he cried.

A cop lunged for him, baton raised. I shoved a pillow over my mouth and screamed, "No!!!" as the baton slammed down.

Yates fell, and the camera lost him. "Students aren't criminals!" the crowd roared at the police. "Students aren't criminals!"

Yates had disappeared in the chaos. "Come on, where are you?" I whispered. I stopped the video and searched the frame. Stopped it again and zoomed in. I kept going while the camera dogged police who were hammering boys with batons and dragging handcuffed protestors to a line of buses.

Finally, I couldn't stand it and I tapped Yates' number, but the phone went to voice mail and I hung up, too afraid to leave a message.

Yates had to be okay. They wouldn't just throw him in jail. They'd take him to a doctor, right? He was bleeding! He could have a concussion! I pulled my quilt around me, imagining Yates crumpled on a dirty cell floor, his sweatshirt soaked in blood.

Even if he was okay, he had to get out of there. But what could he do about bail? His dad wouldn't give him the money. They'd barely talked in over a year. I pressed my hands to my throbbing head. I don't know what made me look over my shoulder right then, maybe a psychic flash, but when I did I saw a tiny red light tucked behind the edge of my curtain.

I threw myself into my closet and shut the door.

Roik monitored my bedroom!

Think, think! I held the phone up to my chest. I didn't know how much Roik saw or heard—or if he was watching me right now. I searched the dark, but didn't see another red light. Maybe Roik didn't dare watch me undress.

Then I realized I was right: Roik *was* in my closet the other day.

I flipped on the light and searched for wires. None. But that didn't mean he didn't put a wireless mike in here. Roik wouldn't be the first bodyguard to pull that.

My closet was packed. Boxes crammed the shelves to the ceiling. Shoes and purses and dirty clothes were piled up on the floor.

The row of garment bags.

I zipped the first one open and tore out the outfit. I felt along the hems and in the pocket and seams looking for something small and black and traitorous. Then I moved on to the handbag and shoes and headband Elancio had so carefully selected—feeling the linings, and checking the heels.

Roik hadn't done this alone. Ho probably told him to do it.

I found the first mike. *Oh no. Oh no. Oh no.* Roik heard Yates and me on the phone.

I ran to the bathroom and filled a glass with water. The mike hissed when I dropped it in. But I knew it wasn't the only one. Roik believed in backup plans.

My hands shook as I tore into the rest of the garment bags, digging into jacket pockets and burrowing into boots. I'd never said Yates' name aloud, but Roik wasn't stupid. He'd heard me talk about running, and he could put the clues together.

There were three more mikes in my closet, and the glass of water was packed like a lobster tank by the time I was done. I climbed up on my chair, and waved a bottle of Peach Kissed nail polish at the camera. "Screw you, Roik!" I said, and brushed over the lens.

Then I fell back on my bed, thinking what the hell were we supposed to do now? Yates was probably bleeding in some filthy jail cell, and if Roik told Ho what he heard me say to Yates, Yates could be charged with grand larceny.

Oh, God, Yates, I love you. You have to be okay.

My stomach plummeted. *No, tell me I did not say that.*

I told myself to calm down, I was just upset because Yates was hurt and in trouble. I was not one of those girls who makes a big drama out of every little thing she feels. Not like Dayla.

Of course I loved Yates. We'd been friends practically our whole lives.

I opened the window and leaned out, inhaling the foggy night air, and trying to clear my head. Obviously, the stress of worrying about Yates and Hawkins and my Contract was messing me up. Making me emotional. Irrational.

That's it, isn't it? I lingered for a moment, fighting the urge to take out Yates' picture as if seeing his face would somehow guarantee he was alive and being cared for. Then I gave in.

His eyes were powered with excitement and his fist was raised. He was a rebel ready to fight the world.

My heart fluttered. *Ugh.* I dropped my face into my hands and wished Dayla was here.

Or Mom.

The box of letters she'd left me was right by my hand, full of all the advice and love she could leave behind. I pulled out a handful of her letters. *Mom, help me. I'm a mess.*

Somehow she knew what I needed to hear. "Love is confusing. Your heart may race when you're together, and ache when you're apart. You will share secrets, and reveal your inner selves. You may feel he's the only one who truly understands you."

The things I'd shared with Yates this week, I'd never shared with Dayla. And Yates had never told anyone what he'd told me about Becca's death.

But maybe that was because Yates and I were such old friends. I kept reading.

"If you want to know how a young man feels about you, watch how he acts. Observe how he treats you."

Yates was risking his life, hooking me up with Father G, smuggling me the phone, urging me to follow my dreams. He knew Hawkins would hurt him, if we got caught.

But Yates probably did this with all the girls he met in Exodus, trying to make up for not rescuing Becca from the man who abused her.

I put Mom's letters back in their box. I still wasn't sure how I felt or Yates felt, and I wasn't even sure it mattered, because in the end, I was leaving and Yates wasn't going with me.

But I needed to know Yates was safe, and I needed to say good-bye.

29

I shoved the little lobster tank of mikes in Roik's hand before I got in the car for school on Friday. "Lose these?"

He didn't even try to deny it. "Can you blame me? What with everything?"

"Yeah, I can. But I'm guessing Ho made you."

And bad little liar that Roik was, he gulped.

The photographers who'd camped out at the Flintridge community gates were gone when we went through. Ho got to them, I thought. For once, I appreciated how Ho vaporized people.

Roik and I didn't talk the rest of the trip which was fine, because all I could think about was Yates and whether he was okay.

The second we hit Masterson, I flew out of the car.

Sparrow was squeezed into the blind spot in the hall where the monitors didn't reach, tapping away on her phone. I hadn't seen her for a few days, since her dad took her to New York to prep for her debutante auction.

"Hey," I said.

Sparrow looked up. Her eyes were bloodshot, and I swore she hadn't even brushed her hair. "What you do want?" she snapped.

I almost walked away, but then I saw her hands were trembling. "Are you okay?"

"No, I'm not okay. Sotheby's sold me to a speculator last night. Eighteen million. Impressed?"

I was horrified. The guy bought her so he could turn right around and sell her to someone else for more. "I'm so sorry, I didn't know. I thought you were just going for an interview."

"Yeah, well, surprise. Dad couldn't wait to auction me off." Her eyes kept flitting to her phone. "So, you obviously want something."

If it wasn't about Yates, I'd have left her alone. "Yates is missing. He was at the protest in Sacramento yesterday, but he's not answering his phone."

She stared at me and I felt her deciding if she should help me. "Yeah, the cops took him in. I saw it last night on a video."

A lump formed in my chest. "How can I find out if Yates is okay? A cop beat him over the head with a baton."

"The police won't tell us if he's hurt, but we can check his release date."

"You know how to do that?"

"Unfortunately, yes." Sparrow tapped away at her screen. "Here's the inmate locator."

I watched her type in "Yates Sandell." He was in Sacramento County Jail charged with disorderly conduct and resisting arrest. No bail. No release date.

"That's not good," Sparrow said. "He's stuck in there until a judge feels like letting him go."

"No, you're kidding!"

"Afraid not." The bell rang for class. Sparrow checked her messages once more, and swore a streak before shoving her phone into her pocket.

We walked into class with the last bell, and Sparrow slammed into her seat. Ms. A studied her for a moment. "All rise for the Pledge of Allegiance."

We stood up, all of us except Sparrow who stared at the floor, shaking her head.

"I pledge allegiance—"

"No, I'm not doing it," Sparrow said.

The rest of us looked at each other. "To the flag—"

"Sparrow, get up," I whispered. The monitors could see her.

"Of the United States of America—"

Ms. A frowned at the monitor and then at Sparrow.

"And to the Republic for which it stands—"

"Sparrow!" I said.

"One nation, under God, indivisible, with liberty and justice for all."

Sparrow raised her head and sat with her chin held high, meeting Ms. A's gaze.

Ms. A took a last glance at the monitor, then she marched up the aisle, and wrenched Sparrow to her feet.

My heart thudded as I saw Sparrow's eyes narrow. "It's a joke," she said. "Liberty and justice for who?"

Ms. A slapped Sparrow so hard, her head snapped back, and she would have fallen if Ms. A hadn't grabbed her arm. "How *dare you* defile the Pledge of Allegiance!"

Sparrow touched her cheek, the slap a brilliant pink.

"You will proceed directly to the track," Ms A told her, "where you will run until I tell you to stop." Then she shoved Sparrow out the door.

Ms. A folded her arms as if she was trying to hold herself together. "The rest of you will take your seats and write an essay about the meaning and significance of the Pledge of Allegiance."

I knew Ms. A was doing this, slapping Sparrow and disciplining us, for the camera in the back of the room, but for some reason, today I couldn't go along. I remained on my feet as each of my classmates sat down and started to write.

"Avie?" Ms. A said.

"I can't," I answered. "Sparrow's right. Liberty and justice for who?"

I felt everyone's eyes on me.

"Aveline, in the hall. Now!" Ms. A pointed to the door.

Holy—why did I do that? I thought as Ms. A marched me down the hall to the spot the monitors missed.

"What has gotten into you, speaking out like that?" she demanded. "You know that could get us *both* in trouble."

I covered my face with both hands. "I know. I'm sorry. I shouldn't have, but—"

"Avie, look at me. This is about Jessop Hawkins, isn't it?" she said, glancing between my face and the sparkly bracelet on my wrist.

"He's horrible. He's taking over my life, and he locked this bracelet on me before I could say no."

"So you don't want to go through with your Signing?"

I shook my head no.

"Do you know someone who can help you?"

"Yes, I think so."

We both turned as we heard footsteps down the hall. "Promise me you will ask if you need help," she said.

"I promise."

"Now go change into your running clothes, and when you get to the track let Sparrow know I'll be down soon."

Out on the track, Sparrow was running in ballet flats. Her uniform skirt was flapping around her thighs and her shirt was so wet with sweat, you could see her bra right through it.

I trotted to the fence and stretched out my quads. No way was I going to involve Ms. A if I made a run for Canada. My classmates needed her. Father Gabriel was the one who had to get me out.

30

No release date. No matter how many times I checked on Friday and then on Saturday morning, Yates' status didn't change. He was locked up like a criminal and all I could do was wait.

By lunchtime I was banging off the walls, so I threw on my running gear. Roik was parked in front of the Sportswall. "I'm going for a run," I said.

Roik paused the TV. "That's what the treadmill's for."

"I need some fresh air. Come on. You can follow me in the car. We'll be back in half an hour."

He rolled onto his feet. "Twenty minutes and you wear a hat, shades, and long sleeves. I don't want you flashing that bracelet around. Oh, and no earphones."

"Sure." Anything to get outside and get out of my head.

I followed the street as it climbed the hill, and ran through the lacy shade. The neighborhood was so quiet, you could almost believe it was the same as it was when I was little.

The hill got steeper, and the road twistier. Roik slowed Big Black to a crawl about a hundred feet behind me. I smiled, thinking that if

I jumped into one of these yards. I could take off down the canyon, and Roik couldn't guess which way I was headed.

My feet soared. I imagined leaping like a deer over fences and Roik trying to chase me in Big Black. He'd never catch me on foot.

I'd gone about a mile when Roik pulled alongside and shoved his phone through the window. "It's for you."

The screen said, "Restricted Number," so it had to be Hawkins calling from Singapore, checking up on me like one of his investments. "No, thanks."

Roik sighed. "Take the damned phone."

I slapped it to my ear. "Hello?"

"Avie!!!!" Dayla's squeal sent me running to a neighbor's driveway.

"Day! Are you home?"

"No, still here in Fetal Fed. But I'm getting out in a few days."

The video was blocked so I couldn't see her face. Maybe the Feds didn't want anybody to see what a Fetal Protection unit looked like.

"You are? That's amazing." Then I remembered what Dad said. "Does that mean you're— Someone's taken possession?"

"No, not exactly."

Dayla sounded like she was playing for the camera. "I mean Dad's considering offers. One guy's even throwing in a condo in Jackson Hole. My brothers are pumped. You know how they love to ski."

"Riley especially."

"He called me this morning. 'Black diamond, Dayla. This guy's the best.'"

I was dying to ask about Seth, but I held off. "I can't wait to see you."

"I've missed you so much."

"Oh, Day, it's been awful without you. So much has happened. I have so much to tell you."

"I can't believe you're getting Signed!!"

"You heard about that?"

"Jessop Hawkins! Did you meet him? Is he cute?"

Day was totally playing for the camera. She knew I didn't want to get Signed.

"No, he's not cute exactly, he's—" Evil, villainous, perverted. "I don't know, you have to meet him."

"Well, I love him already for getting me out of here."

Icy fingers raced up my back. "Hawkins helped you?"

"Yeah, his assistant, Mr. Ho, arranged everything. They wanted to surprise you."

"This is the best surprise ever." I tried to think like Ho. His strategy: bring Avie's best friend back to spy on her.

Sadness swept through me. Dayla wasn't stupid. She had to know what she was doing. "So when do you come home?" I said.

"Not sure. Next week sometime. Ooops, my three minutes are up."

"Call me as soon as you get out."

"I will! Love you, Avie!"

"Love you, Day."

I crushed the phone in my hand. Dayla could be back as soon as Monday. So who told Hawkins about her?

I bet the answer was sitting behind Big Black's steering wheel. Roik would be out of a job once I belonged to Jes Hawkins. Unless Roik proved he was invaluable. Loyal.

To Jes.

That did it. Tomorrow I was telling Father Gabe that I was joining Exodus.

After mass on Sunday, Father Gabe and I tucked into a corner of the rectory away from the windows. He didn't look directly at me and anyone would think he was watching the church grannies teach us girls to dance the Macarena.

"Have you decided?" he asked.

My mouth went dry. Tell him. This is what you want. "Yes, I want to join the Exodus."

"You have no doubts? You are sure?"

"Yes." I wasn't, but how could anyone be absolutely sure?

Father G bit into his doughnut and a comet trail of powdered sugar hit his black shirt. "We will plan for you to leave Thursday afternoon. Your friend suggested a location."

Sweet Fantasies. I nodded, wishing Thursday wasn't so far away. Dayla could be back any minute.

"Your bodyguard will wait outside?"

"Yes, that's the last place he'd want to be."

"*Bueno,*" Father Gabe murmured.

My heart pounded in my ears. I did it. This was real. I was going.

Even though I was scared, I felt a surge of power. Screw Hawkins and Roik. I was taking charge of my life.

"I will contact your father, and tell him you must receive premarital counseling on Wednesday. Then we can discuss the final plan."

"Okay, but what if my dad says no?"

"Your father was married in this church. I will remind him that God does not believe in Signings. Marriage is holy, a sacrament, and Signings defile His gift."

As Father Gabriel watched the grannies and girls dance, I had to ask why he was risking so much to help girls get to Canada.

The Catholic Church didn't exactly have a rep for championing women's rights.

"Father, I don't understand why you help girls like me, why not the poor or the homeless?"

He brushed the sugar off his shirt and didn't answer right away. "The chess players do not care about the pawns. They sacrifice the least powerful so they can hold on to their power. Your leaders play chess with your lives, but what the world does not yet know is that someone else whispers the moves as they play."

I started to pick apart his words, trying to understand what he meant.

"If you will excuse me," he said, and walked away.

Whispers the moves as they play? I glanced over at Sparrow, re- membering what she said after Rowley's lawyer was blown to pieces. This isn't about Paternalists keeping girls safe. Something else is going on.

Sparrow was hugging each girl in her needlework group, and I realized she was saying good-bye. Earlier, I overheard her tell Mrs. Kessler that her dad was shipping her off to her buyer in New York in a couple days.

I walked over and said hi to Sparrow. "Yates hasn't contacted you, has he?"

"Sorry, I wish."

"I saw you saying good-bye to people. So, I guess this is it."

"No, I'll be at school tomorrow." She nodded at Father Gabriel. "Is he helping you?"

There was no point in lying. "Yeah."

"Good for you." She tucked a loose curl behind her ear. "You've got a backup plan, right? In case things don't work out."

"No, I—"

"Any money? A few hundred dollars?"

I didn't have any cash, just the plastic cards that alerted Dad or Roik every time I made a purchase. "No, why would I need that?"

"Because you don't want to be stuck somewhere with no food or gas money or, worse, get held up at the border because you can't pay a bribe."

Come up with hundreds of dollars! Why didn't Yates or Father Gabe warn me?

"I guess Janitor Jake could help me," I said.

"I wouldn't go there. JJ would sell you out in a minute."

"Do you know anyone who—"

"Yeah, sorry, I don't." She took out her phone and peeled off the rhinestone case. "Here. Put this on the phone Yates gave you so you can use it at school."

I blushed. Of course she knew he gave me a phone. Sparrow knew everything.

"Thanks, but don't you need it?"

"Nah. I'm getting a new one."

I slipped the case on my contraband phone. "So where's the best place to talk?"

"Any place you see cigarette butts, that's where monitors aren't."

Sparrow seemed almost relaxed, like she was leaving on vacation, not being dragged away from home. And for that matter, why wasn't *she* heading for Canada?

"Is that it?" I said, "Everything I need?"

"Besides your backup plan, yeah. Leave everything else. You don't want anything that can ID you, like that megaobnoxious bracelet."

I tried sliding the Love Bracelet over my hand again. "I'd take it off in a second if I could."

Sparrow looked like she was about to say something else, but changed her mind. "Do me a favor, will you?"

Weird. Sparrow never asked me for favors. "Sure. What do you need?"

"Dad scheduled a dentist appointment tomorrow first period. So tell Ms. A not to worry, okay?"

"No problem. I'll let her know. "

Sparrow pulled me into a hug, and I was so shocked I didn't let go until she did.

I watched her leave. I didn't have a clue how I was going to come up with all that money in three days.

Three days.

I didn't have a secret bank account like Sparrow. Mom's jewelry was home in Dad's safe, but I had no way to pawn it, other than Janitor Jake.

But jewelry wasn't the only thing in Dad's safe, I thought, remembering the envelope of emergency cash Dad stashed in there after the riots shut the banks down for a month.

A crazy thought flitted through my head: I'd have all the money I needed if I broke in.

Right. Break in and not get caught. How was I going to pull that off?

Sparrow said she couldn't help me, but she knew things nobody else did. Tomorrow, I'd make her talk to me.

32

I didn't get to question Sparrow, because Monday morning, she was gone.

Ms. A made an announcement right after the Pledge of Allegiance, but Portia had the inside scoop. She whispered to Zara and me that while Sparrow's bodyguard went to Tempe to visit his grandma, Sparrow disabled the alarm system, stole the neighbor's racing bike and disappeared.

"She must have been planning this forever," Zara said. "All the money she got by selling her little inventions online."

"You have to admit, the bitch has guts," Portia said.

"Don't call her that," I said, feeling strangely protective. "She—"

Zara snorted. "She's certifiably crazy. You wait. She's going to show up on the news someday. The Paternalists better watch their backs, because she's out to take them down."

"Girls! Eyes on me." Ms. Alexandra strode down the aisle, slapping a copy of *Romeo and Juliet* on each desk.

No one made a move to touch them. Romantic literature had been banned from the Masterson curriculum for months.

Ms. A leaned against Sparrow's desk, her arms folded. "In light of recent events, the administration feels that you girls would be better prepared for Signing by a rigorous analysis of the lies and distortions contained in romantic fiction." She held up a copy of *Romeo and Juliet*. "Who knows what this play is about?"

Sophie raised her hand. "It's about a boy and a girl who fall in love."

"Wrong. It is about two young people who *imagine* they're in love. They meet secretly. Ignore their parents' teachings. Refuse to respect Juliet's father's selection of an appropriate spouse. A sentimental nurse and sinful priest help them deceive her parents. And what is the result? Tragedy."

Ms. A looked at us like we could make the same mistake. "We will read the play aloud and get a feel for it, and then we will analyze it. Zara, will you begin, please."

Halfway through, I realized Juliet was living my life, only four hundred years ago. Her dad arranged for her to marry Paris. Juliet didn't want to get married because she was so young, but her dad wouldn't listen.

And then she met Romeo, the one she shouldn't and couldn't help loving.

My thoughts walked right out of the classroom and climbed on the back of Yates' motorcycle. We sail up an empty desert road, my body pressed against his back, my arms around his chest. Alone. Free. Yates pulls off the road and we stand overlooking the scrub, sharing a bottle of water. A drop clings to my lower lip and time slows and dies as Yates reaches out his finger and wipes it away.

Ms. A called my name and I snapped back to reality. Heat like a prickly rash climbed up my neck.

This was ridiculous. I was out of control, fantasizing about a *friend*—the one who told me he *cared* about me.

I had to stop obsessing about Yates and focus on getting the cash I needed for Canada. Without Sparrow to help me figure it out, I was screwed.

Up at the front, Ms. A covered the board with sweeping cursive. "Romantic love equals lies, deceit, disrespect. Lies to self—lies to partner—lies to family."

Ms. A was only writing down what the administration wanted to hear, but my fist clenched reading it. This was so twisted, what the administration—what society expected us to swallow.

I need that cash. I have to get into that safe.

I felt for Becca's silver dolphin at my neck. *You'd tell me not to be a wimp, wouldn't you, Becca? You'd tell me to ignore how scared I am and figure out the passcode.*

Okay, Becca. Okay. I'll do it.

All day I imagined possible passcodes for the safe. Dad could never remember birthdays or anniversaries. He liked chemical formulas and patent numbers.

By the time Roik came to pick me up, I had a list of twenty, and I'd figured out how to keep Roik busy while I tried the safe. All I had to do was to get home before Dad got there.

But I'd forgotten that Ho had arranged for me to get fitted for my Signing dress. Roik drove me to the designer's studio on Melrose.

The walls were hung with life-sized portraits of girls in white dresses, softly focused so they looked like angelic visions. I stared at a spot on the ceiling while the designer and his assistant pinned the fabric over my body. They fussed with the draping and hem, and complained about how the sparkly bracelet locked on my arm caught on the tissue-thin silk.

I refused to let myself crumple or freak, because that girl in the Signing gown wasn't me. I was a stand-in playing a part, and I'd be long gone before the Signing invitations went out.

The designer was so pleased with how cooperative I was, he called Ho and told him the fitting went superbly which meant that Roik was happy to get me a smoothie on the way home.

Too bad I dropped my mango-papaya-strawberry swirl as we turned into the driveway. The twenty-ounce cup hit the seat and gushed onto Big Black's carpet.

"I'm so sorry, it just slipped right out of my hand."

He pulled into the garage and leaped out to get his cleaning kit. "You go inside."

I set my backpack just inside the front door and slipped off my shoes. Gerard was prepping dinner in the kitchen.

I sneaked into the library and closed the door. A huge acrylic of a neural synapse hung on the wall behind Dad's desk. A push of a button, and the painting swung out from the wall.

I checked my scribbled list of passcodes, hurrying to key in numbers while Gerard pulsed the food processor. The lock gave a loud, indignant beep when I got them wrong.

I'd run through about twenty when I heard a cough behind me. Gerard.

"You set off the silent alarm. Entering an invalid code twice sends out an alert."

I crumpled the scratch paper, trying to hide the evidence, but it crackled like chips. "Mom's ring is in there," I said. "I want to wear it."

He raised one eyebrow and eased the picture back against the wall. "Avie, what's going on?"

My heart missed a beat. "What do you mean?"

"The Headmaster sent out a message about Flight Prevention to parents, bodyguards, and domestic managers. When one girl takes off, it can trigger other students to do the same. The letter listed warning signs, and you've exhibited half of them."

I tried to sound casual. "Oh, really? Like what?"

"A change in activities or friends. Secretive or distancing behaviors. Sarcasm."

"Sarcasm. That's not new."

Gerard sighed. "Avie, I'm trying to warn you."

I could make up a story or I could trust him. Gerard had covered for me in the past, tried to protect me, but how far would he go?

"Whose side are you on, Gerard?"

He glanced at the door. "I can't take sides."

"But you don't want me to be with Hawkins."

"It's not my place to comment."

"I know you don't agree with Dad going out and Signing me to him."

"Your father had to weigh the welfare of hundreds of employees into his decision."

No matter what Gerard said, I didn't believe he was so cold. "So you're fine with standing by and watching Dad sell me off?"

"I can't interfere."

"Okay, I get that you can't interfere, but if I ask you for something—"

"What's going on?"

I jumped about three feet. Roik stood in the doorway, his gun raised. "What are *you* doing!" I yelled.

"Good Lord, put the gun down." Gerard said. "Avie was trying to get into the safe. She's convinced the screwdriver for her bracelet is in there."

I wanted to applaud Gerard for the perfect lie. It was almost true, making it completely believable. "This stupid bracelet's so annoying. Everyone wants to look at it and it catches in my hair when I go to wash it."

"Hawkins has the screwdriver," Roik said. "So there's no point in fooling with the safe."

"Oh," I said.

Gerard folded his arms. "You really should get that bracelet off her, Roik. Once *People* magazine comes out tomorrow, everyone will see it on her. She's enough of a target as it is."

Roik frowned. "It's not my say."

Gerard flicked his hand and strode to the door. "Well, you're the one who has to pay the price if anything happens to her."

I smiled to myself, seeing Roik squirm. Gerard always had a special way of getting Roik to rethink things.

"She can ask Hawkins herself when she sees him on Saturday."

"Fine, I'll do that," I said, and stalked out.

I grabbed my backpack, ran upstairs, and flung myself down on my bed. I was screwed. I didn't have the cash I needed, and Gerard wouldn't help me. Thursday was three days away and if Dayla didn't show up before that, it would be a miracle.

I reached for my secret phone and checked the inmate locator. Yates Anton Sandell. No release date.

When would they let him go?

I knew I needed to make up with Gerard for putting him on the spot with Roik, but the first thing I saw when I came down to breakfast was a copy of *People* on the kitchen counter. Ice water trickled through my veins. The cover was Hawkins locking the Love Bracelet around my wrist.

I picked up the magazine. "Nice. Looks like I've just been given a life sentence. Where did this come from?" I asked Gerard.

"Ho sent it over. He thought you'd like to see it."

Ho wants me to know I can never disappear. "Great. Now I'm famous in grocery stores and 7-Elevens across the country."

Gerard didn't laugh. Obviously, he was still unhappy about yesterday. "I'm sorry," I said, "I'm not trying to get you in trouble."

He slid a power smoothie in front of me. "I'm not angry, but I can't help you. I have a husband and son who depend on me."

"It's okay. Really, I understand."

I tossed the *People* in the trash, never imagining that when I got to school copies would be stacked in the lobby for everyone to take. Someone had framed the cover and stuck it in the school trophy case, because overnight I'd become Masterson Academy's Most Successful Alumna Placement.

Seventh-graders shoved magazines at me in the hall, pleading with me to autograph the covers and squealing at the bracelet peeking out of my blazer.

Ms. A stood sentry at her door to keep them from following me in. "All right," she said, closing the door. "Excitement's over."

Zara passed me a note as I walked to my seat. "My brother's friend got back last night," she said. "He gave me this to give to you."

I unfolded the scrap of orange paper. At first I thought it was a mistake, because nothing was on it except rules about visiting inmates, but then I saw a few words penciled between the lines.

"Miss you. Be back soon."

I closed my eyes. Thank you, thank you, thank you, I said to the universe. Yates was okay. He was coming home.

And he misses me. He misses me!

"Class, let's take up where we left off yesterday with *Romeo and Juliet*," Ms. A said.

We opened our books. Things had only gotten worse for Juliet. Her dad was pissed because she wouldn't marry Paris, so he told her she was worthless and could go live on the streets. Jules went half crazy when Romeo was banished. She was ready to kill herself, because she didn't know if she'd ever see him again.

So when the friar cooked up this plan for her to fake her death so she and Romeo could run off to Mantua and live under an assumed name, she jumped on it. It was Exodus, Shakespeare style.

I envied how Juliet was crazy reckless brave with all Romeo's love fueling her, because unlike her, I wasn't a fictional character.

I was a plain old girl, trying to escape marriage to a heartless, controlling man, and my version of Romeo was hundreds of miles away. And instead of a sympathetic nurse helping me, my best friend was ready to rat me out. Even if my extract went perfectly two days from now, I could end up stuck in the middle of nowhere, because I couldn't get my hands on any cash.

But I guess a part of me had to be crazy reckless brave, because despite the odds, I was going for it. There was one more thing I had to do today before I left and that was say good-bye to Mom.

At the cemetery, a Hispanic family had spread blankets across four graves so they could picnic. The son bounced a soccer ball on his knees like he was showing his mamma his skills. Not far away, a man held the hand of a little girl, clutching a big red paper heart to her jacket.

Mom's corner was empty. After Roik checked out the area, I carried my blanket up the hill.

My heart was heavy, knowing this was the last time I'd ever see Mom, and it felt like I was losing her all over again.

A few rows over, a man kneeled beside a grave. He pulled out a trowel and started to dig. It looked oddly sweet, a big bald man with tattoos on his scalp, planting sunny yellow flowers.

I sat back against Mom's headstone. "I need to tell you that I'm going away. Father Gabriel's helping me make a run for Canada."

I glanced at the car. Roik was completely immersed in whatever was on his phone.

"Yates was supposed to help me, too, but he's in jail. You would have been so proud of him. He got arrested for—"

A hand clamped over my mouth. Cold and callused and smelling of dirt.

I froze as a face pushed up against mine. The guy from a few rows over. "Hi, gorgeous. Let's go for a ride."

He jerked me to my feet, and pulled me behind the tree. Down the other side of the hill, a blue van idled on the service road.

I tore at his fingers, trying to peel them off my mouth as he wrestled me toward the van.

Finally, I shoved my elbows into his stomach. His hand flew off my mouth. "Roik!" I screamed. I thrashed out of the man's grasp, but he reached out and grabbed me around the neck and flattened me against him.

A shot split a branch above us. Roik was flying up the hill.

I struggled to get away, but the hand tightened around my throat. The man fired a shot at Roik, while I dangled in his grip.

The cold mouth of a gun kissed my forehead.

Roik held his fire, poised to shoot. "Drop her NOW!"

"Like hell I will." The guy held me like a shield and my brain emptied of everything I knew about self-defense. Roik and I had trained together at a security camp, but at this moment the only thing in the world was the gun beside my eye.

"Let her go!" Roik yelled.

I tripped on the uneven grass as the guy began to walk me backward down the hill.

"Look at me, Avie. Look at me!" Roik yelled from above us.

I focused on his face, and his lips formed a command. *Claw him.*

I couldn't.

"Avie!"

I threw my hands back and blindly tore at the man's eyes.

"Bitch." His hand fell off my throat. I dropped to the ground as a shot smacked by me.

Then Roik charged past. "Get in the car!"

Below us, the blue van hurtled down the service road.

I crawled to my feet. Blood blackened the man's shirt from a wound below his collarbone. I rushed for the car, the ground heaving beneath my feet. I threw myself inside and slammed down the lock.

Bulletproof glass and armored panels couldn't keep me from shaking. Sirens screamed and cops swarmed the hill. An ambulance braked behind me.

If Roik hadn't stopped that guy, I'd be in that van right now. Handcuffed? Duct-taped? Ready to be someone's— Stop it. Don't go there.

Roik climbed in beside me. "The police want you to come down to the station. Your father's talking to them right now, trying to convince them to interview you at the house."

"Okay."

A cop knocked on the window. Roik stepped out and I watched him bum a smoke and light up. He hadn't had a cigarette in two years.

Roik could have been killed.

His phone buzzed next to me on the seat. "Dad?"

"Avie. Thank God, you're safe."

For a second, he sounded like old Dad, the one I had before everything fell apart, and all I wanted was to go home and feel his arms around me. "The police have agreed to interview you at the house, but first, Roik's taking you to Huntington," he said. "We need to get you checked out."

"I don't want to go to a hospital." A news copter rattled the air.

"Roik said he saw bruises and scratches. That man who grabbed you, he didn't do . . . anything else . . . did he?"

Dad's face sagged like a bad day on the stock market. His big investment threatened. He wasn't old Dad at all.

"No. I'm in *one piece*. No broken *anything*."

"Still, Jessop wants you to be examined."

"You told him what happened?"

"I had to. It's part of your Contract: I have to inform him of any significant life event."

Dad and Hawkins ganging up on me. Well, I would fix them. "Daddy, if I go to Huntington, the place will be swarming with reporters. What story do you want on the news: this one or the one in *People*?"

Dad flinched like Biocure's stock had just dropped fifty percent. "All right. I'll meet you at the house."

Roik hopped into the driver's seat. He gunned the engine and tore out the cemetery gates. Halfway home I realized I'd left my bag on Mom's grave. And the phone Yates gave me, the one I needed if I wanted to get away, was inside.

Cops followed us home and Dad arrived just after us. He went to hug me, but an officer stopped him. "Not until we get her clothes, Mr. Reveare. Everything she's wearing is evidence."

"But she's . . ."

"You can wait in the kitchen."

They told me to strip right there in the library. "In front of a bunch of men!" I cried to Roik. "Can't you do something?"

Roik held up a sheet and I peeled my clothes off behind it. The officers dropped each piece in an evidence bag, but when they demanded my bra, I refused. The guy never touched me under my clothes, I argued, but they weren't happy until they had everything.

I shivered on the stone floor as an officer snapped shot after shot of the bruises on my arm and neck and the bloody scratches on my legs where I'd been dragged through the rosebush.

I couldn't stop feeling the cold metal shoved up against my face or the panicked rush as I tore blindly at my attacker.

Claw him, Avie, claw him.

Bam!

Roik handed me my robe, and I knotted it tight. "Can I go now?"

"We have a few questions," one officer said.

Dad met me in the hall and wrapped his arms around me. "I'm so glad you're all right." He looked like he had when I was ten and broke my arm on the trampoline. Like he never imagined I could get so hurt. "Jessop's plastic surgeon arrived—in case you need a stitch or two."

Cold skittered up my legs. "Right." Hawkins didn't want any marks. Nothing to blemish the landscape.

I felt a sheet of bulletproof glass roll up between me and the world. Everything else was on the other side.

The surgeon examined me in Gerard's office. I trembled as the man ran his gloved fingers over my bruises and the cuts on my thighs, lingering on the two deepest scratches.

Please let this be over.

"Good news," he said, placing a bandage over one cut. "I don't think you'll scar." He opened the door, and the detective was waiting at the kitchen table. "Shall we get started?"

I wrapped my arms across my body. "Can I at least get dressed?"

"This will take just a few minutes."

I sat down and Dusty jumped into my lap. I held her close as I answered the detective's ridiculous questions. Why did we go to the cemetery? What time did we arrive? Was that our routine?

Then a cop showed up with my purse and I held my breath as he spilled it out on the table. First my phone fell out, then the one Yates gave me. The rhinestone Tinkerbell case sparkled under the lights, and Roik looked from me to the phone he knew wasn't mine.

The detective sensed something, because he picked it up and studied the cracked screen. "What do we have here?"

"Give me that," I said, and he swung it out of reach.

"This isn't the perp's?"

"No, it's a friend's."

The cop wiggled the phone at me. "You in cahoots with the perp? You set up this little drama?"

Roik took the phone from the cop and began to tap through the screens.

"What? You think I *arranged* for that guy to attack me? To shove a gun in my face?"

"You wouldn't be the first. Girl under Contract. Doesn't like who Daddy picked out . . ."

Dusty started to growl and thrash in my arms. Everyone turned to the sound of boots clacking down the hall. Gerard appeared at the door, flanked by a German shepherd and a hulk in fatigues and a Kevlar vest. "Jessop Hawkins sent this man to escort you to his compound."

I leaped out of my chair, still holding Dusty. "No. No! I have to talk to Hawkins."

"You know he's in Singapore," Dad said.

"I don't care where he is! He can't do this!" I paced, and Gerard locked Dusty upstairs while Dad got Hawkins on the phone.

"Aveline, I'm glad you called. I was worried about you." Hawkins' voice was oily with concern.

"Yeah, that guy you sent to take me to your house, I'm not going with him."

"I want you to be safe."

"I am safe."

"You're not in a condition to decide that. You need to listen to me—"

"And you need to listen to me. I—"

"I want you in my compound where you can be watched!"

"And I want to stay here with my family!"

Hawkins' silence was long and angry, but finally he spoke. "You're obviously hysterical, so I will ignore your little outburst, but I have decided that you may remain at your house on the condition that the additional perimeter guard stays."

Another armed guard and this time with an attack dog. What choice did I have? "Okay."

"And?"

It took me a second before I realized what he wanted. "Thank you, Jessop."

"You're welcome."

I hung up the phone and grabbed mine off the table. "I'm done answering questions."

37

I locked my bedroom door and ran the bath as hot as it would go. Then I perched on the edge, waiting for it to fill. I wanted that man's touch off me even if I had to boil it off.

The world's a dangerous place for girls.

Roik had said it a hundred times, but I never thought anything would ever happen to me. If it wasn't for him, I'd be in that van. Blindfolded. My arms and legs bound with plastic ties. Duct tape over my mouth. The kidnapper probably wouldn't even bother asking Dad for ransom, because chances are he'd have a buyer lined up. And not one like Hawkins.

More like a guy who'd handcuff me to a bed, and then—

I clutched my bathrobe tight across my chest. *Don't, you're making yourself crazy.*

There was a knock at the door. "Go away!"

"Avie, it's Gerard. Can I come in?"

I turned off the water. When I opened the door, Gerard was holding a tray with Mom's favorite blue teapot and jam sandwiches with the crusts cut off. "I thought you could use a little something to settle your stomach."

My eyes filled. Mom's Bad Day Cure. "Peppermint tea?"

"Of course. Let me set this down."

I nodded, and he nudged the door shut with his foot. He dodged the piles on my floor and set the tray on my bed. "Sit."

I plopped down on my quilt, and he put the napkin in my lap. "Open it."

A stack of fifties was hidden in the folds along with my secret phone. I crushed the napkin to my chest. "Oh."

Gerard held a finger up to his lips and leaned in close. "I told

Roik I'd return the phone to the family. Don't let me see or hear or find a thing," he whispered, and backed away.

Thank you, I mouthed.

When the door closed, I peeked and counted the bills. Eight hundred dollars.

Gerard was telling me to run. I wasn't sure I had the guts to do it anymore—not even with Yates right beside me.

I pulled *Titanic* off the shelf and tucked the bills inside the plastic case. Then I peeled back the credits card to see Yates' picture.

That glance yanked me back to the moment the cop struck him with the baton.

I'm so freaking blind.

Yates doesn't play it safe. He charges right into danger. If he'd been with me today instead of Roik, he'd have thrown himself on that gunman, trying to save me.

I couldn't let Yates anywhere near my extraction. Maybe he wouldn't get back to L.A. in time, but if he did, I had to stop him.

I wasn't like the other girls he'd helped. Hawkins would send an army of Retrievers after me and Hawkins wouldn't care if they killed Yates to get me back.

38

I slammed awake in the middle of the night.

I'll never feel safe again.

As soon as Roik drove me out the Flintridge gates the next morning, my heart started to race, even though Efram, the perimeter guy, was tailing us.

You can't be afraid, I told myself. Or you'll never get away. You'll be Hawkins' prisoner.

My fingers shook as I put in my earphones and cranked up the music. *Call me Ninja Warrior Templar Gladiator.* I shouted the words in my head as we left the nicer neighborhoods. My skin prickled, seeing men sitting on the curb in front of the liquor store, drinking from paper bags, men begging at stoplights, men loitering by alleys, smoking cigarettes.

The world's a dangerous place for girls.

My chest heaved as I sucked in a breath.

Roik pulled the car over. "Son of a— I told them you weren't ready," he muttered. "Avie, you want to go back to the house?"

I combed my fingers through my hair, trying to decide. *I have to go to school. If I don't Roik won't take me to St. Mark's after to see Father Gabe.* "No, take me to school."

"You sure?"

"Yes. I want to see my friends."

Roik insisted on walking me to class. Ho had kept me off the network news, but even Ho couldn't control cyberspace or gossip. Underclassmen stared as I passed, trying to get a glimpse of the bruises under the makeup on my neck. I was sweltering in the sweater and bicycle shorts I wore under my uniform skirt, but I wasn't letting anyone see my cuts and bruises.

Zara taped LEAVE HER ALONE over the window in our classroom door. Ms. A brought me lunch, and arranged for our class to have the track all to ourselves.

Roik was first in the car line when school let out. "I don't think it's a good idea, you going to see that priest today."

For a second, I was scared Roik knew what I was up to, but then I realized he was worried. "It's counseling, Roik. It's good for me."

I can do this, I thought, looking out the Masterson gates. The gates rolled open and the perimeter guy came up behind and tailed us into St. Mark's dicey neighborhood.

Roik walked through the church with me to Father Gabe's office.

I had this crazy fantasy that Yates would be waiting in the confessional, but as soon as we entered St. Mark's, I knew he wasn't. I don't know how I knew, but I did.

It's fine. It's better if Yates stays out of this.

Mrs. Kessler, the receptionist, let Father G know we'd arrived. Roik tried to follow me into Father Gabe's office, but Father G blocked him. "The instruction is private and spiritual. You can wait out here and Mrs. Kessler will chaperone Aveline and me."

Roik took one look at the stack of *Catholic Weekly* in the waiting area and headed for the courtyard.

Mrs. Kessler sat down with her knitting on Father G's couch. When I went to sit beside her, Gabe led me to a door across the room, talking in his priestly voice. "When the Lord joins a man and a woman . . ."

He waved me through, and I was in the priest's dressing room. Sun streamed through two stained-glass windows, smearing color over the room and distorting the cabinets on the walls.

He shut the door behind me, and I was alone.

But then Yates stepped out from between the windows. His dark hair was a mess and he had a bandage above his left eye and he hadn't shaved in days, but he was back. He opened his arms and I leaped into them.

"I was so scared. I saw the cop hit you, and then you disappeared and didn't pick up your phone. I had no idea what happened to you."

"They didn't release me until this morning," he said. "I'm sorry, I probably stink. I drove right through so I could be here."

He held me tight and I squeezed him back, but that only lasted a moment before it became awkward and stiff, and we both let go.

We sat down, facing each other on the bench where Father G probably tied his shoes. My hand lay on the seat between us, and I stretched out my little finger, so I could touch the seam of his jeans without him seeing. I needed to feel he was really there.

Yates' shirt was damp with sweat and he smelled like leather. The sunburn on his cheeks made his eyes look even bluer and there was a narrow band of stubble along his jaw.

I touched the frayed gauze on his forehead. "Don't worry about how you smell. Are you okay? What did they do to you?"

"I'm fine. It's just a cut. Nothing serious. The police had paramedics standing by so they wouldn't get sued."

"But they hit you with pepper spray."

"Yeah. It burned like hell. But you know, it was worth it."

"How could that be worth it?"

"Because after the police attack, we were totally united: fifty student groups from all over California. We held meetings in holding cells, made plans. I'm telling you, Fearless, we're on the verge of a revolution. We're going to take down the Paternalists."

For the first time in way too long, I saw his eyes fired up with hope.

"You really think so?"

"Yeah. All it will take is a trigger, I don't know what exactly, but people will come to their senses and throw them out."

"I hope it's soon." I gave him a huge smile. "I'm so glad you're back. The police took forever to let you out."

"I had trouble making bail, but then some anonymous donor covered it. I wish I knew his name so I could thank the guy."

"If you find out, I'll send him a card. 'Thanks for getting my best friend out of jail.'"

For a moment, Yates didn't move. "I guess with Dayla gone I am your best friend."

The slightly disappointed way he said that drew me closer. *Does that mean . . . ?*

He hooked his finger through my Love Bracelet. "Tell me about Hawkins. Is he as airbrushed in person as he is on TV?"

"No, he saves that for the camera. At home, he sticks with cold and controlling."

"Guess I'll see for myself on Saturday."

"What?"

"Hawkins ordered the Biocure board members to bring their families out to his house so Dad demanded I show up." Yates, reached toward my face, and brushed my hair away from my collar and my heart stopped. *What are you doing?*

"What's this on your neck?" he said.

I slapped my hand over the bruises and looked away. Images strobed in my head: the man's face, the blue van, Roik taking aim.

Yates took hold of my arms. "Did Roik do that?"

I shook my head.

"Hawkins!"

"No," I whispered. "I was attacked."

Yates let go and I saw his hands tremble as they hovered over my arms. "What! When? How?"

"Yesterday."

"Holy— Were you ambushed?"

Yellow crime tape flapped in front of my eyes, but I tried to hold it together. "I was at the cemetery. This man grabbed me and tried to get me into his van."

"You must have been terrified." Yates swallowed and shook his head. "I don't know how to ask, but are you hurt anyplace—else?"

Dad and Hawkins had asked me the same question, but Yates meant it totally differently. Tears trickled down my cheeks. "I got lucky. Just some bruises, and scratches from the rosebushes."

"I don't get it. Where was Roik?"

A gun blasted in my head, and I choked back a sob before I

completely lost it. Yates wrapped me in his arms. "You're okay," he whispered, tracing circles on my back. "I've got you."

I wanted him to hold me and not let go. I wanted to stay like this, the two of us safe and locked away forever.

But the reality was we had less than an hour.

I eased myself out of his arms. "I have to stop crying. Roik's going to wonder what the hell Father G and I were doing."

Yates opened a cabinet and handed me some tissues. I dabbed at my eyes and saw him looking at me intently. Suddenly, I felt warm and shivery at the same time.

It was like that moment in movies, when the guy realizes how he feels about the girl, and suddenly she realizes it, too. Gravity lets go. Love tilts the world on its axis, and the two of them do stupid dangerous outrageous things. Maybe that happened in real life, too. Maybe this was it.

I held my breath, sensing Yates was going to finally tell me how he felt.

But then he turned and closed the cabinet, and the moment was gone, and everything inside me demanded to know why.

Why wouldn't he admit to how he felt? Yates said he *missed* me in his note. What did he even mean by that?

"We should delay your extraction a few days," he said quietly. "Give you some time to heal."

"I don't have any time," I snapped. I wanted to shake him. *Tell me what's going on with us.* My cheeks flared, knowing I wasn't being fair or even smart. "Dayla's coming home."

"Dayla? Why's that bad?"

"Ho, Hawkins' assistant, got her out of Fetal Fed to spy on me. And I'm sure Roik told him about you, too."

Yates cursed under his breath. "You're right. You can't wait. You have to get out of here."

Fresh tears dribbled out, and I dabbed my eyes.

"So, tomorrow," he said, "a woman carrying a red purse comes into the store. You go into the dressing room where she hands you a change of clothes. She distracts the owner, and you disappear out the back into a white Prius."

I tried to focus on what he was saying but it was hard when I kept thinking I was leaving Yates and L.A. forever. "So then my extractor takes me to my next contact?"

"Yeah. I'll be waiting a couple miles away. You'll get out of the Prius and into a different car with me."

My eyes stung. I had to tell Yates now. "No, you can't take me."

"What do you mean, *no*?"

I couldn't bear this. "You have to find someone else to get me out of L.A., and drive me to my next stop."

"No."

"Yes, you have to listen to me. Ho's ruthless. He'll hire an army of Retrievers for Hawkins and he'll tell them to kill you. That's what he does. He *eliminates* problems. He'll eliminate *you*."

Yates glared at the wall.

"Please. Promise me. I can't do this if I have to worry about you."

Yates was quiet for a moment. "I pushed Gabe to let me drive you. Normally, they don't allow you to extract someone you know. If you can't think clearly, you put the whole team in danger."

Yates had fought to be the one to extract me. I took a deep breath. "This is the right thing to do."

"Yeah. We'll get Aamir to extract you. He's good."

"Okay." The clock over the cabinet was ticking down. "Should I call you when I get over the border?"

"No, I'll be a suspect, but you can ask Refugee Assistance in Canada to let me know you made it."

There would be layers of people between us, shielding his connection to me. "I'll never be able to come back to the U.S., will I?"

"Don't worry about that now. Things might change in the future." His voice grew quiet. "You know I care about you, Fearless."

Our eyes locked and his told me everything he'd never said aloud. Then, without warning, he moved closer and our lips touched. Heat streaked through my body and for a moment, all I could do was sit there, stock-still. But then he drew me even closer and our kiss went from surprised to happy then desperate as if our lips knew we only had these few minutes.

We shouldn't be doing this.

I had to let him go. I put my hand on his chest. His heart was beating hard.

Yates laid his hand over mine. "Avie, I know I shouldn't ask this, but do you think that someday we—"

There was a knock on the door. Yates stood up as Father Gabe came in. "It is time," he told us.

"Hold on," Yates said, and filled him in on how they needed to find someone else to extract me. I knew I should listen. It was critical for my escape, but I wanted Yates to finish his question. *Do you think that someday we—*

I was almost sure I knew what he was going to say, because I'd felt it in his kisses and I would have said yes, if he'd finished asking.

But Father Gabe was moving me toward the door. "Yes, you are right," he told Yates. "It will be safer if someone else takes her."

Yates reached for my hand one last time. "You'll be okay. You can do this."

I nodded, trying to hold it together, and then Father Gabe ushered me out of his office.

Someday. We.

I held on to those words and the memory of Yates looking into my eyes, his lips on mine, all the way back through the church, into the car, and then home. Tomorrow night, I'd be in someone's car or truck or RV, hurtling toward the border.

How far from now was someday?

Exodus

40

Thursday felt like a film where the climax was looming and the director was drawing out every minute. I moved through each scene, aware of small, sharp details. Dad wore a blue tie when he kissed me good-bye. Gerard handed me a paper lunch bag with a cinnamon bun "for later." Dusty flapped her front paws when I scratched her belly.

These were the last memories of them I'd ever have.

At school, I counted down the hours and then the minutes. At 2:45, the bell rang, and I felt for Becca's necklace, the only thing I was taking with me, other than the music and pics on Yates' phone.

Good-bye, Sophie, Portia, Zara, Ms. A. I'm out of here.

I checked for the cash and phone I'd stashed in the lining of my purse. Headmaster Gleason would rethink sewing class if he knew I'd used what Masterson taught me to split the seam, insert a pocket, and close it with an invisible zipper.

When I came down the steps, Roik grinned like he had a great big secret.

"What are you so happy about?" I asked.

He opened the car door, and "Surprise!" Dayla burst out.

I gasped like I'd been socked. "You're home!"

Day threw her arms around me and squeezed me tight.

No, this isn't happening!

"I got back like an hour ago, but I had to see you," she said.

"I can't believe you're here."

"Ohmygodohmygod," she squealed, and I bounced on my feet just like her, trying to act like I was totally elated she was back.

Day pulled me into the car. "Let's get out of here before anyone sees me," she said. "I look like crap."

Roik started up Big Black and Dayla shoved back my sleeve. "Is this *the* bracelet?"

"Ugh. Yes."

"At least it's classy. I saw the *People* cover. At first, I couldn't tell it was you with that nasty headband and the cardi over your shoulder."

My brain was screaming, but I forced myself to focus. If I seemed distracted for even a second, Day'd know I was up to something.

Her hair was pulled back, and she wasn't even wearing lip gloss. Her shirt was tight, but her baby tummy was still small.

"You don't look that bad. You look healthy," I said.

"I'm disgustingly healthy. They made us walk every day. Drink milk. Take vitamins." She curled her arm over her stomach.

"Well, that's good for the baby, right?"

She bit her lip like she was refusing to cry. "Fetal Fed is all about what's good for the baby. Look. We even sew our own diaper bags." She held up a bag embroidered with three bears strolling toward a cottage. "Like it?"

Coded into the stitches was "Fetal Fed Sucks."

"Ms. A would be proud," I said.

She grabbed my purse and started fishing around. "Where's your lip gloss?"

I tried to snatch my purse away, but Day held it out of reach. "Give it back," I said. "I'll find it for you."

While she dug around inside, I prayed she wouldn't feel the phone hidden in the lining. "Found it," she said, and waved the pink tube at me.

Roik pulled onto the freeway, heading for West Hollywood and Sweet Fantasies. I had to stop him. "Roik, let's forget about going shopping today."

"No way!" Day said. "I've been locked up for weeks. I'm dying to go shopping with my best friend."

"You sure?" I should have known. Nobody loved shopping more than Day.

Roik butted in. "I have to call Ho if we cancel."

"No, don't call Ho." I needed to alert Yates that our plan was falling apart, but I couldn't, not if Day was watching my every move. I had to throw her off, so I leaned over and whispered, "Have you heard from Seth?"

Day shrank back like she knew the car was monitored. "No." Her face filled up with unsaids. "I'm so over him. I was an idiot, letting him take advantage of me."

And the look she gave me: she was pregnant and trapped and even though she hated that Ho had asked her to spy on me, she was still going to do it.

It hurt, knowing my best friend would sell me out, but it wasn't her idea to betray me.

We turned off the freeway onto Sunset Boulevard. In a few minutes we'd reach Melrose. Drops of sweat trickled down my side.

"Come on," Day said. "Show me the dress."

I took out my Princess phone and pulled my Signing dress up on the screen.

"Are you kidding me?" Day said. It was nothing like the strapless pink dress with shimmery daisies she wore last spring to hers.

"It's totally virgin sacrifice." Whisper-thin white silk falling in drapes from my shoulders. "Lance, the designer, said if I wear a bra and panties it'll ruin the lines."

"Ewww. So, what about your hair?"

"Headband, of course."

"What?"

I dug the words in. "Hawkins *loves* headbands. His mother was a big fan. Lance is designing me one to go with my updo. Swarovski crystals. White satin."

"*Mom* was a headband fan?"

I blinked twice for *Yes, it's exactly what you're thinking.*

Day scrunched up her nose. Yuck.

I nodded, sad that these were the only completely honest words we'd said to one another. "But what about *your* Signing?"

"It's going to be small. Just family. Buck's sons. Dad. My brothers."

"His name's Buck?"

"Bucknell Buchanan. You can call me Mrs. Buck." From the look she shot me, I knew she'd gut me with a hunting knife if I ever tried it.

"Does he hunt deer?"

"He lives in Montana. What do you think?"

Buck Buchanan from Montana. "He doesn't sound . . . Jewish."

Dayla touched the little star hanging around her neck. "Yeah, like my dad said, 'Beggars can't be choosers.'"

"So when is the Signing?" I asked.

"Sometime after New Year's." Day squirmed. "Things aren't quite *settled*."

I got the feeling her Contract was tied to mine. "So you can be my bridesmaid?"

"I made everybody promise."

Right. Day makes sure I go through with my Signing, and then she's shipped off to Montana to start her new life. And as much as I hated her for doing it, I felt sorry for her, too. She'd lost everything. Except Seth's baby.

"We're here. Sweet Fantasies," Roik said.

Roik drove into the gated parking lot with my perimeter guard right behind.

My blouse was glued to my back. What the hell was I going to do now?

41

Sweet Fantasies was done up like a faux boudoir: velvet couches, rosy pink fabric walls, and a domed ceiling the color of vanilla frosting.

"Don't you love this?" Day said. "It's like a giant cupcake."

"Yeah, adorable."

Sergio invited us to relax on little gold chairs while he brought out the merchandise Hawkins had reserved. I angled my chair so I could see the front door. My contact was going to freak when she saw me here with Day.

Day bumped my shoulder. "Sergio doesn't have panty lines."

In that moment, I remembered everything I loved about her, and it broke my heart. "No, stop! Do not make me imagine that."

The minutes to disaster were counting down, but if Day would only go to the bathroom, I might be able to get away.

Sergio returned with an armful of satin and lace, and tenderly arranged each tiny bra and panty set on the table in front of us. "Mr. Jes," he said. "He loves the Naughty Angel collection."

Acid burned the back of my throat while Day stifled a laugh. She picked up a bra that was two lacy straps and a baby blue bow between barely there cups. The matching thong was basically a ribbon. "Does this come in pink?"

"But of course." Sergio hustled off to the panty vault, and Day waved the price tag in my face. "Mr. Jes totally *loves* the Naughty Angel collection."

The doorbell chimed, and a splash of red appeared through the sheers covering the glass. Sergio answered the door, bras hooked over his fingers.

"Why don't you try these on?" I said to Day. "Jes is so generous, I know he'd want you to have some, too."

"Really?"

"Yeah. Go for it. I'll be there in a sec."

"Yay." She pranced away, her arms full of silk.

Sergio brought the woman with the red handbag to the table where I still sat. "I will return in one moment," he told her.

She was Mom's age, toothpick skinny, with a great big yellow diamond on her finger. One of those women who'd survived the Scarpanol disaster, because she was anorexic or a vegetarian.

She fingered a bra on the table. "The detailing is exquisite, don't you agree?"

"Yes, it's really pretty."

She dropped her voice to a whisper. "The car's waiting out back. Go to the dressing room. I'll pass you your clothing. You have three minutes."

"Avie, you have to see this!"

The woman started. "You brought a *girlfriend?*"

"It's not my fault. My bodyguard surprised me."

Her eyes darted to the front door. "This won't work."

It could. All we needed was for Dayla to go to the bathroom. "But—"

"I'm sorry."

"Can't we wait ten—"

"No, it's too dangerous. Do you understand?"

"Chantelle Eternelle, madame!" Sergio reappeared, waving a

dove-grey confection, and I watched my contact stride away. Our conversation was over.

No, I didn't understand how things could have gone so horribly wrong when I needed them to go right. My ride to freedom was just outside the door, and Hawkins had fixed things so I couldn't take it.

My head throbbed, and I nicked a wall as I walked to the bathroom. I wasn't getting out of here. No one was going to risk extracting me today.

I locked the bathroom and typed a 911 message for Yates, but stopped before I pressed send. If I did, he'd come flying right in here and I couldn't let that happen. I cleared the message and walked to the dressing rooms.

Sergio pulled back one of the peach velvet curtains. "Put these on," he said, handing me a pair of satin mules with puffs of marabou feathers. "They will *transform* you."

I jerked the curtain closed, and tossed the mules onto the platform in front of the mirrors. Yeah, they'd transform me into Hawkins' plaything, a gift-wrapped virgin in lacy straps and ribbons. That's what I'd be a week from now.

This couldn't be my last chance to get away. It just couldn't.

"Buck is going to love these!" Day squealed.

Jes would, too. He'd unwrap me like a greedy little boy on Christmas morning. "Day, I think you should take one in every color."

"Okay!"

I heard the woman who was not going to save me tell Sergio she would take the Chantelle set, and then glide past the peach curtains back to her own life. Then Sergio cooed over her and packed her lingerie, while I fought the image of the white Prius speeding down Melrose without me.

When she was gone, I poked my head into Day's dressing room. "My head's killing me. Can we get out of here?"

"Sure." Day was smiling like a kid trying to be brave, but her eyes were filled with tears.

"What's the matter?"

She held out her arms. "I don't want to go to Montana," she whispered. "I don't want to live fifty miles from a grocery store, trapped with some old man I've never met."

"Isn't there anything else you—"

"No, Dad had to pay back the six million. Buck's was the only offer that came anywhere close to what Dad needed. I'm so screwed."

"I'm sorry."

"At least you get to stay in California."

Imprisoned in Hawkins' compound. "Yeah, at least I get to stay in California."

I had to contact Father G. There had to be another way out.

Day gave me a last squeeze. "Sorry. All these hormones. I get so emotional."

Sergio spoke through the curtains in a singsong voice. "Have you decided which fantasies you desire, Mademoiselle Day?"

Day and I looked at each other and burst out laughing. It was too, too horrible. Day picked up the bra and panty sets and handed them to Sergio to wrap.

"You really feel sick?" Day said.

"Yeah, I just want to crawl into bed and go to sleep."

She stuck her arm through mine. "Let's get out of here."

On the way home, Day snuggled up next to me in the car. She made me promise we'd have a sleepover the next night, and then she told me she was meeting with the Headmaster on Monday, and I realized Day was staying glued to me until my Signing.

Hawkins wasn't going to let me out of his grasp.

Thank God I'd told her I was sick. If I hadn't, she'd have made some excuse to come home with me.

Day didn't shut up all the way back to her house, but I couldn't tell you what she said. My mind was spinning, imagining the extraction team debriefing Yates and Father G. Maybe they had a backup plan to save me, but in one week, it wouldn't matter.

42

Roik dropped me at my house, then took off. I walked in, thrown to find Gerard had left early and Dad was home for dinner, until I saw the turkey on the kitchen counter. It was Thanksgiving or the day that used to be Thanksgiving before Scarpanol killed it and Congress buried it so people wouldn't have to suffer four days of mourning families that didn't exist anymore.

Gerard had set the table with flowers and a tablecloth. Dad and I helped ourselves to the meat, and cranberry sauce, and sweet potato casserole. Dad tried to make conversation, but I could barely talk and I definitely couldn't eat. Finally, he gave up.

Later, Dusty shadowed me around my room with her stuffed monkey, Cheech, hanging out of her mouth. I scooped her into my arms. "What am I going to do now, Dusty? What am I going to do?"

The secret phone hummed in my purse and I grabbed for it. "Come out on the balcony," read the message. I hurried to the back balcony and eased the door open. Dusty ran though my feet, almost tripping me.

I stared into the darkness beyond our pool. The yard dropped off so the back fence ran along the street below our house.

A light blinked at me through the hedge. I pressed Yates' number and he immediately picked up.

"Hi."

"Hi," I said. Was he insane? "How did you get past the gatehouse?"

"I rode in in a friend's car. Check out my disguise." A big, wet, black nose and slobbery tongue filled the cracked screen.

It felt good to smile. "Great disguise. So you're a mixed breed?"

"I'm a neighbor walking his dog."

"Oh, now I get it."

"Come down and say hello."

I shouldn't. Ferris was on patrol tonight, but it looked like he was probably up front. "Give me a minute."

I tucked the phone in my jeans. "Ball, Dusty, ball. You want to play ball."

Dusty dropped Cheech and bolted for the stairs. She plowed into the kitchen and did doggy pirouettes at the back door as I picked her ball off the shelf.

I flung the ball across the lawn and she tore into the yard, a white dot bouncing in the dark. I ran toward the pool and Dusty raced back and dropped the ball at my feet. I listened for Ferris and his dog, then I tossed the ball over the low wall that separated the pool from the orchard below. Dusty charged after it, weaving through the fruit trees toward the hedge and iron fence that shielded the yard from the street.

When I caught up, she was crouched by the fence at a spot where the hedge was missing, touching noses with another dog.

Yates clutched the iron bars, waiting for me.

There were cameras all up and down the street, so I approached slowly, trying to remember where they were and to stay out of sight.

"I had to see you," Yates said. He opened his hands, and I wove my fingers into his.

"You shouldn't be here," I said. "It's too dangerous. Hawkins hired a perimeter guard and attack dog."

Yates leaned his forehead against the bars and I rose up on my tiptoes. It was the closest we could get with the bars between us.

"Are you okay?" he said.

"Not really. I can't believe Dayla showed up like that. It was almost as if Ho *knew* what we were planning."

"He doesn't. No one at Exodus would give you away."

I didn't have Yates' faith in them, but what did I know? "What do we do *now*?"

"We try a different place, different time."

It wasn't that simple. "I don't know."

"You can do this."

"That's not it. Whatever plans Hawkins and Ho have for me the next few days, they're keeping them secret."

"Think. Is there anyplace you could ask Roik to take you?"

We were both thinking the cemetery, but neither of us said it.

"What about school?" Yates asked. "Aren't there any holiday pageants or service projects? Events where everybody's running around and you could sneak out?"

Yes. Yes, there was. "The *Sound of Music*. It starts Monday and hundreds of families will be on campus. I can tell Dad and Roik I'm doing makeup. I just need someone to unlock the back gate."

"Would Ms. Alexandra help you?"

"Maybe. Yes."

"Then it's a plan." He stretched his fingers and I matched mine with his so our hands lay flat against each other's. I felt the energy flow back and forth between us.

This may be the last time we see each other.

Ask him, the voice in my heart insisted. Don't let him go without knowing. "What were you going to ask me yesterday?" I said.

Yates hung his head. "I shouldn't have said that. It's not fair."

"Because I'm leaving?"

He nodded and my heart soared.

"What's not fair is leaving me hanging," I said quietly. " 'Do you think that someday we—' How does that question end?"

"Aves—"

"Don't make me beg. It's humiliating."

He stroked my face with the tips of his fingers. "All right. Do you think that someday we could be together despite the thousands of impossible obstacles in our paths?"

Yes danced on my lips. "Yes, I do."

A loud barking came from up near the house. Dusty pawed my leg, whimpering to be picked up. "You've got to get out of here."

Yates' fingers lingered on my cheek while the barking got closer and angrier. Dusty circled me frantically. "Go, go," I said.

Yates stepped back from the fence and put his hand over his heart. I did the same. Mine was beating wildly, hearing the guard come toward us.

Yates disappeared into the dark and I kicked Dusty's ball so it rolled between the iron bars out of reach.

A flashlight beam pinned me to the fence. "Identify yourself!" Ferris yelled.

The shepherd snarled at the end of his leash as I swept Dusty up in my arms. She was trembling even worse than I was. It was all I could do not to turn and check to make sure Yates had gone.

"It's me, Avie," I snapped back. "I live here."

Ferris silenced his dog with a quick "At ease," and it dropped to the ground.

"Actually, I could use your help. Dusty's ball went through the fence."

Ferris loaned me his expandable nightstick since he couldn't fit his arm between the bars. I deliberately knocked the ball too far left, then too far right, so Ferris couldn't resist watching it. Finally, when I was sure Yates was gone, I smacked the ball back to Dusty.

So we're going to try again, I thought as Ferris walked me back to the house. It's not over.

Trust Yates and Father G. It will all work out.

43

I went to school early the next morning hoping to get Ms. Alexandra alone, but she didn't appear until after the last bell. She stood at her desk for a moment, drumming a finger on the wood. "Mmm . . . let's convene in the Tea Garden."

We trotted behind her. "Your assignment is to write a love poem from the point of view of either Romeo or Juliet," she said. "Try to capture their emotions, and we'll return inside and critique."

We scattered, each of us picking a bench or a spot among the camellias. I lay on my stomach on the grass and stared up through the branches.

I knew exactly how Juliet felt: cornered, desperate, sold. Delusional. Juliet thought she had a chance at a happily-ever-after in Mantua. That she could elude her sword-wielding kinsmen, the Renaissance equivalent of ex-military, field-reconnaissance-trained Retrievers.

I tapped my pen on my notebook. I couldn't blame her for risking it all. Romeo loved her. He *loved* her.

I thought back to last night, Yates and I reaching for each other through the bars of the fence, and at that instant I totally got how Juliet knew that loving Romeo was impossible, but love made her crazy, gave her courage, sent hope through her veins.

The poem flowed like my heart was pumping out the words.

Says Juliet

love wields the scissors
love is the escape
love blows through pinholes
love refuses to die

love holds its breath in the absence of oxygen
love defies the weight of the pillow
slips free of the knot

love builds a fire out of hope
love climbs a rope of maybe
love trusts the grappling hook to hold

let the world
tell us no
love is the rusted fire escape
that shouldn't support our weight
but does

When I finished, I read it over and realized that I'd never written anything so true or so real, and I shouldn't show it to anyone. Except Yates.

A shadow fell over the paper, and when I looked up it was Ms. A. "Show me your work," she said, reaching for my notebook.

"I'm not done."

"Show me what you have."

Her brows arched as she read it through. "Oh, dear." She scanned the branches above us. "Get up."

She steered me out from beneath the trees to an open space in the rose garden. "You're in love," she said, her voice just above a whisper, "but not with Jessop Hawkins."

I gulped. "It's that obvious?"

"This is extremely dangerous." She seemed to be keeping an eye on the path behind me. "Do you need my help?" she said slowly.

I didn't want to drag her into this, but I had no choice. "Yes, I'm sorry, but I do."

"All right," she said. "Tell me what you want me to do, and nothing more. The less I know, the better."

First, I told her about Dayla's plan to shadow me at school, and she said she'd try and stop her. Then I asked Ms. A if she would open the back gate Monday night during the play.

She cupped my chin in her hand and sighed. "I so wish it hadn't come to this, but yes, count on me."

As she walked over to Zara, I tore my poem out of the notebook and folded it up into a triangle, and tucked it in my bra. I did it, I thought. I'm set to go. Now, I just had to keep Dayla and Roik from finding out.

44

Hawkins' garage was packed with cars when Dad and I got there on Saturday, and right up front was the red Ferrari that belonged to Yates' dad.

Please tell me Yates is not here.

I breathed in, trying to center myself as Dad and I went through the double doors and stepped onto the landing. The living room below was packed with men milling around with drinks in their hands. A few wives huddled to the side.

Mr. Sandell was holding court by the Simcha painting of slaughtered chickens, but I didn't see Yates.

I ducked behind Dad as Hawkins jogged up the steps to greet us. He shook Dad's hand, then reached over and pulled me to him, locking his lips on mine. I couldn't breathe and I couldn't get away, and even with my lips shut, I tasted his mouthwash and red wine.

When he stopped, I eased out of his arms. "Why don't you introduce me to your guests?"

"I'd love to." Hawkins grabbed the railing. "Everyone! Let me present the future Mrs. Jessop Hawkins."

The entire room turned and started clapping. And that's when I saw Yates, standing by the windows.

I tried to keep my face a blank as Hawkins gripped my elbow and steered me down the stairs. He guided me through the room, talking golf and international markets with the men, and making me show off my bracelet to the four wives who'd come.

I tried not to look at Yates, afraid my face would give away my feelings. But Hawkins led me over to him.

My heart beat rapid-fire.

"Avie, how's it going?" Yates smiled, his blue eyes telling me to relax.

"Yates. It's great to see you."

Yates thrust his hand at Jes. "We haven't met. I'm Yates, Cyrus' son. Avie and I grew up together."

Hawkins shook his hand. "Yes, I've been eager to meet you."

I felt dizzy, this was surreal.

Hawkins squeezed my hand hard. The clink of our Love bracelets rattled in my ears. He gave us a cold, hard smile. "Walk with me," he told us.

"Lead the way," Yates answered.

I wanted to grab him and run for the stairs. My heart jackhammered as Hawkins led us to an empty alcove off the living room, as if to show us a painting there. We were just out of sight of the party.

I stared ahead, even when Yates' hand brushed mine, setting off electric sparks. If I didn't know what Hawkins was capable of, I'd have thought he was casually chatting Yates up. But I knew differently.

"You're at Occidental, studying social justice, correct?"

"Yes, sir," Yates answered.

Hawkins squinted at him. "Social work. An admirable choice, but not one that pays well."

Yates held his eyes. "Actually, I'm more into political activism."

"Yes, that's right. You helped lead the protest in Sacramento."

Hawkins turned to me suddenly, and I couldn't breathe. I was looking a cobra in the eyes.

"I know about you two," he said, his voice low, casual.

"Mr. Hawkins, excuse me," Yates tried. "I'm not sure what you mean."

Hawkins looked at Yates, his voice almost bored. "I know about the messages and the rendezvous at the church. I've been patient. Even helpful." He looked at me. "I bailed your friend here out of jail."

My knees began to buckle. I wanted to reach for Yates, but I forced myself not to.

Yates cleared his throat. "Thank you for bailing me out, Mr. Hawkins, but I assure you—"

Hawkins held up his hand for Yates to stop. "You know why I got you out? Because I can. I have the lawyers and the money and the connections to shape the world any way I want. Bailing you out was a gift for my lovely bride. Now you are in my debt—both of you."

Yates tried again. "Sir—"

Hawkins cut him off. "No. You do not appreciate the situation. Your sneaking around will stop. Now. You will not see or text or talk to each other. It's over. Aveline is under Contract to me. She *belongs* to me. Do you understand?"

The silence sucked the air out of the room. There was only one answer. I nodded.

"Yates, go rejoin the party."

Yates' fists were clenched. "If you hurt her—"

"*You* are the one hurting her with your righteous folly and foolish bravado."

I winced. I wanted to pick up the huge glass bowl on the pedestal near us and heave it at Hawkins.

Yates stood up straighter. His hands were shaking. "Excuse me," he said, and walked back into the crowd.

I shrank back as Hawkins closed in on me. "I know where your boyfriend works." He slipped his hand inside the collar of my dress and stroked my skin with his thumb. "I know where he lives. What kind of motorcycle he rides. If I chose to, I could have him arrested. Or worse. I don't think you want that."

I stared at the wall, not saying a word.

"In a few weeks, you will become my wife. If you haven't read your Contract, I suggest you go home and do so."

My body went cold. I hadn't read my Contract.

"Are we clear?" Hawkins said.

I refused to answer.

"Are. We. Clear?"

"Yes. Yes!" I tore his hand off me and rushed around the corner.

You will never NEVER own me.

I didn't care how dangerous it was, I was getting away from Hawkins even if it killed me.

45

Hawkins made Yates and me sit across from each other at a late lunch that lasted hours. He eyed us like prey while he listened to men report on how the opiate trade had exploded in Eastern Europe and Biocure's profits from the new drug could surpass all expectations.

Despite the happy news, those guys rushed to get out of there, the minute the meal was over. Hawkins made me stand beside him at the door as he said good-bye to each of them, but when Yates came up to us, I clasped my hands behind my back, not knowing what to do.

"It's okay, you can kiss her," Hawkins told him. "You're an old family friend."

Yates' lips brushed my cheek, and I fought the urge to reach for him. Then he walked out, my heart unraveling after him.

Dad was last, and I stepped toward him. "Thanks for loaning us the driver," he told Hawkins.

"Of course. Mind if we have a moment alone?" Hawkins said, nodding at me.

"Sure," Dad said before I could say no. "Take all the time you need."

Dad shut the door, and I stopped breathing as Hawkins took my hands and placed them on his shoulders. He slid his hands down to my waist and pulled me up against him.

His cement-colored eyes searched my face. "Your Signing Profile was incomplete," he said. "It should have mentioned that you need some taming."

My stomach clenched.

Hawkins nuzzled my cheek, gripping the back of my head so I couldn't move. "Read your Contract, darling," he whispered. Then he forced his tongue deep into my mouth.

I squirmed in his grasp, wanting to bite his plunging tongue and knowing it was the last thing in the world I should do.

Finally, I couldn't stand it anymore and I shoved him off me. He stumbled back against the railing, then caught himself and lunged for me. I tried to duck, but he grabbed hold of my hair and jerked me off my feet. I gasped from the pain.

"There are other things you need to learn, Aveline, but I look forward to *those* lessons."

He released me and I ran for the car. Dad slouched in the back-seat, scrolling through messages on his phone. His face was tight, and he didn't look at me as I got in.

Get me out of here. Get me out of here now, I thought, but we barely made it out the gates before I yelled, "Stop the car."

The driver pulled over and I lurched out the door. I stumbled to the brush and heaved. My body shook as everything spewed out and the wind splattered it onto my dress.

Dad came over with a bottle of water and some tissues. "Here."

The sun was already setting, turning the ocean grey. I stood there, trembling and wiping my mouth.

Dad put his arm around my shoulders. "You feel any better now, angelpie?"

I looked at him. He hadn't called me that in a really long time. "I can't do it, Daddy. I can't marry Hawkins."

Dad tensed. "Are you afraid you can't live up to his expectations, because you did a fine job today. I was very proud of how you handled yourself."

"No, you don't understand. I can't be his wife. I don't like him."

Dad's fingers tightened on my shoulder. The waves crashed below. "Dad, I said I don't like him."

"I understand you don't love him. You hardly know him." Dad's phone buzzed furiously and he reached for it.

I grabbed the phone from his hand. "You don't get it. I hate Hawkins. I can't Sign him. He's repulsive!"

Dad wheeled around and looked back at the car. "Keep your voice down!"

"I won't. Can't you see how awful he is? You know Mom would hate him. You know she'd never let me Sign him."

"Avie, shut up!"

I stepped back. Dad had never ever said anything like that to me.

"Everything okay, sir?" Hawkins' driver stood by the car.

"Nothing serious. A little too much wine."

The wind ripped at my dress as I drifted away from him. My heels wobbled on the rocks. "You don't care about me at all, do you? I'm standing here with puke all over me, telling you I hate Hawkins, and you tell me to shut up?"

"I'm sorry. I shouldn't have said that." The phone buzzed in my hand, and Dad reached for me with his eyes. "Could you come away from the edge, sweetheart?"

I shook my head. "No. You're not listening to me."

Dad inched forward. "I promise I'll listen if you come away from the edge. Please." He stretched out his hand, and I wanted to believe him so much I held mine up. He jerked me so hard I fell into him. "Okay. We're Okay now," he said, sheltering me under his arm.

His phone hummed, and I went to throw it, but Dad wrestled it out of my hand.

"Honey, I know it's overwhelming, committing to a life with someone you barely know . . ."

"I know enough, Daddy. And you do, too. You can't tell me he's a good person."

Dad's lips went flat. His eyes darted from me to the car and back. Finally, he let out an exhausted breath. "We need Hawkins. We've got hundreds of families depending on us. These men, most of them are raising kids by themselves. They've got mortgages . . ."

"Can't you get the money some other way?"

"It's too late for that. Jes has been buying up stock. He's close to owning half the company."

I didn't know much about business, but I guessed what that meant. "Jes owns you, too."

"You could put it that way."

"Not a great feeling, is it."

"No, quite frankly, it sucks."

We stood there in silence, Dad biting his lip, and me shaking my head. Hawkins controlled both of us.

"Hawkins suggested I read my Contract," I said.

"What did you do!"

I took a long hard look at Dad. He had no clue about Yates. Roik and Hawkins had kept him out of the loop.

"I didn't do a thing. He just said I should read it. Besides," I said quietly, "if I want to change anything, don't I need to do it before the Signing?"

"I don't think that's possible. Jes and I already negotiated the terms. Your signature is more of a 'formality' than anything else."

"Property," I muttered. "That's all I am. Property."

"Honey, I promise I'll get your Contract out and go over it with you line by line, but right now I've got to answer these calls."

"Fine." I was exhausted.

I let Dad lead me back to the car. He sat me down in the backseat and buckled my seat belt, gently moving my arms as if I was still six.

Dad reached for his phone and started messaging like the future of the world depended on it.

I kicked off my cherry heels and curled up in a ball. My dress stank so bad it was making me sick all over again.

Dad couldn't help me, and it wasn't because he didn't want to. The whole drive home, I kept hearing Hawkins' voice in my ear. *Read your Contract, darling.*

It wasn't an order. It was a threat.

46

I wasn't the only one who'd had a terrible time at Hawkins' party. Something Hawkins said had spooked the Biocure board, because they started showing up at our house before I'd even changed out of my dress.

Dad burst into the kitchen while I was searching for ginger ale. He looked like he could use a defibrillator. "Can you put together some snacks, honey?"

I was too tired to argue. "Sure. What's the emergency?"

"The board's questioning how I'll vote at the next meeting. Some of the members are convinced I'm in bed with Hawkins."

"Can't imagine why," I muttered as Dad dashed out the door.

Once they were shut away in the living room with their beer and cheese crackers, it only took a minute of searching Dad's files to find my Contract. I sprinted upstairs and locked my door. Then I spread the pages out on the floor and kneeled over them.

What do you want me to see, Jes?

I skipped to the end, because Ms. A had warned us that was where they hid the bad stuff. Unlike the earlier sections, I didn't need a law degree to decipher what they meant. I wasn't surprised when I saw the virginity clause, or that my Contract didn't have a four-year college deferral like Dayla's first Contract did.

But I'd never imagined there could be something worse than a virginity clause. I had to read the final pages twice, because I just couldn't believe them.

If I failed to perform my wifely duties, Hawkins could *transfer ownership*.

If I failed to live up to my vows to love, honor, and obey, he could *transfer ownership*.

In the event Hawkins even *suspected* I was unfaithful, he could *transfer ownership*.

He could resell me.

I read and reread the section, but no matter how hard I looked, there wasn't a single sentence stating I had the right to approve who bought me.

My sweatshirt was strangling me and I tore it off. Okay, okay. *Don't freak. Dad hasn't signed it yet. The signature lines are still blank.*

There were two more pages to go, and even though I hoped I'd seen the worst, I knew better than to trust Hawkins. I kept reading.

In the event of an impending transfer of ownership I could buy out my Contract by *repaying* my bride price.

Sure. Because I had fifty million dollars of my own, right.

My hands were shaking so bad by the time I picked up the last page, I almost couldn't read it. But once I did, I dropped it and hugged my arms to my chest.

The Contract was in force as soon as payment was received. That fifty million Dad got from Hawkins a few weeks ago. That was my bill of sale.

Hawkins owned me NOW.

OhmyGodOhmyGodOhmyGod.

Yates called me about an hour later, and I almost didn't pick up, Hawkins' threats echoing in my head, but I was desperate to hear Yates' voice.

"Aves —"

I heard the catastrophe in his pause. "What? What are you going to tell me?"

"Gabe's been arrested."

"No, say it isn't true."

"We think he'll be charged with kidnapping."

"Kidnapping?" Father Gabe was going to prison. Roaring filled my ears.

"The girls he helps are minors. They can't legally give consent, so technically, Exodus is a form of kidnapping."

"Hawkins did this, didn't he?"

"Not sure. His lawyer thinks it came from someone higher up. Someone in Washington."

Things were starting to make a bizarre kind of sense. "While you were gone, I asked Gabe why he risked working for Exodus, and he said the weirdest thing about girls being pawns in a chess game our leaders are playing."

"I wish I knew what he meant by that. Gabe always kept a lot of secrets."

I wrapped my arms around my legs to stop the trembling. "This is horrible."

"Aves, I know it looks bad, but Exodus' plan for you is still in place. All we have to do is get you out of L.A."

"Aamir's still okay with helping me?"

Yates didn't answer right away. "Aamir's gone into hiding. So, I'm extracting you. All we need is a car."

"No, you need to stay away from me," I said. "Hawkins threatened to have you arrested."

"I can deal with being arrested."

"He threatened to *hurt* you."

"If you don't get away from Hawkins he *will* hurt you, Aves, and I'll have to live with that, and it will be much worse than what he might do to me."

I laid my head down on my knees. I couldn't protect Yates. No matter what happened he was in danger.

"I know someone who'll loan us a car," I said.

"Someone you trust?"

A week ago, I wouldn't have hesitated, but now I had to take the chance that Prandip wouldn't betray me. "Yes."

"Then call them."

My fingers messed up when I dialed Dr. Prandip's number and it took three tries before I got it right. Her husband must have thought I was going into labor, the way she told me to slow down and breathe. I heard her tell him she was going upstairs.

Then she promised I could use her car. The person helping me could pick it up at her office. All he had to do was tell the office manager he was from the Mercedes Service Department and would bring it back the next day.

I sent Yates a message. "All set."

Outside, a flashlight beam ran back and forth along our fence. Ferris was on duty, keeping me safe from the bad guys. The only thing was, Ferris couldn't keep me safe from the scariest of them all.

47

Dayla showed up early on Sunday to go shopping for a crib and stroller, then dragged me to Chinatown for dim sum. After, she insisted we go for mani-pedis and to get her color corrected. Just like she had Friday night, Dayla stuck to me like a tattoo. Ho was getting his money's worth out of her.

The next morning, Dayla had a nine o'clock with the Headmaster to persuade him to reenroll her. When she passed by our class, my heart raced like I was out on the track. The Headmaster had to say no. I could not have Dayla shadow me at school today and I could not have her backstage at the play tonight.

In class, the minutes ticked by so slowly it was like waiting for an execution. Ms. A tapped her fingers on Dayla's empty chair.

The Headmaster called Ms. A out of second period, and she didn't return for the rest of the period. When the bell rang for morning break, we all looked at each other and got up.

Dayla was hanging out in the courtyard, surrounded by sophomores, but she brushed them off when she saw me. Her eyes were slits. She was ticked.

"What happened?" I said.

"They wouldn't let me back in."

"That's too bad." I shot thanks to the Headmaster and Ms. A.

"I was sure the Headmaster was going to say yes, but then he called in Ms. A."

"Ms. A said no?"

"Not exactly. She went on and on about how she'd love to have me back, I was such a good student, blah blah blah, I'd definitely benefit from completing the semester, but then she asked if the board needed to weigh in. She'd hate to have my return 'marred by questions about my character.' I can't believe she did that."

Ms. A was brilliant. No father would want Dayla in the classroom infecting his daughter with romantic fantasies. "Maybe she didn't want you to get hurt."

"Bull. She knew exactly what she was doing."

"I'm sorry."

Dayla sipped her latte. "It's okay. I took care of it."

The hairs on the back of my neck stood up. *What did you do?*

"Anyway," she said, "I wanted to tell you Buck's flying in this morning so I get to meet my knight in shining armor."

"I hope he's—" I searched for the right word. "Nice."

Day threw her bag over her shoulder. "Yeah, me, too."

"Call me later?"

"Yeah, we'll autopsy my life." She hugged me good-bye, and I watched her walk away.

If I'd been locked up like she was, who knows what I'd do to get free.

Ms. A was back after break. "Let's resume our lessons on first aid. Today, poisoning." For the last two weeks, she had lectured us on what we called LC. Leading Causes of Death in Children. Drowning. Electrocution. Poisoning. Falls.

She seemed distracted. She dropped her first aid kit when she pulled it out of the drawer and had to search her bookshelf when normally she'd reach automatically for a book she wanted.

We waited, our first aid kits open on our desks. Sophie Park whispered across the aisle. "What's up with her?"

"I don't know," I said, but the hideous tickling sensation up my neck was back.

"Please find your syrup of ipecac." Ms. A fumbled in her kit while the rest of us found our bottles and held them up as we knew she wanted.

She shoved her kit away. "Good. You found it. If a child has ingested poison, time is of the essence. Ipecac can induce vomiting, giving you precious minutes until help can arrive. Some consider it folk medicine, but if you are desperate, it is both powerful and effective. I recommend you keep it in your purse at all times. Is that clear? Who does not understand?"

The skin on my neck pulled tight. Ms. A only said that when she absolutely, positively wanted us to remember something.

She strode over and locked the door. Zara glanced at me. *What the hell?*

Then Ms. A walked to the front row and looked right at the camera like she wanted to make sure it had a clear shot. She smiled, her eyes taking us all in, even the empty seats where Sparrow and Dayla used to sit.

"My darlings. My chosen ones," she said. "I have tried to prepare you for life outside these walls. The administration has decided that this will be my last day."

I shook my head. No, this can't be happening.

She stared hard at the camera. "But I cannot go silently and I cannot go nicely. You are not objects to be sold by your fathers to pay off their debts or buy a new house. And the movement in this country that claims that you need to be protected has created legalized servitude."

Footsteps clattered down the hall.

Ms. A embraced us with her eyes. "Don't let the Paternalists take away your rights without a fight. Don't let them make you weak and dependent. And above all, don't let them silence you."

A fist banged on the frosted glass in the door. "Ms. Alexandra. Ms. Alexandra, you're wanted in the Headmaster's office."

I leaped out of my seat. She hugged me to her, and we were enveloped by fifteen sets of arms.

Keys jerked angrily in the lock.

"I will miss you, my beauties."

"No, don't go, you can't," we cried.

The door swung open and the Headmaster himself stood there. "Girls, you need to release Ms. Alexandra."

We reached out faces and hands for her kisses. Her perfect makeup was streaked with tears.

"Mr. Austin will take over the class while Ms. Alexandra comes with me," the Headmaster said.

Ms. A took a deep breath, and stood up straight like she'd breathed in the power to do anything. Then the Headmaster and Security escorted her out, taking my last chance to escape with her.

Dayla had no idea how she'd just imprisoned me for life. Or, maybe she did.

"If you would take out your workbook on household finances," Mr. Austin said.

I went to close the first aid kit, but then I realized that Ms. A had given me one last lifesaver. I palmed the tiny bottle of ipecac, and dropped it into my backpack.

No, I was not going to give up. It was time to act.

48

Roik crushed out his cigarette when I came down the steps after school. A shiver ran through me. *Now. You're doing this.*

I held out a cup. "Coffee? I put in two ice cubes just the way you like it."

He smiled and took a gulp. "Tough day?"

"Don't pretend you don't know about Ms. Alexandra."

"No, I saw them escort her out."

Roik started the car. The fancy iron gates released us, and he pulled into the street. I looked at the coffee silhouetted in his cup. A quarter was already gone.

I took a centering breath. "I want to see Mom."

"It's not Tuesday."

"I haven't seen her in two weeks, and after next Saturday, who knows when Hawkins is going to let me see her again."

"Hmm. You sure you're ready to face the crime scene?" he said.

I gripped the armrest. "I won't know until I try, right?"

"I dunno. It's late. Sun'll be down soon."

"I was helping with costumes for the play. Come on. Fifteen minutes, that's all I'm asking."

"All right, but the second the sun goes behind the hill, we're out of there."

"Deal." I sat back as Roik pulled onto the freeway.

This is really happening. Dear God, please tell me Yates got my message. I'd texted him from day care lab, but I hadn't heard back.

We sailed past the Million Mother Wall and Roik touched his fingers to his lips and blew a kiss. Billboards loomed over the wall, shouting out warnings. My heart pounded faster with each one.

K-9 Commandos. Keep your home front secure.

Can't afford a bodyguard? Our No-Jack titanium ankle bracelet is guaranteed. We retrieve your girl or we pay you $100,000.

Burning Desire Signing Brokerage. White, black, brown, or Asian. We satisfy your every need.

I tore my eyes away from the window and focused on Roik's coffee cup. *Yes, I get it. The world's a dangerous, messed-up place, and I'm insane to make a run for it.*

There was strength inside me and I needed to find it.

I put in my earphones and pulled up Survival Instincts. Those six angry girls sang to me and I whispered the words along with them. *Call me Ninja Warrior Templar Gladiator G.I. Ranger Samurai Terminator.*

Roik pulled into the cemetery and every muscle in my body tensed. I dropped my earphones on the seat. Crime tape ringed Mom's grave.

Take the blanket out of the trunk like you always do and walk up the hill. You can do this.

"Don't get out yet," Roik ordered.

"Why not? The place is empty."

"Wait for me to check it out. The cops still haven't found the driver of the blue van." I heard a clip snap into his gun, then he climbed out of the car.

I leaned over the seat. Roik had finished his coffee and his Taser lay on the center console. Always carry backup, he liked to say, so I shoved it into my bag.

Roik waved to me to come up, so I grabbed my backpack and started up the hill. The yellow crime tape snapped in the breeze.

I flashed back to the man's hand on my throat, the gun shoved up against my eye. My heartbeat pounded in my ears.

Keep going. Don't stop. I kept my eyes on the green grass, and forced one foot in front of the other. Seventy-five steps up the hill to Mom's grave.

I stood beside Roik, my knees shaking. He shook his head. "You shouldn't be here. It's too soon," he said. Sweat was beading on his forehead.

I hated what I was going to do. "I need to talk to Mom alone. Could you just leave us?"

"No, it's my job to protect you." He wiped his face.

"Look around," I said. "The place is empty."

He gave me a look like something awful was going to happen. "Get back in the car."

"Why?"

Roik grabbed me and pushed me ahead of him. "Go. Get in the car."

"Why? What's wrong?"

And then he doubled over. Vomit spewed from his mouth. "Get—in the—car."

"I'm sorry, Roik."

And I Tased him. He fell on his back, the volts jerking his body as they coursed through him. I picked up his phone and threw it as hard as I could.

And then I ran. Past Mom's grave and over the hill. Behind me, I could hear Roik retch. He could choke to death, lying on his back, but I couldn't help him now. My shoes pounded the dirt service road as I tore for the gate about a half-mile down.

Yates wasn't there.

I dove behind the work shed and pulled his number up on my phone. *Pick up. Pick up. Pick up.* Nothing.

"Yates, I need you to call me now!"

I can't go back. I've got to get out of here. I tore off my uniform and pulled on the sweats and baseball cap I'd grabbed from my locker.

Ripped out my earrings, rubbed dirt over my face, and threw everything except the phone in the dumpster.

Outside the cemetery gate was a neighborhood of dried lawns and chain-link fences. A few houses had lights on, but there weren't any street lamps.

I could do this. Ms. A ran us five miles every day for four years. Thank you, I sent out to her, and I ran into a maze of streets I'd never seen before.

The sun dropped behind the hills. Another twenty minutes and it would be pitch-black.

The neighborhood looked half deserted. Dogs barked and threw themselves at the chain-link fences as I ran by. I veered into the middle of the street. The men who lived here with their kids were probably on their way back from work. I had to get off the streets before one of them spotted me.

The roads didn't go straight. They curved back and forth like a folded-up electric cord, and I ran, wondering how in the hell was I going to get out of there. I punched an intersection into my phone, but it refused to give me a map.

Damn. I've got to get out of here.

I tapped Yates number again. *Oh, please be there. Pick up. Pick up.*

"Avie?"

"Yates! I did it! I got away!"

"You did? Where are you?"

"In the neighborhood behind the cemetery. Can you come get me?"

"I'll be there in fifteen. Find someplace to wait."

Hazy light outlined two boys shooting hoops in a driveway up ahead. I tore across the street as a deep voice called out, "Hey, baby. What you doin' here?"

Chain link chinged like he'd jumped the fence, and suddenly a boy built like a football player was right behind me.

"I can't stop," I told Yates. "Someone's chasing me."

"You know where you are?"

Street sign up ahead. "Just a sec. Jacaranda and Arroyo."

"Slow down, sweet cheeks." The guy chasing me was closing in, so I ran faster, hoping that his size meant he wasn't a distance runner.

"Okay, I got it," Yates said. I heard his motorcycle rev.

Yates told me he'd be there in fifteen, but if Roik got to the car and hit the panic button, the cops would be there in ten.

Footsteps pounded behind me, and I ran flat out. The streets kept curving, and I had no idea if I'd end up back at the cemetery.

Headlights roared right at me and I dodged. A truck passed me, and then braked, and I heard it whine and rumble like it was turning around. I didn't know if the teenage guy was still after me, because I couldn't see or hear him.

I dove into an overgrown hedge. My heart banged as loud as the muffler.

The truck passed.

I waited.

The driver went about a hundred feet. Threw the truck into reverse.

I held the phone against me to dim the screen, and sent Yates the address of the house across the street.

The truck backed up until it was a couple houses away. It idled in the street, high beams lighting up the yards on either side.

A motorcycle roared behind me. Yates? It tore off in another direction. No, don't go away. I'm here. Over here.

The truck driver got out and prowled the yard across the street, waving a flashlight into the bushes. He had a big beer gut, so I knew I could outrun him if I could get past him.

Come on, Yates. Where are you?

The driver moved down to the next house, and a dog started barking and carrying on. The front door banged open. "What the hell you doing in my yard?" yelled a man.

The driver's hands flew up as he backed away. "Nothing, buddy. Looking for my dog. She jumped out of my truck. That's all."

Then he turned toward me like he sensed exactly where I was. I forced myself to breathe. *Remember. Go for the instep. The groin. Get him down, then run like hell.*

I heard a motorcycle coming toward us. I had to get out in the open, because if I didn't, Yates would fly right past me.

The guy hunting me barreled across the lawn.

I jumped out from the hedge and sprinted for the street, trying to make it to the truck's headlight beams so Yates would see me.

The guy saw where I was heading and tried to cut me off, but I dodged him. The motorcycle screamed right for us, but the guy was only ten feet behind me.

I charged into the light. *Hurry, Yates!* I pumped faster and heard the bike slow. I wheeled around, just as Yates knocked the man off his feet.

He fell on his side. "Son of a b—, you broke my arm!"

The bike braked in front of me, and Yates reached for my hand, I leaped onto the bike and we tore out of the neighborhood.

50

I pressed my body into Yates' as we soared through backstreets. He dodged streetlights, and I kept my head down and my face out of sight.

My heart revved as the bike swept me away from Hawkins and into my future.

Yates pulled into the dark alley behind Dr. Prandip's office. He cut the engine and tore off his helmet. I slid off the bike. "I can't believe we made it," I said.

Yates threw his arm around my waist and planted a quick kiss on my lips. "You're fearless."

Adrenaline roared through me. "I'm not. It was you. You told me I could do it."

"Yeah, but you pulled it off." He reached for his phone, his face illuminated as he read. "Okay, we've got your connection out of California."

"That's good," I said, not quite feeling it. Even though I knew I had to make this connection, now it was real. "So far things are going well."

"Yeah, hold that thought." He opened his saddlebags and pulled on a pair of mechanic's coveralls with a Mercedes logo. Then, he slapped a baseball cap onto his head. "Time to pick up the doc's keys."

We hopped the wall into the parking garage. Yates walked to the brightly lit lobby while I crouched by the Dumpster. I stayed hidden while men in suits or scrubs got in their cars and drove off.

Finally, Yates sauntered back through the glass doors. He clicked the keys and a car in the next row blinked its headlights. I was about to stand up when a guy appeared behind Yates. I dropped to the ground and listened hard. *Please don't let it be a cop.*

His steps echoed Yates' like he was following him. I held still, but my heart thudded so I could barely hear.

"You're from Mercedes?"

"Yes, sir." Yates sounded completely relaxed.

"I didn't know you folks pick up at the office."

"It's a service for preferred customers."

I heard first one, then a second door open. I remained out of sight until I heard a car back up and drive away, then I crawled out of hiding.

Yates waited in the front seat. I dove into the back and crouched on the floor while Yates pulled out and paid the garage attendant. Then he swung out of the lot.

Twenty minutes later we were cruising north on an old two-lane highway into the mountains, the radio turned to the evening news. Yates pulled onto an overlook and I climbed into the front seat. "Put this on," he said, handing me the baseball cap.

"Have they put an Amber Alert out on me?"

California had installed computerized signs on every freeway to alert drivers when a child was kidnapped.

"The freeway signs were turned off, so the police must not have a description of my bike or plate number."

The police would question Yates after I got away, Roik would see to that. "Do you have an alibi?" I said.

Yates nodded. "Mrs. Kessler and I are handing out coffee and sandwiches on Skid Row tonight."

I thought of her knitting on Father G's couch so I could be alone with Yates. "Thank her for me?"

"I will definitely do that."

I ducked my head as headlights hurtled toward us. "How long until we get there?"

"About an hour." Yates reached for my hand. "I'm proud of you. You really kicked butt back at the cemetery."

I wove my fingers into his. "I feel bad about Roik. The Taser must have hurt like hell and I probably got him fired."

"You did what you had to do."

"I know. I'm just happy I'll never have to do anything like that again."

Yates kept his eyes on the road. Deliberately, it seemed.

"So where are we going?" I said.

"I can't tell you."

"Right. The less I know, the better." If the cops stopped us and took us into custody, they'd interrogate us. This way I couldn't betray anyone.

Yates shrugged and squeezed my hand. "Gabe told you how you'll be staying in people's homes, how they'll get you to your next connection?"

"Yes. But has that changed now that he's—" *Locked up.*

"No. The plan's the same." Yates shook out his shoulders like the weight of my life was pulling them down. "It's gonna be tough. You've got to be ready to go the minute they say go."

"All right."

"No, I'm serious. You've got to take care of yourself. You've got to eat and sleep whenever you can."

Tension was sewing a line up my back. I wished Yates would lighten up. I didn't want to think about cops or Retrievers or the six hundred other things that could go horribly wrong. "You sound like Ms. A before regionals."

"I'm not joking," he snapped.

"Okay. Okay."

The news murmured in the background. Traffic backed up on the 210 freeway. Lakers ahead by ten. No mention of an Amber Alert for a missing girl.

The city lights were behind us and stars were visible through the trees. Yates raised my hand to his lips. "I don't want anything to happen to you."

"But girls get over the border every day, right?"

Yates hesitated for a split second too long before he said, "Yeah, every day."

That split second had the fast, sharp pain of a razor slice. "You're holding something back. What is it?"

"Avie . . ."

"Come on. Truth. Like it's harder for girls with big price tags and squads of Retrievers on their heels. Believe me, I noticed: Six Million Dollar Dayla lasted, what? Three days on the run? And I'm worth millions more."

"I wasn't going to say that."

"What then?"

"It'll be fine. Trust me. It'll work out."

I took a deep breath and let the steam blow out of me. Yates still wasn't being completely honest. "The girls you helped, how do you know they made it?" I said.

"To Canada? Sometimes Father G gets a postcard."

I imagined my card, glossy red and white maple leaf on the front. *Having a wonderful time. Truly wish you were here.*

Yates rubbed my knuckle like a worry stone. "I'm sorry for freaking you out."

I kept pushing. "And the girls tell you they're fine?"

"No. The cards are blank."

"Oh." I wished the answer was different. "So there's no evidence to trace."

Yates nodded. Finally, he'd admitted the truth.

We drove, listening for breaking news as the road climbed the mountains, twisting and turning. The pavement turned glossy black, and snow crusted the dirt under the pines.

By now Roik would have called the cops. A K-9 unit was probably tracking my scent through the neighborhood. The cops would knock on doors and someone would tell how they saw a guy on a motorcycle pluck a running girl off the street.

I stared into the darkness. The horror of what I'd done flooded me. "The cops are going to drag you in and question you. I should never have asked you to help me."

"Hey." He jerked my hand. "Look at me."

I could barely see him in the half-light.

"We're going to make it. I've got an airtight alibi in Mrs. Kessler, and in two days, you'll be safe in Canada." He nodded ahead of us. "Look."

We'd crested the mountains and started down to the desert. Way below, I saw the lights of a small city through the gaps between the trees. I was crossing the border to Underground.

51

Yates drove down a side road past a tall fence topped with razor wire and through an open gate. Small private planes lined up along a row of hangars. Floodlights lit up the car, and I tipped my hat to hide my face.

A woman carrying a clipboard circled a Cessna. White hair in a bowl cut. Khaki vest with a dozen pockets. Her favorite phrase was probably "cut the crap."

She waved Yates over and squinted at us through the windshield. "Who you looking for?"

"Ruby?"

"Yeah, you found her." She pointed to the small hangar behind the plane. "We've got ten minutes before takeoff. Pull in there and say your good-byes."

Yates drove in and Ruby shut the hangar doors behind us. I climbed out of the car. Grey light filtered through the dusty windows. Big red toolboxes hunched in the corner, and my nose tingled from the smell of oil and metal.

Yates came over as I leaned against the car. My breath caught as he put his hands on my hips and lifted me up on the hood. He smelled like cinnamon and soap and . . . Yates.

I wrapped my arms around his neck as he bent down and peeled off my hat. My hair tumbled over my shoulders. "You're so beautiful," he said, cupping my chin in his hand.

I was dirty and sweaty, and I didn't feel beautiful, but I loved that Yates didn't need me gift-wrapped to think I was.

His lips met mine, tender and sad, and our kisses whispered good-bye, good-bye.

I slipped two fingers into my bra and eased out a little triangle of folded paper. Suddenly, I was embarrassed to show it to him. I wrapped my fist around the paper and pressed it to my chest.

"It kills me to let you go like this," he said.

"Me, too."

"I could come with you." Yates said it like he was just tossing out the idea, but I knew him too well.

I pulled away so he'd see my eyes. "No. You hear me. NO."

"I can protect you."

"Two people traveling together? They'd track us down twice as fast. Besides, you have to return Dr. Prandip's car."

He nodded in surrender. "I hate not knowing where you're going."

And then it hit me, I didn't have a clue where I was going next. I was relying on faith that I'd make it across the border and we'd be together someday. Faith born from the crazy, irrational feelings I had for Yates.

I opened my hand. "This is for you."

Yates opened it as gently as if I'd handed him a flower. The paper crackled as it unfolded, and I stilled myself as Yates swept his eyes over the grey-penciled lines of my poem.

"Love wields the scissors," he said, and I sensed him waiting for me.

"Love is the escape," I answered.

"Love blows through pinholes."

"Love refuses to die."

I smiled, flicking tears off my cheeks when Yates looked at the paper.

Each line we spoke held its hand out to the next and when we got to the end, we said it together. "Love is the rusted fire escape / that shouldn't support our weight / but does."

Ruby jiggled the door. "Time's up."

No, it can't be. I need more time.

Yates wrapped me in his arms. My throat was thick with tears, and I could barely say, "Bye."

"This isn't good-bye," he said, kissing me. "They won't stop us."

"No?" I wanted so badly to believe him.

"No. We are going to be together. In Toronto. Say it. We're going to have a life together in Toronto."

"Okay, we're going to have a life together in Toronto."

A hand pounded the door. "Let's go!"

"When?" I asked.

"I don't know, but I'll find a way."

Ruby hauled open the door and shooed me over to the plane. I buckled in and watched Yates back the car out. He drove away without waving just like Ruby told him to do.

He was taking my heart, and I felt like all that was left was a kite string connecting us. I touched my hand to my nose, hoping some of his smell had seeped into my skin so I could have him with me.

Ruby shoved a headset at me. The control tower gave her clearance and the plane barreled down the runway. I clamped the headset over my ears. Yates was gone and I couldn't stop thinking how Juliet trusted everything to work out with Romeo, but stuff happens. Messages get screwed up. People get it wrong and never find each other.

And love, as powerful as it is, can't fix everything.

Underground

52

The small plane climbed into the air, the engine roaring like a food processor grinding walnut shells. It wobbled in the wind, and I grabbed my seat and held on. The mountains on either side were solid black cutouts and within a minute or two the city lights suddenly ended.

I imagined Yates driving back alone through the mountains and dropping Prandip's car back at her office. I shuddered, wondering if Roik or the police would be waiting for Yates at his apartment.

Yates had to go to classes and work and pretend he wasn't involved in my disappearance, but Ho would hire investigators to hack Yates' phone and computer.

Please, please be okay.

I knew I had to focus on myself right now. I couldn't get distracted. I adjusted the mike on my headset. "Where are we going?"

"You don't have to yell. Mike works pretty good," Ruby said.

I waited for Ruby to tell me where, but she didn't. "That your boyfriend?" she asked.

"He's a friend." Ruby probably guessed that we weren't shaking hands good-bye in that hangar, but if she wasn't handing out information, I wasn't going to, either.

"You got a phone on you?" she asked.

"Yes?"

"Get it out. I need to adjust the settings for the altitude."

I'd never heard of that, but I'd never ridden in a small plane, either.

"Good." She jerked the window open and pitched my phone right out. The window slammed shut, smacking Ruby hard.

"What the hell are you doing! That was mine!"

She rubbed her arm. "Damn. That hurt."

"Why'd you do that?"

"Listen, missy, I'm cutting the trail you left. Making sure your daddy doesn't track you right to that signal."

"That phone wasn't registered to me. My friend got it."

"So nobody knew you had it. Never saw it even once?"

I didn't answer her. Roik knew.

"I see. Then you're better off dumping it in the desert. It won't stop the Retrievers, but it'll slow 'em down a bit."

Now Yates had no way to reach me!

The seatbelt felt like a straitjacket. Here I was, trapped with a crazy lady pilot, going who the hell knows where, no clue if I could trust her.

And, on top of that, she threw out all the photos I'd transferred to the phone. Gone! My pictures of Mom and Dad. Yates. Dayla. Ms. A. Not to mention the songs Yates had sent me. Things I'd counted on to keep me sane while we were apart. Dumped in the freaking desert.

I hit the door with my fist, and Ruby smacked my shoulder. "Don't do that."

Ruby looked like she'd wrestle me out of the seat if I tried anything, but I still glared back at her. "Nobody told me you'd toss my phone."

"Stop your whining. That boy'll walk through fire to see you again. You've got his code and you'll get a new phone in no time. Right now you're free from whoever you're running from. So shape up."

My cheeks flared in the dark. "Sorry."

Ruby ignored me.

The plane crossed a double line of headlights and taillights that went on for miles. The landscape was black except for one or two white-haloed gas stations beside the road. It seemed as if we might be headed for Nevada.

The plane hovered over the highway. Ruby flew without saying a word for a half hour, giving me plenty of time to "adjust my attitude" as Ms. A liked to say. Ruby was ticked and that was the last thing I needed.

"Ah. Thanks for helping me," I said, breaking the silence.

"I'm not helping you," she snapped back. "I'm helping them." Ruby tapped a photo on the dash. Two girls in wet bathing suits, probably eleven and nine, mugged for the camera.

"Your granddaughters?"

"Yep. My grandbabies."

"But aren't you taking a pretty big risk, helping me?" Ruby could go to jail if she got caught. Who'd take care of her girls?

"Maybe. But I couldn't sleep at night, knowing I stood by while my country went to hell. I don't know what's gotten into men these days. At first, I thought they were being protective, but lately I've gotten to wonder if there isn't something else going on."

"Like what?"

"Don't know, but it strikes me as suspicious that when I applied for a government contract, I got rejected, but when I put Mr. in front of my name, it went right through."

Up ahead, carnival-colored lights fanned out along the road. "What's that?" I said.

"That's Wonderland, Alice. But the locals call it Vegas."

The airport was practically on top of the town. The casinos on the Strip glowed like shiny gold, red, and green Christmas presents and the town glittered around them like spilled sequins. But as breath-taking as it was, I saw black hulks of abandoned hotels and neigh-borhoods where whole blocks looked deserted.

The control tower came on, and Ruby warned me to stay quiet. The tower guided us in and Ruby set down the plane. I tensed when we hit the runway, wondering how I'd get through the terminal with hundreds of men's eyes on me.

"Get your hat back on and your shades," she said. "And grab that bomber jacket. That'll give you some heft."

She taxied around to a private hangar. "When I open the door, you come down the stairs and walk right to the car that's waiting. Don't look at me or say anything. Pretend I'm nothing and get out."

A white limo with gold running lights idled by the hangar. I cracked open the door and paused. This could be a trap. Hawkins could afford to deck his Retrievers out in a limo.

But I'd only been gone a few hours and Dad wouldn't tell Hawkins until he had to. Roik was probably still driving around, puking his guts out looking for me.

A guy the size of a sumo wrestler opened the limo door.

I climbed down, knowing I couldn't run. Barbed wire circled the airport. I had money, but no phone, and I didn't know who my con-tact was.

Sumo Guy waited for me to get in, so I said a prayer and he started the car.

The Vegas Strip pulsated with light and music. Huge screens scrolled come-ons. *Jade Wants It Bad. See Her Live at Torrent. Sheila in XXXtasy. Onstage at Tropical Fever.*

Thousands of men clogged the sidewalks in front of the casinos. They laughed, and swigged beer, and shoved each other into the street like we'd driven into the middle of one big party. I jumped when a guy shoved his middle finger at me through the tinted window.

"Don't get excited," Sumo Guy said. "He thinks he's flipping off a high roller."

"All right. Thanks," I answered.

None of this matched what Father G had told me. Small towns. Back roads. Forgettable houses. He said Exodus stops were places that people would never think to look.

I wanted to jump out of the car, but I didn't dare. I didn't know where Sumo was taking me, but I was sure it wasn't a safe house.

The limo inched up the Strip, before it dipped down into an underground parking lot. My whole body tensed. Maybe I should bolt.

I scanned the backseat while Sumo guy parked the car. I wished I still had Roik's Taser. The only thing I could possibly use to protect myself was the bottle of scotch in the limo bar. I wrapped my hand around the neck as Sumo opened the door.

He looked at my raised arm and shook his head like he didn't get paid enough to put up with girls like me. "Tuck your hair in your jacket," he said quietly. "And keep your head down. They got security cameras everywhere." I put the bottle back.

Sumo led me through the flashing, winking, chinging casino. The noise and spinning, strobing lights hammered me, and the smell of cigarettes and beer and greasy buffet food made me feel sick. The room was a maze of slot machines and poker tables and I was afraid to follow him, but even more afraid to lose him.

He whipped out a key card for the elevator and pressed a button. The elevator surged to the top floor, not stopping for anything. The door opened, and six huge guys in suits and dark glasses were lined up across from the elevator.

Retrievers! I threw myself at the elevator buttons, but Sumo splayed his hand over the panel. "Those men have nothing to do with you," he said. "Besides, the elevator won't work without a card."

53

Double doors that looked like beaten gold opened into a circular foyer. The room was opulent in ways that said it didn't have to prove it: a gleaming wood floor, a huge golden bowl spotlit on an ebony table in the center.

Dance music pounded the air, and blue laser beams flickered through an archway to the right. Sumo led me to a small room off the foyer with creamy red walls the color of tomato soup.

Vanilla and musk wafted off the woman who came around her desk to greet me. Her dark hair spilled over her shoulders and the fabric of her perfectly cut shift was obsidian black and textured like a chipped arrowhead. "I'm Magda," she said in a cool, professional voice. "You must be Avie."

"Yes, I am. Hello."

She was probably forty, a Survivor, and I wondered what her story was.

Magda swept her phone off her desk, tapped the screen, and I swear she took my picture even though she didn't actually look at me while she did it. She handed her phone to Sumo guy. "Billy, did you scan her?"

"No, ma'am. Haven't had time."

"That's all right. I'll do it. You can go."

Billy retreated behind the closed door, and Magda took a thick, white wand out of her desk. One touch and it buzzed with blue light.

I took a step back.

Magda crooked her finger at me. "I promise it doesn't hurt. If you would push up your sleeves and hold out your arms."

"What's that for?"

She brought the wand closer. "It's a locator chip detector."

Dusty had a locator chip, I thought, before I remembered Becca got one, too, after her Signing. "I don't have a chip."

"Hmm. That's exactly what someone else said before we found hers under a tattoo of her husband's name. She had no idea the artist had thrown in a little extra."

I pushed up my sleeves and stole glances at her face.

Magda ran the light wand up my left arm. "You're curious." She tilted her head, studied me. "But not about the wand—you're wondering why I survived the Scarpanol disaster."

The light wand hummed behind my neck then traveled down my other arm. "I don't meet a lot of Survivors," I said.

"I'm an ex-vegan. Living proof that a healthy diet can prolong your life."

She passed the wand under my arms, and across my breasts. "Spread your legs, please."

"What?"

"I know, it's shocking, but you wouldn't believe the places we've found chips."

I stood legs wide apart while the wand hummed and crackled around my crotch. Magda switched it off. "Excellent. All clear."

I wasn't sure what to say. "I really appreciate you hiding me."

She smiled. "It's what I do."

I didn't get a warm and fuzzy feeling from Magda's smile. Maybe she was legit, but there were six guys at the door and an elevator that didn't go down unless I had an access card.

"I need a phone," I said. "Mine got lost." I reached into my pocket. "I've got money."

"A phone would be a bad idea right now."

"But I need one. I can't—"

Magda didn't let me finish. "I understand you'd like to call a friend, but doing that would put you both in danger. We'll find you a phone, but not tonight. In the meantime, I think we should remove the bracelet, don't you?"

"Yes, absolutely. Thank you!"

She retrieved a small maroon velvet bag from her desk and loosened the braided ties. A tiny gold screwdriver dropped in her hand, and I held out my wrist.

Magda twirled the screwdriver like she'd done it a hundred times before and slid the bracelet off. I rubbed my skin. *Free. Finally.*

The bracelet dangled from her finger. "Do you want to keep this?"

"No, I never want to see it again."

"Then you don't mind if we donate it to the cause?"

"Sure. Fine."

There was a knock on the door and Sumo stuck his head in. "They're waiting for you," he told Magda.

"I need to attend to my guests," she said. "Billy will take you Backstage, and you can rest and get something to eat. We'll talk tomorrow."

She glided toward the door. "We don't use our past names here. Let Billy know what you'd like to be called. Oh, and Billy, be sure to incinerate the outfit she's wearing."

Billy and I left Magda's office. "Why are you going to burn my clothes?" I asked.

"Because I'm guessing you want to stay gone."

Yes, I most definitely wanted to stay gone.

Billy led me across the foyer away from the pounding dance music. An amp blasted a girl's voice yelling instructions, and men cheered and booed like two teams were battling it out. I caught a glimpse of a guy jerking and spinning around on top of what I guessed was a mechanical bull.

"What's going on in there?" I asked.

"Don't worry about that," Billy said. He took me over to a door marked PRIVATE and punched in a code.

Guards, codes, access cards? I planted my feet on the parquet. "The door's locked."

"For your safety."

For your safety. Yeah, right. I'd heard that lie about a thousand times. "Why should I believe you?"

Billy opened the door enough so I could see a long hall with doors on either side like a typical hotel. "What else you gonna do, miss?"

Stay out here with the party dogs or trust that Billy wasn't locking me up. Not a lot of choices for a girl on the run. I decided to trust Billy. For now.

The steel door shut behind us, squeezing out the party sounds like we'd just passed through an airlock. Creamy scents of shampoo and body lotion wafted in the air and the lighting and carpet were rosy and soft.

My legs went wobbly as I flashed back to Dr. Prandip's serenely lavender waiting room and Sergio's ice-cream-colored underwear boutique. Places designed to make girls relax and feel safe while exploiting the hell out of them.

"Aren't you going to tell me the code?" I said.

Billy started down the hall. "It's Independence Day: 741776. But you don't need a code to get out. Push the release bar. It'll open."

I tested the bar and felt the lock give. When I looked up, Billy was waiting. So what if he thought I was paranoid. I'd been guarded and gated for the last eight years by people I thought I could trust. I had good reasons not to trust people I didn't know.

"Sorry," I said. "I just wanted to check."

"Suit yourself. As long as you stay this side of that steel door," he said, "you can pretty much go anywhere on the floor."

I scanned the ceiling as I followed him. If there were monitors, they had to be in the sconces, because there wasn't anyplace else to hide them.

Billy opened a door and I caught a glimpse of stainless steel. "Kitchen's here," he said. "When's the last time you ate?"

"Not since lunch."

"Dinner's over, but fridge's stocked. Help yourself when you're ready."

Billy lumbered on until he got to an exit sign. He stared me down as he pointed at it. "You do not want to use this unless there's an emergency. You go through here, you're not getting out for twenty floors. Got it?"

"Yeah. I got it."

"Your room's over there."

I don't know what I was expecting when he switched on the light. A set of bunk beds and two twins were crammed into the room along with a couple dressers. Clothes hung off the bunks and littered the floor. Looked like I had roommates. Girls who liked sequins. And stilettos.

What kind of place is this?

"Bed near the window's free," Billy said. "You can put your stuff in that bureau."

I shoved my hands in my empty pockets. "I don't have any stuff."

He nodded. "You're not the first to show up like that. I'll get you a toothbrush. Be right back."

I walked around the room, checking out the closet and the bathroom. The bed that Billy'd said was mine had a puffy white comforter and somebody'd changed the sheets. One of my roommates had written her name on the big bottle of expensive shampoo on the bureau. Splendor.

I angled the picture on the bureau so I could see it: a black girl with her arms around two younger girls who looked like they could be her sisters.

A photo from home. A big bottle of shampoo. It didn't seem as if this runaway was passing through. Splendor *lived* here.

My arms prickled. *This place isn't what I expected at all.* Father G had said I was going to stay in people's houses, and all these rebel grannies and their sons would sneak me from town to town, zigzagging me to the border.

I sat down hard on the corner of the bed. This had to be some kind of mistake.

Billy walked in with pajamas, a toiletry kit, and a plastic bag with a red biohazard symbol. "Put your old clothes in the bag and hang it on your door. I'll see they're destroyed."

"Okay."

"You decide what you want to be called?" he said.

The name popped right out of me. "Juliet. Everybody can call me Juliet."

"Well, Juliet, I got to go back to work. See you tomorrow."

He closed the door and I counted to twenty before I got up and tried it. It was unlocked. Strange.

I wasn't locked in, chained up, or chipped. I was free, but all I had right now was a toiletry kit, pajamas, and a wad of money in my pocket. I felt for the little silver dolphin dangling from my neck.

Becca, if you're up there, could you keep an eye on me—and Yates?

By now he should be back in L.A., dropping off Dr. Prandip's car. I prayed that he made it safely, and that the police wouldn't find the driver who'd chased me through the neighborhood before Yates flattened him.

The huge window looked up the Vegas Strip. Neon lights pulsed, circled, and soared like comet tails. Life outside was one big insane party.

Even if I didn't completely trust this place, I needed to get something to eat, get cleaned up, and sleep. For now I was going to believe this was just my first stop Underground.

54

Food was next after my shower. I wrapped my hair in a towel and peeked out into the hall. The biohazard bag I'd left outside was gone.

Somewhere close by, a girl was crying, big, angry, painful sobs. "It hurts! It hurts!!!"

My heart skipped a beat. *What the—*

I stole down the hall and rested my ear against the door. I couldn't hear actual words, just a girl whimpering and sobbing while another girl comforted her. They seemed to be alone, so I knocked.

A girl with big brown doe eyes opened the door. With those eyes and full red lips, she could have been Dayla's sister. "What do you want?" she said.

Her blond friend sat on the bed in her underwear, a big piece of white gauze taped to her hip.

"Hi, I heard somebody crying," I said.

"Sorry, we didn't mean to disturb you. I'll tell Shae to keep it down." The girl went to close the door, but I put my hand on it.

"You didn't disturb me. I just wanted to know if she's okay."

The girl squinted, and looked me up and down. "Are you . . . Cast?"

"No, I'm Juliet."

Her eyes relaxed. "Shae'll be fine," she said, almost friendly. "Her tattoo wipe's burning and that crappy painkiller they give you is wearing off."

"So she had a tattoo removed?"

"Had to. You know how Magda is about *resale value*. Bitch."

Resale value? "I'm sorry. What did you say?"

The girl threw her hand over her mouth. "Ohmygod, don't tell her I said that. I didn't mean it. She's not a— Promise me you won't say anything?"

"I promise."

"Okay. Well, thanks. See you around." She shut the door in my face.

Now everything clicked into place. Magda sold girls. She was a broker.

And based on that raging party, that wasn't the only thing she sold.

I backed away from the door. I was blind, thinking I could trust Exodus. Crazy to have assumed that everyone Underground would be like Yates or Father G or Dr. Prandip. Honest and good and committed to the cause.

I strode up the hall and grabbed the handle of the emergency exit. I braced for the alarm and then pushed. The door flew open onto a staircase of windowless cinderblock. No alarm.

Fluorescent lights lit up this floor and the other nineteen below it. I could bolt right now, but I'd end up out on the Strip in my cami and sleep shorts, surrounded by horny, half-wasted men.

I retreated into the hall.

Nothing made sense. Father Gabe wouldn't work with people he couldn't trust, right? Not unless they had him fooled. Or he was working for them. A priest cozying up to desperate girls, promising them freedom and he gets, what? A cut of the profits when they're resold? Maybe that was why he was arrested for kidnapping.

No, Yates would know if Father G was corrupt. He's known him for years.

But maybe Yates was fooled, too. He'd basically admitted that he and Father G never spoke again to the girls they helped. Maybe those girls never got to Canada.

Cold cascaded through my body. "I will not be a casualty. I will not be a casualty," I whispered.

Ajax had made me yell that back at him every day at self-defense camp. I saw him with his buzz cut and his oversized biceps, drilling us on how to survive a kidnapping, barking outcomes.

"Best case: you escape or are ransomed. Worst case: you disappear in the white-slave trade."

Had I been kidnapped? I wasn't sure. Nobody had drugged me. Nobody had locked me up. But they'd set it up so I really couldn't leave. I needed tools: food, clothing, a phone.

Ajax barked orders in my head. "You need to have a plan. Observe the surroundings. Know where the exits are. Pay attention to the players and their routines. You need to stay in top condition. Eat, sleep, exercise. You can't make good decisions if you're starving or exhausted."

Okay. Deep steadying breaths. *Slow down. Focus.*

I looked over my shoulder. Ajax always made a big point about how fire inspectors required *multiple means of egress.* I knew where two were, but there had to be another at the end of the hall.

Shae was still whimpering when I passed her room. Signs for CARDIO, YOGA, SHOWER, and SPA decorated the hall like this was some twisted luxury resort.

The hall ended in a wall of beaded glass, but I could tell there was a big, open room behind it. A couple spotlights were still on, and I peeked around the glass.

Two styling chairs stood in front of a makeup mirror. Blow-dryer cords snaked out of a stand. Fifty bottles of nail polish climbed little acrylic stairs, and the counter had more colors of eyeshadow and blush than Dayla did.

Even though I couldn't see the other half of the room, I knew I was alone. I crept across the wood floor.

There was the other exit; two frosted glass doors lit up from behind. The way the light hit the glass, I could tell they led outside. And right next to them were shelves stacked with folded workout clothes. I pawed through them. Yoga pants and racer tops, sweats and warm-up jackets. All sized for girls like me.

I tucked a set under my robe. Now if I had to escape, I wouldn't be in sleep shorts and a skimpy cami.

I pushed through the glass doors into a rooftop garden with a spotlit pool, cabanas, a glass railing around the whole thing. A band rocked the penthouse bar on the casino next door. My hair whipped in the wind as I scanned the roof. There was no way off. This place might be a lush escape, but it wasn't an exit.

Once back inside, I spied what I'd missed before: a dozen racks of clothes—like the costume racks backstage at a theater. Curiosity lured me over. Each rack was labeled with a girl's name. Amanda, Sirocco, Persephone. And the dresses hanging on them were all baby soft or shiny tight and cut so they'd hug and reveal a girl's breasts or legs.

All the hairs on my arms stood up. I'm in a— I couldn't say the word.

Who hides a runaway with a broker? Or worse, a—madam?

I tore back to my room, pulled on the yoga pants and zipped the jacket up to my chin. I pulled the comforter over me and sat with my back to the wall, tugging my sleeves over my hands.

I hooked my hands under my knees, fighting off the spinning in my head. Clearly, the effect of a precipitous drop in blood sugar, Dad would say. He'd tell me to eat, but I knew if I tried to, I'd spew.

55

Neon lights flickered on the ceiling as I lay with the comforter around me. Time seemed endless, even though I'd only been here a couple hours.

I couldn't stop thinking about Yates. Roik wasn't stupid. He probably guessed Yates was involved the minute I took off. And Roik knew Hawkins would be pissed he let me get away. I could see Roik showing up at Yates' apartment so he could beat the crap out of Yates without any witnesses.

Roik wouldn't care how badly he hurt Yates, and Yates' dad wouldn't press charges, not when Hawkins owned so much of the company.

Please, Yates. Please be okay.

I closed my eyes and saw him cradling my hand, heard him say, "Love wields the scissors."

"Love is the escape," I whispered back.

I have to believe everything will work out. That's the only way I can do this.

It was two thousand miles to Toronto and at least a year or two until we could be together, but right now it felt like infinity.

Out in the hall, girls were laughing. I pulled the comforter over my face as the door swung open.

"Could you believe that guy?" a girl squealed.

"He would not give up!" another one said.

"Shh. There's somebody in here," a third said.

My new roommates gathered around my bed. "Oh, she has *no idea* what she's gotten into."

They tried to smother their laughs. "What's her name?" one whispered.

"Who knows."

They giggled about a party trick with a candle and a glass of wine. Shoes clunked on the floor, and someone pulled the curtains shut. The room went black, and I lay there, listening as they fell asleep.

They didn't act like they were being forced to do horrible things. So why were they here? Why was I here?

My spinning thoughts kept waking me up, and I finally stopped trying to go back to sleep when I was too hungry to lie there any longer. I squinted as I entered the brilliantly lit kitchen. Sunshine coated the buildings and the mountains in the distance. Someone had set up coffee, so I took a cup and some cereal and headed for the rooftop.

As I stepped into the sunlight, cool morning air flowed over my face. The sky stretched blue-white in all directions. It was huge, and for a second, I felt completely free.

I lounged beside the perfect turquoise pool and dug into my cereal.

Obviously, I let myself get out of control last night. How genius to hide a runaway with a broker. Nobody'd ever guess, right?

Magda was probably planning on moving me this morning. By tonight I'd be in Utah or Colorado.

But then I realized that she hadn't said anything like, "Get some rest. Big day tomorrow." She asked what name I wanted to use, and promised me a phone, but didn't say when I'd get it.

I put my bowl down and got up. *Stop pretending this is perfectly fine.*

I paced the edge of the rooftop. For all I knew Magda was waiting for Hawkins' Retrievers to show up so she could turn me over for ransom.

And that's when I saw the guy staring at me. Outdoor bar, top floor of the next hotel over. His eyes trained on me like I fit the description of the person he was looking for.

Retriever! I tore across the deck for the frosted-glass doors. I'd almost reached them when one swung open and Billy stepped out and caught me in his arms.

"Let go of me!"

His hands flew off me. "What's going on, Juliet?"

He seemed sincere as if he actually cared, so I said, "A Retriever found me," and pointed to the rooftop bar.

Billy rolled his eyes. "Lowlifes." He walked over to the wall and pushed a button, and the glass around the rooftop fogged up. "That's no Retriever. Just some dude with nothing else to do. He can't bother you now."

"Thanks."

"Don't mention it." He toured the deck, straightened a few cushions, and headed for the door.

"Billy, am I leaving today?"

"I'm not in charge of that. You gotta ask Magda."

"Okay. So when can I see her?"

Billy checked his watch. "She won't be up before noon, but I'll let her know you want to talk." The door closed behind him with a whoosh.

They weren't in a rush to move me. They weren't even thinking about getting me out of here. I could feel my pulse start to race.

They stick you in this place, and it's so nice and pretty you think you're perfectly safe.

Why'd I let Yates talk me into this? Why'd I think I could do this?

I dropped into the pool in my yoga pants and started running. The cold water slapped my chest as I pushed through it. Two laps. Four. Eight. Twelve. Twenty.

You never thought you could run a mile, but Ms. A made you run five. You never thought you could mastermind your escape or Tase Roik, but you did. You can do this. You can make it to the border. But you can't let your fears take over.

I flopped onto the deck and caught my breath.

I didn't know how Anne Frank made it two years in hiding. I'd been Underground less than twenty-four hours, and I was already fighting off the crazies.

56

Backstage came alive at noon: treadmills and ellipticals whirred and blow-dryers were going all out. The kitchen was full of girls in exercise gear scarfing down salads and protein shakes. They were lining up at the window like a show was going on outside. I stole glances at them as I poured a glass of juice.

They were all different. Black, white, brown, Asian, and they didn't look like—*call girls*, my mind whispered. They looked *normal* with their hair pulled back and no makeup on. From the way they acted, laughing and joking with each other, not one of them seemed drugged or hungover.

So why don't they leave here? What's stopping them?

I helped myself to the grilled chicken and salad bar set up on the island. Shae and her roommate from the night before were outcasts at a table in the corner, a five-foot perimeter around them. Shae's eyes were puffy, but she'd stopped crying. She hunched over her plate like she had a secret she was dying to tell.

I heaped carrots on my salad, listening, but pretending not to.

"Magda says I'm meeting someone very special today," Shae said to her roommate.

"She used those exact words? Very special?"

"Yes!"

"So he's prequalified. Wow." The *wow* was an I Wish It Was Me Not You Wow.

"I know!" Shae said.

My brain crackled and I quieted so I could hear better. They were talking about a Contract.

"Did you see a photo?"

"He's okay-looking. I mean, he's not that much older than me. I wish he didn't—"

A blender tore through what Shae was saying, but I didn't need to hear the rest. It was like being back at Masterson, listening to one of those sheep from the other class of juniors, the girls who'd rather get Signed than graduate.

I took my salad over to the window. Men were installing a megagraphic on the next casino over announcing, TABITHA!!! Twenty stories of long tan legs, full breasts, and a thick sweep of golden-coppery hair.

"Wish I had a body like that," somebody said.

The Asian girl with perfect bangs snorted. "I was her roommate. Believe me, it's airbrushed."

Shae spoke up from the corner. "Tabitha lived here?"

The other girls looked at her as a group, stoning her with silence.

Finally, a tall Latina stuffed into an exercise bra separated from the group. She smirked at Shae. "Tabitha was here all summer. Magda set up that deal for her."

"That's disgusting," Shae said. "I'd never do anything like that."

"You already are."

Shae whipped her lunch off the table and shot out of her chair. "Slut."

"Cow!" Latina shot back.

"Come on, stop it, Sirocco," someone said. "Magda'll be pissed if she hears you talking like that."

Shae and her roommate squeezed by me, their eyes trained on Sirocco. "She won't hear about it unless somebody tells her," Sirocco threw at them.

She was two feet away from me, so I ducked my head, hoping to get out of there before I turned into Sirocco's next target. But no such luck.

"You, new girl."

I turned around.

She speared a radicchio leaf and held it up to her mouth. Her eyes narrowed like a cat. "Cast or Consignment?"

It was the second time somebody'd asked if I was Cast. Cast wasn't a who. Cast was a what. "I have no idea."

Splendor, the girl whose picture was on the bureau, piped up, "She's in our room."

"So you're Cast."

"I guess." I had no intention of being Cast, whatever that was, but I definitely wasn't Consignment. Obviously *Consignment* meant girls who were here to be sold. Or maybe resold like a previously owned Mercedes.

"What's your name?" Sirocco said.

"Juliet."

"Ooo, romantic." I could see why Sirocco chose her name. A hot wind that tears up the desert?

But I wasn't about to let her tear me up. "I like it."

Billy's voice came over a speaker. "Debriefing. Ten minutes."

Sirocco relaxed her gaze on me. "Nice to meet you, *chica*. See you around." Sirocco and her friends scurried about, scarfing down their lunches while I sipped my drink.

It was 12:30. I wanted to see Magda and I wanted some answers.

57

I lasted about forty minutes before I couldn't stand it anymore, and marched into the foyer. Madga's office door was closed, but before I could even knock, Billy intercepted me.

"You do not want to interrupt Magda's meeting," he said.

"But I need to talk to her."

"I understand, but you got to wait. Take a seat on this bench. I'll tell her you're out here."

"Thanks, Billy."

I plopped down on the gold-upholstered bench. Vacuum cleaners roared nearby. Last night's party must have left an industrial-sized mess.

There wasn't much to look at around the room besides the big gold bowl on the table in the center and four wall hangings some decorator had hung up. The abstract desert landscapes were embroidered in gold and silver. I glanced at the one right across from me and the name Fletcher jumped out from the pattern, then disappeared.

The head of the Paternalist party? My eyes had to be playing tricks on me.

I stood and examined the hanging behind me. The silk dashes, dots, and curlicues transformed into names and dates. The stitch-code was the same one Ms. A taught us.

The names were clearly in English, but there were other words that didn't make sense when I decoded them. Acronyms? Or maybe a different language? And there were amounts of money stitched in, too.

Secrets. Recorded in silk. It was daring to leave them in plain sight, but maybe it was genius, too.

Sirocco and the other Cast members filed out of Magda's office, followed by Billy. The girls looked me over like I'd annoyed them. "Go ahead," Billy said. "She'll see you now."

Magda was curled on the couch in expertly tailored pants and a sweater that bared her perfect shoulders. She waved me in with her teacup, and kept right on talking into her phone. "I assure you, we're known for our discretion."

A long strip of sage green silk, a needle barely visible in one cor-ner hung over her head. I perched on my chair and stole glances at the cryptic story coded into the pattern of blossoming cherry branches. Names. Dates. Money. Magda was collecting this infor-mation for a reason. Blackmail? Maybe a little insurance policy if she ever got arrested for sheltering runaways.

Magda snapped her phone shut. "Billy said you insisted on seeing me."

Suddenly I felt rude and ungrateful, and then just as quickly I got ticked she made me feel that way. "I thought I was leaving today."

Magda blew on her tea. "Umm. Let's discuss that."

Adult-speak for "you're getting screwed."

"What do we need to discuss?" I said.

"We're having to reconfigure your arrangements in light of recent events in Los Angeles. Everyone's safety depends on it. We won't pass you on until we are sure we aren't endangering you or the vol-unteers helping you."

I should have known Father Gabe's arrest would affect a lot more people than me. What Magda told me sounded reasonable, like there was no question that I was leaving, it was just a matter of when. "Sorry for asking, I didn't understand."

"Yes, I'm delighted we could clear that up, but Juliet, we should talk about your Contract."

I gulped. "Why?"

"Fifty million? I think we both know the dangers facing a young girl with a bounty that size on her head."

My foot started to jiggle. "How do you know about my Contract? Am I on the news?"

"Not as of an hour ago, and I'm sure Jessop Hawkins wants to keep it that way. He'd hate for his political rivals to know that he couldn't hold on to a little sixteen-year-old."

I crossed my ankles to steady myself. "Do you know him?"

"He's not a client, if that's what you're asking."

I nodded.

"You may have realized that I'm a broker."

Wherever this discussion was going, I didn't want to go there. "I guessed when the girls asked if I was Consignment."

"Oh, I wish they wouldn't call it that. I specialize in brokering girls who've landed in unhappy relationships. I arrange for—"

"Transfer of ownership." My tongue tasted like metal.

Magda tilted her head like I'd surpassed her expectations. "I find a better match, one the girl can live with, and I give her half the profits as a dowry."

"I'm not interested."

"Well, it's unlikely I'd be successful in your case. You're simply too expensive. Unless you have a talent I don't know about."

"A talent?"

"Like Tabitha. Surely you couldn't avoid seeing the billboard?"

"She's a *stripper*."

"Tabitha is a talented, charismatic singer who is on track to become a millionaire in the next eighteen months."

"I heard you set her up."

"I put together a group of investors who bought her Contract and bankrolled her show. You're very fit. Are you a dancer, a gymnast? The Dallas Cowboys are paying a fortune to remake their cheerleading squad. A multiyear contract might get you—"

"No, I'm not a dancer. I'm a runner."

"Ugh. Unfortunately, the Olympic Committee pays nothing."

"I'm going to Canada," I interrupted.

Magda pressed a finger to her temple. "It's very dangerous out in the real world."

"Yeah, I figured that out already."

"Eight in ten don't make it across the border."

"I didn't know that." Yates had made it sound like almost everyone did.

"I'm not surprised. Juliet, I'm happy to hide you until the next stage of your extraction, but I think you'd be better off staying here and working for me."

I knew men paid women for sex. And it was pretty clear men came to Vegas to party. And those girls Backstage? They were partying last night.

"No, thanks. I'm a virgin."

Magda banged her teacup on the saucer. "This isn't a *whorehouse*."

"Sorry. I didn't mean—"

"We are in the *entertainment* business. We are *geishas*, not prostitutes. Geishas caress men's egos. We embrace their desire to break rules and have tantalizing secrets. And we *listen*."

"So the girls here don't have sex with people?"

"Sexual favors are not included on our menu," Magda said.

"And you want me to join the Cast?"

"I'm offering you a less dangerous alternative than attempting to cross the border at sixteen with forged documents."

Maybe being a party girl was safer, but I didn't want safe. I wanted freedom and I wanted to dream about my future. *About Yates.* "No, thanks. I mean, I appreciate the offer, but I'm going to try for Canada."

"I understand." Magda arched one eyebrow like she knew she didn't have the whole story. "Perhaps you'd do me a favor, however. We have very special guests tonight, and I could use one more hostess."

Hostess. The word made me want to put on rubber gloves.

But Magda was risking jail to hide me, and if all I had to do was hang out for a couple hours with some guys looking for fun, I'd be ungrateful to say no. "All right."

"Thank you." Magda stood up and pointed out the window at the airport. "Do you see that large jet set apart on the tarmac? It brought in a delegation from Congress."

"They're the special guests?"

"Exactly."

"But won't this place be crawling with security? Shouldn't I hide?"

"Quite the contrary. With the Secret Service outside the door, you couldn't be in a safer place."

I guessed Magda knew what she was doing. If the other Cast members had escaped like me, she'd figured out how to hide them without landing in prison.

"Okay, sure."

"Excellent." Magda picked a phone up off her desk and handed it to me. "This is for you as I promised. But understand that we've placed limits on it for your protection."

I took it from her. "All right, what are they?"

Magda gracefully maneuvered me to the door. "You'll see. Now, go find Helen in Wardrobe. Tell her CHI."

And before I had a chance to ask what CHI was, Magda swept me out.

Backstage. Cast. Wardrobe. This place was one big theatrical production. And all those actresses were girls like me, looking to not get Signed.

I headed back to Wardrobe. So I'd join the Cast for a night. It was harmless. Like being in a play.

Shae strolled ahead of me, her bandage peeking from under her tee. Her friend's words came back to me. *You know how Magda is about resale value.* I clenched my new phone. Magda was amazing. She'd made me think she was caring and generous the way she helped the girls here, but she'd forced Shae into a tattoo wipe so she could get more money for her.

Plus, Magda got me to agree to join the Cast tonight. She had me right where she wanted me and I didn't have a clue if I could trust her.

I had every intention of finding Helen, but she could wait a minute while I checked out my new phone. The yoga room was empty, so I tucked into a space behind the exercise ball rack.

The phone screen went live when I touched it, and my face appeared in one corner. It was the pic Magda took when I first got here. Then the phone snapped a picture of me now and lined it up with the first. "Welcome, Juliet," the screen flashed. Even my restricted phone at home didn't verify like this.

Icons peppered the screen, but not ones I was used to: Current Events, Politics and Government, Science and Industry, Global Affairs, Religion and Society. There were two marked Onstage and Backstage. Finally, I found one for live calls, but when I tapped it, it said, "Function not available."

Magda didn't trust me not to call Yates. Damn.

At least I could see if my disappearance had hit the news. I clicked on Current Events, bypassed Top Stories, and went to Search and typed in "Avie Reveare."

Instead of bringing up links, the screen flashed, "Search denied."

I typed in Dad.

"Search denied."

Biocure.

"Search denied."

Clearly, Magda or one of her minions had programmed the phone to block me. And maybe that made sense if they wanted to prevent someone putting a trace on me. But what if I searched Jes Hawkins?

"Search denied."

Yates.

The screen flashed white, then, "Warning: continued searches in restricted areas will result in revocation of privileges."

English translation: Stop or we'll take it away.

I went back to Top Stories, even though I doubted I was scandal-worthy enough to rank Top Ten. The list popped up and I almost dropped the phone. No, this can't be happening. The top story: "U.S. Pressures Canada to Close the Border." I clicked on it.

"Canadian officials report that the United States government has threatened to cut off exports of American pharmaceuticals to Canada unless it closes its border to Americans seeking asylum."

Americans seeking asylum like me. The U.S. was blackmailing Canada into cutting off the exits.

I kept reading. "This move by the U.S. would jeopardize the health of millions of Canadians suffering from diabetes and heart disease. The Canadian prime minister responded that he will not buckle to American bullying despite warnings that the embargo could triple the Canadian death rate within six months."

Canada wanted to save us, but their citizens were going to raise holy hell once people started dying.

How long before Canada gave in? A week, two? I had to get out of here.

But what about Yates?

Even if the police didn't charge him with helping me escape, he would never be able to join me.

A voice came through the speakers overhead. "Juliet, please report to Wardrobe. Juliet, Wardrobe." I scrambled to my feet as the voice continued. "Tonight's guest list is now posted. Please familiarize yourself before this evening's event."

The phone screen automatically switched to a photo gallery of men. I scrolled through them as I scurried off to Wardrobe. Senators, congressmen, a couple congressional aides. The same dirtbags who were trying to cut off Canada.

Wardrobe was crazed. Girls rushed around in shortie kimonos and expensive underwear while two men in silky shirts and perfectly done eyeliner worked on faces and hair.

Helen was tall with siren-red hair, an Adam's apple, and a phone that never left her hand. With heels on, she towered over everyone in the room, even the guys. As I approached, she pointed at two of the girls. "You and you. UVA cheerleaders. You're assigned to Senators Wagner and Sanders in the Sportslounge."

"Hi, Helen, I'm Juliet."

Helen looked me over like I'd come to audition. Then I saw a flicker in her eyes like she knew exactly where she'd seen me before.

Please, please don't say anything, I thought.

She pointed a long green fingernail at my head. "So you're the last-minute addition. As if I didn't have enough to do."

"Umm. Magda told me to tell you CHI?" I said.

"Capitol Hill Intern. Hmmm. It has possibilities. Now, the hair. Normally I would suggest a headband—"

My mouth dried up like a cotton ball.

"Politicos just love the naughty conservative look, but I think *bangs* and a smoky eye." Her voice dropped about six octaves. "What do you think, *Jul-yet?*"

"Perfect," I squeaked.

She led me over to the stylists. "Ah, my miracle workers. The look: CHI."

Helen did a checklist on her fingers. "Bangs, smoky eye, pale pink lipstick. Outfit: silk blouse, pencil skirt, thong, enhancer bra, sheer black stockings, heels. Remember. Sexy, not slutty."

Stylist One scurried off to wardrobe while Two shoved me into the chair. I waved into the mirror. "Hi, I'm—"

"Honey," he said, "we've got no time to gab."

One and Two exfoliated, polished, groomed, and mascaraed me like I was getting ready for the runway. Meanwhile, Helen cruised the room, adjusting clothing and makeup, checking hair, and ordering girls to hurry up and get it together.

A couple of hours later when I slithered into my skirt, Helen clapped her hands. "Places, everyone," she cried. "It's Showtime."

We lined up at the big metal door in our tight dresses and cheerleader outfits. Sirocco squeezed in front of me. "Listen, new girl," she said. "If a guy starts putting his hands places you don't like, tell him you need to *freshen up*. But save it for when you really need it, 'cause you can only do it once."

"Why?"

"Magda's rules."

Helen stood beside the door, her head held high. "As you enter Onstage, remember: these men carry the weight of the nation. They want to unburden themselves, and you will lighten their burden. You will *listen*."

We marched past her, and Billy escorted us across the foyer. My snug skirt barely gave as I walked. My skinny heels sank into the carpet, and I teetered on my tiptoes. The style boys had unbuttoned my blouse for a glimpse of my pink silk bra. Any resemblance I had to Letitia Hawkins was gone.

All I had to do to keep Magda happy was to hang out with these guys for a couple of hours. Smile and pretend I was having a good time. Compared to everything else I'd been through, this would be easy.

Polished and packaged like a Capitol Hill intern, I entered Onstage.

60

Onstage was a big open room. The sky was twilight blue beyond the floor-to-ceiling windows, orange-red couches warmed the room, and the eternal lights of the Strip danced below.

A dozen men hung around the foosball, pool, and air hockey tables. Their suit coats were thrown over chairs and their ties were torn off. The girls spread out like bees over a rosebush, handing out drinks. A buffet was set up, and I smelled ribs and sausage and burgers from across the room.

I hung off to the side, not sure how to do the whole congressional geisha thing. But Magda didn't wait for me to catch on. She stuck her arm through mine and propelled me over to a tall man with silver hair. "Senator Fletcher, I don't believe you've met Juliet."

I held out my hand and forced a smile. "Senator." The real live head of the Paternalist Movement. The guy who'd transformed me and my girlfriends into property. He'd probably masterminded both the Twenty-eighth Amendment and closing the border with Canada.

"Well, aren't you something?" he said. "You look good enough to get a man impeached. How much?" he asked.

My mouth dropped. Magda shot me a "get that smile back on your face" look. She placed her hand on his arm. "For display only, I'm afraid. I'm brokering her Contract. The latest bid is fifty million."

"Fifty!"

"She comes with partial ownership in a manufacturing concern."

"So she's investment grade." Fletcher paused like he was considering making a bid. My cheeks twitched from holding my smile in place. What the hell was Magda doing, telling him all this real stuff about me?

Finally, Fletcher shook his head. "Nope, I'm just a humble public servant. Besides, the wife would probably frown on the deal."

"Wives. So inconvenient." Magda crooked her finger, and a blonde in a too-tight cardi set bounced over. "Senator," Magda purred, "I think Amanda would be interested in learning some of your billiard secrets."

Amanda guided him away.

"Why'd you tell him about the fifty million and my dad's company?" I asked.

Magda dropped her elegant accent. "Because he's old and married, and he probably thinks I'm inflating the number to impress him."

"So he thinks you're lying."

"Exactly. Ready to meet our guests?"

Magda strolled me around the room, introducing me and making each of the senators and congressmen tell me which committees they controlled. I smiled and listened to them talk, but I couldn't stop thinking how if Ms. A was here, she'd blast them right out of the room.

She'd tell them what she thought of their laws. These guys had conspired to keep girls out of college. Made it a crime to run from a Contract. And now they were imprisoning us in our own country.

Magda left me at the air hockey table with a senator from Kentucky and a congressman from Illinois. The congressman handed me the puck. "Ready to play?"

"Sure," I said, skimming the puck onto the table.

"We playin' teams?" Senator Kentucky asked. Sirocco nuzzled up against him with a plate of sliders. "I'll be on your team," she said.

I bent over the table, ready for the first round, when the congressman pressed against me. He whispered something nasty in my ear about an intern and a cigar. Every cell in my body wanted to smash my heel into his foot, but I forced myself to grit my teeth and smile. Perv.

Senator Fletcher waved his pool cue. "Don't molest the girl, Paul. You can't afford her."

The congressman eased off. "So you're luxury goods."

"Very," I told him, smacking the puck into the goal.

"Nice shot." The congressman raised his glass. "Gentlemen, a toast to Senator Fletcher and his action group for persuading American universities to put women's safety first."

By keeping us out!

The men raised their glasses to Fletcher, and Congressman Paul ran his hand down my back. "Now you wouldn't want to go to college, would you?"

I gripped the plastic puck tight. "No, Congressman, I can't imagine anything more fulfilling than being a mother."

"Spoken like a true patriot. We can fix this country, but we need every seventeen-year-old like you to start popping out babies. We lost half our workforce," he said. "Half! No babies. No workers."

"Seventeen's too old," Fletcher said. "There are only four million seventeen-year-olds in this country. If we could lower the Signing age to fifteen we could triple the number of births in the next three years."

Fifteen! They wanted to pull girls out of school their freshman year.

"Forget fifteen. You'll be lucky if the old lady voters don't demand eighteen," Senator Kentucky said. "That Rowley girl getting shot on the Supreme Court steps today has them all riled up!"

My knees turned to Jell-O and I had to lean on the table. *She was only sixteen.*

Congressman Paul smacked the puck into my goal. "Senator, our office has surveyed women across the country and most have never heard of Samantha Rowley."

I lined up for the shot.

Samantha died for nothing, because women didn't know about her. Of course they didn't. How would they hear about her? Their restricted phones? The Sportswall?

Disgust flickered on Sirocco's face, and then she slinked over to the aide and slid the phone out of his hands. He grinned as she played with it and asked questions like she'd never seen a phone before.

Congressman Paul fingered the ends of my hair. "These old men can be pretty boring."

I wanted to rip his arm out of the socket. "I don't mind. All anybody ever talks about around here is clothes."

His cell buzzed in his pocket and he turned to answer it.

Thank God. A reprieve.

The senator with the bow tie playing pool against Fletcher was getting looser and louder. His name was Perue, and Amanda had refreshed his drink at least three times already.

Senator Perue looked down his cue. "I'm telling you, we can solve the workforce problem and the media'll make us into heroes."

Suddenly, Bow Tie had an audience, because half the guys in the room stopped what they were doing. Magda strolled over to our table.

"Well, what do you suggest, Perue?" Fletcher said.

Perue took his shot, and two balls dove into pockets. "Orphans," he answered. "We've got millions of orphans in this country and the states are choking on the costs of keeping up the orphan ranches. If we Sign girls out of those ranches at fifteen with Contracts in their hands instead of releasing them Unsigned at eighteen, we can increase the birthrate and those ranches will turn a profit."

"Interesting," murmured Fletcher, the dollar bills practically glowing in his eyes.

"And gentlemen, it's the right thing to do," Congressman Sung said, tipping his drink at Perue. "Under current law, those girls lose their homes on their eighteenth birthdays."

Magda echoed him. "Yes, they're kicked out into the streets oftentimes with nothing more than a toothbrush, a backpack, and a twenty-dollar bill."

"That's awful," Sirocco said.

"Think about it," Perue continued, "these girls can go to a loving home and not be exposed to the dangers on the streets."

They were talking about girls like they were pound puppies.

I'd never thought about girls who didn't have fathers to look out for them. Dad had tried to make a good match for me, even though he screwed it up. And I knew he felt bad he couldn't get me away from Hawkins. What if some bureaucrat who didn't even know me arranged my Signing—somebody who only cared about the money?

"And we should think about imports," Perue said.

"Well, Europe's not helping us," Fletcher said. "Half the continent's considering a ban on women traveling to the U.S."

"We don't need Europe," Sung answered. "You all know Jessop Hawkins?"

My jaw locked and I couldn't swallow. I tried to look bored, but hearing his name amplified every sound in the room.

"He flew back from Asia this week with thirty Nepalese girls he found at the Indian border. Eight- to twelve-year-olds, he bought off traffickers taking them to brothels in Mumbai."

"He saved their lives," Magda said.

"Yes. Now they have a real chance at a future," Sung declared.

"To the American dream!" Congressman Sung lifted his glass in a toast and the men joined in.

Sirocco nudged me to hold up my glass. In their twisted view of the world, Hawkins was a savior—but those little girls were still going to be treated like things to be sold.

"Ah, Mr. Vice President!" Madga exclaimed.

Everyone turned as he walked in. And I wondered why they didn't look surprised. He wasn't on the guest list. Vice President Jouvert cut the Paternalists to shreds in his speeches, but here he was, ready to party with them?

Magda walked over to the basketball-player-turned-politician, and offered her cheek for a kiss.

As handsome as he was with his light green eyes, creamy brown skin, and bleached smile, I barely looked at Mr. VP, because the girl on Jouvert's arm was Sparrow. She stood there, giving off serenity and disdain in her five-inch heels and tight purple dress. Her curly hair was pulled off her face, and her eyes were made up like bird wings.

Sparrow caught my eye and batted her lashes at me in warning.

Mr. VP threw himself on one of the couches and Sparrow sat down beside him. The men gathered around them, but not one said a word to her.

"Who is that gorgeous creature?" Congressman Paul asked Sirocco.

"That's Persephone."

Sparrow didn't look at me, but I couldn't keep my eyes off her.

Magda slid into an open seat on one of the couches while the Cast members perched on the backs. I hovered until Sirocco jerked me down beside her.

The Veep asked for a burger and a scotch, then said, "I'm glad you're all here. I'd like to share the outcome of my meeting."

"So it was successful?" Magda asked.

"Another trillion in loans and investments."

The men rocked the room with applause. "And what do we have to do to get this?" Senator Fletcher asked.

Mr. VP smirked like it was all so easy. "Merely continue on the path we're on. Our friends are very pleased with our progress. I've committed to continuing our efforts to segregate the sexes and to deny federal contracts to companies that employ women. We don't have to put that into law. We can just let federal agencies know it's our unwritten policy. Of course, once the Twenty-eighth Amendment passes, we can do whatever we want."

You bastards. Pretty soon we won't have any rights at all.

Sparrow leaned into the Veep, and ran her hand down his leg. I couldn't believe it. Not Sparrow. What had Magda turned her into?

My head started to spin. I had to get out of here.

I stood up and, even though I felt Magda's eyes on me, I didn't stop and I didn't turn around. If I stayed, I'd explode.

61

Back in Wardrobe, I tore off my costume and threw on running shorts. I needed five or six miles on the treadmill to keep my thoughts from blowing out the walls.

Closing the border. Orphans for profit. And Jessop Hawkins was in the middle of it. All these schemes weren't just about guys getting baby brides or rebuilding the workforce. This was so much bigger. But how? Who exactly was involved?

I wished I could call Yates or Ms. A, and tell them what I'd heard.

People had to know about this. Women had to hear what they were doing.

As I went past the styling station, my eyes caught on the scissors somebody'd left out. Long, luxurious hair. All men wanted to touch it, run their hands through it, yank it.

I picked up the scissors and cut.

I won't be anybody's baby doll. Someone has to stop them. Cut.

Those senators and congressmen, all they want is to hold on to power. Cut.

Show the voters how they personally brought the economy back to life. Cut.

They don't care that Samantha Rowley was murdered. Cut.

This is a chess game, just like Father Gabriel said, and they are using us girls like pawns. Cut cut cut. I put down the scissors.

But who's paying them to do it? Who does Father G suspect?

I had to get out of the country. The U.S. was completely messed up. No way anybody could save it.

High heels clacked across the floor, and Helen appeared behind me in the mirror. "Gracious me! You look like an—emu. One that was attacked by whatever large, vicious animal attacks emus and tears off their feathers."

"I'm done looking like a good girl. I refuse to be some perv's fantasy."

"Mission accomplished." Helen ran her fingers through the spiky remains of my hair. "But if I may refine the look?"

"Sure."

Helen pushed me into the chair. Snip here. Snip there. Gel. A little mousse.

"Ta-da," Helen said. "Fierce. Uncompromising. The kind of girl who walks out on a room of slimy politicians—but I imagine you have experience dealing with men in high office."

We exchanged a look. "Don't worry," Helen said. "Your secret's safe with me."

She whipped out a lip brush and went to retouch my gloss.

"I don't get how they can do it," I said.

"Who?"

"Cast. I don't get how they can stand dressing up and having dirtbags paw them like that."

Helen draped herself over the other chair. "They all have their reasons. Your roommate Splendor? She's banking money so when her little sisters turn sixteen she can buy their Contracts."

"I didn't know that."

"You haven't been here very long."

"Helen?" Sparrow called from the other side of the room.

"Over here."

"Is my coat finished?"

"Sorry. I had to do an intervention." Helen got up as Sparrow came around the glass wall. "Ten minutes and you'll be ready to fly," Helen promised, walking away.

Sparrow leaned against the counter, a big croc bag over her shoulder. "Like the hair, Juliet."

"Like the name, Persephone," I shot back.

"I couldn't resist the irony. Hades' plaything, get it?"

"Yeah, I do."

The sewing machine whirred in the background. I'd seen pieces of a coat laid out last night, but I never guessed Helen sewed like a pro. I watched Sparrow pick through the rows of lipsticks.

"I'm impressed." Sparrow applied a fresh coat of gloss. "I wasn't sure you'd have the guts to run." For a second, I felt like she'd slapped me. She shrugged like I was wrong for being insulted. "I'm just saying it's hard."

"Yeah, but I made it."

She smiled and her whole face brightened. "This is so great you're here. You've joined the revolution."

"I'm only here a couple of days," I said. "I'm going to Canada."

"Oh." She dropped the gloss back in its slot. "Good luck with that. But I guess in your fantasy world, love is so powerful it can move mountains. Or borders."

"You've never been in love. If you had, you'd understand."

Sparrow glared at me. "You don't know *anything* about me. You're not the only girl who's ever fallen in love."

I stood there, stunned. Sparrow had never, ever dropped even a hint that she cared about someone.

"Here's what *I* don't understand," she said. "You heard the way those men talked back there, how they're happy Samantha Rowley's dead so they don't have to deal with her anymore. You heard what they're planning to do to women in this country, and you don't even care."

I wanted to smack her. "I care."

"So what are you doing about it?"

"What are *you* doing about it," I shot back. "Other than partying with those jerks and letting them get off on rubbing their hands all over you."

Sparrow smirked. "I can't believe, you really have no clue. I thought you'd figured it out. You're usually so per-cep-tive. Such a good *listener.*"

Then, I got it. That's what Magda said geishas did—listen. It's what Helen instructed us to do before we went into the party. We were supposed to listen as these guys spilled their secrets. We were living, breathing recorders. Witnesses.

"You're spying," I said.

"I'm gathering information."

"Almost done!" Helen called out. "You can be on your way."

Sparrow snapped open her croc bag and pulled out her phone. "Magda got you a phone, right?"

"Yeah, but she put controls on it so I can't make calls."

Sparrow's fingers danced over her screen. "Yep, there you are. Oooo. Outbound calling disabled. Let's fix that. One two three. Done."

"Thanks," I said, even though I knew Magda would be ticked if she found out.

"Happy to help a friend," Sparrow said. "Listen. I'm heading out to D.C. for a few days, and I'm sending you a little software fix. It hunts for paternal controls and breaks through them. You can send videos of two minutes or less to millions of women before the controls turn back on."

"Kind of like a scrambler?"

"More like an unscrambler. And it allows people to forward your messages, but not to trace them back to you."

"Did you invent this?"

"Almost. I stole it from a defense guy and modified it."

"So, why are you giving this to me?"

"Because I know that deep inside, you hate the Paternalists almost as much as I do. And someday, you'll want to stop them." Sparrow bent over to whisper in my ear. "We have to be the voices of Gen S, just like Ms. A always said."

A rush of prickles shot from my shoulders to my fingertips. Sparrow was up to something, but clearly, she wasn't about to tell me what.

Helen sashayed toward us, waving the pomegranate-red coat like it was a matador's cape. "Ready." Helen held the coat while Sparrow slipped into it and cinched the belt. The rolled collar and big sleeves made her look like a ninja.

"It's gorgeous," I told Helen. "How did you get to be such an incredible seamstress?"

"Ten years as a Vegas showgirl. You either sew your own costumes or spend half your take-home pay on cheap satin and plastic sequins."

"Okay, I gotta run," Sparrow said. She embraced Helen. "Thank you."

"Be naughty," Helen said, "but not too naughty."

Then Sparrow reached for me. "Come on, give me a hug. If you're not here when I get back," she said, squeezing me tight, "I'll see you in heaven."

Sparrow strode off, but I stood there, mesmerized by the way she walked in that deep red coat, so cool and tall and detached. Persephone, ready to kick butt in the Underworld.

I wasn't Sparrow. I wasn't a rebel obsessed with a cause. I was just an ordinary girl, trying to have an ordinary life. Get an apartment.

Go to school. Get a job. Fall in love. All those things girls did in movies from when I was young.

"His name was Imran," Helen said, keeping her voice low. "MIT student. Indian. Fabulously wealthy. They met online. Tragic story. Absolutely tragic."

"What happened?"

"I really can't—Magda would kill me if she knew I'd told you any of this, but let's just say Persephone is committed to getting revenge on our nation's leaders."

The skin on my neck pulled tight. Not the first time I'd heard someone say that about her.

Helen handed me a dustpan and broom and pointed to the hair on the floor. I started sweeping.

Screw it.

I'm not Sparrow and I don't want to be a witness.

I don't want to be a voice for Gen S.

I want to go to Canada. Love Yates. Be free.

Let Sparrow be the witness. The sex spy.

"I'm not Cast, Helen."

"I knew that the minute I saw you, Juliet. You don't have that protective shell the rest of the Cast has. Besides, girls like us, we write our own scripts."

We locked eyes. Maybe Helen had chosen to be a woman or just to dress like one, but she'd definitely made a choice most guys didn't. "Is it wrong that I don't want to be part of the revolution?" I said.

"No, baby, it's not wrong." Helen pointed to a spot I missed. "You're in love. And God knows, I envy you."

"It's not like I'm giving in. I'm not a collaborator. Not like those Consignment girls."

"Harsh. Those are merely poor little lambs who've lost their way."

"I have a dream about how my life could be. I don't want to give that up."

"Then that's what you've got to do, hon. But you need to know that if the revolution wants you, it's going to find you."

"Not in Canada, it won't."

"I hope you're right, Juliet," she said, holding up the trash can. "I'm a sucker for romance."

I emptied the dustpan into the trash. A couple of days and I'd be back on the road, headed for Canada. I couldn't wait.

62

I lay out by the rooftop pool, soaking up the morning rays as I ate my cereal. Behind me, the doors swung open and I heard someone pad across the deck. Sirocco set down her coffee and eased onto the lounge chair next to me.

"That party last night, not what you expected, Juliet?" Sirocco seemed softer today, as if she'd lowered her defenses, or maybe she was just tired.

"Yeah, the Vice President in bed with the Paternalists. I didn't see that coming."

"Sick, right?" Sirocco leaned back and tipped her sunglasses over her eyes.

I remembered what Helen said about how all the Cast have stories, and I wondered about Sirocco's. "Can I ask why you're here? Is it for the cause?"

Sirocco looked at me over her glasses. "I couldn't do this if I didn't believe, but Magda paid off my Contract. A year from now, I'll have paid her back and I'll be on a plane for Barcelona."

"Spain." I imagined floating in the turquoise Mediterranean. "Sounds heavenly. Lying on the beach—"

"No, more like sitting in a classroom. Cinema studies at Universitat de Barcelona."

"You want to be a filmmaker?"

"*Historias de amor*. Love stories."

"We need love stories."

"Yes, all Hollywood makes now is garbage: guns, drugs, war, murder—"

The phone Magda gave me vibrated in my robe pocket. *That's weird.* "It's a message from Persephone, but she used a timed release. She sent it a half hour ago."

"Maybe she didn't want to wake you."

I pressed play. Sparrow was standing on the Capitol Hill steps. "Sorry to stick you with this, but in case anything happens, someone needs to know the truth. I'm sending a message to the media and copying you. Remember, we're the voices of Gen S."

Sparrow held a lighter up beside her face. "Just because I choose to go out in a blaze of glory, doesn't make me crazy. See you in heaven."

Sirocco peered at the screen. "What the—"

I leaped up and charged through the outer door, crying, "No, no, no!" down the long hall through Backstage. "Magda!" I burst into the foyer. "Magda!" The lounge was empty, and I hammered the controls for the Sportswall. "Turn on. Dammit. Turn on."

Magda flew into the room, her silk robe half tied. "What the hell is the matter?"

"Something horrible's happened. I think Sparrow set herself on fire!"

"Sparrow?"

"Persephone!!"

Magda wrenched the control out of my hand. Eight screens went live with a special report. Shaky video showed a fire burning on the Capitol steps. Whoever held the camera ran forward so you could see a person in a red coat sitting cross-legged like a Buddha.

My knees let go and I crumpled onto the couch. "No! Sparrow! Why did you do this?"

"Are you absolutely sure it's her?"

"Yes, she sent me a video telling me good-bye and she pulled out a lighter—"

The camera caught an emergency crew running forward with extinguishers. They crowded round the fire, blocking the view.

Magda lowered herself down next to me. "What have I done? How could I have let her go?"

A newscaster came on: "We're here on Capitol Hill where a homeless man died after dousing himself with accelerant and lighting himself on fire. Authorities claim this was a protest designed to send a message to Congress to focus on job creation."

"What?" I said. "No! They're lying."

"They're erasing her." Magda folded her hands like she was praying and pressed them to her forehead. "They can't keep the media from reporting, so they're reframing the story."

The newscaster looked so polished and clean you'd never suspect he was feeding you a load of crap. "Congressman Blake responded to the news, saying, 'More than ever, this shows how important it is to pass the legislation we've created to address our economic crisis.'"

I muted the wall. "Sparrow sent a message out to the media. They'll know that story's a lie."

"The government will bury it," Magda said, shaking her head. "They'll find witnesses to confirm their account." She picked up my phone. "Can you show me her message?"

Sparrow looked deep into the camera. Her hair flowed down her shoulders, and she looked as innocent and pure as Botticelli's Venus, but her voice was cold and hard as marble.

"Hello, America. My name is Sparrow Currie, and I have a message for our esteemed leaders.

"You've told me and my friends we should get married and have babies. You say it's to rebuild the nation, but it's really more complicated than that, isn't it, Mr. Vice President?

"You allow our fathers to decide who we marry. You prevent us from driving, voting, earning money, or deciding what's right for our own bodies.

"Until now, you've been able to hide the fact that you have conspired with members of Congress, pretending to oppose the Paternalists while accepting bribes and directing the rewriting of American laws. I am going to expose you. I have proof.

"For the last eight years, I and my friends have been treated as children, but now we're women. We're not your slaves or your property."

Sparrow raised a bottle of clear fluid and began to pour it down her coat sleeve and across her chest and along her other arm until long, dark stains ran down the fabric. Then she tossed the empty bottle over her shoulder.

"The revolution has begun," she said. "My blood is on your hands."

Sparrow flicked the lighter, and Magda cried out as the coat exploded.

I felt it blow a hole right through me. How could Sparrow do this to herself? And for what?

Magda stumbled to her feet. "I need to think."

The Sportswall was frozen on the commentator's face. "Homeless Man Incinerates Self" read the headline, but up in the corner I could see the figure in the flames.

Sparrow had to be insane. Normal people just don't do things like this.

Helen and the other girls rushed in. "Is it true? Has something happened to Persephone?" Helen cried. She swayed in front of the screens. "I sewed her that coat. She begged me to finish it before she left." The Cast huddled around her and I fled to the pool.

The sky was clear yellow and the deck was hot below my bare feet. I shut my eyes, but I couldn't shut out the eight screens of Sparrow in flames.

Those liars stole her death and used it for their own purposes.

"Bastards!" I yelled.

Down below, the poolside DJ cranked up the dance music. I picked up a chair and strode to the railing to pitch it over, and that's when I realized: Sparrow expected that to happen.

I put the chair down.

Sparrow made sure I could speak out if her voice was silenced. She knew Fletcher and the Paternalists would never stop lying, never stop selling out girls. They'd keep doing it until someone made them stop. If she couldn't, she expected me to try.

And I was angry enough to do it.

I pulled up Sparrow's video. Once I touched the unscrambler icon, the software would charge off to unlock paternal controls and deliver her video to every female in the country—all of us whose double-X chromosomes had turned us into slaves.

And the message couldn't be traced.

I held up my phone and looked right into the camera eye and hit record. "No more feeding us lies, and telling us it's the truth. That wasn't a homeless man who set himself on fire on Capitol Hill. That was my friend and this is her message."

I touched send.

63

I stayed out on the deck, wanting to be alone. Twenty floors below, speakers pounded over a pool where men who were totally wasted chanted in a raging chorus.

Maybe I'm not so rich
Maybe I got no money

But I'm gonna make you hunger, ba-by
Beg for it, ho-ney.

I shut my eyes, trying to force out the world, and imagined Yates wrapping his arms around me, resting his head on mine. If I could just talk to him for a minute. Not even a minute. Thirty seconds. Fifteen.

I wrapped my hand around my phone. My fingers hovered over the keypad and I tapped out the first nine digits of his code.

I hit clear.

You can't call him. He's a suspect. Besides, he might not even have his phone. Roik could have forced him to turn it over.

My thumbs scrolled up and down the screen like they didn't want to listen to me tell them no. And then I realized Sparrow had sent me two more time-delayed messages. A voice message marked OPEN NOW, and a recording, FOR MAGDA'S EARS ONLY.

What— I clicked on OPEN NOW.

I had to turn the volume up, because Sparrow was talking just above a whisper. There was water running in the background, making me think she was locked in a bathroom. She didn't even say my name, just started talking.

"I'm trusting you. Do *not* open the file for Magda." Sparrow went quiet while the recording continued to play the sound of water gushing.

I waited, listening hard. *Is that it?*

A moment later she returned. "Remember how Father Gabe suspected that the Paternalists had *help*? Well, I found out who."

My heart started pounding, seeing the grenade coming for me.

"Last night, Jouvert told me the truth. He just doesn't know it."

I dug my fingers into my hair. *What did you do, Sparrow? Tape Jouvert? Trick him into confessing?*

"What I learned is too dangerous for mere mortals like you and me. Let Magda handle it—and you, you stick to your plan."

My head began to shake, hearing her tell me to go to Canada.

Then Sparrow laughed, quiet, and sharp-edged. "Maybe you're right that love can give you the strength to do anything," she said, "but I'll never know."

Click.

I dropped the phone on the lounger and shoved it away with my foot. Stared at it like it might sink teeth into me.

"Juliet!"

I wheeled around, and Billy was running toward me. "Magda wants you, now!" He pulled me out of the lounge chair, and I snatched up the phone. "Let's go!" he said, pushing me in front of him and shoving me through the door. He punched in a code and as I tore down the hall, I heard the metal rattle of a security gate coming down.

Girls rushed around Backstage, grabbing clothes off racks and shelves. I blew past them, heading for Magda's office.

I burst into the foyer. Magda's office was wide open and she stood behind her desk, punching in the combination of her wall safe. "Well, it's the star of the hour," she said, seeing me.

The hangings were ripped off the walls and crammed into the open duffle on her desk. Magda flung open the safe, and I shrank back as she pulled out a gun.

I flashed back to the icy gun against my cheek. My head spun, but I tried to focus. "What's happening?"

Magda stuffed some ammo clips in her bag. "You're what's happening." She shoved her phone in my face. "Look closely." It was me, beaming Sparrow's message, and over my shoulder was the rooftop bar of the casino next door. "You might as well have given out our address."

My stomach twisted. "Oh, my God."

"You should have talked to me."

"I'm sorry."

"I understand you were angry, and you didn't want the Paternalists to get away with their lies, but right now Retrievers are passing photos around downstairs. We've got to get you out of here."

Billy burst in. "Everything's secure."

Magda shoved a stack of passports and a roll of cash into Billy's hands. "I called François, and told him the girls need a holiday in the Caymans. You have to get them to the airport."

I stood there, confused. "I don't have a passport."

Magda looked at me hard. "You're not going to the airport. You're going with me." *Don't ask where* was written all over her face.

"Do you know how to use a gun?" She held up a second one.

"No. I don't like guns."

Magda threw it in the bag. "Well, that might change. Go grab some warm clothes."

The gun lay on the folded hangings.

"Don't just stand there," Magda snapped. "Get going!"

I ran back to Wardrobe. A tall, black man in an elegant suit was tearing through a cabinet. He turned around, and I realized it was Helen. She'd shaved off her hair and stripped off her nails. Helen strode toward me, carrying a down jacket and hiking boots, and every girlie thing about her was gone. She held out the clothes. "You'll need these," she said.

I took them and grabbed a shirt and jeans off the shelves. "Are you going with Sirocco and the girls?"

Helen looked ten years older than she did the night before. "Don't I wish. No one loves the Caymans more than I, but I'm destined for other things."

She slid a cigarette case out of her pocket and flipped it open. Inside was a screwdriver and a tiny pair of wire cutters. "We've spoken to the management several times about how unreliable the elevator is."

I'd turned Helen's and everyone else's life inside out. "Helen, I'm sorry. I didn't mean to mess things up like this."

She shrugged. "Occupational hazard," she said, and shooed me into the dressing room.

I pulled on the jeans. "You've been so kind. I don't know how to thank you."

Helen tossed a sweater and cowboy hat through the door. "Survive. Live happily ever after. And promise me you won't do anything as foolish as Persephone."

"Promise."

"I hate good-byes," she said, and when I pulled back the curtain, she was gone, but she'd left me something. Zipped into the inside pocket of the down jacket was a Canadian passport with Sparrow's picture, but another girl's identity.

Why did Helen give me this? I wondered as I rushed back to join the others. But even more importantly, why didn't Sparrow use this to escape to Canada?

The girls clustered with their bags in the hall. Magda was in the midst of them. She'd stripped off her makeup and traded her dress for jeans and a sheepskin jacket.

Billy shook his head at me, but Magda said, "It's a risky business. You know that. Take care of them, Billy."

She went to each girl, whispered something and kissed her good-bye before she sent her down the emergency exit. All the girls had gone down when the phone in the foyer rang. Stopped. Rang again.

"Shouldn't we answer that?" I said.

"No." Magda jerked her head at the exit. "Let's go."

Stairs spiraled down and we ran flat out. We passed landing after landing, but just like Billy said, there wasn't a single door.

The duffel bag on my shoulder swung wildly as I pounded down the stairs, throwing me off balance. My knees burned. I flashed back to the million times Ms. A ran us up and down the bleachers. She must have guessed that someday at least one of us would need it.

Magda and I hit the bottom. She punched in a code, and the door opened into a corner of the garage caged off from the rest.

Wheels screeched and we dropped to the floor. We scurried behind a van, listening to the growl of an engine, prowling a few rows away. It braked. Heavy footsteps patrolled the perimeter of the cage. Then the metal banged like someone hit it, and a man yelled, "There's a separate exit!"

The engine revved. Took off.

I ran down the aisle after Magda. She tore the tarp off a huge, black pickup truck. The sides were coated in dried mud like it had just come out of the mountains. We threw the bags in the backseat and jumped in.

Madga guided it out a back gate. Then we charged down a service road and left the Strip behind. My heart pounded in my ears. We passed pawnshops, tattoo parlors, and broken-down neighborhoods with crumpled cars parked on dead lawns.

"See anyone following us?" Magda asked.

It was hard to tell through the tinted windows, but none of the drivers or passengers around us looked like they were checking us out. "I don't think so."

"Good. You know how to drive?" Magda asked.

I shook my head. "No."

"Well, you've got six hundred miles in which to learn."

"Where are we going?"

"Idaho. I know a place we can hide." Magda pulled a pair of men's sunglasses from under the seat and tossed them at me. "Put these on and pull your hat down. We don't want anyone looking at us twice."

Her voice had changed. The polished, elegant tone and diction she had upstairs was gone. She was an entirely different person. The strange thing was, I couldn't tell which Magda was the real one.

64

The two-lane highway ran straight, and we were the only ones on it when Magda told me it was my turn to drive. We didn't stop. The truck was charging along at seventy. Magda clutched the steering wheel and lifted up so I could slide into her spot. I shoved my foot on the accelerator, and she dropped into the passenger seat.

Seven thousand pounds of steel and power in my hands and I was *driving*. I checked the mirrors like I'd seen Roik do. Adjusted the seat. Felt the tires vibrate through the wheel.

I couldn't see Magda's eyes behind her big aviator shades, but she sat facing me, her arm over the seat, scanning the road in front and back of us.

I was glad I had to watch the gas gauge and the speedometer and the mirrors, because every time my thoughts drifted, they skidded into imagining the Retrievers hauling me out of the truck cab. They'd be careful with me, because they had to return me in perfect condition, but it probably didn't matter how much they roughed up Magda.

Why are you running with me? I wanted to ask. Magda could have just turned me over to the Retrievers. She barely knew me. I wasn't one of her girls.

About an hour outside of Vegas, I finally remembered Sparrow's message for Magda. I needed to give it to her now, not when we were in the middle of a face-off with the Retrievers.

I pulled up the message FOR MAGDA'S EARS ONLY, and shoved the phone at her. "Here, it's for you from Sparrow."

Magda glanced at the display and then turned her back to me. She put in earphones, and from the corner of my eye, I saw her fingers play and stop and replay the recording.

Play. Stop. Replay. Play. Stop. Replay.

Finally, she pulled out the earphones and handed the phone back. Her mouth was a thin line. "Did you listen to it?"

"No."

Her eyes flickered and I realized she didn't believe me. "Put that phone where you can't lose it," she said, unzipping her duffel bag. Then she loaded both her guns and put them in the glove compartment.

I stuffed the phone into my jeans.

Magda didn't intend to hand me over. Clearly, I'd seen too much, men in high places selling the country's soul, and Magda and the Cast listening and recording it all. She didn't trust me out in public, even though Hawkins would make sure I wasn't out in public at all.

Night fell and we kept going.

We tuned through the radio, picking up satellite signals of sex jockeys and evangelists. We went back and forth between music stations until we gave up on finding anything decent, and let the basketball games run one after another.

I'd never seen anyplace so black or so empty as Nevada. Pinpricks of light in the mirror grew larger and larger until headlights thundered up alongside and then charged past.

Magda put her hand on the glove compartment each time one went by. If a driver came alongside and didn't pass, I was to brake hard and duck. Every time one sailed by and didn't look back, we'd both let out our breath. We'd lucked out that time.

Our luck changed after we crossed the Idaho border.

"That's weird," I said.

"What's weird?" Magda leaned over to look at the dash in front of me.

I pointed up at the mirror. "Somebody was behind us for miles and then they just disappeared. They didn't turn or pull off. They're just gone."

Magda rolled down her window. "Slow down a little and listen."

We weren't alone. There was another truck out there, its engine churning in the dark, but the headlights were off.

"It's pitch-black. How can they see where they're going?" I said.

"Night-vision goggles. Speed up, but do it gradually." Magda pulled out her phone. She didn't even say hello to the person who answered, just, "They found us. Just south of Twin Falls."

Magda set both guns on the seat between us. Dashboard light slicked the barrels. I had a crazy sick thought that maybe Magda got them out for us. Kill the witnesses. Save the movement.

"Why don't you just drop me off?" I said.

"What do you mean?"

"The Retrievers don't want you. They want me. You can leave me in the middle of the road. Drive away. Avoid the whole dying-in-a-rain-of-bullets thing. I can keep quiet about Jouvert."

She rested her hand on one of the guns. "It's not that simple."

"Yeah, I get that I saw things I shouldn't, but I know how to keep secrets. And Jes Hawkins will have me locked up in Malibu. I won't be a threat."

She didn't answer me. Her eyes were riveted on the road behind us.

And right then all the weird pieces fell together. "Those aren't Retrievers, are they?" I said.

Magda didn't waste time looking guilty. "No, they're not."

"So who are they?"

"Federal agents, I'm guessing."

I tried to breathe against the crazed spinning in my chest. I'd stumbled onto crimes some powerful people did not want exposed.

"You lied to me," I said. "You knew the whole time who was chasing us."

"So what if I lied? Would you have acted differently?"

"No-o, but that's not the point. I've been lied to half my life." *Truth matters.* "They're going to kill us, aren't they?" I said.

Magda stuck her hand under the seat and pulled out a bunch of keys. "I'm not sure. Assume their job is damage control."

Damage control? "You mean yes! Why don't you just say it? Yes, they want to kill us!"

She twisted a key off the ring. "All right, they might kill us, but not until they know what evidence we've got and where it's hidden."

"Like the wall hangings."

"How do you know about that?"

"I know stitch-code."

"Right, of course you do." Magda tore off her jacket. "Listen. I'm going out that back window, so hold the wheel steady and when I yell 'Now,' you hit the gas. Okay?"

"Okay."

She crawled over the seat and slid open the back window. I held my breath as she slithered into the truck bed.

The other truck was still out there, and it sounded like it was getting closer. Magda crouched in the back. The truck's running lights caught on the lid of a big, steel box she'd opened. She tossed things out of the box, the lid slammed, and I heard the scrape of metal.

Magda sank down until she'd disappeared, and the metal box inched toward the tailgate until it was right up against it.

The other truck thundered behind us, then light suddenly blasted into the rearview mirror, half blinding me. I glimpsed Magda's hand on the tailgate, and she yelled, "Now!"

I slammed the accelerator and the truck took off. The tailgate burst open and the steel box soared into the air.

Brakes shrieked behind us. The box crashed on the pavement, bounced, and flew, lid open like a giant steel moth throwing itself at the coming headlights.

The other truck swerved, but too late. Tires squealed and metal screamed.

"Keep going!" Magda yelled.

I pushed the accelerator to the floor. Magda crawled back through the window and over the seat. She pulled on her jacket, her whole body shaking. "You did great back there, but let's change places," she said. "I'll drive the next section."

"Do you think they're gone?" I said when Magda had the wheel again.

"No, we slowed them down, but we didn't stop them."

"What do we do now?"

"We keep going." She stared out into the dark. "I know there's someone you care about. Here's my phone," she said, pushing it at me. "Call him."

"But you said—" I didn't finish.

My eyes filled with tears as I tapped in Yates' code. Good-bye. I could feel my heart tearing from my body. How could I say it?

The phone rang three times, and then a slight click and silence. I swallowed, afraid of who might be on the other end. "Yates?"

"Avie! Are you okay?"

Scenes flashed through my mind. Yates waiting for me by Mom's grave, showing up at my house with his friend's dog, laughing with me at Riding Buddies, disappearing after Becca's death. He'd always been a part of my life.

"I'm in trouble."

"You sound like you're hurt."

I'm not hurt, I'm going to die. "We're on a highway in—" I stopped myself, guessing his phone could be tapped. "Some guys are chasing us."

"Jeez, no!"

"We're trying to outrun them, but—"

"Hawkins can't keep us apart. I love you, and I'll find a way to get to you, even if he hires a hundred guards."

I licked away a tear at the edge of my mouth. "It's not Hawkins. These aren't Retrievers."

"Then who the hell is it?"

"We're not sure, but I got caught up in something huge. Father G was right—what's happening, it goes way beyond the Paternalists. The Vice President's involved."

"The VP! You think those are government agents chasing you?"

I nodded, the yes stuck in my throat and Magda squeezed my arm. "Say good-bye. Now."

"I love you." My voice shattered. "I'm sorry. Good-bye."

"Avie!"

I broke the connection. If I was going to die, I didn't want Yates to die, too.

Magda's eyes darted from the road to the rearview mirror and back. "Pull the card on my phone and bend it in half. There are pliers in the glove compartment."

I did as she said.

"Now toss it."

I cracked the window and the little plastic and silicon card was swept out of my fingers. Phone numbers, addresses, and who knows what else Magda didn't want those agents to discover.

"We'll get rid of yours, too," Magda muttered. "But not yet."

Hearing that, I realized she hadn't given up completely. There was a slim chance we might survive.

65

Magda and I turned away from each other. Stared out into the dark. I felt as empty and cold as the night we were driving through except for the sputtering flame of knowing I didn't want to die like this.

We drove with the windows open, even though it was freezing outside. We didn't talk. Didn't play the radio. We listened hard for the sound of an engine.

Magda's guns lay on the seat between us. I set my hand down on one without looking at it. Flashed back to icy steel on my cheek. My heart pounded, but I didn't take my hand away. I saw myself shove the gun into the guy's ribs. Bam.

"Teach me how to shoot," I said.

"Not now."

"I want to live."

"This isn't the movies. If I try to teach you now, you'll only end up getting hurt."

"As opposed to being totally defenseless and getting killed?"

Magda didn't answer. She pointed at two sets of lights up ahead, one right on the other's tail. The one in back hugged the first so closely I didn't see why it wasn't pulling out to pass.

"Why are you smiling?" I asked.

"Because I love welcome parties." She crammed a gun into her belt. "Get your stuff together."

I had no clue what was going to happen next, but I did what she said.

The two trucks slowed down up ahead. Magda blinked her lights and yelled, "Brace yourself!" She wrenched the wheel, and slammed on the brakes.

"What are you doing!" I screamed.

We skidded past the trucks and sailed off the road. Dirt exploded over the hood. The truck hurtled through the brush, rocks pelting the windshield.

We banged to a stop.

"Get out!" Magda grabbed her bag and threw open the door. I jumped out into the cloud of yellow dust.

Flashlight beams swept through the haze. Magda was running for them and I ran after her.

Up on the road, one of the trucks idled while the other was turning around.

The men behind the flashlights were scrambling down the embankment. "Maggie, you okay?" one of them called out.

Magda raced up and threw her arms around him. "Still in one piece. Let's get out of here."

He helped us up to the road while the other man got on his phone. "Sheriff, we ran into an abandoned vehicle down on Highway—"

We crawled into the truck bed and slid under a tarp lashed to the sides. I lay down on the hard plastic liner, the tarp stretched over us like a coffin lid and the truck took off, heading back the way it came.

They called her Maggie. *That's got to be her real name.*

Her friends in the other truck were covering our tracks. Pretending to be concerned citizens, waiting for the local sheriff. But how far ahead of the bad guys were we?

The pickup roared up the highway. The truck bed stank of manure and cement dust and the raised diamond pattern on the liner bit through my jacket and jeans. I could feel Maggie's gun lying beside my thigh. Ready.

Wind banged the tarp over us like a drummer. "How long before we get there?" I yelled.

"Couple hours. Maybe more," she yelled back.

"It's freezing back here."

"It's only going to get colder."

She wrestled with a metal box, then slapped something small and folded against my chest. "Wrap this survival blanket around you— and cover your head."

The papery metallic blanket crackled as it unfolded. We both wrapped up burrito style, but I still shivered under the foil. Maybe it would have kept in my body heat if I'd had any left.

Time passed, but there was no way to tell how how far we'd gone or how close we were to where we were going, and my pulse wouldn't slow down. The guys chasing us were still out there and even though we'd dodged them this chase wasn't over.

They won't stop until they know we're not a problem anymore. I wondered if they'd do it fast. A bullet to the head? Or if they'd interrogate us until they found the evidence we had.

Tears ran in hot trickles into my hair. I'd messed up so badly. I shouldn't have let anger screw up my thinking. I should have waited until we crossed the border to send out Sparrow's message.

If we live, if I get to Canada, I have to leave Maggie the phone with Sparrow's tape of Jouvert and I have to disappear. That's the only way I'll be safe.

Suddenly, we were slowing, turning off the highway. The tarp sighed and went quiet, and I lay completely still. The tires crunched over something like snow.

The truck cruised along slowly. Braked like we were hitting traffic lights. "Are we there?" I said.

Maggie rustled in her foil wrap. "No, we're on the outskirts of Boise, but I think we're safe for now. I doubt they'll track us into the mountains."

I lay back. Soon, we started climbing and the road got bumpier.

I wanted to believe Maggie, I really did. But it felt as if she had decided a long time ago that lying worked better for her than telling the truth.

Salvation

66

When the truck stopped after what could have been an hour or maybe two, Maggie and I crawled out from under the tarp. We were parked by a big, black building with a cross on top. "Welcome to Salvation," she said.

Hills spotted with pine trees rose up on either side of the little valley we were standing in. The moon reflected off the snow and the rooftops of cabins. It smoothed out the fields and caught on the blades of a dozen windmills.

Close to the church, the cabins clustered together, but as the valley stretched away, the houses were farther and farther apart. The lights were off in all of them except one.

"Is this a town?" I asked.

"Not exactly. It's for people who don't trust towns. Or governments," she added. She grabbed her duffle. "You want us in the Bunker?" she called to the guy who drove us in.

"Nah, sis. Heat's not on. You kin stay at the house tonight."

I don't know what blew me away more. That this place had a

Bunker or that the guy was Maggie's brother. He came around the truck. "Let me carry that," he said, taking my bag. "So who's your friend, Maggie?"

I decided then and there I was done with lying. "I'm Avie."

"Rogan."

"Thanks for—" My throat got so tight, I couldn't finish.

"Sure. No worries."

We trudged through ankle-deep snow to his cabin and climbed the rough-hewn wooden steps to a small covered front porch. A white dog with grey and black splotches leaped up to greet us as we walked inside. Warm yellow light filled the main room. A sofa and chairs sat by a woodstove, and a table big enough for a family separated the sitting area from the kitchen.

"Nellie and the kids are asleep," Rogan said. He fed wood into the stove before tossing us a couple sleeping bags. "Bathroom's back of the kitchen."

Maggie and I rolled out the sleeping bags on the rug by the stove and slid in.

Safe. For now.

67

I woke to the smell of frying sausage. My eyes weren't even open when I heard a woman say in a hushed voice, "I don't want her staying here."

"Shush now, Nellie," Rogan said. "She's family and she's in trouble."

"I understand she's in trouble, but she's never put family first. Not you. Not me. Not her son."

My eyes popped open. *Son?* There were obviously volumes of Maggie's story that were classified.

Rogan said something I didn't catch. Maggie was asleep on her side a foot away from me. Her mouth twitched, and I wondered why we were here if Nellie hated her so much.

"I won't let her hurt that boy."

"Luke's almost a man, Nellie. He can handle seeing her."

"Do I have a voice in what goes on in this house?"

"Of course you do. We're partners."

"Then respect my feelings," Nellie said.

Maggie opened her eyes. She had been awake and listening, and when she saw me looking at her, she warned me with a look not to ask about what I'd heard.

"All right. They'll move into the Bunker," Rogan said.

"Thank you. And I promise I won't say anything."

"That's all I ask."

Then everything was quiet except for the griddle. Maggie and I lay still.

I heard Rogan say, "Kids outside?"

"Sarah's feeding the goats, and Jonas is up to his usual. When do you expect Luke and the others?"

"Before supper. That the second breakfast you're fixing today?"

"I'm guessing those two didn't eat much yesterday."

"You're a kind woman, Nellie Paul."

"Go on. Get out of here."

I watched Rogan pull his jacket back on. He was pressed, buttoned-up, tucked in, and polished even in jeans and a work shirt. Clean shaven, not a hair out of place. The front door opened and shut. Maggie waited a minute, then faked a yawn. She crawled out of the bag. "Morning, Nellie. Good to see you."

"Maggie."

"Mind if I wash my face?"

"Not at all. By the time you're done, food'll be ready."

I waited another minute, then got up. "Hi, I'm Avie."

"Nellie."

After hearing Nellie stand up to Rogan, I expected her to be tall, but she was tiny and lean in her overalls and flannel shirt. Her hair was pulled off her clean-scrubbed face like she didn't have patience for unnecessary things.

"Thanks for letting us stay here," I said.

She nodded. I rolled up the sleeping bags. "What should I . . . ?"

"Oh, just leave that. Come get something to eat."

Nellie'd set two places at the table. She slid a plate with eggs and sausage in front of me. I took a slice of bread, spread it thick with butter and cherry jam, and dug in.

"This is delicious," I said. Then I took a sip of milk. It wasn't from a cow.

Nellie eyed me. She was in her thirties, I guessed, a survivor. "You don't seem *fancy* enough to be one of Maggie's girls."

I didn't look like a call girl, that's what Nellie meant.

"I'm not one of her girls." I don't know why I felt I had to stick up for Maggie. "You know, they're not . . . the girls don't have sex."

"A penthouse full of girls in a Las Vegas casino. What *do* they do?" Nellie said.

I shrugged. "They're like, I don't know, entertainers. The guys just want to have fun and the girls play pool with them."

"So what are you doing with her?"

"Maggie's helping me. I ran away from home after my dad signed my Contract."

"You don't like who your dad picked?"

"He sold me to get money for his company." I saw Nellie frown. "Besides," I added, "I'm in love with someone else."

Nellie's frown softened as she flipped the last sausage. "Is he coming here?"

"No. He's meeting me in Canada."

Nellie paused, and then said carefully, "So you're not planning on staying?"

A little warning bell triggered in my head. Maggie layered everything she did with secrets. One wrong word, and who knew what trouble I'd cause. "Maggie can explain better than I can."

"Explain what?" Maggie stood right behind me.

"How you're just visiting," Nellie answered. "How you're taking this girl to Canada." She looked at Maggie like she was challenging her to lie.

"That's the goal," Maggie said. She pulled out her chair, and her face transformed. She was Magda: smooth, cool, deceptive. "Mmm. Elk sausage and homemade bread. You're an amazing cook, Nellie."

The door burst open, and a little boy about five or six ran in, followed by a girl a few years older swinging a pail. The boy threw himself at the table. "I'm Jonas," he said to Maggie. "Who are you?"

"Your Aunt Maggie."

"I don't remember you."

"It's been a while."

The girl, Sarah, put the pail on the floor. "Can I hug you, Aunt Maggie?"

"That's up to your mama to decide."

Nellie gave a nod, and Maggie drew in Sarah for a hug. The kids sat down with us at the table.

"Our brother's gone for a ride," Sarah said. Maggie's face paled, before she said, "When's he coming back?"

"Around suppertime." Sarah looked at her mother. "Can Aunt Maggie come to supper?"

Nellie froze, a plate in her hand. Maggie shook her head. "It's too much, Nellie. I know that."

I saw Nellie nod, and Maggie turned to Jonas. "Tell me about your goats." Jonas started talking nonstop about his favorite goats while I ate my food and listened.

I wondered what Nellie was thinking. She knew Maggie and I were in enough trouble that Rogan and four other men drove off in the middle of the night to save us. But why would Nellie think for even an instant that Maggie and I intended to stay?

And Luke, Maggie's secret son? Things were going to get really interesting here around suppertime.

68

Sarah and Jonas wanted to give me a tour after breakfast, but Nellie told them they weren't skipping school, and besides, Maggie already knew her way around.

I stood on the porch, the snow so bright I had to squint to see. Besides the cabins I noticed the night before, trailers dotted the valley. There were windmills next to almost every house, but only one big barn. The black walls of the barn and church twinkled. They were covered in solarskin. Wind and solar power kept this place alive.

The harder I looked, the more I saw what wasn't there—like mailboxes or satellite dishes. No store or school or post office.

The door banged open behind me. "You ready to see the Bunker?"

I turned, and Maggie tossed me my duffle and sleeping bag. "Sure."

We walked toward the church, lugging our bags. By almost every house, chickens the color of maple syrup perched in the open doors of coops while one or two brave ones tried out the snow. In one yard, red and blue plaid shirts rocked like sheets of cardboard pinned to a clothesline.

"Our luck's improving," Maggie said. "It's going to snow tonight."

More snow didn't sound lucky when we were headed for the border in the next couple days. "Why's that good?" I said.

"Barnabas and John—they were the ones driving the other truck last night—they'll be back in a few hours. The snow'll cover their tracks. We can sit tight for a week and hope the guys following us decide we've left the state."

I could feel myself wanting to believe Maggie's fantasy about how the snow would save us, but so far things hadn't been that magical. "The feds know who you are. They know you have a brother. I can't believe you think they won't find us."

"Avie, this place, these people, they're off the grid. They got rid of IDs, credit cards. They don't take salaries or pay taxes or do anything else to clue the government into their existence." Maggie opened a door on the side of the church.

"I thought we were going to the Bunker," I said.

"Almost there," Maggie answered.

"Did you grow up here?"

"No, a few hundred miles away. I stayed here, though, several years ago when I decided to take a break from law and revisit my life choices."

I was dying to ask, *What life choices*, but I knew Maggie'd never answer that. "What kind of law did you practice?"

"Civil rights."

I felt like every new thing Maggie told me turned my thoughts about her inside out.

Sunlight poured into the church even though the windows were narrow slits in the three-foot-thick walls. A skinny balcony circled the church hall. We walked up the main aisle through rows of long wooden tables and benches. Up on the wall in front, a simple cross hung between a Star of David and a yin and yang.

"I've never seen a church like this," I said.

"It's not just a church. It's also the school and community center."

Behind the dais, a staircase led up to the balcony. Maggie punched a code into a panel on the wall and the door in front of us un-latched. I unzipped my jacket.

"You might want to keep that on," Maggie said.

I left my jacket open. "How long has Salvation been around?"

"Hmm. Forty years, maybe. It started with army veterans like Rogan."

When Maggie opened the door, I saw four rough wood steps be-fore the rest disappeared in a black hole. She reached for a lantern just inside the door and lit it. I followed her down. "Was Rogan in the Middle East?" I asked.

"Saudi Arabia, then Iraq, then Afghanistan. He returned with a healthy distrust of authority and a hatred for Al Qaeda, the Taliban, and other oppressors of the human soul."

At the bottom of the steps, Maggie held up the lantern and said, "Ah, the Bunker. Our home away from home."

I dropped my bags. My breath clouded in the light and I zipped my jacket back up. The room was huge, bigger than the church hall overhead. The walls and ceiling and floor were all flat, dead grey.

The corner closest to us was set up like a kitchen with a sink and camp stoves. Folded canvas cots were piled to one side. Maggie car-ried her duffel bag over to a padlocked cabinet at the far end as I walked along the shelves that ran the length of the walls. They were loaded with jars of hand-canned cherries, pears, and tomatoes, and stacked with gallon cans labeled water, flour, oats, powdered milk. Sacks of beans and rice were piled as high as my waist.

This wasn't just a storeroom. No wonder they called this the Bun-ker. These people were ready for a catastrophe.

Maggie pointed to a walled-off corner. "Chemical toilets. Sorry. No shower. But I know a few women here who might take pity on us and lend us theirs."

"There are other women?"

"Forty, forty-five, depending on who's still here since the last time I visited."

I heard her spin a lock and watched her open the cabinet. She held the door, blocking me from seeing what she was doing, but I caught a glimpse of what she pulled out of her duffel and stuffed in there: the wall hangings with their secrets. Stitch-coded names, dates, and details that could blow a hole in Congress.

She snapped the lock back on.

"Are there more places like Salvation?" I said.

"I'm convinced there are. Half the men in Rogan's platoon vowed they were going rogue once they got back to the States."

I looked over at the camp cots, thinking I should pick one out and set it up, but all I wanted was to get the hell out of there. The way that cold, grey ceiling curved over us, I felt like I was in a coffin.

I blew on my hands. "It's freezing down here."

"Yeah, we could use some long johns."

I hauled a cot out of the pile and unfolded the aluminum frame, dropping my duffel onto the faded khaki fabric.

Pipes squealed as Maggie tried the faucet in the kitchen. "Well, we've got plenty of cold water," she said.

"How long are we going to stay in Salvation?"

"Until things cool off. Those agents aren't going to leave Idaho until they think we have."

I stuffed my freezing hands into my pockets, thinking about them prowling around like wolves, trying to sniff us out while the U.S. cut off our escape. "But we've got to get out of here before the border's closed."

"There are other ways out of the country," Maggie said.

I was just about to ask how when a voice called out, "Who's down there?"

A woman in a red down vest stood on the stairs with her arms crossed. She looked ten years older than Maggie. With her short spiky hair and round glasses, she looked like one of those tiny, endangered owls.

"Is that you, Beattie?" Maggie rushed forward as the woman clambered down the steps.

"Maggie! I heard Rogan came and got you." They hugged with

their eyes closed, whispering to each other in a way that made me nervous. Maybe Nellie didn't know what Maggie was really up to, but I was sure Beattie did.

When they broke apart, Beattie turned to me. "Who's this?"

"I'm Avie. I'm—"

"She's traveling with me," Maggie said.

Beattie pursed her lips like she was trying hard to keep her questions to herself. Instead, she ran her eyes over my cot and said, "This is wrong. You can't stay here."

Maggie shrugged, but Beattie reached for my sleeping bag. "You'll stay with us."

"Thanks, but don't you think you should ask your partner first?" Maggie said.

"Cecelia's not here."

"I'm sorry."

"We haven't broken up. She's at a med school in Honduras until May, teaching and picking up some new skills."

"Keisha won't mind company?"

"I think our daughter will be happy to have company, especially someone from Outside."

"Fine," Maggie said. "Lead the way."

I followed them out, feeling like I'd crossed another border. Outside Salvation, women couldn't marry each other. The Paternalists didn't mind if two men married—less competition. But women who didn't want men were lucky to be left alone. More than one had been raped to "teach them a lesson."

The sun blinded me as we went outside. I shaded my eyes as boys in leather boots and long jackets and girls wearing prairie dresses over their pants ran past us, yelling, "Mornin', Pastor Beattie."

Beattie wasn't just a Survivor, she was a Servant of God. I'd never thought any place could be stranger than Vegas.

69

Sunlight bounced off the snow so Beattie's bathroom glowed pink. I stood under the shower, hot water raining down, loosening up the muscles in my back. A big purple bruise on my knee ached, and I found two more thumb-sized ones on my hip, but other than that, I was fine.

The soap dish cradled a block of handmade soap. I brushed my finger over the rose petal floating under its cloudy surface, remembering how Nana Stephie sometimes had soap like this. I held the bar up to my nose, and *breathed*.

I'm okay.

I made it to Idaho.

Maybe everything will work out.

I ran the creamy soap over my skin. Maggie had hidden us up in the mountains far off any main road. If Salvation wasn't on any map or in any government database then maybe we really were safe.

And the border was just a couple hundred miles from here. A couple hundred miles to Canada, and if we were careful and lucky, Yates and I might even find each other there.

I imagined standing on tiptoes in a crowd, triple-checking my phone and counting down the agonizing minutes until Yates came through the airport arrivals gate. He appears and I yell, "Yates!" People open a path between us as he rushes to me and I leap into his arms.

The water suddenly went cold and I hurried to turn it off. I reached for a towel and heard Maggie and Beattie through the door, their voices hushed and tense. I crept over and cracked the door open.

"You think it's a death squad?" Beattie said.

I held my breath and Maggie mumbled a reply.

"Your brother's name's not on anything," Beattie said. "I don't see how they would track you here."

I missed Maggie's answer.

"Even if the border's closing, you can't leave now. They know there are only two routes you can take."

I shut the door and sank onto the stool by the tub. The night flashed back to me: speedometer ticking ninety, the steel box sailing like a deadly butterfly, Maggie screaming, "Hold on!," the rain of rocks on the windshield.

My clothes lay across the toilet. I slipped my phone out of my jeans and turned it on. The reception was zero and the battery barely holding on.

I'd be in Canada right now if it weren't for this.

I muted the phone and scrolled through my files. Sparrow's messages were still there, including FOR MAGDA'S EARS ONLY.

It was begging me to open it. *Right, like I don't have enough trouble, I need more?* I tapped on the first message Sparrow sent me from the Capitol steps.

Seconds away from torching herself, and there she was smiling, her eyes alive with a weird, almost religious ecstasy like some arrow-riddled saint right out of a Renaissance painting. She raised the bottle, and her final words played in my head. "See you in heaven."

"Why'd you do it?" I whispered. *Why'd you kill yourself and leave me with this mess?*

I saw us back at Masterson, Sparrow tinkering with one of her little inventions and muttering under her breath while Ms. A shared Congress's latest indignity to women. I had been close enough to hear Sparrow say that the world would close its eyes until blood ran down the Capitol steps.

And I remembered thinking, she'd do it. Sparrow would waste them all. Maybe Sparrow had always been unbalanced, or what happened with the boy she loved who'd destroyed her, but I didn't want to end up like her.

I don't want to die for the cause. Well, maybe I should have thought of that yesterday before I blew my cover and everyone else's.

Maggie rapped on the bathroom door. "Can I get in there?"

"Just a sec." I stuffed the phone back in my jeans and pawed around for my underpants.

"Great. The sky's clear, so after I shower, I'll take you out for a shooting lesson."

I lost hold of my towel and had to grab for it. "Today?"

"You have other plans?" she said.

I hated how smug she was, saying that. "No."

"Okay, then."

I pulled on my jeans. Learning to shoot another human being wasn't okay. It would never be okay, but I couldn't escape the fact that I needed to defend myself.

When I came out, Beattie was sitting by the woodstove, jotting notes from the *Challenge of Faith*. "I left a hat on the table," she said. "I doubt you're used to this cold." The hat looked like it was brought back from the Andes with llamas circling the crown, and two long skinny ties, made from the same heathery brown wool as the rugs covering the couch and floor.

I waited by the window, holding the hat, and twisting and untwisting the ties around it.

"Nervous?" Beattie said.

"I hate guns." My fingers wouldn't stop moving. "*You* don't believe in guns, right?"

"Personally, I wish guns were only used for hunting. But I'm forced to admit that we're perilously close to TEOTWAWKI."

"What's that?"

"The End Of The World As We Know It." Beattie's voice quieted like she was quoting a religious text. 'When the government collapses and anarchy reigns, we must protect ourselves from those who would do us harm.' It's the reason Salvation exists."

Beattie seemed so rational. "You really believe in The End Of The World As We Know It?" I asked.

She peeled off her glasses and folded them tenderly. "You lived through the chaos. Is your world anything like it used to be?"

I choked back the rush of tears. Life as I knew it ended the day Mom died. "No."

"Avie, knowing how to do something is different from using that knowledge. Buddha and Jesus are my guides, but if my life's on the line, I'm calling on Smith & Wesson."

"Almost ready," Maggie called.

Beattie stood up and eased the hat out of my fingers. "You poor, sweet girl, " she whispered, guiding the hat over my hair. I closed my eyes for a moment, and felt her mother's hands fuss with the scarf around my neck. I stood there, not moving, holding on to the tenderness of her touch.

Maggie strode into the room. "Let's go!" A bulging canvas bag hung off her shoulder.

Beattie squeezed my elbow. "Keisha should be here by the time you get back."

Maggie handed me some mittens. "You'll want these," she said, and showed me how to fold the tops back so they turned into fingerless gloves.

Fingerless, so they wouldn't interfere with squeezing the trigger.

I jerked them on and followed her onto the porch. *You're learning how to survive*, I told myself as we tramped down to the snowbanked road. *You learned how to drive, now you're going to learn how to use a gun.*

But the other part of my brain wasn't about to listen to that crap. Shooting a gun isn't like learning to drive, it yelled back.

When you're driving, the point isn't to kill someone.

Piled snow lined the road from the church, past the barn and the twenty or so houses closest to them. The plowed part of the road stopped a few hundred feet ahead of us.

I walked next to Maggie. I didn't see anybody at the windows, but I swore I felt eyes on us. Even the goats in the pen beside the barn seemed to be watching us as we went by.

"It's about two hundred miles to the border from here, isn't it?" I said.

Maggie shook her head. "No, it's closer to six hundred."

"Six!"

"We're in southern Idaho. It's a long state."

I swore like Roik did the time a guy scratched Big Black's paint.

"Are you *blaming* me?" Maggie said, her head cocked, ready for a fight.

Six hundred freaking miles. And according to Beattie, there were only two roads that could get us to the border. If I wanted to survive, I needed Maggie. "No, no, I'm sorry."

"I don't like this any more than you do, but I'm going to try like hell to get us out of this in one piece."

"Okay."

The quiet was broken by an engine rumbling and tires thumping over bumpy ground. We watched a pickup with monster tires come around the church.

"John and Barnabas are back," Maggie said. They waved as they drove by, stopping at a small cabin up ahead. "We need to thank them for helping us last night."

She said it in a strangely nervous way. And when I saw a young guy in a sheepskin jacket get out of the truck after the other two, I was pretty sure I knew why.

He took one look at us and stomped off in the opposite direction. Maggie followed him with her eyes, but she kept her face from showing how she felt.

The two older men climbed up on the back of the truck. The one with the big gut and ripped down jacket yelled out, "Jemima, I brought you a present!"

Nobody could beat Maggie at hiding the truth, but now I saw her lips part as she stared at the tall, slim guy with the greying ponytail sticking out from under his cowboy hat. She gave a little shake of her head. *Oh, Maggie. You've got it bad.* He was something she wanted, but couldn't have.

The two men wrestled with the front end of a claw-foot tub. Maggie picked up the pace. "Those idiots, trying to get it out of the truck by themselves. It's cast iron." She raised her voice, and it almost sounded like she was smiling. "John, wait up."

A girl a little older than me rushed out of the cabin, the pockets on her tool belt slapping her thighs. I guessed she was Jemima. Maggie climbed up beside the men, and I stood next to Jemima on the ground. We waited for Maggie and the men to turn the tub on its side and inch it to the tailgate.

They lowered it down, grunting and swearing and trying to brace themselves, as Jemima and I clung to the curled lip. The weight buckled my knees, and I dug my boots into the snow, afraid if I lost my grip the thing would crush me.

We set it down gently on its feet, and all stood there panting. "This is gorgeous, Dad," Jemima said. The tub was nicked in places and stained near the drain hole.

"Found it at a salvage yard. You said you wanted one."

Jemima's face shone, and my heart squeezed, seeing the look she gave her dad. It took me back to the day when I was ten, and Dad put Dusty in my arms for the first time and made me promise to brush her and play with her and hug her every day.

My heart kept squeezing, thinking I'd never see him again. *You don't know that,* I tried to tell myself. *You don't know what's going to happen.*

We hauled the tub into the cabin and set it down in a corner on the rough wood floor. "We've got flour to drop off," the father said, and headed for the door. The other man—Barnabas, I guessed—tipped his hat at us, and I swore that even though Maggie stood right where she was, her heart followed him back to the truck.

What's your story, Barnabas? The shadow on his cheeks. The wrinkled shirt and stained jacket. He looked like he'd slept in those clothes and not just last night.

Maggie picked a hammer off a sawhorse table and turned it in her hand. "So this is your Build?"

"Sure is," Jemima said. "Caleb and I should be done by May."

Curtains hung in the windows, but pipes and electrical wires climbed the unfinished walls. The kitchen cabinets didn't have doors or a countertop yet, but heat poured from the woodstove.

"Why's this called a Build?" I asked.

Jemima gave a little shake of her head. "A Build's when you build a house together so you know you'll be good together. Don't you do anything like that where you come from?"

"No. I wish." I imagined Yates bracing a cabinet while I screwed it in place. I could see us someday, sweaty and covered in sawdust, collapsing beside each other on the floor when we were done. "And when you finish your Build, you get married?"

"Not always," Maggie said under her breath. She glanced up and realized we'd heard her. "But Jemima and Caleb will."

"This is so cool," I said. All those hours working side by side, you'd know each other so well, and you'd have *built* something.

"You want to help?" Jemima said. "I've got doors that need sanding."

Before I could say a word, Maggie took hold of me. "Sorry, but she's mine for the next hour."

"See you later," I said.

Barnabas called to Maggie from the porch of the next house. "You left your gun bag on the gate. You planning on doing some shooting?"

"Avie and I are going out to the pasture. I'm going to teach her."

Barnabas cocked his head at me. "That right? You want to learn how to hunt?"

"Not exactly," I said.

"Everyone should know how to handle a gun," Maggie said.

"That's right. TEOTWAWKI," he said.

A shudder ran through my shoulders, and I tried to shake it off. My own end of the world was lying in wait outside Salvation. Two men with guns and night-vision goggles and one big-ass reason to want me silent.

"I got a target you could use," Barnabas added.

Maggie thanked him, and I could see her not quite smile. She was holding back, like she wasn't sure she should allow herself to.

We waited in the road while Barnabas got the target. "Ugh, my tongue's sticking to my teeth," I said.

"You're dehydrated. It's the cold, plus the altitude." Maggie unclipped an insulated bottle from her belt. "Here. You have to drink constantly so you don't get sick."

Dehydration? No, more like nerves, I thought, swigging the water.

Barnabas came back and we walked out to the pasture together. He glanced at the trees on our right. "He's up on that slope, watching, if you want to talk to him."

I saw Luke leaning against a pine, his arms crossed. Even the tilt of his cowboy hat felt defiant.

Maggie shook her head. "I don't intend to force myself on him. Me showing up here is shock enough."

"Your choice. How about you give Avie a safety lesson while I put this target up?" he said.

When Maggie took out her gun, I forgot about Luke. The gun was black steel. Not elegant or sleek, but so ugly you wouldn't forget its job was to kill.

The safety lesson was simple. Don't point a gun at anything you don't want to shoot. Keep your finger off the trigger until you're ready to shoot. Keep the gun unloaded until you're ready to use it.

I played back the night before, the loaded guns on the seat while we dodged the men chasing us. Maggie didn't have any emotional conflict weighing her down. She would have shot to kill.

I don't want to kill anyone. I just don't want to die.

Maggie checked to see the clip was out. She fit the gun into my palm, and laid my index finger along the barrel. Then she curled my other fingers around the handle and set my left hand over my right. Across the pasture, the black shadow of a man flapped gently in the wind.

The black metal chilled my bare fingers and the flashback from the cemetery caught up with me, blurring my vision. No fear, I thought, pushing it away. I'm taking charge of my life. I refuse to be a victim. *No fear. No fear. No fear.*

I was concentrating so hard, I didn't notice Barnabas beside me until he pushed down on my hips to shift my weight.

I got the sights lined up, and put my finger on the trigger.

"You're too tight," he said. "Squeeze too hard, it'll throw your aim off. You have to be gentle. Peaceful. When that gun goes off, you should almost be surprised it fired."

"Okay." I shook out my muscles like Ms. A taught us to do before a track meet. *No fear. No fear.* I took a deep breath and squeezed. Click.

"Okay," Barnabas said. "Now open your eyes and try again."

A couple more tries and Barnabas shoved in the clip. "This is a nine millimeter. When you fire, the muzzle's going to flip. Maintain the right tension, and it'll snap up about forty-five degrees, then your hands will drop back into firing position."

I was glad Target Guy was an outline. Glad he didn't have a face. I got him in the sights and found a quiet place inside me. Eased the trigger back. Bam!

The shot echoed so loud I could almost see the sound.

"I think you got him," Barnabas said.

"Really?" I couldn't see the hole, but I felt an unexpected sense of exhilaration.

He adjusted my stance, had me fire a few more rounds, and told Maggie, "She's all yours."

Maggie kept me out there until the target was tattered. Most of the shots had missed Target Guy's vital organs, but she still said, "That's good enough for now."

My ears were ringing, but I felt oddly satisfied. Next time, I wouldn't be a weak little girl with no way to defend herself. Next time, I wouldn't be an easy target.

"Thanks for teaching me, Maggie. I know I haven't exactly acted grateful."

"It's okay." She looked off into the distance. "Sometimes we wait too long to do things we know we have to do."

The sky had clouded over. Maggie and I tramped back toward Beattie's as scattered snowflakes drifted down. "Pray it lets loose," Maggie said. "The more snow, the safer we'll be."

71

We'd cleared the pasture when we heard someone strumming a guitar. It was hard to tell where the song was coming from, and the notes were slow, hesitant, as if whoever was playing had almost forgotten the song. A man began to sing in a soft, gravelly voice.

I was snow blind
lost in winter

my heart as frozen as the ice on the birch
then you came along,
thawed me out,
gave me water
Your love, darlin',
is my rebirth

The song touched the places in me that knew lonely and lost and the brand-new one that knew love. I hadn't heard someone sing a song like this in a really long time. Not since Scarpanol broke a hundred million hearts.

The song got louder as if the singer had found the words and his fingers now remembered every chord. "That's Barnabas, isn't it?" I said.

Maggie quickened her pace like she wanted to get out of there. "Yeah, he builds guitars. He's probably checking the tone on that one."

You brought the sun
and the hours of solstice
you forced the green
and the leaf from its curl
You lifted seeds on the wind of tomorrow
Sweet summer lover
my heart's rebirth

I trotted alongside Maggie, watching her face shift as if she was reliving a love story from the moment she'd fallen in love to when she'd lost it.

Her eyes darted to a small wood building nestled up next to the barn. The door was cracked open and the music drifted from inside. Maggie slowed as we got closer, and finally, she sighed and handed me the gun bag. "I'll meet you back at Beattie's," she said.

I lingered at the gate, listening to the last words of the song, and I knew Barnabas had written it.

I've trekked the wasteland
I know its hunger
Felt the cut of the wind
On the tundra's white sheet
The day that you leave me
Let the wolves claim my body
There won't be enough left
For winter to eat

It was obvious: Maggie had left and broken Barnabas' heart. And while I didn't have the whole story, I guessed she'd broken Luke's, too.

I could see her doing it, she was so obsessed with saving the world, she didn't care about what happened to either of them. *I'm not like that. I will never give up on Yates and happiness to fight some battle I can never win.*

I'd only taken a few more steps when I realized that maybe I already had. The moment I'd sent out that message from Sparrow, I'd joined the struggle, whether I was ready for it or not.

72

Snowflakes swirled in front of my face, and I nestled my nose in my scarf. The temperature must have dropped twenty degrees now that the sun had been swallowed up by the clouds.

I'd barely passed the barn when the church door opened, and children spilled down the steps. Sarah and Jonas raced toward me, a dozen younger kids chasing after them while the older ones held back. Spying me, girls who looked twelve and thirteen crushed to-gether with their hands over their mouths.

In about ten minutes, there wouldn't be a single person in Salva-tion who didn't know Maggie and I were here.

Jonas barreled into me, and threw me off balance. "Come meet our goats!"

"Okay," I said.

"But first I got to get them inside. It's gonna snow hard tonight."

Children gathered behind Jonas, checking me out. A little boy spoke quickly in Spanish to his older brother. The brother swaggered up to me—all four feet of him. "Who are you?" He had on a camouflage jacket that looked like somebody'd cut it down to fit him.

"I'm Avie." Maggie had told me not to say much, to let her handle people's questions.

"You're not from here. Where are you from?" he said.

Sarah pushed through the crowd. "Hector Flores! You're not sup-posed to ask where she's from or where she's going. Didn't you listen to the teacher?"

I should have guessed the children would talk about me when they saw me earlier with Beattie, but it shook me up to hear it.

Sarah tugged me toward the barn, shooting a nasty look at the crowd. "Go on, get out of here." She wore a pink calico dress under her winter coat, but even the bigger boys stepped back.

Jonas climbed the fence and dropped into the goat pen. Droopy-eared goats almost as tall as he was surrounded him and nosed his jacket. "You want food, you got to go inside."

Sarah shoved me into the barn and pulled the door closed. "They're too curious for their own good."

I unwound the scarf from my neck. The barn smelled of alfalfa and goats and disinfectant. Electric lightbulbs dangled from the raf-ters, and light glinted off a scythe on the back wall. There was a row of them hanging there like this was Death's walk-in closet. And be-low them on the floor were contraptions with iron wheels and long spidery metal fingers that came right out of *Little House on the Prairie.*

"Do you have horses?" I asked.

"They're in winter pasture," Sarah said. "We'll bring 'em back late spring."

She grabbed a handful of sunflower seeds from a bin and dashed down the row of pens, tossing the seeds into the bedding. "Best get out of the way," she said.

I climbed on a hay bale as goats bolted through the barn's side door. Sarah and Jonas worked as a team, wrangling them into their pens.

Jonas pulled me off the hay bale over to the first pen. "This here's Emmeline, and that's Rosalind, and over there's Geraldine and her baby Pluto." He took me down the row, introducing me to thirty or forty animals.

"You've got a lot of goats," I said.

"We got a lot of people to feed," Sarah said, with a note of pride in her voice.

She moved among the goats, whipping off their quilted coats. She tossed them to me and I stacked them. They were sewn from faded scraps of clothing. Nothing was wasted here.

Sarah crouched beside a nanny and smeared something that looked like Vaseline on her udder. "They can get frostbite here and on their ears if you don't put salve on them."

"You know a lot about taking care of goats," I said.

"I'm Jemima's apprentice. I know how to milk and shear, and I'm learning how to doctor them. Jemima's teaching me to make cheese."

"Sounds like a big job," I said.

"Everybody has a job here. We're a community," she answered.

I thought about how Mom and Ms. Alexandra would have loved seeing Sarah take charge like this. How they'd admire Jemima for building her own house.

A big, black nanny bumped Jonas in the shoulder. He threw his arm around its neck and rubbed it hard. "Goats are messy, but I like them."

The barn door opened, silhouetting a man in a cowboy hat in grey white light.

"Luke!" Sarah called as he shut the door behind him.

"Hey, Miss Muffet!"

She ran up, arms held out. Luke grabbed her hands and spun her off her feet.

Jonas leaped off a bale of hay onto Luke's back and sent his hat flying into a stall. He wrapped his arms around Luke's neck, and clung to him like a monkey.

"If Emmeline eats my hat, you're going to buy me a new one, little brother," Luke warned.

Luke spun faster, his eyes trained on Sarah. I sauntered over to the stall and managed to snatch the hat out of Emmeline's mouth. The whole time I was keeping an eye on Luke, Maggie's mystery son.

A big open smile creased his tanned cheeks. His light brown hair curled around his ears. He wore a sheepskin jacket over a sweatshirt, but that wasn't why his shoulders looked big. Luke was all muscle.

I almost laughed, hearing Dayla gush in my head. "OhmyGod, he looks like that Greek god, you know, the one with the hammer!" Day could never keep her gods straight.

Sarah had squealed with laughter, but now she cried, "Luke! Luke! Put me down. I'm dizzy."

Luke slowed until her feet touched the ground, then he peeled Jonas off his neck. "Aren't you going to introduce me?" he asked them.

"This is Avie," Sarah said. "Aunt Maggie's friend."

Luke looked me up and down, his oak-brown eyes trying to figure me out. "Hello, Margaret's friend. I'm Luke."

I handed him his hat. "Emmeline only dented the brim."

"Thanks." He dusted it off on his jeans and stuck it back on his head. The way he kept his eyes on me made me think he was more of a listener than a talker—just like his mom.

"It's nothing," I said. "You saved my life."

Jonas grabbed his arm. "How'd you save her life, Luke?"

"Ah, don't listen to that. She's making up a story," Luke said. A bell jangled, and Sarah yanked Jonas' sleeve. "That's Momma's cowbell. We gotta go."

Luke lingered at the open door. Snow tumbled from the sky like somebody was shaking it out of a basket. Nellie stood across the road on her front porch, watching Jonas and Sarah hurtle toward home.

Luke stuffed his hands in his leather gloves. "You can tell your friend Margaret, I didn't come to save her. I came because my pa told me to."

"Sure, I can tell her, but she's not exactly my friend."

"Then what are you?" he said.

I lowered my eyes to the floor. His boots were scuffed and a deep scratch cut across both toes. "I'm not sure. We're on the run together."

"Yep. That's Margaret. First sign of trouble, she runs. She's all about saving herself."

Maggie had done plenty of things I didn't like, and I did not know all the history here, but I couldn't walk away without defending her at least a little.

"Look, I'm sure you have good reasons to feel the way you do, but just so you know, she didn't leave Vegas until she made sure that twelve other girls got away safely. She's not all bad."

"So you trust her?"

I snorted. "No!" I said, instantly wishing I hadn't.

"No surprise in that," Luke muttered.

I tried one more time. "Maggie's complicated. She has lots of secrets—" I stopped, thinking if I said any more I'd probably make things worse. "You know, if you've got questions, you should ask her yourself."

"All right," Luke said, and he tipped his hat at me. "See you around, Avie."

I watched him cross over to his house. He'd lost his mom, too—but not the way I did. When Mom died, my heart felt like it was cut up into pieces. I wondered if it was worse to be abandoned.

Snowflakes melted on my cheeks like tears as I hurried toward Beattie's cabin. Up ahead, a man carrying a shotgun came out of his house, and clambered down his porch.

Snow rained on his shaved head, and his black eyes were pinned on me. "You, *chica!*"

Flashbacks exploded in my head. The gun against my eye. The hand on my throat. I forced myself to breathe as I clutched the strap of the gun bag. I sped up. Beattie's was a few hundred feet ahead.

The man leaped toward me through the snow, no coat over his thin shirt. His feet were completely bare. He was going to cut me off. I couldn't reach Beattie's before he got to me.

He swung the shotgun up so it was pointed right at me. "Stop. Do not move." His eyes were wild, like he was seeing something else entirely in front of him—not me, but an enemy.

I froze. I had the gun, but he'd shoot me before I could put the clip in. I wished someone would look out the window. There had to be people in the houses on either side of us.

The man scowled as he blocked the street in front of me. "You are an Outsider. We have rules. No Outsiders."

Don't panic. You have to think, think how you're going to get away from him.

"You got a gun in that bag?"

I knew lying could get me killed. It took all my strength to answer. "Yes."

"Put it down."

I fumbled with the strap on my shoulder.

"NOW!"

I dropped the bag. My heart pounded in my ears, making it

impossible to think. Sweat trickled down my side, and I wished I could unzip my jacket, but I didn't dare.

Isn't anyone going to help me?

"Mr. Gomez!"

The man took his eyes off me and focused on someone behind me. I wanted to turn around and look, but I was afraid to move.

"Who is that?" the man called out.

"It's me, Luke Stanton, Mr. Gomez." Luke sounded like he was greeting an old friend, like he didn't see the barrel pointed at my face.

Gomez squinted and shook his head. "Luke Stanton?"

I listened to the delicate crunch of Luke's boots moving closer.

"Yeah, Ramos, you know. Rogan and Nellie's son."

Luke came up beside me and laid his hand between my shoulder blades. "If I shove you, dive to the left," he whispered.

Ramos' eyes relaxed. "Luke. Where you been, man?" The gun barrel began to lower toward the ground.

Luke shrugged. "Working with Barnabas in the shop. Doing some trapping." His hand fell off my back. "This here's Avie."

The gun swung back up. "She's an Outsider. We don't allow no Outsiders."

Snow caught on my eyelashes, but I didn't blink. My legs couldn't hold me up much longer. "Avie's a refugee," Luke said quietly. "You helped refugees in the army, didn't you, Ramos?"

Ramos nodded like it was all coming back to him. "Yeah, we bandaged them up. Got extra food for the babies."

"You did a good thing, helping refugees."

"Only good thing I did in the war."

"My dad says the same thing." Luke and Ramos shared a look. "We're giving this girl sanctuary, if it's all right with you."

Ramos looked at the snowflakes swirling around us. He swiped his hands over his scalp, then he looked down at his bare feet, confusion on his face.

Without another word, he turned and walked toward his house

and I didn't move an inch until the door closed behind him. "Thank you," I said.

Luke picked the gun bag off the snow. "Let's get you to Beattie's."

I tried to take a step, but couldn't. Luke put his arm through mine. "Ramos probably won't bother you again. The war messed him up. He gets like this sometimes."

Luke walked me to Beattie's like a fireman removing a victim from the scene of a blast. I got the feeling he wasn't helping me because he liked me. It was more like he wanted to prevent Ramos from doing something that might send him over the edge.

At Beattie's porch, Luke hung the gun bag over my shoulder. In that brief moment, standing inches apart, I saw hints of Barnabas in his face. The eyes, the deliberate set of his mouth, his brow.

"Thank you again," I said.

He nodded like I'd embarrassed him, then the door opened, and Beattie stepped out on the porch. "Luke. I see you've met Avie."

"Yes, ma'am." Luke hunched his shoulders and didn't meet Beattie's eyes.

"Why don't you come inside?"

"No, thank you, Pastor Beattie. I best be getting home." He stepped off the porch.

"Carry a message to your mama for me?"

"Yes, ma'am. What is it?"

"Please ask Nellie if she will grant us the pleasure of your company at dinner. Six o'clock."

Luke's head snapped up. He kept his voice completely calm, but he was ticked. "Yes, ma'am." Then he spun on his heel and walked off without saying good-bye.

Beattie took the gun bag off my shoulder. "You are white as a ghost. Something happen?"

I told her about Ramos and Luke coming to my rescue.

"Luke," she said. "Always cool under pressure. But sometimes I wonder if there's a storm inside that boy."

"Is Maggie here?" I asked. Dinner was going to be really interesting.

"No. Did she stop at a neighbor's?" Beattie said.

"Oh, she must still be with Barnabas." I tried not to show I knew about their past and Beattie tried to hide a smile.

"Hmm. Not entirely unexpected," Beattie said. "Come warm up. Keisha's napping. She was up all night while the Johnston baby made up its mind to be born. The midwife's still there, tending to the mother."

I curled up by the fire under a soft throw. I was so tired. So very, very tired. Still, as I dozed off, I couldn't help picturing Luke's face. There was a quiet strength there, like granite—all smooth will and determination.

Yates would have tried to grab the gun from Ramos, but Luke got him to put down his weapon just by talking to him. I wished I was more like Luke. Calm under pressure. Able to keep more of my feelings under control, even when everything around me was going up in flames.

I pictured Luke back in the barn, twirling his little brother and sister. His broad smile and chestnut-colored eyes were the last things I remembered before my thoughts drifted completely away.

73

I slowly eased into consciousness, watching Keisha set bowls out on the table. The room wasn't completely in focus. Maggie was cutting what looked like cornbread. Beattie was in the kitchen.

"Why are you putting out five bowls?" Maggie asked Keisha.

"Beattie invited Luke."

"You didn't," Maggie snapped at Beattie. "I told you I don't want to pressure him."

"You're not, I am. And given that this could be the last chance he will ever have to get to know you, the two of you need to sit across the table from one another."

Keisha caught me staring. "You're awake."

"Not really. My head's pretty fuzzy."

Keisha was even prettier than in her picture. Flawless, caramel-colored skin and thick black eyelashes. The kind of gorgeous that, if she lived in L.A., would turn her Contract auction into a live broadcast.

Beattie handed me a glass of water. "You need to keep hydrated."

"You guys are obsessed with hydration," I answered, but the water tasted so fresh and pure, I drank the whole glass.

"Well, are we going to wait for our guest," Maggie asked, "or are we going to eat this food while it's hot?"

Beattie checked the clock over the mantel. Six-thirty. Her smile was calm, almost sad. "No, we can sit down."

We linked hands for grace. Beattie thanked God, Allah, and Yahweh for protecting Maggie and me on our journey. I wondered if she ever added a little thank-you for Smith & Wesson.

Keisha filled my glass. "Have you ever been to Disney World?"

Beattie and Maggie burst out laughing. "You just helped birth a baby this morning and you want to talk about Disney World?"

"Nobody around here's been," Keisha said back. "So, have you?"

"No," I said, "but I've been to Disneyland."

"We used to go all the time when I lived in Florida."

So Keisha didn't grow up here. "What did you like best?" I asked.

"The teacups. I know they're not exciting, but Mom and I used to spin as fast as we could, and when we got off, we'd stagger around, holding on to each other so we didn't fall down."

"Yeah, I remember the teacups, but my mom and I always rode Dumbo together."

"The one where you press the lever and make the Dumbos fly?"

"Yeah." I smiled, feeling Mom's arms around me, letting me control how high we went.

"Are there any new rides?" Keisha asked.

"I don't know. I haven't been there in a while." I didn't want to tell her Disneyland was closed except on weekends and holidays, and girls my age never went there anyway. Bodyguards hated crowds.

"I heard you're running from a Contract."

My mouth dropped open. I glanced from Maggie to Beattie, not sure what they'd told Keisha or what they wanted me to say.

"Don't look at me," Beattie said.

"Obviously, somebody said something," Maggie said.

"I guess I mentioned something to Nellie," I said.

"Tell one person, you've told the whole town," Beattie said.

"Oh, I didn't know." I bent over my bowl, my cheeks flaming.

"Why did you run?" Keisha asked.

"There's someone, a boy I'm . . . seeing."

"What's he like, your boyfriend?" Keisha said.

"He must be very special," Maggie muttered into her chili. "She dumped a millionaire for him."

"A millionaire?" Keisha gasped. "You could have been rich."

"Keisha. Don't be shallow," Beattie said.

Keisha winced, but she still looked at me, expecting an answer.

"He was cruel. Completely controlling," I said.

"But your boyfriend's nice?"

Nice didn't describe Yates. Risking prison to help girls escape? I searched around for the right word, but all I came up with was, "He's really caring."

"And I'm guessing he's cute," Keisha said.

I bobbed my head, embarrassed at how that made *me* look shallow. "Yeah."

Keisha asked who Yates looked like, and named some TV stars I used to watch on the kids' channel. I picked a guy with dark hair, but that was basically the only similarity. The worst thing that actor ever had to deal with was being chased by paparazzi.

"What is your boyfriend doing with his life?" Beattie said.

"He goes to college, and works part-time at a restaurant. He volunteers at church."

"What is he studying?"

"Social justice."

"A cru-sa-der." Maggie drew out the syllables, baiting me to look at her. "No surprise there."

"Why?" I said.

"Because that's what you are."

"No, I'm not." Mom was a crusader. Sparrow, too. But definitely not me.

"Then how'd you end up here?"

I glared at Maggie, wishing I could smack that smug smile off her face. She was pushing me like she wanted me to get angry.

"You could have stayed silent when the government lied about Sparrow, but you didn't."

"Yeah, but that was just me acting on an insane impulse. I'm not like Sparrow."

"Then why did she choose *you* out of all the girls around her to deliver her message?"

Because she knew I'd do it. Because she knew how I felt about the feds sticking it to us. "I'd never do what Sparrow did."

"What did she do?" Keisha said.

"She set herself on fire on the Capitol steps," Maggie answered.

"She what?"

Beattie reached across the table. "It's a form of political protest. Throughout history, people have immolated themselves to bring attention to war and oppression."

Keisha ignored Beattie's hand. She turned to Maggie. "But how could she do that!"

"Because she was deadly passionate about her cause."

Maggie was ticking me off. "No," I said. "Sparrow was *sick*. People who are passionate about a cause might be so obsessed they take crazy risks or neglect their families or make their entire existence about the cause. But only ones who are really *sick* throw away their lives. Sparrow did *not* have to die."

Maggie's mouth went flat, and I guessed I'd touched a nerve talking about people who neglect their families.

"You regret blasting that message," Maggie said. "And not because you're stuck in backwoods Idaho. You're mad, because you know that now you might never get that perfect life you dreamed about in Canada with your cute, caring, socially aware boyfriend."

A blast of heat roared through me.

"Maggie—" Beattie tried, but Maggie ignored her.

She tapped her finger on the table, punctuating each word. "You can cross that border and reunite with your boyfriend, but your life will *never* be normal. He's probably already seen Sparrow's video, and he's going to ask you about what went down in Vegas. And when he finds out that you're hiding what you've witnessed—that you have evidence that can help bring down the very people he's fighting—"

She was completely wrong. Wrong about me. Wrong about— "You don't know anything about Yates."

"You're fooling yourself."

I stood up, dizzy, hot, and ready to shove Maggie out of that chair. "Screw you." I grabbed my bowl off the table.

She thinks she knows everything. But what if she's right about how I'll never be able to keep Vegas a secret, how Yates will never let it go until he knows the truth?

There was a knock at the door. No one moved, then Beattie chuckled. "I guess we've got company after all. Since you're up, Avie, why don't you get the door."

Great. Now Maggie could face her unfinished business, just like she was making me face mine. I wrenched open the door.

"Hi."

Luke stood in the doorway, a pie steaming in his hands. "Sorry I'm late. Nellie sent this. It's apple berry."

I could feel my cheeks turn as pink as the berries under the crust. "Come in. We saved you a place."

"Hi, Luke," Keisha said as he approached the table.

"Hi, Keisha."

I wondered vaguely if there might be something between them—it's not like there were too many people our age here.

Luke took the empty place across from Maggie. I smiled to myself. Her turn to be in the hot seat.

I was not disappointed. Keisha poured Luke some coffee. Beattie cut into the pie and Luke leaned back in his chair and said, "Who's chasing you, Margaret?"

She sipped her coffee all cool and collected. "It's best we don't discuss that. Let's talk about something else."

Beattie passed around the pie, and Keisha and I exchanged glances. The tension was thick.

"I hear the trapping's been good this year," Maggie tried.

"Yeah, bobcat. Some beaver."

I pictured Luke with a bobcat slung over his shoulders, like a Viking Warrior with golden fur framing his face.

"Barnabas tells me you're building a mandolin," Maggie said.

"I'm doing the sanding is all."

Maggie's smile was as tight as a guitar string. "How's school coming?"

Heat was coming off Luke's body, and I caught his warm soap smell. "I'm almost done," he said. "I'll have my diploma come April."

Beattie piped up. "He's done well, Maggie."

Maggie weighed her fork before she spoke. "I've got funds set aside in case you'd like to go to college. I could arrange an identity for you."

I barely knew Luke, but even I knew Maggie was screwing up.

"I'm not like you," Luke said, his voice warning her. "I *like* it here. I've got everything I need."

"I talked to your father—"

"Which father? The one you ran out on or the one you palmed me off on so you could go to college?"

Maggie flinched, and I almost felt sorry for her. "I haven't had a chance to talk to Nellie and Rogan, but Barnabas and I hope you'll continue your education—"

Luke pulled a thick book out of his jacket and slammed it on the table: *Stillness at Appomattox*. "I read plenty."

Maggie stared at the cover.

"I don't want your world," Luke said. "Full of theories and philosophies and high-minded principles—but not one ounce of what counts." He stood up, almost knocking over his chair. "Thanks for the coffee, Pastor Beattie."

I was surprised by how gently Luke closed the door on his way out.

"Happy now?" Maggie snapped at Beattie

Keisha and I hunkered down over our pie.

"Yes," Beattie said. "Finally, you're talking."

We finished the pie in silence, and the way Maggie choked hers down it must have tasted like regret. I didn't know why she'd done what she did, but she was living with the consequences. Maybe that's why Maggie had blistered me with that speech about how I could run off to Canada and reunite with Yates, but my life would never be normal again. Because she'd learned that sometimes what you did couldn't be fixed and it couldn't be erased.

I only hoped that, as far as I was concerned, she was wrong.

74

Keisha got me alone in her room after dinner, and bombarded me with questions about Yates and what it was like to have a boyfriend.

And each one I answered made my heart ache. I didn't know if he was safe. If Hawkins was having him tailed. How long I'd have to wait to contact him after I got to Canada, *if* I got there.

Then Keisha wanted to hear all about the world outside Salvation. About fast food and fashion and music, and while I tried to answer, I kept having to explain why I never got to go to arcades or movie theaters or music concerts—places where it was dark and crowded, and Roik couldn't control the situation.

I had to explain that love songs had basically disappeared now that hardly anybody fell in love anymore. How most shopping malls were boarded up, because there weren't many shoppers, and girls could only go to secure gated ones like the Beverly Center. It wasn't the world Keisha remembered. And it wasn't one Beattie'd ever told her about.

I spread out my sleeping bag on Keisha's rug, and she dozed off. But when I closed my eyes, I couldn't sleep.

Finally, I sat up against her bureau and wrapped the sleeping bag tight around me. Outside, wind blew the icy snow so it sounded like rice hitting the windows. Keisha was burrowed down in her covers, and I couldn't shake a story she had told me.

Her older brother had sold her to Cecelia for a Camaro. Custom paint job, V-8 engine, spoiler, aluminum rims.

Cecelia knew Keisha's mom from the army, and when Cecelia heard she'd died, she tracked down Keisha's brother. He didn't want an eight-year-old hanging around his neck and was a day away from dumping her at an orphan camp. All Cecelia had to do was toss him the keys and he was gone.

Keisha's brother threw her away like she was trash.

I covered my face with my hands, glad no one could see me. The world was full of messed-up things but I'd never really thought about anybody's life but mine. I lived in my rich-girl cocoon, completely focused on what *I* was going through. What *I* didn't get to do. I had passed the L.A. orphan ranch probably once a week for five years, but did I ever think about the girls inside?

The girls I went to school with, Dayla, Sparrow, Portia, Sophie, we didn't have a lot of freedom, but none of us had a brother who'd sell us for a *car*. None of us became escorts like Splendor so we could buy out our sisters' Contracts.

No, we were protected by gates and bodyguards and dads who could afford to feed us and clothe us and send us to a fancy school.

I laid my head down on my knees, feeling horrible. *I'm so selfish.*

Even when Mom made me go to church and serve that free Thanksgiving dinner, the next day I barely thought about the people I'd seen. But not Mom.

She always met someone who would be her next crusade. Somebody who needed a heavier coat or qualified for free medical care they didn't know about.

I remembered getting mad, because the day after Thanksgiving was supposed to be *my* day with Mom, but she'd be out, taking care of somebody else.

I heard her calm and loving voice in my head. "If I don't speak up for people in need, honey, who will?"

Mom wasn't silent. She cared about people and fought for them. Yates, too. It's time I did the same.

75

It snowed for a day and a half, blowing so hard that I couldn't see past the porch rail. Somewhere out there, agents were hunting Maggie and me, and I had no clue how close they were to finding us.

Stuck inside, unable to get out and run, I bounced off the walls like a squirrel in a cardboard box. The electricity in the cabin was barely cranking, and it wasn't like Beattie had a Sportswall to distract me.

She and Keisha tried to keep me busy, kneading bread and playing marathon card games, but I couldn't keep Yates out of my head. I was sure I'd set the dogs on him by calling him from the truck. The feds chasing Maggie and me probably intercepted the phone signal.

And you didn't have to be a genius to guess that if Hawkins hired Retrievers to track me down, the first thing the professional hunters would do is monitor Yates' phone. I had no way to warn him even through a friend, because my phone was completely useless. No reception, or at least that's what Beattie told me.

Maggie kept to herself by the fire, holding a beat-up paperback, but rarely turning a page. I felt her eyes on me every time I circled the room, and when, around noon on the second day, I started to pace along the windows she snapped, "Would you stop that, for God's sake. No one's looking for us in this."

I glared at her. "You know damn well they are," I said.

If a look was a shove, Maggie's would have nailed me to the wall. "The only thing you can think about is saving your own skin," she said. "Nothing and no one else matters."

"You're wrong," I threw back.

"I wish I was."

I turned my back on her, hating Maggie for believing that about me, and hating myself for the things I'd said and done to make her believe it.

The wasp sting of what she said was still sharp hours later when the snow finally quit. Maggie made me give her my phone, and she took off to see Barnabas. She'd barely left before Beattie took me out to the porch and handed me a pair of cross-country skis. "Being snowbound can bring out the worst in people. I recommend a dose of fresh air," she said.

It wasn't going for a run, but it was close enough, I thought. I stuck my head in the house. "Keisha, you want to ski with me?"

"Not unless I have to," she called back.

Beattie smiled. "Winter's not her season." She wrapped a bright red scarf around my neck. "We don't want the neighbors mistaking you for a deer."

The wind had scooped the snow into white drifts and blue hollows, and it sparkled like someone had poured sugar sprinkles over it. Across the road, a boy and a girl were digging out a chicken coop while their older brother pushed snow off the roof of their house.

I headed for the far end of the valley. Jemima waved as I passed the barn. She was brushing off the solarskin with a broom while Caleb dug out the solar water barrels.

Running on tiptoes up the frozen valley, I got into a rhythm. *Left right glide breathe left right glide breathe.* It felt good, pushing my body after being cooped up so long. My head began to clear, but the cold and the altitude made me feel like I was dragging a parachute. I had to stop, drink, and catch my breath every hundred meters or so.

Someone had been this way already today. I followed the snowshoe tracks until they veered off and headed up into the pines.

At the last house in Salvation, a half-dozen doghouses on stilts poked above the snow. Huskies lounged on the roofs, ignoring me. Then a man with a braided beard hauled a dog sled into the yard. The dogs sprang up, barking and yipping and spinning on their chains. I watched the man harness them to his sled and bang! The sled shot straight across the valley and disappeared behind a hill.

Look at them run, I thought. Those dogs live to pull that sled. They're not conflicted about whether to go. They just go.

I wish I could be like them. Running for joy, not worried about what's ahead or behind.

But instead, I was out here, trying not to blow up from inside, thinking of everything I'd done and hadn't done. What I should do now.

The narrow valley went on for a mile more. I focused on what was in front of me, until my thoughts began to straighten out like the tracks my skis had carved in the snow.

All I can do is go forward. I can't go back and change anything I did. I just have to keep going.

When I reached the end of the valley, I turned. The sun had colored the distant peaks blush pink against a sky as clear blue as Venetian glass.

It was beautiful, I thought, trying to catch my breath. Like a picture postcard of the most idyllic place on earth. Except that it wasn't where I should be.

I need to stop fighting Maggie. I need to work with her to get the evidence we're carrying into Canada where it will be safe.

I need to be the person that Mom and Ms. A expected me to be. The person Yates believes in. That's the only way I can have a happily-ever-after.

Because I couldn't live a lie with Yates. Or myself.

I fit my skis into the tracks they'd made and headed back to Salvation. I'd only gone a hundred yards when Luke stepped out of the woods. Spying me, he walked forward, a rifle strapped to his back, his snowshoes sinking into the snow, and then waited for me to catch up.

"Nice to get out," he said. His brown eyes welcomed me.

"I was going crazy shut up inside," I said. "I needed to clear my head."

"Did you?"

I smiled at the peace flowing through my body. "Yeah, I think I did."

"The mountains'll do that." A quiet smile lit his face.

"I can see why you'd never want to leave here."

"I got basically everything I need."

I couldn't resist trying to open him up. "Is there anything you don't have that you'd like?"

"Not really, but—" I felt him change direction. "I guess just once I'd like to compete in a rodeo. Barnabas took me to one in Idaho Falls last year."

"Yeah? What event?"

"Barrel racing. I've got a mare who takes turns like nothing you've ever seen. I think we could take the prize."

"Is she at winter pasture?"

He smiled. "How'd you know that?"

"Sarah."

"Yeah, we'll herd Sweeney and the rest back up here in April."

"So why can't you compete?"

"Well, we don't leave Salvation much, and not having a legal identity makes it difficult Outside."

"Yeah, I guess it would." Being with Luke was easy. I wanted to linger here in the frosted beauty of the woods. "Were you out hunting?" I said, nodding at his rifle.

"Nah. Hunting season's in the fall. I was checking my traps, but I carry the gun in case I run into something."

"Like what?"

"Wolf."

I swallowed. "I didn't know there were wolves out here."

"Don't worry. They usually don't come around when elk's plentiful. They wouldn't bother hunting a scrawny little skier."

"Scrawny?"

"Compared to an elk." Luke ducked his head. "I'm sorry about the other night. I guess I ruined your dinner."

"Too late. Maggie had already accomplished that."

"She give you a hard time?"

"Yeah, but everything she said, I needed to hear."

"Truth hurts sometimes."

Luke was a good guy. It seemed wrong and a waste that we'd be gone in a couple days, and he was no closer to knowing Maggie than he was before she showed up. This was probably their last chance to fix things, and Luke was too angry and Maggie too closed off to try.

"Maggie heard you the other night," I said. I saw a glimmer in Luke's eyes. "I know you're really angry with her—"

Luke groaned and looked away. "Could you leave it alone?"

I'd backed off on way too many things in the past. I had to say something that would get him to talk to her. "Maggie won't tell you what she's been working on—but if you knew, you might—"

"I might, what? Forgive her?"

"I don't know if you'd forgive her—but you'd realize that she cares deeply about people, and justice, and she's put her life on the line to save others."

"For someone you say you don't trust and you claim is not your friend, you think pretty highly of her."

I smiled at my contradictions. "You guys should talk to each other. We're leaving and there's a really good chance you'll never see her again."

Luke was quiet for a moment. "I guess that means there's a good chance I'll never see you again."

He was looking at me with something like—curiosity, or waiting. I bent down and checked my bindings. "Maggie and I are heading out as soon as we can. Canada's border might be closing, so we need to get out before it does."

Luke turned and was listening hard. Way off in the distance, I heard a whirr like an engine or a chain saw. "We've got to get back." He jerked me to my feet and took off.

The sound got louder and louder the closer we got to town, turning into an air-churning roar. We raced for the shelter of the buildings. Whatever was making that noise was coming from the road to civilization.

76

We were almost to the barn, when Maggie burst out of the wood shop, her shirt undone under her jacket and her jeans crammed into her boots. Her hair was wild around her face and she slammed a clip into her gun. "Do you see anything?" she yelled.

"It's a snowmobile," Luke answered. "Stay here," he told me, and ran ahead.

I undid my skis and tossed them aside. Maggie dragged me behind a woodpile, and we looked past the church to the way we'd come in the other night.

Barnabas dropped to his knees beside us. He was carrying a sleek black weapon that looked like the lethal love child of a rifle and a crossbow. It was fitted with a scope and a steel-tipped arrow. A silent assassin.

"Definitely a snowmobile," he said. "We're looking at two riders max."

"You think it's the guys who were after us?" I said.

"Don't know, but if it is, they'll be carrying an arsenal," he answered.

My hands felt hopelessly empty. The gun Maggie gave me was back at Beattie's, a hundred yards away.

Barnabas stood up. "I'm going up on Ramos' roof. Get a clean shot when they come around the church." He bounded across the road.

I peeked over the stacked wood. At every house, men and women were out on their porches, and each one of them had a rifle in their arms. The sound came closer, and they ducked down or retreated into the shadows.

A dot of red strobed through the trees. Nobody moved.

A snowmobile zoomed up to the edge of the woods, and the person on the back got off. His legs broke through the snow crust, and he stumbled to get his footing in the thigh-high snow. The snowmobile turned around and tore off. The person it left behind lumbered toward the church, arms flailing as he tried to steady himself.

Maggie peered through a stubby little scope. "It's a young guy. If he's got a weapon, it's under his clothes."

I could see Barnabas from where we crouched. His crossbow was trained on the intruder. I bet fifty more ex-military were ready to blast the guy's head off as soon as he got closer.

"I don't know about this," Maggie muttered. "You don't use a snowmobile to surprise someone."

The guy had to be crazy or completely clueless. If he knew anything about these people, he'd know you don't show up in Salvation unannounced.

And that's when I realized who it was. I grabbed the scope from Maggie and took one glance before I leaped up. "Yates! Yates!"

"Avie!" he cried, and started running toward me.

Maggie tried to grab me, but I twisted away and scrambled out into the open. "Stop! Don't move!" I shouted.

I ran up the unplowed road, sinking to my knees in snow. "Don't shoot! Don't shoot!" I yelled. "He's a friend."

Tears blinded me before they froze on my cheeks. I ran, but I couldn't breathe. The air was so cold and thin, and Yates so close and yet so far away.

I slipped and fell, and Yates bounded toward me. "Stay right there," I yelled. "I'm coming."

The snow had soaked my pants. They stuck to my knees and almost pulled me down.

I fell into his outstretched arms. "Yates. Yates! I can't believe you're here."

He crushed me to him. "You're alive," he said, like he was trying to make himself believe it.

"Stand down!" I heard Barnabas yell. "Stand down, everyone, until we see what we've got here."

I locked my arms around Yates' neck. "You found me." My lips met his, and we drank each other in, frozen lips and warm breath. *I'm not dreaming. You're real.* "I didn't think I'd see you again. Not for months."

His eyes were red, and he hadn't shaved in a couple of days. "I told you I'd find you," he said. He went to kiss me again, but I held him back. "Wait," I said, "there are about a hundred people watching us."

Yates rested his head on mine. "Okay, as long as I can hold you."

"How did you get here? How did you find me?"

"I caught a ride with a trucker delivering tortillas to Salt Lake. He found me a ride to Boise."

"And who was that guy on the snowmobile?"

"The pastor at the Pentecostal church. I told him I was looking for Salvation."

"But how did you even know to look for this place?"

"Mrs. Kessler got a call from a man who said he had a message from Helen."

Helen, you diehard romantic, thank you.

Yates jerked his head like something caught his eye. "Check it out."

Barnabas, Ramos, Rogan, and a dozen other people marched toward us, weapons in their hands. "This doesn't look good," Yates said.

"It will be okay. I'll tell them you're a friend. They don't need to worry about you." I kept my eyes on Ramos. He was twitchy, but at least he had boots on. Luke was nowhere in sight and I wondered if anyone else could keep Ramos from losing it.

"What's with the guy with the crossbow?" Yates whispered.

"Barnabas? He's a carpenter. He builds guitars."

"That's a special forces weapon."

"He's ex-military. A lot of people here are."

"Great."

The crowd stopped about twenty feet away. They talked in low voices, while Barnabas came forward. "Who's this, Avie?"

"My name's Yates." Yates straightened up and trained his eyes on Barnabas. They were the only weapons Yates had.

"All right, Yates. Why are you here?"

"I came to help Avie."

"How do we know you're for real?"

I moved in front of Yates, daring them to shoot me. "He's my friend. He helped me escape my Contract."

"Open your coat, Yates. Let's see if you've got any weapons on you."

Yates raised his arms. "Sure, check me out. I'm not packing." He tore off his coat and held it over his head while he turned around so everyone could see he was clean.

It was way too cold to put Yates through this little show. "Okay, he did what you wanted," I said. "Are you satisfied?"

Barnabas looked at me just long enough to let me know he didn't take to being pushed around, then he nodded at Yates. "Go ahead. Put it back on."

Beattie'd been watching from inside the crowd, but now she stepped around to the front. "The Council's asking for a meeting. I think it's clear this young man is not an immediate threat. Everyone, you can go about your business. We'll let you know when the Council's ready to meet."

Yates and I stood there while the crowd broke up and people returned to their houses. I couldn't figure out why the Council was so amped up. It was obvious Yates wasn't dangerous.

"Is there someplace we can be alone?" Yates asked. "How about the barn?"

Forty goats and Jonas and Sarah barging in and out. "Definitely not." I turned Yates toward the church, and that's when I saw Luke behind us. I don't know how he'd circled around without us seeing him, but he did.

"This way," I said.

77

We knocked the snow off our boots and stepped inside the church. It was dim in the falling light. I led Yates up to the balcony, holding on to him the whole time. I didn't trust him to really be here, feeling almost as if he could be just a figment of my imagination.

"It's a little warmer up here," I said.

"Not much." Yates lowered himself to the floor and propped his back against the wall. He took my hand and drew me onto his lap. My heart pounded as he slowly unzipped his coat, then mine.

We pressed together, soaking in each other's warmth. I looked into his blue, blue eyes and wondered if he could see the selfish, messed-up parts of me. I was changing and I wanted him to see that—not the rest.

"I can't believe you're here," I said.

"Believe it."

"You could have gotten killed."

"Yeah, but I couldn't stay in L.A., knowing they were hunting you. I couldn't do it."

I needed to tell him about Sparrow and the secret files I was carrying.

He pressed his lips to mine and there were no words, just touches, kissing away Now and Reality and This Can't Be.

"You'd better not be doing what I think you're doing!" Beattie's voice cut through the church.

We froze. She was staring at us through the railing and Maggie was with her.

"And at the feet of our Lord Jesus," Beattie moaned.

I looked up, and the cross was right over our heads. I fell off Yates. "Sorry, Beattie!"

Yates scrambled to his feet. "Sorry. Didn't mean to be disrespectful . . ."

Beattie laughed. "Oh, get down here."

We came down the stairs, and Beattie met us on the landing. "Time to summon the Council," she said.

That didn't sound like a good thing, not the way she said it.

Beattie pushed open a door on the landing I hadn't noticed before. She stepped into a windowless room and fiddled with a panel. Recorded church bells clanged over our heads—just like a special ring at school to tell you there's an assembly.

"Brace yourself for the fireworks," Beattie muttered.

Maggie leaned against a wall while the Council assembled. Beattie made Yates and me sit down beside her at a table. The first person in the door was Ramos. He picked at a spot on his cheek and stared at me and Yates.

"We'd better let Maggie do the talking," I said so only Yates could hear. "I don't want to screw up and tick these people off even worse."

The rest of the Council arrived: Rogan and Nellie. Barnabas. Jemima and Caleb. Mr. and Mrs. Flores. I hadn't met the others, but soon all the chairs at the long table were taken. Then Luke came through the door and Rogan tried to send him home.

"You can't keep me out," Luke fired back. "Council meetings are open to everyone over eighteen."

Rogan gave Luke a look that said there would be hell to pay when he got home. I didn't have a good reason for not wanting Luke here, just an uncomfortable feeling that he was judging Yates.

Beattie had barely called the meeting to order, when Ramos jumped in. "We have rules. No Outsiders!" He jerked a finger at Maggie. "First she brings her—" I cringed as he targeted me. "And then he shows up." Ramos pointed to Yates. "It's no good!"

Beattie folded her hands on the table. "Maggie's not an Outsider, Ramos."

The man across from me leaned back and hooked his thumbs in his belt. "I want to know why you're here."

He was talking to me, but Nellie must have seen me hesitate. "She's running from a Contract," she said quietly.

"That right?" the man said.

I nodded.

"What about you?" he asked Yates. "How do you fit into this?"

"I'm her friend."

"Boyfriend?"

"Yes."

Luke was very still and I could feel him paying attention to every little thing.

"Great." The man slapped his leg. "Now we're going to have some GD Retrievers sniffing around."

"I don't think so," Yates said.

I shot a look at him. *Why did you say that?*

"Your dad is trying to break the Contract."

I shook my head, finding it impossible to believe. "How do you know?"

"Gerard. He told me your dad is trying to lead a coup at Biocure. He and some of the board members found a new shareholder rich enough to buy Hawkins out."

"So, I'll be free?"

"Looks like it."

The shock made me dizzy. *Free.*

"What about you, Maggie," Rogan said. "Why'd you come? You never brought any girls here before."

Maggie cocked her head at her brother.

"You're mixed up in something," he said.

"It's time to come clean, Maggie," Barnabas said. "This boy managed to find you. You know the others are probably right behind him."

Ramos eyed her like a wolf about to spring. "What's going on here?"

"Calm down, Ramos," Beattie said.

"You tell us what's going on!"

"It was my fault." Everyone turned to me. "I angered some power-ful people."

Ramos leaped up. "Who? Who's coming for you?" His hand hov-ered over a knife strapped to his thigh.

Yates was on his feet. "Hey, back off."

"Mr. Gomez," Beattie said calmly, "if you would take your seat, please."

Yates and Ramos glared at each other. The table was hot with tension. I held my breath as they lowered themselves into their seats.

"Maggie," Barnabas said. "Tell people the truth so they know what you're up against."

Maggie approached the table with her head bowed. Her hands were on her hips and I got the feeling that the fight she'd been wag-ing against the Paternalists was wearing her down. "You know I sup-port the Resistance."

Rogan shook his head. "You promised you'd never bring it here."

"I didn't plan on it," Maggie said.

Maggie had dragged me into this deeper than I ever wanted to be, but I couldn't let them stick the whole blame on her. "Maggie didn't intend to come here. The federal agents showed up just like that and we had to run."

Ramos jabbed his finger at me and I wanted to shrink into obliv-ion. "You telling us the feds are after you!"

"That's right," Maggie answered.

"Then you tell us what you got us mixed up in!" Ramos said.

"All right. But before we do, I think anyone who doesn't want to know, should have the option to leave," Maggie said.

"I agree," Beattie said. "Anyone who wants to, may go."

No one got up.

The Council grilled Maggie and Yates and me.

Listening to Maggie answer them, I learned things I'd never have gotten from the news reports. After the Scarpanol disaster left the economy barely breathing, men were mostly focused on protecting their families and holding on to their homes. The Paternalists rode into office with a promise to rebuild and not enough women voters to stop them.

Maggie laid out what she'd learned in her years of partying with the Paternalist leaders, how Fletcher and his gang were quietly and systematically limiting what girls and women could do, and how she'd uncovered that Vice President Jouvert was secretly supporting them.

"But the President has railed against the Paternalists," Rogan said. "I guess this explains why he hasn't been able to cut them down to size, not with his own VP working against him."

"Someone's got to expose Jouvert before he's nominated for president next year," I heard Barnabas mutter.

"So you two are witnesses," Nellie said. For the first time I saw her look at Maggie with sympathy.

"We're not just witnesses," Maggie told her. "We're carrying evidence that could impeach Vice President Jouvert and force Senator Fletcher to resign if we can get it in the right hands."

That's when I realized that, despite everything I'd heard Maggie reveal, she hadn't said a word about Sparrow's final, deadly message now back in my pocket.

"Who's going to touch your evidence?" Rogan said. "Any news service or blogger who puts it on their site's going to get shut down."

I thought about Sparrow's software. The government couldn't kill millions of copies if I could blast them through the paternal controls to every Princess phone in the U.S.

"Right now there are people inside the government and out who support Gen S rights. I know at least one congressman who's sympathetic," Maggie said, "although he's keeping it quiet." She smiled ironically at me. "You met him."

Congressman Paul? I was shocked at first, but it made sense. His hands all over me and his tongue in my ear? He was playing the loyal Paternalist jerk in front of his congressional dirtbag friends.

Barnabas and Maggie laid out the plan they'd been working on. The three of us would ski out in a day or two and make contact with Exodus in eastern Washington so they could pick us up and hide us. Now we had to move up the timetable and add Yates.

The Council calmed down after hearing we were leaving, but then things turned red-hot.

"Something's bothering me," Ramos said, turning to Yates. "You said Pastor Isaac drove you out here on that snowmobile, but how did you find him?"

"I asked a bunch of ministers around town how to find Salvation. He was the only one who didn't think I was looking to be saved."

"You talk to Reverend Frank?"

Half the people around the table exchanged looks.

"Yeah. He said I'd find salvation through prayer and reading the Good Book. What's the problem?"

"He left us a few years ago under bad circumstances," Rogan muttered.

"I sincerely hope," Beattie said, "that whoever's looking for you doesn't find Taylor Frank."

"Or those snowmobile tracks that lead right to us," Barnabas said.

"I don't understand," I said. "Won't you be safe after Maggie and Yates and I leave?"

Barnabas shook his head. "Whoever's after you won't stop until they've eliminated the danger." He looked from face to face. "Nobody who's seen or talked to you or harbored you in their home is safe."

Yates clenched his jaw and swallowed hard. I gripped his hand.

You didn't do anything wrong, I told him with my eyes. Yates shook his head.

"Stop scaring everyone. You don't know that, Barnabas," Beattie said.

"I was in Langley for six years. I know how they think."

I glanced at Yates. "CIA," he whispered.

I respected Beattie, but I trusted Barnabas to know what they would or would not do.

"We'll leave before sunup," Barnabas said. "Luke, Rogan, we need to go warn people what's coming. Maggie, take Yates and Avie back to my house and get the packs ready. With any luck, you three will be gone and I'll be back in Salvation before the bad guys get here."

I got up from my seat. Luke glanced at me and turned away. I couldn't read his face, but if I was him, I'd be mad as hell if some Outsider arrived and blew my life apart. My neck was pink hot. That easy friendship Luke and I had out in the woods was gone. Yates felt for my hand, but I pretended I didn't know he was doing it.

Maggie stood in the doorway. She wouldn't let Yates and me out until she saw Ramos go inside his house. As we went down the steps into the open, she kept her eyes on his house, and her hand on her gun.

She never said it, but it was obvious: she didn't want Ramos killing us before we had a chance to make things right.

79

It was barely any work to put the packs together, because every house kept a couple bug out bags ready to go. That's the beauty of TEOT-

WAWKI, I thought, going through the equipment in the bags. If you believe you could be attacked at any time, then you always have what you need to survive: duct tape, signal mirror, compass, topographic map, matches, hand shovel, knife.

Maggie walked Yates and me through how to use each item. How to find a route on the map. How to fire up the Kelly Kettle so we'd have drinking water. How to dig a snow trench so we wouldn't freeze to death.

"Why do we need to know this?" I asked her. "It's not that far to the main road, and it's not supposed to snow."

"Actually, we decided it's too risky to go out that way. There's a back way, a trail we use to take the horses down to the wintering grounds. From here, it's about ten miles to Horseshoe Bend, but there are homesteads closer than that."

The back way. I guessed that was where the guy with the dog sled disappeared to earlier.

We were almost done packing when Jemima stopped by. "Here," she said, handing me a stack of pants and shirts and a woolly hat. "I rustled these up for you and Yates. Those clothes you're wearing won't keep you anywhere near as warm or dry as these."

The second I touched the pants I knew they weren't castoffs. They were expensive survival gear. I tried to hand them back to her. "These are too nice."

"Keep them. Everybody'll be safer. "

Get wet and cold and we put everybody at risk. Not just Maggie and Barnabas. If we survived, they survived.

"Tell them thank you for me?" I said.

Jemima waited until Maggie stepped out of the room before she said, "Caleb and I thought maybe you'd like some privacy. If you want to use our cabin tonight, it's yours."

My cheeks burned. I wasn't sure how I felt about spending the night alone with Yates.

But he looked Jemima in the eyes. "Thanks, sounds great," he said.

"It's not finished," she warned. "There's no running water or electricity, but the woodstove works."

"We don't need anything else, do we?" Yates said.

I shook my head no, and wrapped Jemima in a hug. "This is really sweet of you."

"You're like Rapunzel and the prince," she said, her voice fairy-tale soft. "Or Romeo and Juliet."

"Yeah, I guess we are."

"Thanks, again, Jemima," Yates said. He kissed me on the cheek. "I'm going to go take a shower."

Jemima let herself out and I got back to stuffing the packs. I was in love with Yates, so why hesitate about spending the night together?

Because I barely know him. I swallowed. Not true, I told myself. *I've known Yates my whole life.*

But not like this.

Maggie and I finished up the packs. When Yates reappeared, he wrapped both arms around me and nuzzled my neck. "Thought I'd never get that tortilla smell off me."

"You smell good," I said, my heart beating like a rabbit's.

"Come on," Maggie said. "Let's get these packs over to the back door."

Yates and Barnabas were each going to carry twenty pounds more than Maggie and me. Still, I wondered if I'd make it ten miles with a full pack. I hadn't broken any records earlier when I wasn't lugging a thing.

Keisha showed up, carrying a steel pail with a dish towel over the top. "Beattie sent you a picnic dinner," she said to us. Warm, delicious smells of bread and some kind of stew wafted into the room.

Maggie tossed me a sleeping bag and lobbed a second one at Yates. "Go on. Enjoy the time alone. After tonight, we'll be stuck together until we get out of this."

Yates and I stood on Barnabas' porch, sleeping bags slung over our shoulders. "Ready?" he asked, swinging the pail toward Caleb and Jemima's.

I looked into his eyes. I wanted time alone with Yates, no interruptions, no threat of being discovered by Roik. But I wasn't sure about the rest. "Yes, totally," I lied.

Cold burned my cheeks, but I was too hot to cover my face. I was conscious of every little thing: snow crunching under our boots, a guitar singing into the night, my flashlight's blue-white oval, Yates' shoulder bumping mine.

The moon wasn't up yet, but the sky was so coated with stars it was like looking at it through gauze. I paused in the middle of the road, needing a moment to center myself before going into the cabin.

"What are you thinking about?" Yates said.

"How much I've changed."

He pulled me along the path. "I don't think you're different. I just think you're *more*."

"More of what?"

We stepped up onto the porch. "More of what I've always liked about you: you're ballsy, independent. Real."

Mom's voice whispered in my ear. *Choose the man who thinks you are beautiful just the way you are, who wants to hear what you have to say, who urges you to follow your heart.*

I smiled at him. "Thanks."

Yates opened the door and we stepped into the echoey dark. I reached for the light switch, forgetting there wasn't one. We passed our flashlights over the room. A hurricane lamp stood on the half-built kitchen counter. The room smelled of freshly sawed wood, and Caleb or maybe Jemima had lined up the hammers and screwdrivers and boxes of nails in a tidy row on the sawhorse table.

"Jemima said the firewood's on the back porch."

I followed Yates out and held the flashlight while he loaded up his arms. Then I lit the lamp while he got the fire started. The wood walls glowed golden yellow, but I could still see my breath.

I lifted the towel off the pail. A loaf of bread sat on top of two plates. When I lifted them, a small crock of stew steamed in my face.

I came around the corner with the food. Yates sat by the stove, the fire glow lighting his face. He smiled at me as he blew into a large air mattress.

"Let me know if you get tired," I said.

My fingers fumbled with the ties on the sleeping bags. I rolled them out and they lay side by side, before I realized how awkward and useless they were this way. I didn't look up, but I felt Yates watch me zip them together.

"Done." Yates spread the air mattress in front of the woodstove. Flames crackled in the stove's iron belly and we sat cross-legged on the mattress and pulled the sleeping bag over us like a quilt.

I dished out the stew and Yates tore into it. "When was the last time you ate?" I asked him.

"This morning. I caught the $2.99 All You Can Eat Flapjack Special at the Rise and Shine Diner."

I watched him eat, marveling that he'd ridden to Salt Lake in a tortilla truck and searched Boise until he found someone who'd take him to Salvation.

You promised you'd find me, and you did. But you probably shouldn't have.

I took a deep breath. I'd come clean at the Council meeting. I didn't have any secrets from Yates anymore.

"You know you might have to hide out in Canada with us?" I said. "You probably won't be safe in the U.S."

"I know."

Those men pursuing us weren't going to give up until Maggie and I were permanently silenced. "Are you sure you're ready to give up your life in California—school, all your friends, the movement?"

Yates dropped his fork on his plate, and gently ran his finger down my cheek. I tilted my face toward his. "I gave up my old life when I joined Exodus," he said. "The minute I did my first extract, I knew I'd have to run someday."

I nodded as he took my empty plate from my lap. He slipped his hands into my hair and pulled me ever so gently closer. "Forget about the world right now," he said. His mouth brushed mine, and our lips did a shy, slow dance.

Together, apart, together—my feelings jumbled with each touch. Excited, afraid, sure, unsure.

We fell back and drew the down bag over us like a tent. In the green-tinted dark, our jackets crackled, and we felt for the zippers and teased them open. We murmured between kisses, our bodies pressed together, warmth flowing through the layers of cotton and flannel separating our skin.

Yates slipped his hand under my shirt and clasped the tender skin of my waist. I drew in my breath and he went to pull away. "I want you," I whispered, and knitted my fingers into his. "But I'm not ready."

He rested his forehead on mine. "We don't have to do anything. I'm not in a hurry. All I really want is to lie here with you and be together."

His eyes told me he meant it.

I got very still. Here we were in this funny little cabin in the middle of nowhere and as wacky as this place was, it was filled with love. The love Caleb and Jemima were building into it, and the caring Keisha and Beattie showered on us, and the love Yates and I felt for each other.

I guided his hand back to my waist, carefully setting it down outside my shirt. I wasn't ready to sleep with Yates, but I knew I would be someday, and for now I wanted to hold on to that hope for someday as hard as I could. I smiled and lifted my face to kiss him.

We moved slowly, our fingers exploring and mapping each other's bodies. Starting, stopping, talking. Each moment so rich with everything we'd been denied that Salvation and Time and the World and Fear disappeared.

80

I lay on my side, watching the flames through the grate in the pot-bellied stove. Yates slept, one arm tucked over me, hugging me to his chest.

If he wasn't next to me, I'd swear everything that had happened that day was a free fall of my imagination. But Yates was next to me and he was real.

I could be free. Soon, Hawkins might not own me anymore. I turned that over and over in my head like something I'd picked up and didn't quite recognize.

Hawkins wasn't the kind of guy who just gave up. Even if Dad forced him out of Biocure, Hawkins wouldn't go quietly. I counted the days and realized he'd launched his campaign. I doubted either he or Ho wanted me to turn up on the talk-show circuit and tell my story: "Ex-fiancée Dishes About Soon-to-Be-Gov."

Even if I was legally free of Hawkins, he probably wasn't out of my life.

"You're awake," Yates murmured. "Can't sleep?"

I snuggled in closer. "I'm fine. Just thinking."

"What about?"

"About Hawkins and my Contract." I saw Dad and me standing on the edge of the cliff. Dad telling me that Hawkins had trapped him, too. "Dad's probably thrilled somebody's buying Hawkins out. He hated Hawkins taking over."

"Your dad's leaving Biocure."

I flipped over so I could see Yates' face. "No!"

"Yeah, he has to give up the presidency and all his stock as part of the deal."

I shook my head. "I can't believe it. Biocure was Dad's baby."

I saw Dad rattling around our empty house, turning on the

Sportswall and watching for about a minute before he clicked it off. The only thing Dad had was work. And me.

Dad give up Biocure for *me*? The enormity hit me: his life's work. His *dream*! "I need to call him, but I can't. Not from here."

"It'll be okay. In a few days, we'll be in Canada. You can call him then." Yates reached over his head and felt around. I jumped as his icy phone brushed my skin. He sat up and played with the screen. "Here. I was going to save this, but . . ."

There was a picture of me and Mom eating fish tacos on the boardwalk at Venice Beach. Then the picture blurred and changed to me and Dayla at her Sweet Sixteen, smiling madly, waving our arms to the pounding music. Then the photo changed again to Dad lying on the couch with his eyes closed and five-year-old me asleep on his chest, a sea of picture books on the floor beside us. I checked the number in the corner of the screen. Three hundred.

"And I loaded them onto a site, PhotoForever, so no matter what, you'll always have them."

I set my hand on my heart. "How did you—"

"Roik searched your digital files, trying to track you down. After Hawkins and your dad fired him, Roik sold them to me."

Roik's help never came cheap. "This must have cost you a lot."

Yates shrugged. "Don't worry about it."

But Yates didn't have access to a lot of money. The only thing he had was . . . "You gave him your motorcycle."

"Yeah, but bikes can be replaced. Your family can't."

I was smiling, but I was choking up. "How did you know?"

"After your phone signal died, I figured Ruby made you toss it. The way you took off so last-minute, I guessed you must have left the other things you wanted to take."

"Yeah, I lost everything except you."

"Except me."

It was still dark when the bells started ringing. Bong bong and then a clang like a giant alarm clock gone crazy. Bong bong clang. Bong bong clang.

"What time is it?" Yates said.

I grabbed his phone. "Four A.M."

"What's going on?" Yates pulled on his jeans.

Bong bong clang. We could hear people calling to each other outside.

"I don't know," I said, fumbling around for my sweater, "but it doesn't sound good."

"Barnabas didn't say anything about this?"

"No, nothing."

I jerked back a curtain. Lights were coming on in houses. Doors banged, and I saw men and women rush into the street, their arms full of bundles. "People are heading for the church and they've got their kids with them."

"Then we'd better go, too."

We grabbed our boots and started lacing them. Someone banged on the door. Caleb stuck his head in. "You gotta get to the church. Bring your lantern, sleeping bags, any weapons you got."

"What's happening?" I said, even though I had a sick feeling I already knew.

"Not sure, but I expect we're going to be under fire. I got to go get Jemima."

"Go," I said. "We'll be right behind you."

We broke up the fire, and left it to burn itself out. By the time we got out to the road, all but a couple houses were dark, and I guessed they'd been abandoned. The alarm bells had stopped, but the air echoed with the panicky sound of goats bleating and banging around in the barn. Their squeals filled me with fear.

A few stragglers ran ahead of us, flashlights jumping over the snow and guns slapping their backs.

"Come on, hurry up," Beattie yelled from the church steps. "Get inside."

Yates and I started to run.

Siege

82

Inside the church, Beattie went from family to family, clasping people's hands, her face calm and reassuring as she tried to get them to take a seat.

Children whimpered and moms shushed crying babies. Keisha and Jemima were stone-faced. They wore down jackets over their nightgowns and jeans underneath. Their bug out bags lay at their feet.

This was what The End Of The World As We Know It looked like.

Barnabas took the podium. "We have reason to believe that a military force will reach us within minutes." He was cool, factual like he was addressing soldiers, not families with children who'd been torn out of bed. "The camera at the base of the road caught a vehicle equipped with tractor treads heading this way. I estimate twenty on-board."

"How long before they get here?" Beattie asked.

"Twenty-five minutes. Half hour. Families should get their children settled in the Bunker while the Council takes a head count to determine who's missing. Then armed adults should take positions at the windows."

Women gathered their children and herded them toward the basement. Mrs. Gomez glared at me. "It's all your fault," she yelled. "You did this!"

My heart pounded as the whole room pinned me with their eyes.

Ramos pointed at Maggie. "Put her and that girl and her boyfriend out on the road so the feds find them. We don't need to protect these people. They're Outsiders."

Yates leaped up before I could stop him and went for Ramos, but fortunately Luke caught hold of him. He leaned in, saying something only Yates could hear. I held my breath until Yates lowered his fists. Thank you, I said to Luke with my eyes.

"We are not throwing anyone out," Barnabas declared. "Right now we've got to focus on what's coming at us."

"Barnabas, the Council reports one unaccounted for: Spoke Coleman," Beattie said.

"He took off with his dog team yesterday," someone added. "Hasn't come back yet."

Barnabas asked for volunteers to bring weapons and ammo up from the Bunker. When he headed for the stairs, Yates and Luke followed him, and I trailed after them.

Down in the Bunker, the gas was lit under an enameled coffeepot and left to brew. A teenage boy was fitting frozen blocks of meat around milk jugs in one of the large coolers.

Women were setting up cots and zipping children into sleeping bags. Lanterns on the floor lit their faces like campfires.

Jemima wandered the room while Sarah dogged her, asking, "Who's going to milk the goats in the morning? Who's going to let them out and make sure they've got water?"

I took Sarah by the hand, and led her over to Jonas, who was curled up in a ball, his cowboy hat pushed down over his face.

"Are you okay, Jonas?"

"Hector said the soldiers are going to kill Emmeline and Pluto and eat them."

"No, no," I said, easing his hat off his face. "They won't hurt the goats." *Or will they?* I thought. *You don't know what they'll do.*

A woman rocked on the next cot, breastfeeding a tiny, tiny baby. She looked stunned like she'd barely slept in days.

And just beyond her, I saw Luke and Yates hauling guns out of the locked cabinet. They were flat tan like a desert tank, and the muzzles and barrels and all the other parts had a brutal, no-shit, we're-at-war look.

Salvation's going to war. And it was my fault for sending out Sparrow's message so everyone could see the Vegas Strip behind me. The phone weighed down my pocket like a stone and I felt helpless, not seeing any job I could do or way I could help.

Back up in the church hall, Barnabas outlined how he thought things would play out. "These agents have probably been told we're antigovernment extremists hoarding a stockpile of arms. They'll search our houses and the other buildings and conclude we're in here. They won't storm the building immediately, but they'll look for vulnerabilities to exploit. Meanwhile, we will observe how they operate. We've got eight cameras under the eaves and another half dozen in the trees. Most important, we will not fire first. We will only fire in self-defense."

Barnabas stepped back from the podium.

83

We turned off the lanterns and waited silently in the dark. Men and women stood on the balcony in pairs, keeping watch through the narrow windows, Yates and I along with them.

Until then I hadn't noticed that the thick walls were angled so a person could fit comfortably against the windows or that the windows were positioned at chest height on both levels. Now I saw how every window had an inset that could be raised to accommodate a gun. I flipped the little panel up and realized it was inch-thick acrylic. The Bunker, the bulletproof windows, the balcony that circled the room. The entire building was designed to withstand an attack.

The moon lingered on the snow, casting long shadows that reached for the church.

The big room hummed as the boiler cranked out a pitiful heat and the ventilation fan turned. Yates and I huddled together, shivering through our clothes.

The feds showed up barely a half hour after we'd taken our places. The vehicle Barnabas had spotted on the surveillance camera crawled over the snow, looking like a kid's toy, not a transport carrying enough troops and assault weapons to blast some serious holes through these concrete walls.

"It stopped," Yates whispered.

The troops got out, and even though they were wearing snow camouflage, their dark weapons stood out in the moonlight against their white suits.

"Let's get a count, people," Barnabas said quietly.

The troops jogged over the snow. I caught whispers. "I count eighteen." "My count's twenty."

Yates and I watched them fan out to the houses along the road. Four would disappear inside a house, then a few minutes later, come out and wave signals to the others. They headed up the valley toward the houses on the outskirts.

"I'd better get to the control room," Yates said. "Barnabas asked me to help monitor."

I crept down the balcony behind Yates and stepped into the control room. Two rows of monitors displayed images caught by the cameras rigged near the roof and in nearby trees. Everything within a hundred feet around the church appeared in at least one screen, and Barnabas sat watching them.

"I don't believe this," I said. "Nobody up here even has a radio, but—" I waved my hand at the screens and wires snaking everywhere.

"We *choose* not to let the outside world interfere in our daily lives," Barnabas said, "but we're not fools."

Something struck me then. "Beattie told me phone reception's spotty up here, so how did Maggie reach you when we were in trouble?"

He didn't even blink. "We have a micro cell tower, but we turned it off once you two arrived. We didn't want to make it easier for them to track you down." He got up from his stool and left Yates and me with the flickering screens.

For an hour, we watched the figures on the screen get smaller and disappear from view. Yates wrapped his arms across me, but no matter how tightly he held me I couldn't get warm. He buried his face in my hair.

"What did Luke say to you?" I asked. "To make you leave Ramos alone?"

"He told me Ramos would gut me like a trout and I was no good to you dead."

I was about to say I preferred him alive, when I saw troops converging in the road and heading right for the church. "They're back."

Yates looked up. "We've got to tell Barnabas."

I forced myself to breathe before I reached for the gun jammed in my pants.

"I wish I knew how to shoot," Yates said, watching me check the clip and shove it in place.

"No, you really don't."

84

Yates stood behind me at the window. The sky was ash grey, but there was enough light to see that the men in snow camo had retreated to the edge of the woods.

"What do you think they're waiting for?" I whispered.

"Dawn, maybe? They thought they'd surprise us, but now they've got to rethink their plan."

Tension was tying everyone in the hall like taut strings crisscrossing the room. Across from us, Luke and Rogan framed a window, guns propped beside them. Sunlight struck the window, glaring like a spotlight on the thick acrylic.

"I can't see a thing," I said.

"Let's check the cameras," Yates replied. We kept low and scurried to the back room where Barnabas was fixed on the center screen.

"They're approaching on the east," he said.

"With their bayonets out?" Yates said. "What the hell? Do they think they're going to cut through the walls?"

"No, they're doing what I would do," Barnabas muttered.

Cameras captured every thrust as a dozen men stabbed the solarskin and jerked their weapons back. The sparkling black fabric tore into ragged pieces that fluttered onto the brilliant white snow.

"They're trying to cut off our electricity," I said.

Barnabas nodded. "They're sending us a message, letting us know that they're going to eliminate our energy sources. First, the solar-skin, then the windmills. They'll force us to use our generator, and burn up our fuel. They know we're not going anywhere and no one's going to show up to save us."

"But we've got computers, a cell tower. We could call for help," I said.

"The minute we turn on that tower, they'll jam the signal."

"So we don't even try!"

"No, we wait until they're not paying attention."

A bullhorn bored through the church's thick walls and bullet-proof glass as if they didn't exist. "Margaret Stanton and Aveline Reveare."

My stomach plunged, hearing the distorted voice utter my name. Maggie and I crept toward the southern wall, keeping out of sight of the windows and the faceless, nameless agent demanding our presence.

"You are wanted on charges of sedition against the United States Government for violating the Patriot Act. We ask that you surrender into our custody."

Oh, my God. I crossed my arms and pressed them to my chest as my body started to shake.

Barnabas appeared over Maggie's shoulder. "Hard to resist a polite request like that."

"What's sedition?" I said.

Yates came up beside me. "It's treason."

"Not exactly," Barnabas said. "It's attempting to overthrow the government by force. It's one way they prosecute terrorists."

My heart pounded in my ears so hard I almost missed what Maggie said next. "Yeah. After they torture them."

Images flashed in my brain like shuffled cards. Agents holding me underwater. Electrodes ripping my body. A needle plunging into my arm.

I started to laugh. This was unreal. I was pinned down by a federal death squad, and suddenly, my best option was to die in a hurricane of bullets.

I could feel myself losing control and the laughter running away with me, and I wanted to stop, but I couldn't, even as I heard my laughs turn jerky and hysterical like the barks of an injured dog. Yates tried to put his arms around me, but I slapped them away.

Then my breath was gone like someone had shoved a wad of cotton down my throat. "I can't breathe, I can't breathe," I gasped.

Yates grabbed my arms and held on. "Stop! Look at me!"

My lungs screamed for air, and I tried to pull away.

Yates swept my feet out from under me. I fell to the floor and he pinned me with his knees, and clamped a hand over my mouth. I twisted under him, but he pressed down harder.

Get off me! Get off me!

"Avie. Avie! You're hyperventilating. You need to quiet down— breathe through your nose."

I strained to push him off. Yates' blue eyes were dark as deep water. "You have to trust me," he said, and pressed his thumb over my nostril.

Trust you? Get off!

"Stop fighting me and breathe!" he ordered.

I hate you, I thought, pulling in hard through my one open nostril. It wasn't enough. It was like trying to breathe through a straw.

"Long, slow, deep breaths," Yates whispered, looking me in the eyes as he held me down.

My lungs began to fill and my breathing steadied. Yates took his hand away from my face and fell off me, his expression tender and scared. "Are you okay? Did I hurt you?"

I lay there for a moment, grateful Yates would never know what went through my mind when he was on top of me. I reached for his hand. "It's okay. I'm fine now."

Slowly, I sat up and let my head fall back against the wall. I was sure everyone would be staring at me after my breakdown, but they weren't. They were too busy watching the movements out in the snow.

85

For the next three hours, we watched the agents hitch a windmill to their vehicle and either pull it down or mow it down. After each one crashed, the bullhorn demanded that Maggie and I come out. After the fifth or sixth windmill went down, I heard a door slam and people yelling in the control room. Later, Mrs. Gomez came out, her face crimson as she glared up at me on the balcony.

But at the same time, I thought I was seeing a miracle as Luke wandered over to Maggie. They stood together, talking in a way that shut out the rest of the room, and their faces were thoughtful and a little pained. Luke was asking her questions, and Maggie was steeling herself to answer. A part of me was glad they were taking down the walls, even if they were doing it because they realized time had run out.

The Council kept telling us to sit tight and wait to see what happened next, but by midafternoon, everything changed.

"Y'all are going to want to see this," a man called from his post.

Beattie took one look out the window and bolted for the Bunker. "We can't let Jemima witness this," I heard her say as she flew past.

Yates and I pressed into a window niche. Two agents had dragged a nanny goat from the barn. People whispered all around us, speculating on what the feds were up to. The nanny was fighting hard. The men probably outweighed her by at least a hundred pounds, but she bucked and reared and threw them down the whole distance from the barn to right outside the church.

I recognized her. It was Emmeline.

The two men positioned her as if they wanted us to have a clear view. Emmeline struggled and stomped as a third man walked up. The two held her tight, and the third pulled a knife from a belt at his waist.

A gasp swept through the church like a gust of wind. The man thrust the knife under Emmeline's jaw and drew the blade down her neck. She bucked and fell, forcing the men to their knees.

"He cut her jugular," someone said.

Blood spurted from her neck, brilliant red on the blue-white snow. Emmeline jerked and the men let go. Her legs churned and then she collapsed.

I gagged and had to turn away.

Behind me, I heard footsteps, and Jemima threw herself against a window. She screamed, and pounded the thick acrylic with her fist until Caleb pulled her away. Her family surrounded her as she sobbed.

"It's over," Yates said.

Outside, Emmeline lay, a dark heap in the blood-splattered snow.

"Sadists." I turned my back on the scene, and my eyes swept over Jesus up on the cross. I felt a rush of anger at how pointless he looked, hanging there.

The bullhorn squealed and we all looked toward the sound.

"Come out if you care about your children."

My body went cold. For a moment, the church was chillingly silent.

"Screw you!" a man yelled back.

"You can burn in hell," yelled another.

Ramos marched over to the American flag and tore it from the wall. Furious Spanish spewed from his mouth as he strode to the center of the room and climbed on one of the long tables. His wife grabbed for his hand. "Get down, Ramos. You want to be a target?"

He shook her off. "This is our country! Ours! We fought for it!" He waved the flag in the air defiantly and began to sing. "'My country 'tis of thee, sweet land of liberty—'"

My heartbeat quickened as a dozen voices joined his. "'Of thee I sing.'"

The flag whipped over our heads, and for the first time I got that this song was about people like us here tonight who'd been pushed down and attacked by the government that was supposed to keep them safe. My voice rose up with Yates' and merged with the others.

"'Land where my fathers died! Land of the pilgrim's pride!'"

One by one people joined in until we all sang as one, "'From every mountainside, let freedom ring!'"

The room resonated with righteous anger as people sang six more verses I didn't know. Their anger was a presence I could almost touch, and when Ramos climbed down from the table and hung the flag back in its place, I told Yates, "I'm not scared anymore. Is that insane?"

"No, it's not," he said, as we saw Ramos embrace Maggie. "Everyone is united now."

Behind us, I overheard Barnabas tell Beattie, "It's time to change plans."

86

"Council meeting," Beattie called out. A dozen men and women left their posts and disappeared into the back. Yates and I watched for movement outside until they reappeared a few minutes later.

Barnabas took the stage. "I've got an announcement." The whole room hushed and every eye was on him.

"The situation isn't playing out the way we thought. This is a clandestine operation, and to get these agents to stand down, we need to bring it out in the open. Maggie and I and the Council have come up with a plan we think makes sense."

I could feel the whole room go still.

"We have access to a piece of software that can broadcast a distress call to a large population that we believe will be sympathetic to our situation."

I wrapped my hand around the phone in my pocket. Barnabas was talking about the software Sparrow put on it, the software I used to send out her video. Maybe by using this phone I could finally help save Salvation.

"But to be most effective, the device needs to be carried out of the valley to a higher elevation, the top of Phelan's Ridge."

People gasped, some muttered under their breath. *"Go for help?"* I whispered to Yates. "How the hell is anyone supposed to do that? We're *surrounded*."

"Maybe there's a way out of the church we don't know about," Yates said.

"We're asking for volunteers," Barnabas continued. "A two-man team. It can be men or women, who will exit the church under cover of darkness, then climb to the top of the ridge and broadcast the distress call."

Around the room, families gathered and huddled together. Jemima and Caleb wrapped their arms across each other and linked hands.

I searched the room, wondering who would have the guts to try.

"We think it best that expert marksmen remain here to defend the church."

Ramos' wife grabbed his shirtfront and shook her head. Luke and Rogan pressed their lips together, and I saw how they would have been the first to volunteer if they weren't such good shots.

Barnabas set his hands on his hips. "The volunteers need to be in good physical shape. They're going to have to climb that ridge before the moon rises, and reach the top by a designated time. Then we'll turn on the cell tower. We'll only have a few minutes before the agents realize what we're doing and block the signal."

"No!"

I saw a woman force down Jemima's raised hand.

"Stop, Mama, I want to do this," Jemima said.

"No!" Her mom grabbed her and pulled her close. "We have to stay together," she cried. "If we die, we die together!"

Jemima struggled in her grasp for a moment, and then gave in and embraced her mother back.

I gazed over this room of families and I realized what I had to do. I laid my hand on Yates' chest. "I want to volunteer."

He wrapped his hand over mine. "I'm glad you said that, because I was about to tell you the same thing."

I smiled up at him.

"You're not scared?" he said.

"Scared to death, but I did this. I brought these men here."

"It wasn't just you. We both did." He leaned down and placed his lips on mine. We gave each other a sad, slow kiss, then turned to face the rest of the church. "We'll do it," I called out.

The room went silent for a second, then an older man snorted out a laugh. "Ha! You! We should put our faith in you! A girl who fell to pieces just hearing those men out there say her name!"

I stared at the floorboards. It wasn't enough to want to help them, I had to be strong and focused enough to do what needed to be done.

"Yeah? Well, I'll tell you," Yates answered back. "You don't know what Avie can do when she puts her mind to it."

"Yates—" I warned.

The whole room was waiting, and the man who'd called me out waved his hand like he was writing me off. "Little rich girl from L.A. She can't even speak up for herself!"

"He's wrong," Yates said. "Tell them about Roik—about how you got away from him."

And I realized I wasn't a poor little rich girl anymore, afraid to try or waiting for people to save me. I held my head up and told them about Father G's arrest and Aamir bailing, about coming up with a new plan, me giving Roik the drug that made him sick and making him take me back to the cemetery where I'd been attacked days before. I told them about Tasing Roik, then running through the dark, sketchy neighborhood, dodging the guys chasing me, before Yates picked me up.

"Well, that's good enough for me," Nellie said, turning to her neighbors. "Is that good enough for you, Mr. Oakley?"

The man who'd written me off cocked his head and nodded. "Yep, I think so."

"All in favor of these two volunteers," Barnabas said. Hands went up all over the room. "All opposed." I wasn't surprised to see some doubters.

"Okay," Yates said. "Tell us what you want us to do."

Barnabas and Maggie took Yates and me into the control room. Luke came in after us. A map was spread out on the table, and one of the silk wall hangings was folded up beside it. "There's an escape tunnel," Maggie said. "It goes from the Bunker to a hatch under Beattie's back porch."

"So where do you want us to go?" Yates said.

Maggie pointed to a pencil-thin valley on the map. "We're here. There's a trail to the ridge."

Luke frowned and almost elbowed her aside. "The trail's hidden under three feet of snow. You need to follow the stream that runs behind Beattie's and the houses to the east. The land will start to rise, and you'll follow the stream another quarter mile before you start climbing."

"We can't use skis," I said, "not to get up the ridge."

I remembered how hard it was just to ski up the valley and that was flat. Now I'd volunteered to hike in the snow.

"You'll start out on skis and then switch to snowshoes farther on," Barnabas said. "You'll have to travel without a headlamp to keep from being spotted." His voice was matter-of-fact, barely disguising that he knew our attempt to get to the ridge was a long shot.

Luke. Keisha. Jonas. Sarah. Jemima and Caleb. Nellie, Rogan, that tiny, tiny baby down in the Bunker. They were depending on us to be brave and strong enough to go for help.

Yates was strong and brave. *Can I really do this?*

Luke glanced from me to Yates. "You'll have to cut your own trail, but the woods aren't thick and if you keep Salvation behind you and keep climbing you should be okay."

"Yeah," Barnabas added. "While Phelan's Ridge would be the best, any ridge should work."

"What time do we need to get to the top?" Yates said.

"Eight o'clock. We'll launch our diversion, then we'll turn on the cell tower."

"What kind of diversion?" Yates said.

Maggie stood up straight, and Barnabas slipped his arm around her waist. They gazed so deeply into each other's eyes that I sensed before Maggie opened her mouth what she was about to say.

She turned to us. "I'm going to surrender."

My heart stopped. "No! You can't!"

"I have to, Avie. I owe it to my family to protect them."

"But those men, they'll—"

Maggie held up her hand to stop me. "I need you to take the evidence—this wall hanging and the rest of it—and get it to a friend of mine in Washington, D.C. Will you please do that for me?"

I paled, knowing what I'd be carrying. My throat tightened, and I had to force out my promise. "Yes, I'll do it."

Yates rested his arm on my shoulders and I wove my hand into his. "What do we do once we make the call?" Yates said.

"Once they cut off the signal, you'd better get going."

Maggie tapped the map and ran her finger over the mountains

and then west through a jagged valley. A two-lane highway north cut across it. "If you can get here, the ranchers in this valley should help you."

"Folks who live up here don't countenance the government interfering in people's lives," Barnabas added.

Yates measured the distance with his fingers. "It's about six miles. We can do that."

I swallowed. *What if I'm not strong enough to do this?* The responsibility for all those lives was on my shoulders.

"Avie, we can do this, right?" Yates said.

I caught movement on the monitor to my right as a man in snow camo darted from one tree to another. I opened my mouth, but I couldn't answer.

"Can you guys give us a minute alone?" Yates said. The others cleared the room. "Avie, tell me what you're thinking."

"I—I—"

He turned around until he faced me, then he set his hands on my waist and leaned in until his head rested on mine. "Tell me," he whispered.

"If I fail, everyone here dies."

"Listen," he said. "We're in this together, and if I didn't believe we could do this, I'd have fought you going."

When I looked up, Yates was waiting.

I wanted to be Fearless, the girl he thought I was. The girl that Mom and Ms. A believed in. "Okay. Let's do this."

87

Barnabas and Luke sat us down and went through all the details. The timing. The terrain. All the things that could trip us up or get us killed. Like the creek we needed to follow, but didn't run straight and was disguised in places under the snow. Or the agents who might be out on patrol. Chances are, Barnabas said, they'd stay close to the church, but he couldn't guarantee it.

Or the goats who'd spent the whole day without food or water, suffering with big, swollen udders that needed to be milked. They'd pitch a fit when we entered the barn. "Don't even think about feeding them. Just get the packs and get the hell out of there," Barnabas told us.

He and Luke went quiet when Maggie walked in. She clutched the ends of a makeshift banner, torn from a bedsheet.

I SURRENDER.

My eyes filled, but I blinked to make them stop.

"Where'd you find the paint?" Barnabas said.

"It's beet juice. Nellie suggested it. You ready to film my testimony?"

"No better time."

They sounded like an old married couple talking about a project in the garage. Yates shook his head. Don't say anything.

Maggie sat at the folding table and asked me to stand across from her and hold up the wall hanging so she could see it. Barnabas turned a camera on her and Maggie started her testimony.

"I, Margaret Stanton, do solemnly swear to tell the truth, the whole truth, and nothing but the truth."

Luke leaned against the wall with his head bowed. His eyes were closed, but he was listening hard.

For the first time since we'd met, I believed everything Maggie said. She was a U.S. citizen. Georgetown Law grad. Clerk for Supreme Court Justice Ruth Ginsberg. Dozen years at a D.C. law firm. Six civil rights cases argued in front of the Supreme Court.

"Five years ago," Maggie said, "I began to suspect that there was a deliberate and organized effort to restrict the rights of women in the U.S. To investigate the possibility of such a conspiracy, I opened an escort service in Las Vegas, Nevada, catering to men in the highest ranks of government and industry.

"I was present at meetings and informal gatherings in which government policies, laws, and practices were discussed. My testimony here provides reasons to conclude that a conspiracy exists to deny women and girls their civil rights."

She nodded to me to hold the hanging higher, then began to unravel the convoluted story. Names and dates. Deals and political favors. Players on five continents. Cash. Lines of credit. Multibillion-dollar loans.

I flinched the first time I heard Hawkins' name, but not all the times after that. Maggie had never met him, but he was friends with the key Paternalists, and they linked him to all kinds of political deals. Expose the Vice President, and Hawkins could be the next to fall.

When Maggie was done, Barnabas shut down the camera. I watched Luke go over to Maggie and rest his hand beside hers on the table. *Hug her!* Say good-bye, I wanted to tell him, but something passed between them that I didn't understand, and Luke walked out. Maggie stood up.

"What about Sparrow's last message?" I asked. "Was that in the testimony you just gave?"

"No. Barnabas will put a copy on the thumb drive along with it."

Barnabas linked my phone to the computer and did the same with the camera. When the thumb drive was ready, he threaded it onto a chain, and I hung it around my neck, knowing I'd crossed a line I could never cross back over.

"Hold up your shirt." Maggie had folded the hanging into a narrow strip, and I chewed on my lip as she wound the silk around my waist.

"You can do this," she said, pinning the end. There wasn't an ounce of pity in her eyes. She was Magda. Committed. Unyielding.

Yates gave my arm a squeeze. "Yeah, she's fearless."

No I'm not, I wanted to say, but I kept my mouth shut. If Maggie was going to walk out in front of the guns, I needed to suck it up.

"You need a minute?" Barnabas said.

"No," I said, looking at Yates. "I think we're ready."

88

Down in the Bunker, the piled sacks of rice and beans had been moved away from the wall, revealing a small metal door with a handle at the bottom.

People surrounded Yates and me as we neared the door, wishing us luck. Luke insisted on reviewing the route, and warning us about places to look out for where the snow might give way and throw us into a creek.

He went to turn away, but I reached for his shoulder. I rose up on my tiptoes and left a kiss on his cheek. "Take care, okay?"

He looked into my eyes, and I saw a flicker of what might have been if things had played out differently. "*You* take care," he said.

Keisha waited by the entrance, her cheeks slick with tears. I held her close. "I'll see you again," I said, "and we'll go to Disney World and ride the teacups as many times as you want."

"And Dumbo, too," she whispered.

"Time to go," Yates said, clicking on his headlamp.

I pulled on my hat and gloves. Zipped my jacket.

We bent over and stepped into the tunnel and the door shut behind us. Silence. Goose bumps ran up my arms, and I hugged my sleeping bag to my chest. The dirt walls were so close I could touch them with my elbows.

Yates stretched his hand back. "Avie, where are you?"

I took his hand. "I'm right here."

"Holy mother. I've got to get out of here," he said, pulling me forward. "It smells like a grave."

We half ran, hunched over, the dark shapes of wood supports appearing and disappearing in our headlamp beams. I counted our steps. Beattie's house was about a hundred and fifty feet from the church. It took us seconds to go the first fifty. At sixty-five, I squeezed Yates' hand tighter. Eighty. We were right under the circle of agents.

I heard the bullhorn call my name, but that was impossible.

They can't hear you. They can't hear you or see you or shoot you so keep going.

Yates sped up as the tunnel zigzagged around a boulder. Fifty feet to go.

And then the tunnel ended. Overhead, we saw the trapdoor between two supports. "You've got the oil, right?" Yates was panting and his face was white, but I couldn't tell if that was him or the headlamp.

I pulled out the tiny can Barnabas gave me. "You okay?"

"I'll be fine once we get out of here."

I squirted the hinges and the springs on the sides.

"This better work," Yates said. "Any noise and we'll have a dozen guns in our faces." We braced ourselves and pushed, but the door didn't move.

Yates swore, and slammed it with his fist. "Come on. Open!"

He was scaring me, banging around like that. I grabbed his arm. "Hey, take a breath. Maybe there's a latch or something they didn't tell us about."

We felt around with our fingers, but couldn't find anything. "The damned thing's probably rusted shut," Yates said.

"You want to try more oil?"

"Go ahead. We've got nothing to lose."

I soaked the hinges and springs until they dripped. We flattened our palms against the wood.

"Now!"

We pushed until I could feel the veins in my head. Then the door gave and the hinges made a loud, horrible screech.

Yates' headlamp glared in my face. "Son of a—"

We waited, listening for boots on the porch or men wading through the snow.

"Let's try working it up and down," Yates whispered.

The metal gave little squeaks, but we could feel it give. "Okay, now." Yates let go.

Please, please, please don't make a sound. I slid my fingers away, and the door eased up like Open Sesame.

Yates hoisted himself up and then pulled me out. We lowered the door and crouched next to it. White walls of snow probably four feet deep surrounded us on three sides.

"Look, there are the steps," I whispered. We rolled our sleeping bags over to the side of the house we hoped was away from the church.

Yates traced his headlamp beam along the edge of the porch. "We've got to get to the ridge by eight, but the feds could be standing right out there."

"Yeah, but maybe they didn't hear anything, because of the snow."

We began to dig, scooping the icy snow with our hands, afraid that the sound of a shovel could give us away. My gloves froze, burning my skin, but I bit my lip and kept going.

"Almost there," Yates said.

"Stop. Our headlamps."

I fiddled, trying to move the tiny switch, but I couldn't get it.

Yates reached over and turned it off, then his lips reached for mine. We held each other in a long, deep, death-defying kiss.

"I love you," he said when we broke apart.

My breath caught and my eyes filled. "I love you, too." It sounded like we were saying good-bye.

89

We slithered on our stomachs, inching our sleeping bags in front of us. The silence amped up the noise my jacket made over the snow so it sounded in my head like ripping Velcro. Everything inside me wanted to get up and run.

I couldn't see Ramos' house. Rogan had watched the agents take it over earlier in the afternoon. Half, he warned us, were probably inside catching some sleep, while the other ten were out here in the dark, listening, waiting.

I kept my head up, but snow shimmied into my sleeves and up under my jacket. We crept toward the creek, and I listened for the sound of water, afraid I wouldn't hear it until it was right under us.

The moon wouldn't be up for a while, but I could see the outline of the barn against the starry night. It wasn't an impossible distance, but right now it felt like it. The fallen skeletons of windmills lay in our path. The snow had been torn up by the tractor treads and boots, and for once I felt like we'd caught a break.

The church bells began to ring like Salvation was being called to celebrate Sunday service. Gong gong gong gong.

I scrambled forward and tagged Yates on the leg. "What's going on?" I whispered.

"I don't know. You think they're trying to cover for us?"

"Maybe."

We got to our feet, but before we took two steps the bells stopped. We froze. Yates clutched my hand, and I knew he was weighing the odds.

Then the bells rang out again. Dong dong dong ding dong dong dong. I heard the faint sound of singing. *Good King Wenceslas looked out.*

They were singing for a reason. To distract the agents? To hide the sound of our footsteps?

Dong dong dong dong *dong* dong.

"Listen to the beat," I said. "It's even—like footsteps."

We took off for the barn, the snow crunching under our weight. *Brightly shone the moon that night though the frost was cruel.*

The words sang in my head as we bounded through the snow. Five verses carried us past chicken coops and empty houses, and at the last verse we climbed over the fence into the goat pen.

The bug-out bags were supposed to be stashed under bales of hay on the north side. Yates took hold of the side door. "Remember. Get in and get out."

I braced myself for the frenzied bleating of forty hungry goats, and Yates pushed the door open. We leaped inside and it closed with barely a rattle.

"We made it," Yates said.

I felt for him. "Something's wrong."

The goats milled in their stalls, banging the wood walls like they were shoving each other. "The goats aren't bleating."

Dong dong ding dong dong. *Frosty the Snowman.*

Yates slid his headlamp off and swept the beam over the closest stall. The goats jerked their heads, their eyes wild. Each had a thick silver band fastened around its mouth.

"What *is* that?" I said.

"Duct tape." Yates dug into his pocket. "Some psycho taped their mouths shut."

"They'll starve."

"Hold this." Yates shoved the headlamp into my hands and unfolded a knife.

"Wait. What are you doing?"

"I'm going to cut the tape." He threw a leg over the stall, and I grabbed hold of his sleeve.

"You can't. I hate it, too, but the agents will hear. We have to leave them like this."

Yates shook his head. "I hope hell reserves a seat for the guy who did this," he said, folding his knife.

We unstacked the hay bales and found the bug-out bags. We tied sleeping bags to two of them, and Yates pulled on the one Barnabas was supposed to carry and helped me on with the other.

I fastened the straps across my chest and the belt around my hips. It was so heavy I couldn't stand up straight.

"You okay?" Yates said. He pulled my straps tighter. "We can lighten your pack."

It was twenty pounds heavier than the one I was supposed to carry. "But we don't know what we need. We could guess wrong."

And leave out the one thing that could save our lives.

"There's still room in mine."

Yates' pack was stretched to breaking. "Let's go," I said. "Figure this out later."

I turned back toward the goats. *I'm sorry.*

"Frosty the Snowman" was still going when we left the barn. We ducked behind the wood shop and over to Barnabas' back porch.

We dug in the snow by the top step, found the tips of the skis, and slid them out. The poles and a flour sack with boots inside came out along with them. Yates crept up on the porch and lifted a couple pairs of snowshoes off the hooks. We tied them to our packs and lashed our snow boots over them. When I slid on the frozen ski boots, my feet went numb. Yates swore under his breath.

How the hell am I going to get up that mountain now, I thought, sagging under the pack. We shoved our feet into the clips.

"Go ahead. Lead the way," Yates whispered.

I'd skied the valley two days before, but it was ten times harder carrying the pack. My skis didn't glide. I had to push them forward with each step. Every move, every breath was a struggle and felt deafeningly loud. Behind us the bells pealed out "Joy to the World," but all I felt was fear that any second one of those special ops guys would catch sight of us and cut us down.

The land dipped a little toward the creek, pulling my skis along. I could hear Yates behind me. *I'm not alone. Yates is here and we're doing this together.*

I didn't look around, because what was the point in looking to see if the agents were stalking us. All I could do was pray they hadn't heard us, that they were guarding the church, amazed by the holiday concert of the bells.

I fought my body to keep going. *It's flat now. What's going to happen when you have to climb up that ridge?*

I kept my eyes targeted on the end of the valley and the mountain we were going to climb. The creek was off to my right, but from the sound, I wasn't sure how close. We passed the silent cabins and trailers until we reached the last house. The mountain rose up right behind it.

I turned to Yates over my shoulder. "We need to find the creek." I lifted up each ski and moved sideways over the snow, planting my poles, afraid I'd slip on the bank and fall into the water.

Then I saw a narrow gap in the snow.

We followed the creek. There wasn't a trail, but the trees were far enough apart that we picked a way up that looked like it might work. Luke had warned us to look out for rocky places where the snow might be a thin layer hiding a slick of ice.

How were we supposed to see *that* in the dark?

At first, the slope was gradual. I jogged from foot to foot, planting my weight so I didn't slide back. A hundred meters later, I was bent over, winded.

I was broiling in my jacket, and the hanging wrapped around my waist itched like mad. I tore at the snaps by my neck. "It feels like we're trying to ski Mount Everest."

Yates went around me. "Let me cut the trail."

We started up again, stopping every couple hundred feet. My lungs burned and I felt like I had bags of clay tied to my feet.

I couldn't see Salvation through the trees, but I could hear the bells. "O Come All Ye Faithful." I imagined families huddled together on the church floor in the dark, singing until their throats ached, trusting us to get them help.

"What time is it?" I said.

"Just after seven-thirty. We need to switch to snowshoes or we'll never make it."

A half hour to get to the ridge or we wouldn't catch the cell and bounce our distress call out of here. People would die.

We unclipped our skis and my breath caught as I changed boots. My feet curled up, because even thick socks couldn't keep out this cold. I wiggled my boots into the snowshoe straps, and Yates crouched down to tighten them.

I stumbled a few steps, the frame flapping at my heel. "I feel like I'm wearing clown shoes."

"You'll get used to it. Walk like normal, but lift your knees high so you clear the snow."

Yates started between the trees and I climbed after him. With each step, the snow collapsed, and I sank up to my ankles. It was like trudging through sand. Then I tried walking in Yates' footsteps, but his legs were so long I fell twice before I gave up.

We crisscrossed our way slowly up the hill, nailing our poles into the snow. Step. Sink. Step. Sink. Breathe. My heartbeat pounded in my ears.

Looking down, I saw our trail. We'd barely made any progress. "Why don't we go straight up? This zigzagging is taking forever."

"Yeah, but there's less chance we'll slip and end up wrapped around a tree. It's not that far. We'll get there."

"If it was summer, I could run this easy."

"Yeah, and you'd totally beat my ass."

Step. Sink. Step. Sink. The cold made my forehead ache.

I began to see faces in front of my eyes. Sarah with her angel-blue eyes. Dimpled Jemima. Keisha and her brilliant smile. Luke.

I can't fail. They're depending on me.

And then I remembered a scorching-hot day back when I was eight. A cancer fund-raising walk with Mom and Dad in Pasadena. Halfway down Colorado Boulevard, I told Mom I didn't want to walk anymore. "You don't have to," she told me. "But see these names on my shirt? I have to keep going for them."

I didn't understand then why those names scribbled on her shirt mattered so much, but now on this cold, dark mountainside I did. "I'm going to dedicate this walk to Salvation."

"Oh, yeah?"

"Yeah, every single step of it." I stamped my foot in the snow. "This step is for Beattie."

"Beattie," Yates echoed.

"This one's for Keisha."

"Keisha."

"Maggie."

I ran through every name in Salvation I could remember. Luke. Barnabas. Nellie. Jonas. Sarah. Rogan. Mr. and Mrs. Flores. Hector. Mr. and Mrs. Gomez. All the goats.

When I ran out of names, Yates said, "How about Father G?"

"And Ms. A."

We ran through all the girls in my class, even Dayla, then Yates said, "Your mom."

An avalanche blew inside me and I had to stop. I stood there, panting, my heart aching for her.

"I wish I'd gotten to know her better," Yates said.

"Me, too." I felt like crying, but I didn't have any tears. Every day I'd never have with her, everything I'd never know about her hit me like a rain of shrapnel. "She left me letters before she died, so I could open them on my birthdays. There are at least ten more waiting in Dad's safe at home."

Yates held out his hand and pulled me forward. "You remember what any of them said?"

"I remember this one page where she wrote 'See all the ways I love you,' at the very top. Then she covered every inch of it with 'I love you.' She wrote it a hundred different ways. Capital letters. Lowercase. Wavy lines. Straight. Different-colored markers."

I love you. I love you. I love you.

Yates turned around. "You know what I'll never forget? Your mom's face the day you stood up on Bruiser's back and rode him around the ring."

I couldn't help smiling. I had sailed around the big arena, no saddle, no reins, my arms spread out like wings, feeling like I could do anything. "Mom kept telling me to try—that I could do it as long as I didn't let fear stop me."

"She was a smart lady."

I pulled in a deep breath like I was filling myself up with Mom's strength and love and belief in me. I held it in for a moment, imagining that power flowing into my arms and legs, then I let it out. "Okay," I said. "I'm dedicating the rest of the way to Mom."

Yates shook his pole in the air. "To Mom."

I reached for his hand and held it. "You should dedicate this to Becca."

Yates face stiffened and he tried to turn away, but I jerked his hand so he'd meet my eyes.

"Becca is looking down at you right now and, listen to me, she is proud of her brother."

"Avie—"

"She forgives you, Yates. You don't have to spend the rest of your life making up for not being there for her that day. This, what we're doing now—it's enough."

He closed his eyes and took in a deep breath, and as he let it out, his face changed. I could almost see, touch, the pain lifting off his body. Then he opened his eyes, and smiled sadly at the night sky. "Are you listening, Becca? This is for you!"

"Ready?" I said.

"Ready."

We planted our poles and the slope got steeper as we went. I slid backward a little with each step.

Another fifty feet and Yates turned around. "Hand me one of your poles." He twisted it until it was shorter than the other and gave it back to me. "We've got to crab-walk up the last part."

We didn't have time to walk. We jogged sideways like we were climbing up crumbling stairs with shoeboxes tied to our feet. My throat hurt, it was so dry. Yates had a canteen, but just thinking about the icy water made my teeth hurt.

When we get to the other side, we can stop. We can set up the kettle and rest. But now we have to get to the ridge.

Yates pushed hard the last hundred feet. I wanted to stop and catch my breath but I knew we couldn't.

Mom, help me. Help me get to the top. The summit's so close.

And then, finally, we were there. Yates wheezed, his hands on his hips. "We made it," he said. "Six minutes to go."

My head spun as I glimpsed Salvation through the trees. It looked small and forgotten in the deep blue snow. "I can't hear the bells."

"That doesn't mean there's a problem."

I hoped Yates was right.

I pulled my phone out of my jacket and turned it on. Pulled up Sparrow's software and got ready to do a blast. If the software worked, we'd break through the paternal controls and reach millions of grannies and girls my age. Someone would hear me and go for help.

No reception.

We waited. I ran through the message the way Barnabas had coached me. Remember: calm, not hysterical.

"Two minutes." Yates waved the phone over his head, but nothing. Then we saw the spinning globe. "We've got a connection."

I took a deep breath. Right now Maggie was waiting by the church doors, ready to step out, wave the banner, and offer herself up.

I had to be worthy of her sacrifice. "I'm ready."

Yates moved me into the shadow of a tree and turned his headlamp on me. "Now."

"This is Salvation, Idaho. We're under attack from armed federal agents. Please send help! We are barricaded in our church. Over a hundred men, women, and children, and we need help now. Salvation, Idaho, northeast of Boise. Please send help now!" I gave out the latitude and longitude and hoped whoever was listening was writing this down.

Yates waved his hand. "Got it. And it's gone!"

It's gone. "We did it." I fell into Yates' arms. "We actually did it."

"Yeah, we did," he said, holding me close. "You and me, Fearless."

We'd gotten past the guards, kept going when the trapdoor wouldn't open, dragged ourselves up the mountain in time to catch the transmission. We'd kept each other going.

A gunshot cracked the air.

91

"Maggie!" I screamed. Yates buried my face in his chest, smothering my cries. I hammered his back with my fists, and he held me as the gunshots got louder, furious. Salvation was firing back.

"Go ahead, scream," he said in a strangled voice.

I stopped pounding and clung to him. "Oh, why did we even try?"

The firefight exploded below, and I saw in my mind the children huddled in the Bunker, while all the good and decent people I'd come to know were at the windows, fighting to stay alive.

A hundred people under attack from the government that was supposed to protect them. "This is murder, Yates. It's murder!"

"We can't let the government bury this. The tower is still open," he said. "We should keep broadcasting until they shut us down."

I staggered back, and wiped my face with my mittens. "Okay, yeah, you're right."

Yates turned the camera on me. I tried to keep my voice steady, but I heard it breaking up. "Please, please help us. This is Salvation, Idaho. Federal agents have opened fire and we're firing back in self-defense. Please help us."

Yates sent out our blast, then tipped the screen so I could see it. "Barnabas sent us a video."

"What's on it?"

The grey, grainy footage was from one of the cameras trained on the church. It showed Maggie stumbling down the steps, her head ducked in the feds' high-watt spotlights. She was holding the banner up in front of her. I SURRENDER. The words were unmistakable. I SURRENDER. The camera focused on the message, and gunshots exploded. Maggie sailed backward and slammed to the ground. The banner billowed like a flag then collapsed over Maggie's fallen body.

"Those bastards!"

The video ended. Down in the valley, the hailstorm of gunshots continued.

"We have to try to send this out," I said. "People have to see it. They have to know what's happening here."

Yates nodded and turned the headlamp back on me. "In one, two, three—"

I held my voice steady even though I felt like screaming. "This is Salvation, Idaho. Please help us. Federal agents have attacked us. They shot and killed a woman trying to surrender. This video is proof."

Yates linked up the video, and the undeniable truth blasted into cyberspace. "Let them try and cover this up," he said.

A moment later, the globe stopped spinning and faded from the screen. "The tower's dead," Yates said, handing me the phone.

I swung my arm back, ready to pitch it into the dark.

Yates took the phone out of my hand, and I let him zip it into my pocket. "You did the best you could," he said.

"But it didn't make any difference. They killed Maggie, and now they're probably going to kill everyone else."

"Not if help arrives. And you've guaranteed that they won't get away with what they did here tonight. The world will know what happened."

The gunshots slowed. "Come on," Yates said. "We need to get out of here." He bent down and pulled on his pack.

I felt like lying down in the snow. Lying down and going to sleep and never waking up.

Yates eased the pack straps over my arms and fastened them across my chest, then he took my hand and walked me to the other side of the ridge.

92

We started down. I began to count the seconds between gunshots like a kid listening to thunder cracks.

"We can turn on our headlamps," Yates said. "They won't spot us in the valley."

The second I flicked mine on, I wished I'd kept it off. The slope fell straight down. "Oh, no."

"I know it looks bad," Yates said, "but I think once we get down about three, four hundred feet, it flattens out."

Pines dotted the slope, so I couldn't see the bottom. "I hope you're right."

We sank in the deep snow and our feet slid with each step. The lamp on my forehead swept like a searchlight over Yates, the snow, and the trees. Everything inside me felt floaty, disconnected. My legs swam through the snow, while my thoughts circled my body.

My mouth was dry and my throat hurt. "Can we stop? I'm thirsty."

"Sure. But let's get a little lower, find someplace flat."

Yates took a step, and I heard the loud scrape of metal meeting rock. Yates flung out his arms, but he was already falling.

"Yates!"

Snow exploded like surf, throwing him forward into the air. His headlamp beam flashed—off on off on—as he tumbled. Head, then feet, over and over, I saw him swept away in a roar and rush of white until he finally disappeared in the darkness.

"Yates!"

He must have stopped, because I couldn't hear him. His head-lamp had been torn off and lay in the snow below me.

"Yates!"

He didn't answer.

"Yates, why aren't you answering me!" I stood completely still, listening hard, but I didn't hear a thing.

I plunged down the hill, following the churned-up snow. "Yates, answer me!"

Maybe he got knocked out. Maybe he's buried. I have to get to him. He could be suffocating.

I knew I should be careful, but I couldn't slow down. I passed one of his ski poles. His hat. The half-buried headlamp. I fought the spinning in my head, and the fear tearing at me.

Then I saw the end of his trail: a thick black pine half buried in snow. He'd plowed into its branches.

I felt like *I'd* hit the tree.

He's dead.

I staggered toward the tree, its silence killing me. *No! He's not! He can't be. He can't be!*

"Yates? Yates, where are you?"

His moan was so short, so quiet, I almost missed it. "Yates?"

I saw where he hit. That side of the tree was clean, the snow that caked the branches had shaken free.

I bent down and swept the dark with the lamp until I saw him. Yates was caught in the branches, splayed out like an insect in a spiderweb. His head was shoved back and his face was a road map of blood and snow.

His hand was close enough for me to reach out and touch. "Yates, it's me. I'll get you out of here."

I dropped my pack and untied the folding shovel. I dug down until I got to a hollow under the tree. I crawled in, and looked up. Yates was woven into the branches farther up than I could reach, his right foot twisted at a bone-breaking angle.

Moving him's a bad idea. Ms. A's first aid lessons stressed waiting for the paramedics, because moving people who are injured can make the injury worse. *I don't have a choice.* If I left Yates in this tree, he would freeze to death before I could get help.

Holy crap. How am I going to untangle him? His pack and

snowshoes have to come off, but one wrong move could send him crashing.

The quiet magnified every sound. Yates' moans. The creak of the branches above me. The gargling cough that set my heart into shock.

I scrambled out of the hollow. Blood streamed from Yates' nose and the gash above his right eye.

I flattened out on the snow and stretched onto the web of branches. It gave beneath me as I gently reached out to turn Yates' head. I hesitated, brushing the snow off his hair. *If his neck's broken, I could paralyze him, but if I don't . . .*

Please, I begged as I turned him. *Please be okay.* Blood gushed from his nose and more dribbled from his mouth. He coughed and his hand jerked. *Thank God.* He couldn't stay there, but if I pulled him out onto the slope he'd sail down it like a runaway sled.

I've got to dig a ledge. Set up a snow shelter like Maggie taught us. A vision of her last minutes flamed in front of my eyes. *No. No. Can't think about that now. I have to take care of Yates.*

I shoveled on my knees, cutting a shelf into the hill, trying to ignore the cold burning through my pants. The shovel got heavier and heavier, and I knew I should stop and eat or drink something, but how could I when Yates was hanging there like a smashed Christmas ornament?

"Avie?"

I whirled around, not sure if that was really Yates or just a voice in my head. "Yates?"

"What happened?"

"You hit a tree."

"You okay?"

I reached out and squeezed his hand. *You're asking if I'm okay?* "Yeah, I'm fine. I'm getting you out of there."

Yates tried to bend forward. "Shit. My ribs. Feels like somebody beat the crap out of me."

"You hit the tree pretty hard. What else hurts?"

"My leg's okay, a little beat-up, but I think my ankle's wrecked. Ow, crap, my hand."

Broken nose, ankle, ribs, smashed-up hand. Yates was alive, but he wasn't in great shape. "Give me a minute. I need to figure out how to get you out of here."

I studied him and the pack like I was making a last move in Jenga. A branch was wedged between his back and the pack. The pack had to come off. I couldn't pull that much dead weight. But if I unhooked the straps across his chest and hips while the others were on his shoulders, the pack could drag him down. With his feet tangled up like that, it could snap his leg.

"I'm taking off your snowshoes," I told him.

Twigs caught my headlamp and icy needles slapped my face as I crawled into the branches. I tore at the straps around Yates' boots, but my hands were useless, fat claws. Yates jerked his leg, cracking his snowshoe into my face. I yelped, momentarily blinded by the pain.

"I'm sorry!" He said it like he was ashamed.

"I'll be okay. It stings, that's all."

One snowshoe, then the other clattered through the branches. Now the hard part.

I slid close to him. "We have to get you out of this pack. Can you turn toward me at all?"

Yates tried to move his hips. "Can't. I'm caught on something."

Screw it. There's no other way.

"I'm going to unhook your chest strap and slide the shoulder strap over your injured hand, but you have to try and hold on to the pack with your other hand so it doesn't fall."

We both held our breath. I unlatched the strap and Yates moaned as we got his arms free. "Now the waist strap. Ready?"

The pack tore away, wrenching his shoulder back. Yates let go of the pack and we clung to the branch as it bucked under us. The darkness below crashed and splintered.

Then, very gradually, inch by inch, I got Yates out of there.

Yates crawled and slid and collapsed onto the ledge I built, but I couldn't rest. I was a plane-crash victim crawling through wreckage, trying to survive.

Somehow I dragged Yates' pack out of the hollow. Set up the kettle, wrapped a sleeping bag around him.

Rest Ice Compression Elevation. My hands moved on their own, packing a snow pillow under his ankle, dabbing blood off his face, and closing the cut above his eye with duct tape. His nose was bent and his eye had swelled into a gashed nectarine. Yates winced and sucked in his pain as I worked.

He was hurt in ways I didn't know how to fix, but I had to shut that out and focus on what I did know. Ice his eye. Splint his ankle. Immobilize his hand. And keep up his body heat, because if Yates didn't stay warm, I'd lose him. I slogged back up the hill to get his hat.

You're not going to make it. He's too hurt to walk, and when the sun comes up, the feds will find your trail.

I snatched his hat off the snow. *Shut up. I don't want to hear it.* His headlamp was right above me, and when I had it, I turned and saw Yates wrestling one-handed with his pack.

If the feds find us, they'll execute us. They'll kill us, and then they'll destroy the hanging and erase all the files on the drive.

Face it. This could be the end.

Yates waited for me. He'd found two cups and filled them with cocoa. "You need to drink, Fearless."

I sat down and took the cup from him. I sipped the thick, sweet chocolate and stared at the star-dusted sky while gunshots burst like faraway fireworks. "This would be romantic if it weren't so horrible," I said.

Yates winced and wiped cocoa off his front with his sleeve. "Yeah, not really my idea of a great date. Next time, let's rent a movie and get take-out."

I smiled at him trying to make me laugh. "What kind? Chinese? Thai?"

He wiggled the fingers on his good hand. "I was going to say pizza, but yeah, I can still do chopsticks."

I held my cup in front of my mouth. I couldn't keep up the banter. *This can't be the end. I can't believe we're supposed to die out here, not after everything we've been through.*

I looked over at Yates' crumpled body. His crushed hand. The splint we'd sawed from a branch and duct-taped to his ankle.

Maybe I'm the only one who's supposed to survive. The one who finishes the mission. I jerked to my feet. *No. No. That can't be the plan.*

"Time to build a snow shelter," I said.

Yates grabbed my hand. "You know you have to leave me."

I tore mine away. *He can't possibly know what I'm thinking.* "I won't abandon you."

"I can't walk. I can't even crawl. You can't drag me for ten miles."

"But the feds could show up here in a few hours." *Think about it. They'll kill you.*

Yates stared at me with his one good eye. "It's all right. I *know* you love me. But if you stay, it's double suicide."

I pushed down on the hanging that was tourniquet tight around my chest. Go and I might save lives. Go and I could pass on the hanging and Maggie's death wouldn't be a waste. Go and I sacrifice Yates.

"I hate this," I said.

"I do, too."

Me staying was pointless. Romantic and loyal and totally pointless when I'd only end up dead or in prison. "I'm not going for me—"

"You don't have to say it. I know."

I leaned over and brushed the hair away from his forehead, and gently kissed it. There weren't words inside me to say what I felt.

"The moon'll be up in another hour or two," Yates said. "You could rest. Wait until then."

"Yeah, but now," I said, dragging myself to my feet, "I've got to build that snow shelter."

It was harder than I thought, digging a trench big enough for Yates to move around in. And sawing through pine branches and weaving them into a roof over his head sucked away most of my strength. By the time I'd packed snow over the top and wedged a flour sack filled with snow into the opening to make a door, I wondered how I could make it all the way to the highway.

I lit an eight-hour candle and set it on a tiny shelf. One candle could keep you from freezing or at least that was what Luke had promised us.

The shelter walls glowed pale gold in the candlelight. Inside this cocoon, we couldn't hear gunshots.

"I'm really tired," I told Yates.

"Then lie down," he said. "I'll wake you in an hour."

Before I went to sleep I put Maggie's gun where I could reach it, and placed the clip next to it. I curled into Yates, careful not to touch his injured side. He wrapped his good arm over me.

I won't let you die alone. I'll bring back help.

94

Someone's out there. My eyes flashed open, but my brain was a couple steps behind. Yates lay beside me.

The eight-hour candle had burned to a stub. *What time is it?*

"Hey, you in there. You okay?"

The man's voice chilled me right through. I felt for Maggie's gun and, fumbling, shoved the clip in place.

The agents found our trail. They followed us. "Yates. Yates, wake up," I whispered, but he barely stirred.

We're trapped. I put on a headlamp and blew out the candle. Aimed the gun at the sounds outside. *I'm not going down without a fight.* My hands shook, and I couldn't breathe, the gun was so heavy.

A shovel broke through the snow. My heart jumped into my throat.

"Hey, anybody home?"

The snow door pulled away, and a guy's face filled the opening. I cocked the trigger, and he spun away from the door. It was still night out.

"Whoa! I'm going. Don't mind me. I was just checking to see if you're hurt."

I trapped him in my headlamp. "Put your gun down!"

"Gun's on the sled." He was backing away with his hands up. He had on a beat-up parka made out of animal skins and a sled team waited below.

"Don't move."

"Listen, I'm going," he said. "No need to point that at me."

I crawled out of the shelter, my heart pounding. The guy towered over me. One kick to the head and I'd be dead.

I stood up and faced him, my hands shaking. This was a real live human being and either he'd been sent out to track us down and execute us, or he was a Good Samaritan who'd stumbled on us in the middle of the night.

Good Samaritan. What were the chances of that?

A dog started to whine and the man turned his head. "Quiet, Gracie."

The headlamp beam lit his braided beard. A fed would never wear that parka or a beard like that—not unless he was undercover. This guy could be telling the truth. "Who are you?"

"My name's Spoke."

"Are you a fed?"

"No, I promise. No government ties whatsoever." The man inched toward his sled.

The sled looked familiar. "Are you from Salvation?

"Yeah, I'm headed back there."

"Don't. It's under attack."

"Yeah, I know. I saw it on the news."

"The news?"

"Yeah, saw the footage in a bar of those bastards taking out Maggie and then the shoot-out at the church."

"People saw?"

"Hell, yeah! Didn't you hear the news choppers?"

"No. Are they—is it over?"

"Shooting stopped once the local officials showed up."

Oh, my God, we did it. "Yates, we did it!"

"Hey, are you the girl who sent out the distress call?"

"Yeah, that was me."

"Damn. You need anything?"

"Can you help us? My friend's hurt. I need to get him to a hospital."

"Sure, I can do that. Closest one's probably Boise. But maybe you could put that gun down?"

Spoke picked up the shovel, and with short, brisk strokes, began to dig Yates out while I tore the snow away with my hands.

"You two are heroes," Spoke said. "I'm telling you, the President's going to have to answer for this. I bet both him and Jouvert are gonna find themselves impeached. Gunning down innocent Americans like enemy combatants—"

My heart stopped. *Americans?* "No. Wait. How many died? Do you have any names?"

Spoke stopped digging. He leaned on the shovel and bowed his head. "There were two bodies outside the church," he said quietly.

I saw the white surrender flag settle over Maggie's body. "One was

Maggie and the other—" The last bars of a love song echoed in my head. "It was Barnabas, wasn't it?"

Spoke nodded. "Had his arms around her when he died. Twenty years, and he never got that woman out of his blood."

I couldn't stop the tears rolling down my cheeks. "And what about inside the church?"

Spoke went back to digging. "Looks like the agents didn't get inside. You saved a lot of lives tonight. You should take comfort in that."

Luke, Beattie, Keisha, and everyone else. They were alive.

The roof I'd woven of pine branches appeared from under the snow. Spoke tore them off, and together we lifted Yates onto the sled. He was half conscious and we tied him down, wrapped in the sleeping bags. I kissed the side of his face that wasn't bruised. "Spoke's going to take you to the hospital."

Yates was struggling to keep his eyes open, fighting to talk through the pain. "If you want to try for the border, it's okay," he said. "I can meet up with you in a few weeks."

I felt the thumb drive dangling between my breasts. It was going to take longer than a few weeks to put Yates back together, and it seemed as if my plans had changed. "No, I think I'd better stick around for now."

I kissed him lightly on the lips.

"Love you," he said, his voice failing.

"Love you." Always and forever.

"Sun'll be up in a couple hours," Spoke said. "You can wait here, or you can follow the sled tracks. Either I'll come back or I'll send someone for you."

Spoke gave the command and the dogs took off. I watched the sled sail over the snow, leaving me alone in the silent night. Slowly, I gathered the equipment together and drank tea and ate some bread before I pulled on my pack.

The moon was huge and the sled tracks were so clear I didn't need a headlamp.

I wasn't going to sit there and wait to be rescued.

I strapped on the snowshoes and walked, knowing exactly where I was going and, for the first time maybe in my life, knowing who I was. I was Fearless.

1. At the beginning of the book, Avie thinks she is going to go to college and perhaps fall in love. How has this been changed by the Scarpanol disaster?

2. Avie's father surprises her by "contracting" her into marriage. Why does he do it? Do you think he was right or wrong?

3. Avie thinks she has no choice but to honor the "contract" and marry Jessop Hawkins, but Ms. Alexandra tells her she has several options. What choices does Avie have and which would you choose?

4. Avie's father keeps tabs on her in many ways. How does he monitor what she does? How would you feel about living like that?

5. Why do you think the Paternalists came to power? They say they want to protect American women. Do you think that is true, or is it a lie?

6. How do you think American men have been affected by the loss of their wives, daughters, sisters, aunts, or mothers?

7. Yates, Father Gabriel, Sparrow, and Maggie Stanton help the resistance in their own ways. Why did each join the movement and how do their reasons differ?

8. Father Gabriel tells Avie that even though the country's leaders are "playing chess with girls' lives…someone else whispers the moves as they play." What do you think he means by this?

9. As Avie disappears into Exodus, she is shocked that the Underground isn't the way Father Gabriel described. What big surprises does she have to deal with?

Discussion Questions

St. Martin's
Griffin

10. Avie's classmate, Sparrow, decides to set herself on fire on the steps of the Capitol building. Why does she do this? Are there things we don't know about her?

11. At what point does Avie decide to support the revolution? What motivates her?

12. Avie volunteers to go for help during the armed siege in Salvation. Why does she do it? What would you do?

13. At the beginning of the book, Avie says, "I'm not fearless, but I loved how he called me that." At the end, she says, "I am fearless." How has she changed?

14. What do you believe will happen to Avie next?

15. The author wanted to write a book that when people finish reading it they would say, "I think that could really happen." What parts of the story feel real to you? What do you feel might happen if the U.S. lost a large number of women?

To connect with Catherine Linka, like her Facebook page,
facebook.com/CatherineLinkaAuthor,
and follow her on Twitter, @cblinka.

For more reading group suggestions,
visit www.readinggroupgold.com.